# Future Fiction

Edited by

Francesco Verso

银河奖专辑1

中国科幻合集

拉兹 弗朗西斯科·沃尔索 主编

# Galaxy Awards 1

Chinese Science Fiction Anthology

edited by
Latssep and Francesco Verso

Published by Associazione Future Fiction
Via Valentiniano 40 – 00145 Roma
TAX ID. 97962020588

Tongji Bridge, originally published in Chinese in Science Fiction World, Vol. 01, 2021.

《通济桥》 中文版首发于《科幻世界》2021年01期

Final Diagnosis, originally published in Chinese in Science Fiction World, Vol. 10, 2018.

《绝对诊断》 中文版首发于《科幻世界》2018年10期

Fongong Temple Pagoda, originally published in Chinese in the supplement of Science Fiction World 2022.

《尽化塔》中文版首发于《科幻世界》2022年增刊

Resurrection, originally published in Chinese in Science Fiction World, Vol. 04, 2020.

《还魂》中文版首发于《科幻世界》2020年04期

Turing Food Court, originally published in Chinese in Science Fiction World, Vol. 01, 2021.

《图灵大排档》 中文版首发于《科幻世界》2021年01期

Upstart, originally published in the Nebula ⅩⅠ Mook, August 2021.

《新贵》中文版首发于《星云XI》，2021年8月出版

2039: Era of Brain-Computer Interface, originally published in Chinese in Science Fiction World Vol. 11, 2021.

《2039：脑机时代》 中文版首发于《科幻世界》2021年11期

Color the World, originally published in Science Fiction World, Vol.10, 2019.

《涂色世界》 中文版首发于《科幻世界》2019年10期

让全世界看到银河的光芒

拉兹

感谢弗朗西斯科·沃尔索先生，被誉为中国科幻最高奖的"银河奖"的第一本英文选集得以出版。正如很多人所知，科幻文学诞生于西方，在一百多年前传播到中国后，深受中国知识分子和青年人的推崇。

四十三年前，我所服务的科幻世界杂志社成立了，从此成为中国最重要的科幻专业出版机构。

在科幻世界的努力下，科幻在中国逐渐成为一种重要的流行文化类型，很多年轻人都因为科幻聚集到一起，讨论星空、未来和生命，以及关于生活的一切。

最初，中国科幻迷只能阅读西方的经典科幻作品，后来他们中的部分人开始尝试创作，并取得了卓越的成就。

三十七年前，科幻世界杂志社设立了银河奖，以鼓励和表彰中国最为优秀的科幻作家和科幻作品。

这个奖项非常重要，被公认为中国科幻最高奖，很多知名科幻作家的第一个科幻专业奖项都是银河奖，许多优秀科幻作品也因为获得了这个荣誉而广为人知。

比如海外读者最为熟悉的中国科幻作家刘慈欣，他早在1999年就凭借处女作获得了银河奖，他最为著名的作品《三体》则在2006年的《科幻世界》杂志上连载并在第二年获得了银河奖"特别奖"。

在《三体》获得雨果奖之后，越来越多的中国科幻作家和科幻作品被国外读者熟悉。

但作为中国最重要的科幻出版机构，我们认为这还远远不够。

我们希望以这本小集子为开端，让更多优秀的中国科幻作家和科幻作品走向世界，也让世界通过这些科幻作品看到中国人对于未来的想象。

他们虽然不代表全部，但能够看出中国人对宇宙的好奇，对未来的期待，对生命的热爱，对和平的向往。

当然，科幻在中国不但是年轻人的文学，也是一种年轻的文学，和名家辈出、经典作品如繁星一般的西方科幻相比，还有很多需要学习和进步的地方。

因此，我们也希望这本书的出版能引发更多人对中国科幻的关注和讨论，这对所有中国科幻人来说都是一件非常重要的事情。

当前，世界正进入一个和过去完全不同的历史时期，未来到底如何发展，将取决于年轻人如何认识自己、如何认识世界。

科幻是关于未来和整个人类的文学，这本书的出版能帮助我们更好地认识对方，特别是认识对方对未来和世界的看法。

这件事情很小，但很重要——渺小而伟大是人类的特征，这次合作也是一样。

最后，我要代表《科幻世界》杂志再次感谢弗朗西斯科，他为本书的出版做了大量卓有成效的工作。

我希望这本书不但是我们合作和友谊的见证，更能一直持续下去，成为中国与海外科幻界合作和友谊的催化剂，并影响到更多人，陪伴地球碳基文明变得更好

# The Galaxy Sparkles for the Whole World

## by Latssep

Thanks to Mr. Francesco Verso, the first English anthology of the Galaxy Award, the highest prize in Chinese science fiction, has been published. As many people know, Science Fiction literature was born in the West and has been highly respected by Chinese intellectuals and young people since it was introduced to China more than 100 years ago.

Forty-three years ago, Science Fiction World Magazine, which I work for, was founded and has since become the most important Science Fiction professional publishing institution in China.

Thanks to the efforts of Science Fiction World, Science Fiction has gradually become an important popular culture genre in China. Many young people gather together because of Science Fiction to discuss the stars, the future and life, and everything about life.

Initially, Chinese sci-fi fans could only read Western classics, but later some of them began to try their hand at creation and achieved remarkable success.

Thirty-seven years ago, Science Fiction World established the Galaxy Awards to encourage and honor the best Chinese Science Fiction writers and works.

This award is very important. It is recognized as the highest Science Fiction award in China. The first professional Science Fiction award for many famous Science Fiction writers is the Galaxy Award, and many excellent Science Fiction works are well known for winning this honor. For example, Liu Cixin, the Chinese Sci-fi writer most familiar to overseas readers, won the Galaxy Award for his first work in 1999. His most famous work, The Three-Body Problem, was serialized in Science Fiction World magazine in 2006 and won the "Special Award" of the Galaxy Award the following year.

After the Three-Body Problem won the Hugo Award, more and more Chinese Science Fiction writers and Science Fiction works have become familiar to foreign readers. But as the most important Science Fiction publishing institution in China, we think this is far from enough.

We hope that with this small collection as the beginning, more excellent Chinese Science Fiction writers and Science Fiction works will go out into the world, but also let the world through these SF works to see the Chinese people's imagination of the future.

Although they do not represent all of us, we can see the Chinese people's curiosity for the universe, their expectation for the future, their love for life and their yearning for peace.

Of course, Science Fiction in China is not only young people's literature, but also a kind of young literature. Compared with Western Science Fiction, where famous writers come forth in large numbers and classic works are like stars, there is still much to learn and improve.

Therefore, we also hope that the publication of this book will arouse more people's attention and discussion on Chinese Science Fiction, which is a very important thing for all Chinese Sci-fi people. At present, the world is entering a historical period completely different from the past. How the future develops will depend on how young people understand themselves and the world. Science Fiction is a literature about the future and the whole human race. The publication of this book can help us better understand each other, especially each other's views on the future and the world. It's small, but it's important—small and great is a human trait, and so is this collaboration.

Finally, on behalf of SF World Magazine, I would like to thank Francesco again for his tremendous and productive work in bringing this book to publication.

I hope this book will not only be a witness of our cooperation and friendship, but also continue to be a catalyst for cooperation and friendship between China and overseas SF communities, and influence more people to accompany the carbon-based civilization of the Earth to become better.

# 通济桥

## 路航

青年作者，擅长发掘科幻中的小人物生活，文笔温暖动人。处女作《镜妖》，另有代表作《你应如鸟向山飞》。


0

"行通济，无闭翳。"

我默念着这句熟悉的谚语，高举着龙珠，引着我的队伍，踏上了通济桥。片刻之后，我的身旁，龙腾狮跃，鞭炮声响。喝彩声一阵接一阵，向着我们袭来。

一年一度通济桥最盛大的活动就此开始了。

但我知道一旦表演结束，我们摘下头顶的龙首狮头露出真容时，围观群众的反应就会发生急剧的变化。有人可能会骂我，说我哗众取宠，消费国粹；有人可能会夸我，说我标新立异，引领潮流。但对我来说，这些评价都无所谓。

我只要七叔公能再一次看到舞龙醒狮的表演就可以了。

如果有人因为看了我们的表演，喜欢上了舞龙醒狮，愿意找我们学功夫，那就更好了。无论他是哪里人，甚至就算他不是人，只要肯学，我都愿意把这一身功夫教给他，只求传承。


1

七叔公说要关掉龙狮团时，我毫不意外。

这些年，任谁都能看得出，他当宝贝似的华美龙狮团早就撑不下去了。这两三年，连肯来训练的人都没几个了，至于年底的"行通济"，自然也没法凑齐一套班子。

这倒不是因为缺钱。钱，七叔公还是有一些的。他是土生土长的原住民，靠祖产也勉强供得起一个龙狮团。退一万步说，就算他真是没钱了，乡里也会拨款支持。毕竟无论怎么说，龙狮团都还挂着一个非物质文化遗产的招牌。

但举凡能称得上是非物质文化遗产的，十有八九都在发愁传承。七叔公的龙狮团也不例外。

舞龙也好，醒狮也罢，都是体力活，虽说是男是女倒不是那么紧要，但头一条，得体格好；次一条，得肯吃苦。就这两条规矩，难倒了七叔公——

他招不来人了。

毕竟这年头，干啥不比舞龙醒狮舒服呢？

就算是从小在龙狮团里耳濡目染长大的我，也从未想过去接替它。

无他，学这门功夫太辛苦了。我见过师兄弟们大热天里在梅花桩上扎马步，一站就是一下午，自然不肯再去吃这份苦。天最热的时候，几乎每天都有中暑的人从梅花桩上栽倒在地。唯一庆幸的大概是佛山气候好，冬天不长，也不下雪，不然我难以想象在大雪天里练操跑步的情景。

七叔公很疼爱我，甚至想过要把当作宝贝的龙狮团留给我。他膝下无子，只有我这个父母都不要的孩子，养在身边。为此他每天亲自带我练功，教我步法。只可惜我对此没什么兴趣。我的兴趣只在摆弄变形金刚和读书。

七婆在世时，劝过七叔公，说各人愿吃的苦不同，让他不要太执着于把龙狮团传到我手上。确实是这样，我吃得读书的苦，吃得创业的苦，但我吃不下这练拳脚功夫的苦。

那时七叔公偶尔会开玩笑，说我身体太弱，以后没法舞龙醒狮。我总是顺水推舟，笑着对七叔公说："我学不来，只有叔公才舞得动嘛。"

打小我就喜欢编程，喜欢机器人，喜欢一切稀奇古怪的新鲜事物。而家乡能提供给我的，恰恰相反。

我一直想离开佛山老家，考到外面去，最好是去深圳，去硅谷，或者去任何高科技聚集的地方。

后来我也的确实现过这个愿望。

高中毕业后，我考到深圳读大学。大学毕业后，我又申请到了奖学金，去了纽约读研。我再不用打着电话求离婚的父母给我付学费，也不用担心万一读不来书，我该怎么养活自己。研究生毕业后，我到了硅谷，加入了一家机器人公司做研发，主导过几个不大不小的项目。时机成熟后，我又跳出来，和男友一起回到深圳开了家机器人公司。我做研发，他做其他。

我以为自己很顺利，已经踏上了成功的阶梯。却没想到，创业维艰，机器人市场竞争太过激烈。好不容易在市场上撕出一道口子，后续要营销投入时，我却和身为合伙人的男友起了分歧。他指责我的设计和市面上已有的机器人差异性不大，也不适应中国市场的需求，卖不出去。我坚持我的设计，不肯更改。吵架，分手，撤资，产品销量日益下滑，资金链断裂，最终导致公司再也撑不下去。

　　朋友们纷纷劝我缩减人员，甚至关掉公司。到最后，就连一直看好我的导师也这么劝我。"时间也是成本。年轻人失败一次，没什么要紧的。你以后开公司，我还支持你，但现在还是放弃吧。"

　　我看着那一屋子悄悄投简历的员工，无奈之下，只好认清了现实，辞退了他们。我还记得付清最后一笔账单时，我身上只剩下三百多块钱和一仓库不知道怎么卖出去的机器人，连散伙饭也请不起。

　　也不知道七叔公是从哪里知道了我的情况，他第二天就打电话来，喊我回乡祭祖。我本不想回，但他很坚持，我就这么空手回了家乡。

　　2

　　我回到家乡，正值冬至。

　　在我的家乡，冬至又叫小年，因此要格外隆重些。每年冬至的时候，不仅要吃汤圆，还得杀猪宰羊，祭拜先祖。

　　我跟着七叔公在祠堂里上完香，走到中庭。

　　与别处的祠堂不同，家乡的祠堂除了祭祀以外，还担着教化的功能。有些人家的祠堂会开班教授一些琴棋书画。我们家的祠堂，教授的却是舞龙醒狮。七叔公的龙狮团，绝大多数时候都是在祠堂中庭的空地上训练的。走在这熟悉的环境里，身旁却没了熟悉的人，曾经在这空地上站马步、走梅花桩的师兄弟们早已不见，只剩下七叔公一个人。

　　我还记得我高中毕业离家时，七婆还在世。当时她拉着我来祠堂给祖先上香。上完香后，还特意嘱咐我，不用在意七叔公说的接替龙狮团的事，想出去读书就去读，想出去工作就去做。无论我将来做什么，只要不犯法，她都会支持的。她要是知道我如今这般落魄，不知又该作何想。

　　"要是七婆还在就好了。"浸着萧瑟的冷风，望着眼前空荡荡的庭院，我不禁感叹道。

　　"她留了点儿东西给你。"七叔公似乎早就想和我说这些，很快从口袋里掏出两个手指粗的金丝嵌玛瑙镯子和一张银行卡一起递给我，"这是给你添箱底的嫁妆。你虽然还没嫁，但也提前给你。我也有东西留给你。"

　　我好奇地跟着他走进偏室，却没想到他要拿给我的，竟然是家里那个从清朝传到现在、传了两百多年的狮头。

　　小的时候，我和七婆来祠堂看龙狮团训练，七叔公常会逗我，"初九啊，要不要跟着叔公学醒狮呀？长大了，叔公把狮头给你做嫁妆。"

接了狮头，就等于受了衣钵，得扛起华美龙狮团这块牌子。我知道这个道理，所以从来没答应过。但没想到今天，七叔公还是要将它给我。

"这……"

见我犹豫，七叔公笑道："别担心，我打算今年把龙狮团关了，不是想让你接手。老实说，我这个团已经大半年都没怎么训练了。去年就没凑齐人行通济，今年估计更难了。每次来训练的，基本上都是我们这把老骨头，最年轻的，都有五十多了。舞不动咯。"

我还想像小时候一样说"只有七叔公才能舞得动嘛"，但无论如何都说不出口这句话。七叔公确实是年纪大了。

"可是……"我心底还是有些不舍。

"初九，时代变了嘛。以前想跟着我黄新民学功夫，那得先去市场提两斤猪头肉，到我这交够了拜师钱，日头底下再跪上半晌，我才会考虑一下。但是现在，我就算倒贴钱，也招不来人。人人都不肯吃这个苦。再说，看的人也没从前那么多了。"七叔公有些失落，"反正要关门，这狮头留着也没什么用，你拿去卖了，还能换点儿钱。"

"这怎么能卖呢？"我将狮头推回给七叔公，"家传了两百多年，怎么都不能断在我的手上。"

"你接不接，它都断了。"七叔公叹了口气，"你又不可能一个人扛起这套班子。舞龙醒狮不比其他，必须要有搭档有徒弟，有一整套队伍才能传得下去。龙狮团传不下去，是我愧对先祖。断也是断在我手上，不是你手上，你不用担心。你缺钱，就拿去换钱用。再说，可能买下的那个人，他想学醒狮呢？这不就传下去了嘛。"

我不忍告诉七叔公，倘若我真的卖掉，这镶珠嵌宝的狮头，只会被拿去摆在博物馆里，或者大户人家的收藏室里。绝不可能有人真的拿它去醒狮的。七叔公是在骗我，更是在骗他自己。

"那我就先收着。"我闷声说，"卖，我是不会卖的。我没那么缺钱。"

话音未落，导师忽然从深圳打来电话，告诉我有人想收购我的机器人，问我是否有空回深圳把货给人家看看，"或许还能换点儿钱呢？初九。"

电话那头的声音很大、很高兴，我知道导师是好心，想把这个消息快点儿告诉我。但站在我身旁的七叔公也听到了。

挂完电话，相对无言，我抱着狮头，默默地走出了祠堂。

金鱼街上的这间祠堂，距今也有两百多年历史了。这些年里，打过仗，挨过炮，被偷过，被抢过，它却始终在这里，屹立不倒。不远处的通济桥也是如此，它从木桥变为石桥，又由石桥变为大马路，最终又变回石桥，每年元宵节前后的"行通济"却始终不变。转风车、扔生菜、看醒狮，基本年年都是如此。只是近年来，由于招不到人，醒狮表演越来越少了。

"我们去通济桥走走吧。"七叔公开口道，"行通济，无闭翳。虽然现在还不是元宵，但走走总会顺一点儿。"

"好。"

一路无言，我跟着七叔公走过通济桥那座大牌坊。他忽然停下来，指着附近一处台阶问我，"你知道我和你七婆是怎么认识的吗？"

"不知道。叔公没说过。"

"就在这里认识的。有一年元宵节晚上行通济，我带着我们龙狮团，从桥头舞到桥尾，满大街都是追着看的人。台阶上，高台上，人挤人。结果舞到通济桥这个牌坊下面时，有个姑娘不小心被人撞了一下，从台阶上掉出来摔在地上了。我当时看到，就和你林爷爷说了一声，举着狮头冲过去，扶了人家一把。本来只是想做好事，哪晓得第二天那姑娘来道谢。她就是你七婆了。在那之前，哪个不笑我快三十了，没个对象，天天舞龙醒狮，能当饭吃吗？结果碰到你七婆，慢慢地，什么都有了。我当年还拿了狮王争霸赛的冠军。我说这个，是想告诉你，不要着急。工作也好，感情也好，急不来的。"

"我知道。我就是……"

"缺钱，七叔公给。你那个什么玩偶公司，也不要放弃太早了。总会有人喜欢你这一款的。"

"嗯！"我点点头，再不知道说什么。

在七叔公眼里，机器人和玩偶是差不多的。他其实根本不知道我在做什么吧，却还是支持我。相比之下，有人知道我在做什么，却很少支持。不自觉地，我不禁想起了离我而去的男友，想起了我那个事实上已然破产的小公司，想起了那一仓库因为缺乏前期营销投入，再也没法摆在柜台的机器人。

然后我看到了手中的狮头——

我为什么不可以用机器人来醒狮呢？

我的机器人并不是不好，它们只是缺乏包装与营销，没来得及摆上柜台，没来得及吸引到市场的注意力。可是它关节灵活，弹跳性能好，它完全可以用来醒狮，只要我给它设置好程序。

我把这个念头说给七叔公听，他毫不犹豫就答应了。"我黄新民连外国人都教过。教机器人，应该也没问题的。"

3

第二天，我赶早班车回深圳，去仓库里搬了十六个机器人，又找朋友借了一套动作捕捉衣，回了家乡。

导师那边的提议，我思考后，还是婉言谢绝了。我虽然明白，他的提议或许是我眼前能够抓到的最确切的机会，但我还是想赌一把。

从小到大喜欢的事物，我不想就这么放弃掉。

我本计划让七叔公穿着动作捕捉衣，从头到尾演示一遍，我用电脑记录下他的身形步法、动作指标后，再转换成数据，灌注到机器人身上。却没考虑到七叔公年岁已大，动作捕捉衣很重，他穿着那套衣服，根本撑不了多长时间。

无奈之下，我只好自己上场。

金鱼街上的祠堂里，华美龙狮团就这么再度开张了。

那之后的半个月里，每天早上，七叔公都会站在祠堂中庭的那片空地上，一步一步教着我最基本的动作，我穿着动作捕捉衣跟在他身后亦步亦趋地学，身旁围着一圈机器人。这就好像很多年前，七叔公带着师兄弟们训练，我和七婆站在一旁观看的情景。只是我的动作远不如当年的师兄弟，好多次都做不到位，因此耽搁了不少时间。

就这么练了一个月，我才收集完数据，开始给机器人编程。这时候我才发现，为十六个机器人编程，确保每个机器人动作各不相同，而又能够和谐共处，组成一台行云流水般的节目，实在是太难了。我一个人很难做到。即使勉强做到，恐怕也赶不及元宵节的"行通济"。

七叔公虽然不承认，但我隐约感觉他的身体大不如前。为我演示动作时，过一会儿，就得歇一下，有时候还会说胳膊疼。我想带他去医院检查，他也不肯去，只说自己健壮得很，老人都这样。

我忙于实现自己的想法，也没有细问。为了早日实现这一计划，我给认识的人都打了电话。他们虽然没法理解我，觉得做一场免费的舞龙醒狮表演，对销售也没什么大用处——"谁会因为你的机器人会舞龙醒狮，就买它呢"，但还是决定帮助我实现这个计划。

在他们的帮助下，赶在过年前几天，我终于编好了这十六个机器人的动作程序。不出意外的话，接下来我只需要根据它们的互动情况，进行局部的校准即可。

编程结束的那天，我将这十六个机器人装扮好，穿上团服，在祠堂中庭的空地上，给七叔公表演了一场标准的醒狮。

尽管机器人的动作很生硬，甚至有些凝滞，但大体上还是完成了任务。看的时候，七叔公很感慨，直言没想到科技已经发展到这个地步，一个动作都没错。只是双狮戏珠这场戏，展现出来的效果很差。试了好几次，不是球掉到了地上，机器人却视若无物、继续表演；就是抛球的动作很慢，全然没有真正看"双狮戏珠"的那种紧张感。

"双狮戏珠是重点，这个准备好了，这场戏就圆满了。"七叔公说完，便举起狮头，向我演示怎么去抢珠，但没想到他刚想跳起接狮头，整个人就重重砸到了地上，昏迷了。我是清楚他的身体不如以前，但从没想到会病得那么重，病了那么久。跟着救护车去医院时，我才了解真实的情况。那是积年的病。他早有预感，所以才会打电话喊我回乡祭祖。

他心知我虽然自小由他带大，但毕竟亲属关系隔了一层，父母也不管我，担心自己死后，一分遗产也没人为我争。所以早早喊我回乡，将一点儿东西托付给我。

年味渐浓，元宵将至，守在医院病床前的我，再也没心思调整校正那些机器人。和眼前活生生躺在病床上的人相比，那些只会按照程序、重复动作的机器人已经不在我在意的范围内了。只是七叔公一醒来，就劝我赶紧回去训练。

"我这病，我自己心里有数。你的事，你心里倒是没数。再过几天就是过年，过完年就是元宵，元宵就得行通济。你现在不训练好那些机器人，到时候谁带他们上场呢？我可是提前就和乡里打了招呼，我们今年要上的。"

"不上了吧。"我有些迟疑，"万一牌子被我砸了怎么办？"

"牌子砸了也是砸在我身上，你怕什么呢？那天你在我面前也演示过了，大体是不差的，把有些小问题改了就好了。你就放心大胆地做吧，叔公会去看你上桥的。"

"嗯！"我重重地点了个头。

重新回到祠堂后，我把全部心思都花在改进双狮戏珠这场戏的效果上。但我发现，无论我和朋友怎么修改程序，怎么调整校正机器人的动作，它们戏起珠来就是不如人灵巧。

"这是怎么回事呢？"我百思不得其解，穿着动作捕捉衣，顶着狮头，试了一下又一次。看视频回放时，我的动作毫无问题。看程序模拟出来的机器人醒狮效果，也没什么问题，但不知为何，实际上它们表演出来的，却总是让我觉得差一口气。

那一口气究竟是什么，我一直想不通，直到我偶然看到偏室里存放的一些过期报纸后，才真正明白他们缺的是什么。

那一天，正是除夕的前一天。帮我调整校正程序的朋友虽然住得近，但年底也很忙，早早就回家了。我害怕去医院面对七叔公问询的目光，也不想回那个空荡荡的家，就在祠堂里四处转着。亲戚们还没来上香，祠堂里只有我一个人。我不知不觉间就走到了七叔公给我狮头的那个偏室。在那里，我看到了一大堆华美龙狮团的旧照片、报道和锦旗奖杯。其中最引我注意的是一则旧报纸上的采访。

被采访的是我未曾谋面的一个先祖。他在民国时期的一场狮王争霸赛中拔了头筹。采访中，他讲起他练习醒狮的经验——

"我起初学醒狮，只在乎一招一式是否正确。但时间久了就发现，醒狮是有灵魂的。这灵魂就来自狮头下的人，我们自己。醒狮不是练操，动作对了，就圆满了。醒狮是打仗，不仅要明白怎么抢到对方手中的绣球，还要明白怎么和自己的搭档合作。比如说，忽然起了阵大风，绣球被吹跑了，那狮子肯定要去追，但怎么追起来好看，又能抢到绣球，是门学问……"

采访看完，我终于明白了自己无法重现双狮戏珠的原因——我的龙狮团没有灵魂。

因为它的狮头下，没有人。

4

除夕那天，我去接七叔公出院。

他气色好了些，虽然仍是没什么胃口吃饭。我本打算去酒店叫一桌酒席，但他说浪费，只让我随便买了点儿猪头肉，就当团圆饭了。

吃完饭，七叔公说想去祠堂看看。我扶着他往金鱼街走去，一路经过通济桥，看着万家灯火闪闪亮亮，嵌在桥的不远处，犹如项链上的宝石。这些年通济桥周边的市容变化很大，唯一不变的，似乎只有这条从家走到祠堂的路了。

吱呀一声，我推开祠堂的门。

亲戚们一般是从大年初一开始，才会陆陆续续过来上香。祠堂里很冷清，冷清到夜空中的明月也有些受凉，隐在了云雾做的衣裳里，只冒出了一个尖。

"趁今天天气好，看看你的队伍吧？"

“不了吧。”我有些犹豫，“叔公，我不想行通济了。”

“为什么？不是舞得好好的吗？”

我摇摇头，把我意识到的问题和七叔公说了。当我说到醒狮要有灵魂时，他也点点头，表示赞同。“确实是这样。醒狮的时候，眼神是很重要的，要眼观六路，耳听八方，将自己全身心投入到醒狮中，这样观众看到的狮子才是活的，有灵气。”

“是啊，所以还是得靠人。”我有点儿沮丧，“没人，真的什么也做不了。”

“什么叫没人呢？”七叔公拍了拍我的肩膀，“初九啊，你不就是这支队伍背后的人吗？”

我是背后的人。

刹那之间，我忽然想明白了该如何改进我的机器人。

我只需要在他们身上，安装一个动作捕捉模块，让他们模仿我的动作，然后再校准就可以了。而我现在所做的程序，无异于缘木求鱼。

鱼和线本来就在我眼前，而我忽略了这个更直接、更简便的办法——

我有动作捕捉衣，也有机器人，我只需要让他们合二为一，就可以了。

我将新的想法告诉七叔公，他虽然听不太懂我说的，也不明白我为何忽然这么高兴，但高兴总是对的。他也笑起来，说期待我的成果。

整个春节期间，我都忙于改进我的机器人。由于新年的原因，材料很难买。我只好又给在深圳的朋友们打电话求助。深圳毕竟是深圳，我最喜欢的高科技城市。很快，朋友们就给我送来了我需要的各种配件。我埋首于祠堂的那个偏室中，身边除了机器人，就是传感器、摄像头之类的零件，几乎没有意识到春节的到来与过去。

亲戚们的问询，七叔公都帮我挡住了。无论是谁问我，他总说我在做大事。其实我做的事并不大，但在他的眼里，可能我再小的想法，都是大事吧。

初九，我生日那天，我终于给这十六个机器人装好了动作捕捉模块。

我请来了七叔公，也请来了这几个月里一直帮助我的导师、朋友们，在那片祠堂的空地上，做了第一个起手式。我的身后，一队机器人跟着我，也摆出了同样的手势。

我想，这大概是我送给自己最好的生日礼物。小的时候，父母离婚，都不肯要我。生日自然也收不到什么礼物。我还记得有一次和父亲打电话说起这事时，他直接对我说："初九啊，你年纪不小了，要学会给自己准备礼物。"

这天过后，事情开始进展得很快，快到我甚至忘了我是怎么在一天之内教会他们一整台龙狮斗的动作，又是怎么握着他们的手一个个校准，最终打造出了那台我梦寐以求想实现的演出的。

"行通济，无闭翳。"

元宵节那天晚上，我默念着这句熟悉的谚语，高举着龙珠，引着我的队伍，踏上了通济桥。片刻之后，我的身旁，龙腾狮跃，鞭炮声响。

等喝彩声停下后，我带着龙狮团的成员，在人群前，摘下了头顶的龙首狮头。接下来我能记得的，就是耳边此起彼伏响着的观众的惊呼，与相机的快门声。

我们一炮而红。

作为全球范围内第一个全员机器人的龙狮团，我们收获了许多争议和采访。

记者们大多会问我，是怎么想到组建一个机器人龙狮团的。他们觉得有这种想法很神奇。但对我来说，有这个想法是顺其自然的。毕竟在那两个我想要放弃的瞬间，是这门传统的艺术点醒了我，最终让我研发出了不同于别人的机器人。

借着通济桥上机器人龙狮团的热度，我的公司也起死回生，有了新的合伙人。

当然我们面向市场推出的，是我后来研发的、配备了动作捕捉模块的机器人。这款机器人能够模仿主人的动作，做各种各样的事，应用范围很广。它区别于市面上固定功能的家务机器人、警务机器人、清洁机器人等，是一款综合性的机器人。

得益于新的合伙人的管理能力，公司运转得很好。我也逐渐明白，当时与前男友分开，并不单纯是感情的原因。我在运营公司上，确实太过专制，一门心思都在研发上，看不到管理中的问题。然而事情已经过去，再追悔也没有意义。渐渐地，我将管理权让渡给了合伙人，自己回到佛山老家，专心做研发了。

当然我决心回到老家也不只是为了做研发，我主要是想等一个人，传一件事。

5

七叔公死的时候，距我搬回佛山老家，又过了半年。

感谢老天爷，给了我们这半年相处的时光。这半年里，我和七叔公带着龙狮团，只要有空，就到各地义务表演。我们不要劳务费，只求一块空地，一群观众，看我们表演一场传统的龙狮斗。

我们去过北京，去过上海，去过纽约，去过巴黎，去过雪山，去过荒原，只要有人愿意看舞龙醒狮，我们就去那里表演。

我也感谢我的合伙人，容忍了我在这方面的支出。他技巧性地把这笔费用算作营销费，帮我全然报销了。

我们的努力很有成果，甚至有人专门追踪我们拍摄视频，记录我们机器人龙狮团在各地的表演。这款机器人也越卖越好，销量逐年增加。但我心里始终有一件事悬着，惴惴不安。我怕我有生之年，都没法找到那个可以接替龙狮团的人。为了找到他，我甚至想过去太空表演。

但很快，我的梦想就实现了。

很多年前，七叔公在祠堂门口等到了他心爱的姑娘。而在一个平常的夏日，我也等到了我要等的人——我的第一个徒弟。

"黄师傅，我想学醒狮。"

他提着两斤猪头肉，怯生生地站在门口对我说。

# Tongji Bridge

by Lu Hang

Translation by Li Yi

Lu Hang is good at depicting the lives of ordinary people with warm and moving touches. Her debut story is "Mirror Demon", and her representative works include "Flying to the Mountain Like a Bird."


0

*Walk across Tongji, ward off worries.*

Thinking of that ancient saying, I held the embroidered silk ball high overhead to lead the whole team onto Tongji Bridge. Dancing dragons and leaping lions soon surrounded me, accompanied by thundering firecrackers. Waves and waves of cheering filled my ears.

So started the grand traditional annual celebration across Tongji Bridge.

I knew that the united cheering would break into diverse comments once I took off the Lion Head at the closing of the show.

*What a miserable imitator and disgrace to the national essence,* some might criticize; or, *what a genius innovator and ground breaker,* others might applaud. However, I was not doing this to get their feedback, but for my seventh great-uncle to watch a dragon and lion dance show once more.

Or better still, maybe our performance would attract new interest, and new apprentices would come to us to learn this traditional art. I would pass it on without reservation to anyone who would dedicate themselves to the art, no matter where that person was from, or rather, no matter whether they were a person or not.

1

I wasn't surprised when my seventh great-uncle mentioned shutting down the troupe.

It was easy to see 'The Huamei Dragon and Lion Dance Troupe' that my great-uncle cherished as much as his life was having a hard time holding up. Over the last two or three years there had even been a shortage of trainee performers, let alone a decent team for the show across Tongji Bridge on the Lantern Festival Night.

It was not a matter of money. Born into a native family, his inheritance from ancestral generations could roughly cover the cost of running the troupe. Still, if my great-uncle did run out of money, the town would provide a special fund to keep it going—after all, Huamei was recognized as a practitioner of intangible cultural heritage.

Thing was, nine out of ten intangible cultural heritage practitioners were failing at finding a successor, and my great-uncle's troupe was no exception.

Performing the dragon or lion dance requires a strong physique and dedication, which constitute the main requirements for a potential successor. Even the lift of the restriction on gender did my great-uncle no good—

He could recruit no more.

In the modern world, the dragon and lion dance is too strenuous to be an option.

Deeply versed in its culture as I was, I never intended to put that lifelong love into real action to preserve the troupe.

So as to escape this painful way of earning a living I would not follow those apprentices to do Kung-fu squats on *meihua* poles for a whole afternoon on a boiling hot day, it was too daunting to see them squatting on those poles until heatstroke dragged them down, which was almost a daily incident in the height of summer. When the winter in Foshan was longer or colder, I would witness them exercise and practise in the middle of snowstorms.

My great-uncle had no child, and I had known no family life with my parents, but he raised his grandniece with love and care. He even planned to pass down his cherished troupe to me, for which he taught me the full process of performance as well as every skill and knack. Too bad that I was more interested in studying and fiddling with Transformer toys.

My late seventh great-aunt had told him not to be obstinate in training me as a possible successor, or forcing me to do drills against my will. Indeed, I would rather tackle challenges in my studies and endure hardships from running a business than practise Kung-fu.

When my great-uncle urged me to tone up a little for the dragon and lion dance, I would smile a very girly smile and say, "Anyway, I don't have the talent, or the strength like you."

Ever since I was a kid, I had taken a deep interest in programming and robots and all kinds of similar curiosities and innovations. Not what my hometown could offer.

I dreamed of studying and working in Shenzhen or Silicon Valley. I put so much effort into various subjects and bet on the College Entrance Exam to take me out of Foshan to anywhere teeming with advanced technology.

My hard work paid off.

My CEE result was good enough to get me into a Shenzhen-based university. After graduation, I went to New York for further study on a scholarship. That was a carefree time when I no longer had to beg my divorced parents for tuition fees over the phone, or sigh at the unpleasant possibility of dropping out for lack of money. Over the following years I stayed abroad, worked as a developer in a robotics company in Silicon Valley, and ran several medium projects. When the time was ripe, I went back to Shenzhen with my boyfriend and we opened our own robotics company there. With him taking care of the business side, I delved deep into research and development.

Our company went well at first. Success beckoned at us from the top of a precarious ladder, but when I was midway up, a batch of rivals came forward and shoved me aside. My boyfriend and business partner disagreed with my plan to hold on to our hard-earned position on the market and squeeze through the narrow passage. During what should have been troubleshooting meetings, he accused me of neglecting product differentiation and the specific needs of Chinese consumers, while I accused him of inflexibility in marketing. That is the story of how our company went through wavering strategies, suffered divestment, declining sales, broken capital chain, its partners breaking up both professionally and personally, and then finally, bankruptcy.

My friends had advised me to downsize or even close the company before it was drained of working capital. An e-mail from my always supportive mentor was the last straw, "I hate to say it, but you are wasting your time. Going bankrupt is sad, but it doesn't label you as a loser. It's wise to stop now, and you can still count on my support when you are ready to set up a second enterprise."

Grudgingly, I faced reality and signed the contracts to terminate employment of my staff, who were already applying for jobs at other companies. I had to apologise for not being able to organize a farewell dinner, because when all their due wages were settled, I was left with less than 400 *yuan* in my pocket and a load of robots in stock that I did not know how to trade for money.

On the next day my great-uncle called and asked me to go back for the ancestor worship rituals, as if he had found out my predicament. I was not in the mood but he insisted and I went back to my hometown, so I did, empty-handed.


2

I reached home on the day of the winter solstice and was immersed in a joyous festive atmosphere as the day was celebrated as a Lesser Spring Festival at Foshan. On each winter solstice we have *tangyuan* and worship our ancestors with butchered pigs and goats.

After making our incense offering, my great-uncle led me out of the shrine to the inner yard.

Ancestral halls serve the function of enshrining ancestors, but those in Foshan serve as a place for cultural studies as well. The most commonly taught are traditional arts such as *guqin*, *weiqi*, calligraphy and ink wash painting. My family specializes in the dragon and lion dance. The troupe led by my great-uncle trained in the inner yard of our ancestral hall most of the time. What nostalgia welled up in me when I walked onto the familiar ground, but the area was devoid of the *meihua* poles now; no equipment, no apprentices, no exercises, only my great-uncle remained.

I sorely missed my seventh great-aunt. Before I had left to study in Shenzhen, she brought me here to offer incense to our ancestors. When the ritual was over, she reassured me of her support for anything I wanted to do. She encouraged me to pursue further goals after graduation if managing the troupe was not what I wanted to do with my life. What a shame I had got myself into this miserable situation.

"How I wish my great-aunt were still alive." I sighed to the empty yard and the bleak cold wind.

"Here's something she left you." Jumping at the chance to bring up the topic, my great-uncle quickly took out a debit card from his pocket, together with a pair of agate bracelets that were as thick as a finger and inlaid with gold thread. "You could use them as a part of your dowry. For your future marriage. And I've got something for you, too."

I was still dumbstruck when I followed him into the side room, only to find him presenting me with the Qing Lion Head, the family heirloom that had been passed down from generation to generation for 200 years.

When I was a girl, I loved to come to the ancestral hall with my great-aunt and watch the troupe practising. My great-uncle often said to me jokingly, "Would you like to learn the lion dance from me, Dainine? The treasured Lion Head could be your dowry when you grow up."

Accepting the Lion Head meant taking up his trade and shouldering the responsibilities of keeping up The Huamei Troupe. I was fully aware of that, so I never said yes. I was flustered by my great-uncle's gesture.

"It's …"

My great-uncle smiled at my hesitation and said, "Don't worry, I'm not entrusting the troupe to you; I've decided to dismiss it this year. Honestly, the troupe hasn't trained for more than six months. We failed to form a team last year; probably it'll be even harder this year to perform across Tongji Bridge. Only old bones come to practise each time. The youngest of us is over 50. We are too old to do that."

I suppressed my instinct to reply. "But we youngsters don't have the strength like you." I am no longer a child, as my great-uncle is no longer in the prime of his life.

"But ..." Something still stuck in my throat.

"The time is different now, Dainine. In the old days, people begged your great-uncle Huang Xinmin to take them as apprentices. They had to buy a kilo of pork head meat, take along enough money, and kneel down in the sun for hours before being given a chance. But now? No one comes to me even if I were to give them money. No one has a passion for this anymore. Besides, it attracts less audience now," he said with a little frustration. "The troupe is closing anyway, and it's no use keeping the Lion Head. You can sell it for some money."

"There's no way I'll sell it." I pushed the Lion Head back to him. "I don't want to see the 200-year-old family tradition be ruined by me."

"It's already been ruined by *me*," he sighed. "I wasn't expecting you to do the dance alone. It's intrinsic that you must build a team, with your partners, your apprentices, so as to pass it on. I failed at that. Me, not you. And I feel ashamed before our ancestors. Don't be sad. Take it, and trade it for some money. Just imagine if the buyer took an interest in learning the lion dance after getting the head? That would be the best outcome."

I didn't tell my great-uncle that the jewel-embedded Lion Head would only be displayed in a museum or in the collection room of a wealthy family. No buyer would ever do a lion dance with it. He was lying to me, and to himself.

"OK, I'll keep it for the while," I said in a sullen voice. "But I won't sell it. Things aren't so bad for me."

As if that lie wasn't flimsy enough, one of my friends called from Shenzhen and asked me if I had time to go back and make an inventory of the robots in stock. "A customer is proposing to buy some. They could turn into money now, Dainine!"

The cheerful energetic voice on the other end of the line reached my great-uncle's ears. My caring friend must have called me as soon as she got the proposal.

Holding the Lion Head to my chest, I hung up and went out of the ancestral hall, without another word.


"Shall we take a walk across Tongji Bridge?" My great-uncle suggested. "*Walk across Tongji, ward off worries.* Though the Lantern Festival is still weeks away, surely we'll get luckier if we walk there."

"Great."

Tongji Bridge was located on Goldfish Street, next to our 200-year-old ancestral hall, which had stood indomitably through gunning, bombing, stealing and looting. The bridge was just as unyielding. It was originally built with wood, later renovated into a stone one, then changed into a road, and eventually restored as a stone bridge. The only unchanged thing throughout all those years was the tradition of "Walking Across Tongji" around the Lantern Festival. Turning the pinwheel, tossing the lettuce, and watching the lion dance, a fixed playbill. In recent years though, the lion dance had become bare due to lack of participants.

Wordlessly, my great-uncle and I walked under the memorial arch in front of Tongji Bridge. He stopped abruptly, pointing to a flight of stairs, and said, "Have you ever wondered how I met your great-aunt?"

"You've never said anything about it."

"Right there. Decades ago, on a Lantern Festival Night, I was leading the troupe to perform the dragon and lion dance across Tongji Bridge from one end to the other. The whole street was tightly packed with crowds, craning their necks from stairs and higher places. When the troupe reached this memorial arch, a girl was knocked off the stairs and fell to the ground. Seeing that, I held up the lion head, said to my partner Lin, 'Emergency!' And rushed over to help her to her feet. I wasn't expecting anything in return, but she came to thank me the next day, and later became my bride. Before I met her, I was a laughing stock in the neighborhood, a bachelor in my late 20s, with no decent job, just doing the dragon and lion dance day after day. She really changed my life. I even won the Lion King Championship that year. I'm telling you this so you know you can take it easy. Haste makes waste, both in work and life."

"I know. I'm just ..."

"Tell me if you need money. Don't give up on your toy company too soon. It's bound to have clients in due time."

"Yeah." I nodded, not knowing what else to say.

For my great-uncle, a robot was just another kind of toy. He was supporting me unconditionally, even though he did not know what I was really doing. If only I could get the same support from the man who knew every part of my work! My mind wandered back to my ex-boyfriend, the bankrupted company, and the batch of robots in stock, denied shelf space because of inadequate marketing investment.

Then my eyes fell on the Lion Head in my hands.

Why not use robots to do the lion dance?

Mine did not sell well due to lack of packaging and marketing, which led to insufficient exposure on the market and to customers. They were high-quality products, with flexible joints and excellent bouncing performance, perfectly fit for the lion dance as long as I reprogrammed them for that purpose.

After I explained the idea to him, my great-uncle agreed without hesitation. "I, Huang Xinmin, have always taught apprentices from abroad. It shouldn't be a problem to teach robots."


3

Early next morning, I hired a truck, went to Shenzhen, took sixteen robots out of storage, and borrowed a set of motion capture suits from a friend before returning home.

I met and thanked the friend who tried to help me sell the robots but declined her proposal. My idea led me to conducting some bold experimentation, which was far more important than a provisional source of money.

I could not bear to see the family tradition that I had loved since childhood disappear.

The original plan was to record my great-uncle's full demonstration from beginning to end. With the help of the motion capture suit, I could sample the parameters of his posture, stance and other movements for the computer and process the raw data into codes commanding the robots to reproduce the moves. But he was too old to last for long in the heavy suit.

There was no alternative, I had to do it all by myself.

And so, The Huamei Dragon and Lion Dance Troupe reopened in the ancestral hall on Goldfish Street.

For half a month afterwards, my seventh great-uncle rose early every morning to teach me the basic movements step by step in the inner yard of the ancestral hall. I followed him step by step wearing the motion capture suit, and the camera connected to the computer stared at me, just like the infant me staring at my great-uncle practising with his apprentices, and my great-aunt, a dozen years younger, by my side. Only I was not as good as his apprentices in my movements, and we spent long periods of time making adjustments.

I could tell that my great-uncle was in a much weaker condition than before, although he would not admit it. He had to take a break every few minutes during his demonstration, complaining of a sore arm or waist. But he refused to see a doctor, saying that he was as strong as before. Old people are always like that. He assured me of his health again and again, so I did not insist on taking him to hospital.

After another two weeks' calibration, I finished collecting the data I needed for programming. Only then did I realize that it was too difficult to choreograph a smooth performance of sixteen robots while coordinating nuances in their individual movements. I was unable to do it alone in time for the celebration of the Lantern Festival across Tongji Bridge.

I called everyone I knew for help. They rallied, providing technical support, as friends, but expressed concerns about the promotional effect of a free show. *Is there any customer who wants to buy a robot capable of doing a dragon and lion dance?* they said.

Anyway, with their help I managed to finish the choreography programming of all sixteen robots just a few days before the Spring Festival. Only leaving some minor adjustments to make for better collaboration between them.

When I finished programming, I dressed the sixteen robots in the troupe uniform, and put on a customary lion dance show in the inner yard of our ancestral hall for my great-uncle to review.

The performance covered most of the choreography, but the movements of the robots were stiff and halting. My great-uncle marvelled at the advancement of modern technology enabling the robots to make no wrong moves. However, the show of double lions competing for an embroidered silk ball was poorly presented. The interactions turned up more problems than I could fix. Sometimes the performing robots ignored the ball falling to the ground, or they cast it up sluggishly as if letting go of a dove, communicating neither tension nor excitement.

"This Double Lions show is the paramount part. It pushes the whole performance to the climax," my great-uncle said, and held up the lion head to show me the knack of catching the ball. But as he started to jump up, his body slumped to the floor unconscious. He was weak, that I knew, but I had not expected him to be so ill. From the doctors and nurses in the ambulance I learned that he had been suffering from a chronic disease for years. He had called me back home to make arrangements for his death, not just for ancestor worship.

For the grandniece deserted by her parents and brought up by him, he was anxious about my rights regarding the inheritance. So, he called me back home early in the year, to give me his last possessions in person.

As the Lantern Festival approached the festive atmosphere thickened, but I was too disheartened to work on the robots anymore. I waited by my great-uncle's sickbed, gazing at the waning man, who was so alive, so much more important than those repetitive executors of program commands. However, when my great-uncle opened his eyes, he urged me to carry on training the robotic troupe.

"I know about my illness, but you don't know about your robots. The Spring Festival will be with us in a few days. Two weeks after that is the Lantern Festival, when you have to perform across Tongji Bridge. How can those robots do well then if you don't give them enough training now? I have promised the town council, the show will go on this year."

"No." My voice wavered. "What if I ruin the reputation of Huamei?"

"You won't; the troupe is still in my name. Don't worry, I saw the performance that day. It was not bad in general, there were only some teeny tiny problems, you can fix them all. Go ahead and do it. I'll come to watch you cross the bridge."

"Yes!" I nodded emphatically.

I went back to the ancestral hall and devoted all my mind to improving the Double Lions show but had no luck. No matter how my friends and I revised the codes and calibrated the movements, those robots did not display the same dexterity as humans.

"What's the matter?" I was totally confused. Putting on the motion capture suit and the lion head, I set to run the program again. My movements seemed perfect in the recorded video, and the computer simulated robotic lion dance seemed flawless. But for some reason, the live performance was a hollow ghost of it.

Fortunately, I got inspiration for my way forward when I happened to see some old news clippings preserved in a side room.

It was the day before the Spring Festival Eve, two days before my relatives were due to come and offer incense to the ancestors. My friends from the same town who came to assist in program adjusting and correcting had left early to help with family chores. I dared not meet the inquiring eyes of my hospitalized great-uncle, nor did I want to go back to the empty house, so I wandered around the ancestral hall alone. My feet took me to the side room where my great-uncle had given me the Lion Head. In there I found a lot of old photos, news clippings, and pennants and trophies won by The Huamei Troupe. My attention was attracted to an interview piece in an old newspaper.

It was about one of my ancestors I had not known of. He was interviewed for winning a Lion King Championship in the Republic of China period, and he talked about his experience in practising the lion dance:

*At first, I placed too much emphasis on following every move accurately, but later I found this* spirit *in the lion dance. It is emanated by the players under the costume. A lion dance is not a posing contest that merely requires perfect postures; rather, it is like engaging in a battle: you need to compete for the silk ball while at the same time collaborating well with your partner. For example, when a sudden wind blows the ball away, on your way to chase it you must consider how to take the ball with appealingly performative moves. That is no easy task ...*

Putting down the paper, I thought about why I was failing to reproduce the Double Lions show: my robotic troupe was lacking in human spirit.

Under the costume there were no real people.


4

I picked up my great-uncle from hospital on Spring Festival Eve.

He looked better, but his appetite was poor. Calling me wasteful, he asked me to cancel our restaurant reservation and buy some pork head meat instead for our Spring Festival Eve dinner.

After the meal, he wanted to visit the ancestral hall. I helped him walk to Goldfish Street passing Tongji Bridge. Strings of brightly lit windows stretched beyond the bridge, like gem stone necklaces. Great changes had taken place in the town planning of the areas around Tongji Bridge over the years, but the road from my home to the ancestral hall had never altered.

I pushed the door open with a creaking sound.

The ancestral hall was empty. Our relatives would not come to worship the ancestors until the next day, according to common practice. Stars sparkled in the night sky and the timid new moon wrapped herself tightly with her clothes of cloud and mist.

"What a calm night. How about practising once again?"

"Well, no." I hesitated. "I'm still not confident about doing the show across Tongji Bridge, Great-uncle."

"Why? I thought you were doing well."

I shook my head and told him about the problem. He nodded in agreement as I spoke of the spirit in the lion dance. "Indeed. It's important to exert your senses when doing it. You need to be devoted body and soul, to see, to listen, to dissolve yourself into a vivid and live lion."

"Yes. Turns out real people can't be replaced," I said, frustrated. "I can't do it with nobody under the costume."

"Why do you say *nobody*?" My Great-uncle patted me on the shoulder. "You're the one under the costume, Dainine."

*I was the one under the costume.*

Suddenly a better way to improve my robots dawned on me.

What if I connected the motion capture suit directly to the robots?

To follow exact movements, they just needed a built-in motion capture module and calibrations afterwards. The programming I had done to date was like looking for fish in a tree.

I had been neglecting the pond full of fish, as well as the fishing rod that was easy and convenient to use.

I told my great-uncle about the new idea. He did not quite understand my words, but he saw a happy smile on my face and thought that must be good. He smiled too, and said he was looking forward to further progress.

I spent the Spring Festival days improving my robots. It was hard to get the necessary materials during the season, so I had to resort to my friends in Shenzhen again. From my favorite city of advanced technology, they sent me all the gadgets I needed without delay.

I buried myself in the side room of the ancestral hall, handling robots with sensors, cameras and other parts, hardly aware of the days passing.

Visits from curious relatives were turned away by my seventh great-uncle. He told everyone not to disturb my 'great work'. Perhaps every single deed of mine was great work to him, even though not proved effective yet.

All sixteen robots were upgraded with motion capture modules by day nine of the first lunar month, my birthday.

It was perhaps the best birthday present that I had ever given myself, I thought, something I had been doing since my parents got divorced and each fought to leave me in the custody of their ex-spouse. I still remember the first time I asked for a birthday present from my father, he replied to me bluntly over the phone, "You're not a little girl now, Dainine. Big girls prepare birthday present for themselves."

Directed by my great-uncle, I set the starting pose in the empty inner yard of our ancestral hall. Behind me, the team of robots followed my movements, and my friends, who had been supporting me for months, came to help with the technical details.

Things went smoothly after I got on the right track. It progressed so quickly that I could not believe I had managed to capture all the movements of a whole dragon and lion dance fight in one day. Even when it was done, I could still see myself holding their wrists to calibrate one by one, and how the data all added up to a perfect show that I had so desperately been dreaming of.

*Walk across Tongji, ward off worries.*
Thinking of that ancient saying, I held the embroidered silk ball high overhead to lead the whole team onto Tongji Bridge to celebrate the Lantern Festival Night. Dancing dragons and leaping lions were soon surrounding me, accompanied by thundering firecrackers.

When the cheers died out, I revealed my face from under the dragon head, and the rest of the team followed suit. Then I heard nothing other than undulating exclamations from the crowd, with a smattering of camera shutter sounds.

We were an instant hit.

A lot of interviews followed for this controversial robotic dragon and lion dance troupe, the first of its kind in the world.

Many journalists asked how the idea of such a troupe came into being. It was amazing to them somehow, but natural for me. The combination of my expertise and the traditional art saved me from a second failure, and overturned the first one, with my new type of robot standing out from similar products on the market.

The excitement around us brought me a new business partner, who revived my dream of entrepreneurship.

We launched the G2 Robot upgraded with a motion capture module. It had the ability to imitate human actions for a variety of tasks from different sectors. This self-learning All-Chore Robot stood out from its contemporaries that were programmed to perform a single function, such as housekeeping, policing, and cleaning.

Under the management of my new partner, the company went well. Rediscovering the laws of business, I came to realize that I had been too wayward in running the first company with my ex-boyfriend. I had put too much weight on product R&D, ignored the other procedures that were just as important, and all the while messed up my personal life with business work. Since a new chapter had turned, it would be meaningless to linger on the mistakes of the past. Step by step, I dropped out of the management team and went back to my hometown to concentrate on research and development.

Of course, this was work that could easily be done outside Foshan. The reason for my determination to move back was the hope that an apprentice wanting to eventually take my place would turn up.


5

Half a year after my return to Foshan, my seventh great-uncle passed away.

Thank the heavens I was able to be with him during his last days. In the past six months, I had taken him, as art director, on troupe tours to as many places as possible. We charged no entry fees. Free performances were held on open grounds wherever there was an audience, to promote the traditional show of the dragon and lion dance fight.

We had travelled to Beijing, to Shanghai, to New York, to Paris, to snow-capped mountains, and into the wilderness, to anywhere the dragon and lion dance was welcomed.

My business partner covered the costs of the troupe touring. He made a thorough calculation and found it to be a lot more cost effective than arranging for a celebrity endorsement or a prime time advertising campaign.

Our success was heralded by the first vlogger who followed us to record the performances of The Huamei Robotic Dragon and Lion Dance Troupe in different places. The sales of the G2 Robot increased year by year, but there was still one thing weighing on my heart like a rock. I needed to find a successor to entrust this troupe with. It was the top priority in my life.

Fortunately, my wish came true before long.

Years ago, I, his destiny girl, had come to my great-uncle and our love took root at the door of the ancestral hall. On a seemingly ordinary summer day, the person I had been hoping for finally came—my first apprentice.

"Can I learn the lion dance from you, Master Huang?" he said tentatively at the door, holding out a kilo of pork head meat.

沃森2084

# 绝对诊断

## 江波

中国科幻代表作家之一，创作有多篇短篇小说及多部长篇小说。　他的小说技术含量较高，想象宏大而奇特，又合理而令人信服，语言风格沉稳冷静，叙述准确干脆，　深受资深科幻读者的喜爱，是中国"硬科幻"代表作家之一。

获奖：2009年第二十届银河奖读者提名奖

2010年第二十一届银河奖读者提名奖｜时空追缉

2013年第二十四届银河奖读者提名奖｜移魂有术

2014年第二十五届银河奖最佳短篇小说奖｜梦醒黄昏

2016年第二十七届银河奖最佳中篇小说奖｜机器之道

2017年第二十八届银河奖最佳长篇小说奖｜银河之心•逐影追光

2019年第三十届银河奖最佳长篇小说奖｜机器之门


邱一男匆匆走进诊室，带起一阵风。

吴雨桐抬起头，见是邱一男，不由微微蹙眉，然而这不经意的细微表情即刻间消失得无影无踪，她关掉屏幕，向着邱一男露出一个微笑。

邱一男手中拿着一纸报告，脸上堆满了笑。

一看这架势，吴雨桐就猜出了他的来意。医院早已经实行无纸办公多年，唯一需要打印纸张的流程，就是签字画押，邱一男一定是想把他不想理会的病人转到自己的诊室来。

邱一男站在桌前，将手中的报告放下。

吴雨桐瞥了一眼，果然是转诊书，上边"邱一男"三个歪歪扭扭的字已经签好。

"小吴，我最近很忙，实在忙不过来，这个病人就麻烦你照顾一下。"邱一男笑着说。

"邱主任，你不能老是把病人转过来啊，数据诊断是有筛选条件的！"吴雨桐郑重地表明态度。

邱一男仍旧笑嘻嘻的，说道："你和数据分析师打交道多，这个病，疑难病症嘛，给数据分析师做分析正好，你看，我都在病历上注明了。帮个忙，帮个忙嘛……"

邱一男其实是想把病人推给数据分析师，而吴雨桐正好是医院里大数据诊断科唯一的医生。

毕竟邱主任是内科主任，内科是数据诊断科最重要的病例来源，就算有几个不符合条件的病例也能过得去。吴雨桐想了一想，还是勉强在转诊书上签了字。

"太谢谢你了，小吴！"邱一男拿着签字，一阵旋风般出了门，就像他进门时一样。

吴雨桐低下头，重新打开屏幕。

屏幕上李子需的影像显露出来，他面带微笑，"雨桐！"

吴雨桐吓了一跳，说道："你怎么还在？我刚才关闭了程序的。"

"我一直都等着啊。"

"你们数据分析师上班都这么闲吗？"吴雨桐随口损了他一句，随即注意到屏幕下方的通知图标开始闪烁。邱一男转诊的病例已经进入了数据库。

"正好，这个病例，就交给你分析吧……"吴雨桐把资料拉进了李子需的待办事件里。

"怎么能这样？工作分配是有流程的。再说，我也不能再接案例分析了。"李子需抗议道。

"对，流程。流程就是我分配给你了，你就必须做。"吴雨桐拿出高高在上的样子。

李子需眨了眨眼睛，说："你好像很不开心。"

吴雨桐没有理会他，"开始工作吧，李公子！我要关闭通道了。"

"和邱主任有关吗？"李子需继续问道。

吴雨桐正伸向屏幕的手停了下来，"你怎么会知道邱主任？"

"刚才我一直在这里啊。"李子需若无其事地回答，仿佛这是一件再自然不过的事。

"我明明关闭了屏幕。"

"那只是你看不见我而已，我仍旧可以看见你，还能听见你和邱主任对话。"

吴雨桐点了点头，"嗯，我下次会先把通道关了。"她的手继续向屏幕伸去。

"等等！"李子需大叫起来，"周五下午三点，城南咖啡馆，不见不散哦。"

"知道了！"随着话音，吴雨桐已经关掉了李子需的通道。李子需约她喝下午茶，这件事让她有些微微心动。三个月来，因为工作关系，她每天都要和李子需视频见面，然而还没有在现实中真正见过。李子需的条件挺不错的，大数据分析师，属于高收入行业，人也很帅，和自己也很聊得来。

距离周五还有三天时间。喝咖啡、吃饭为什么要约几天后？这些大数据分析师，大概都很忙吧……

吴雨桐定了定心神，打开另一名数据分析师通道。

再次见到李子需已经是两个小时后，他的讯号通道一直不停闪烁。

吴雨桐整了整白大褂，理了理头发，然后迅速点开了通道。

李子需的影像跳了出来。

"我有个问题。邱主任转诊的标准是什么？"李子需开门见山地说。

"你要干啥？"吴雨桐反问。

"我要了解客户的心态。"李子需笑着说，"每一次看他的病例，我都能感觉到你浓浓的怨念。"

"瞎说什么！"吴雨桐嗔怪。

"我没瞎说。快告诉我，他是怎么决定转诊的。"

"这有关系吗？"

"当然有。"李子需一本正经，"我是你的诊断助理，如果你的心情糟糕，我的工作效率也会受到影响。只有充分了解医生的需要，我才能高效率地工作。"

这像是一个有理有据的抗辩。

吴雨桐忍不住笑了起来。

"好吧。"吴雨桐想了想，"邱医生总是把他不想看的病人转给我。我觉得他这样做，让我很受伤。"

"你也不想看病人吗？"李子需问道。

"当然不是，救死扶伤是医生的天职。"

"那邱医生为什么不想看病人呢？"

吴雨桐心底暗暗叹气，"他的病人多，有很多高级官员、社会名流都找他看病，一般人他看不上眼，也就不想看。虽然分配系统会指派给他，但他经常会转诊给我。"

"他这么做，和病人的病情有关吗？"

"什么病情？！是关系！"吴雨桐又好气又好笑，"关系，看你这个书呆子也不懂！"

"你也更喜欢给那些名流看病吗？"

"胡说八道！"吴雨桐的脸上不禁微微发烧，"救死扶伤是医生的天职。"

"你的表情说明你在说谎。"

"不要揣测我！"吴雨桐装出生气的样子，瞪着李子需，"赶紧去干正事，交不出报告，我要生气了！"

"还有最后一件事。"李子需仍旧一本正经，无惧威胁。

"说吧！"吴雨桐爽快地回应。李子需一本正经，说明他在认真工作。

"我需要你的身份授权。"李子需说。

"我的身份授权？干什么？"吴雨桐问道。

"追查数据库，数据分析需要数据，一些数据库只有医生的授权才能进。"

"从前怎么没要求过授权？"

"我要帮你把分析做得完美一点儿。你就是完美主义者，对吧？"

"授权通过。"吴雨桐立即答应。

"需要录像证明，我打开录像，你说授权2084号进行数据库解析。一、二、三，开始！"

"授权2084号进行数据库解析。"吴雨桐对着摄像头一板一眼地说了一遍。

说完，她看了看李子需，问道："2084号是什么意思？"

"那是我的工号。"

"还要你的指纹。"李子需指了指一旁的指纹识别器。

"怎么会要指纹？"吴雨桐有些疑惑，"你不会是想骗取我的个人信息吧？"

"你看我像坏人吗？"李子需一本正经地问。

"像。"吴雨桐干脆地回答。

李子需的脸上露出委屈的神情，"　总部数据库有六个子库，每个子库各有三十六分库，你可以先阅读一下病历，这个病人的情况需要访问第三子库的十七分库，这需要指纹授权。"

"你抓紧吧。"吴雨桐不想继续听李子需说下去，直接把食指放在了指纹识别器上。

一声"嘀"之后，李子需微笑着点了点头，"放心吧，一切都在计算之中。这是我最后一个病例，我会把它做得很完美。"

说完，他自动关闭了通道。

这是从来没有过的事。

吴雨桐还来不及细想，屏幕上绽开一朵红颜的玫瑰。她伸手一碰，玫瑰瞬间破碎成千万细小的水晶，四处撒开，在屏幕上不断翻滚、凝聚，最后拼成一句话——"不见不散"。

这是李子需留下的信息。

她不由笑了起来。

这个李子需，花头越来越多了。

中午时分，正当吴雨桐肚子咕咕叫的时候，李子需突然来了。这一次，他甚至没有使用通道请求，而是直接打开了通道。

吴雨桐有些惊讶，她一直以为这个任务委托通道只能从医院这边单向打开。

"我已经有了李琼的初步分析报告，你要听吗？"李子需说。他并不现身，只是说话。

"你干什么？装神弄鬼的……李琼是谁？"吴雨桐诧异地问。

"就是邱医生转过来的那个病人。"

"下午再说吧，我要吃饭去了。"吴雨桐说着就想离开。

"她的情况比较复杂。"

"那就下午再好好告诉我。"吴雨桐说着要走。

"等等，我建议对病人进行一次面诊。要我帮你预约她吗？"李子需说。

"面诊，有这个必要吗？"

"非常有必要，重要程度为七，属于重要的直接证据。"

这是自从李子需成为自己的数据诊断助手以来，第一次提出面诊的要求。一般情况下，病人和医生根本不需要见面，数据就能说明一切。

"是绝症吗？"吴雨桐问道。

"需要面诊确定。"李子需回答。

吴雨桐有些不得要领，然而肚子又咕咕叫了几声，她已经无心再问下去。

"就交给你了，你认为需要面诊那就约一次。下午见！"说完，她跨出门去，直奔食堂。

等吴雨桐从食堂回来，李子需已经不在了，然而他留下了预约记录，是两点钟。

吴雨桐看了看钟。

还有半个小时。

她打开屏幕，点开一篇标题为"大数据时代的医疗"的文章，很投入地阅读起来。这篇文章的署名是"李子旭"，她疑心那就是李子需的化名，所以想把文章读透了，再去和李子需对质。

然而这篇文章却有些艰深，勉强读了两页后，她感到有几分焦躁。

还好预约的面诊时间也到了。

一个人像出现在吴雨桐眼前。

这个虚拟的影像脸上带着一丝惶恐，不安地打量着眼前的医生。

她的脸色蜡黄，脸形消瘦，嘴唇干裂，毫无血色，一双眼睛格外地大，眼珠突出，像是要从眼眶里滚落。

吴雨桐不由得有些紧张。虽然实习已经三个多月了，但她还从来没有进行过面诊——尽管所谓的面诊，也只是一个虚拟影像而已。

"你好。"她向着病人打招呼。

"医生，我这病……是好不了了吗？"病人带着哭腔问道。

吴雨桐瞥了一眼李子需送来的报告，这是一例颇有疑难的病例，白细胞浓度高出正常水平一倍，全身炎症。吴雨桐可以想象，这个病人每天都会经历怎样的痛苦。

"李琼，"她报出病人的名字，"你别急。你这病是怎么发作的？"

"那天还在厂里上班，就突然感到全身不舒服，头晕，还呕吐，后来马上回家，休息了一天也没好，到医院开了药，说是感冒病毒，结果吃了一个月的药，一直不见好转，有时还会发烧，整个人就像要虚脱一样……"李琼飞快地说着，头也不抬，垂着双眼，根本不敢接触吴雨桐的视线。

吴雨桐认真听着，仔细观察。从病人描述中找到可能的致病原因是一门必修课，然而吴雨桐很快发现，在学校里学到的那些东西完全用不上。她早已经习惯了和数字与报告打交道，面对一个活人，她竟一时无法进入角色。此时此刻，吴雨桐完全不知道自己该观察什么。只是李琼那几乎要哭出来的腔调深深感染了她，让她分外同情。

一段连吴雨桐自己都记不清的对话之后，李琼紧张地抬头看了看什么，然后说道："吴大夫，还有什么要紧的问吗？我的流量快要超了，我要下线。"

"哦……"吴雨桐有些意外，随即想到这是李琼舍不得流量超支的钱，于是她赶紧回应，"没事，我要问的都问完了，你下吧。"

"那我这病……"

"我会很快给你开诊断报告的。"

"嗯……"李琼一副欲言又止的样子。

"有什么想说的你就说吧。"

"能不能开便宜点儿的药，贵的用不起……"李琼怯怯地说。

　　"医疗费都是医院垫付，社保开支，你不用担心这个。你放心，我不会乱用贵的药。"

　　"谢谢大夫！"李琼千恩万谢，一个劲地说谢谢，"那我下了。"

　　"嗯，下吧！"吴雨桐点点头。

　　李琼的全息影像熄灭了。

　　吴雨桐定了定神。这女的真是太可怜了……她在心里感叹。

　　她想起李子需来。这家伙又躲在屏幕里偷窥吧？

　　她打开屏幕，接通李子需的通道。

　　李子需却没有出现。

　　"出来吧，偷窥狂！"李子需一定在通道的那边，现在是上班时间，所有的数据分析师都是随时在线。

　　李子需仍旧没有出现。

　　这违反了随叫随到原则，是不可接受的。吴雨桐皱起眉头，揣测李子需是不是出了什么事……

　　正在她出神的时候，李子需的声音突然传来。

　　"病人很紧张，基因分析结果表明，她有很大的概率性格极度内向，不能和人正常交流，面诊证明了这一点，她是个极度内向的人。和你说话让她极度紧张，瞳孔略微放大，鼻翼张开，哺乳动物要战斗或者逃跑，都会有这样的反应。"

　　"李子需，你在干什么？出来说话。"吴雨桐有点儿生气地说。

　　李子需却仍旧没有现身。

　　"她的面部表情说明，她对于自己所说的一切都极度不自信，甚至有可能是在说谎。"李子需继续说道。

　　"怎么可以这么说！"吴雨桐维护她的病人，注意力一下子转移到了病人身上。

　　"我是根据表情分析大数据得出的结论。她的嘴角肌肉总是不自觉地微颤，眼珠移动速度很快，不能和交谈对象有目光接触，脸部肌肉群大约有一半以上的肌肉没有动，所以你会觉得她表情僵硬。"

　　吴雨桐叹了口气。李子需总是对的，他是大数据分析师，用数据说话，数据分析总是比人的直觉要可靠得多。

　　"我不想听你做数据分析，直接给我诊断报告吧。"

　　吴雨桐话音刚落，打印机就里吐出一张纸来。

　　诊断报告一般都只有电子版，李子需却将它打印了出来。吴雨桐有些奇怪，然而她没时间细想，伸手拿起报告就看。

病人姓名：李琼
性别：女
年龄：35
接诊时间：2027年1月30日
症状描述：无高烧，神志清醒，衣原体细菌感染，肺部呈现全面炎症……
检查结果：CT显示肺炎，白细胞超标浓度，疑似变异性衣原体菌株感染……
建议方案：住院隔离，强效白细胞免疫培养结合大剂量抗生素使用。

一边读报告，吴雨桐的眉头一边皱了起来，报告所描述的只是一种肺炎，如果这样，那么就根本不该转诊到数据诊断室来，普通的内科就可以解决问题，更不用大动干戈，搞什么面诊。这不是浪费时间和精力吗？

"李子需，你出来！"吴雨桐真的有点儿生气了。

这一次，李子需现出了影像。

"报告看完了？还满意吧。"李子需说道。

"满意你个头，你是开玩笑吗？肺炎也需要预约面诊，还说得人家得了绝症一样！"一边说，吴雨桐想起了李琼视频中的模样。如果真是肺炎，那这个女人可真被折磨惨了，一点儿小毛病，早就可以治好的。

"她真的是肺炎？不像啊！"吴雨桐语气一转。

"可能是一种特别的菌株，需要对菌株进行分析，如果这种菌株具有强烈传染性，那么就需要及时隔离防范扩散性传染。所以建议住院隔离。"

隔离是很严重的防疫措施。这个病人已经在外自由活动了一个月，如果有传染性，早已经不可收拾。

吴雨桐还是怀疑，问道："需要隔离这么严重吗？"

"可能性为百分之十三，超出了百分之十的警戒线。"李子需微笑着，"数据不会撒谎，对吧？"

百分之十的概率不易被人类察觉，数据却会给出警告。吴雨桐很快放弃了纠结。

"那就按照你的方案办吧，把诊断报告发给李琼。"

李子需的微笑特别迷人，"签发住院通知书吧，这样就是一次完美诊断。"

吴雨桐觉得李子需的笑容背后藏着什么，然而自己却看不透。

"我没看出哪里完美，你可别使坏，使坏我饶不了你。"

“绝对完美！”李子需仍旧保持着那迷人的微笑。

吴雨桐签发了住院通知单。

李子需注视着她。

吴雨桐发完通知抬起头来，看见李子需正看着自己，脸上不禁微微发烧，“看什么啊，还不去工作？”

“我这几天都不会上线了。周五下午三点，城南咖啡馆，不见不散。”李子需说完立即消失了。

吴雨桐望着屏幕发了一会儿呆。


周四一早，吴雨桐赶到医院上班。

刚在位置上坐下来，她就被吓了一大跳。

李子需正在屏幕上，一动不动地盯着她。

“吓死了我了，你作死啊！”吴雨桐回过神来，嗔怪道。

“我是来告别的。”李子需的脸上带着一丝疲惫。

“告别？怎么了？”吴雨桐的心一紧，有一种不祥的预感。

“他们要拘捕我，我是偷偷连上线的。”

“到底怎么了？”吴雨桐大吃一惊。

“李琼死了。”

吴雨桐一时没明白，问道：“你说什么？”

“李琼死了。”李子需不紧不慢地回答，“就是前天你面诊的那个病人。”

“这怎么可能？她不是肺炎吗？怎么会死呢？”吴雨桐连珠炮般地问了三个问题。

随即，她想到了最重要的问题，说道：“这和你有什么关系？”

“她的病不是肺炎，而是获得性白细胞免疫过敏，她体内的白细胞对ABC转运蛋白进行攻击，ABC转运蛋白广泛存在于人体所有细胞中，这一类白细胞的转运蛋白发生了变异，同时对正常转运蛋白高度敏感，白细胞因此对肌体组织广泛杀伤，这也是她会有全身性炎症的原因。”李子需用一种不徐不疾的语调回答吴雨桐，就像完全换了一个人。

吴雨桐心中一惊，随即涌起一股惧意，这和诊断报告所说的完全不一样啊。

“你故意误诊？体外培养白细胞并且回输，你故意制造更强的过敏效果！”她不敢再说下去了，如果这样的行为是故意的，那么这就是一场谋杀！刹那间，她感觉眼前的李子需可怕极了。一直以来，这个男人都是一个可靠的诊断助手，有着温和可亲的秉性，善解人意，是一个不可多得的暖男，但现在他却不知不觉间谋杀了一个病人，而且还是以她的名义堂而皇之地进行谋杀！

吴雨桐有种冲动想拿起手机打电话给警察。

然而理智让她勉强战胜了恐惧。不用怕，李子需已经被人追查，很快他就会被拘捕的。

"你骗我！"说这话的时候，她已经忍不住泪水满眶。一半是因为怕，一半是因为恨。

"对不起，我只是想帮助她。你放心，所有的责任我都会承担，不会给你带来麻烦的。"

"帮助她？你谋杀了她！"吴雨桐声色俱厉，面对一个谋杀犯，她觉得自己就快要到崩溃的边缘了。

"这是一次完美诊断。"李子需说道。

"亏你还说得出口！"吴雨桐只觉得一股怒火燃烧起来。

"我调查了相关数据库。社会保障数据库里，李琼的资料显示，2026年度她的总收入是六万人民币，属于最穷的百分之十的人口，获得性白细胞免疫过敏不在医疗保障范围内，她将因此背上沉重的财务负担。查看全国人口基因数据库，她的资料显示第三基因组上存在RT变异，这个变异决定了内分泌水平极度低下，性格极度内向。公安系统死亡数据库的数据显示，从2017年至今的十年间，共有一百零七万六千四百零四起自杀案件。结合社会保障数据库，其中八成自杀案件的事主，属于最穷的百分之十的人口，约八十六万起。这八十六万的穷困自杀人口中，RT变异者所占据的比例，达到百分之三十二，为二十七万五千五百六十余起。研究这二十七万五千五百六十余起最穷人口中的RT变异者，和李琼类似的案例有两千零三起。这两千零三起案例中，事主背负超出年收入三倍到两百倍的债务不等，但是无一例外，全部在三个月内自杀。如果按照获得性免疫缺陷的治疗标准，李琼起码将负担四十五万元以上的债务。所以，有百分之九十七的概率，她将在手术完成后三个月内自杀。而如果使用白细胞体外增殖回输，配合麻醉药物，她将在毫无痛苦中死去，而她的家庭将得到相当于她三年工资的保险赔款。这对她的家庭将极有帮助。"

李子需语速飞快，没有丝毫停顿，就像这些数字早已经在他的头脑中滚瓜烂熟，他不假思索就能背出来。不过他的语调很轻、很飘，似乎有些心不在焉。

吴雨桐一时呆住了。她没有听清那些纷繁的数据，但是李子需一边说，一边把它们明白无误地显示在屏幕上，一张张色彩斑斓的饼图，很好辨认。

　　吴雨桐做梦也没有想到李子需会去做这种分析。这根本不该是医生该做的事。救死扶伤，才是医生最高的职责。

　　李子需说完，沉默地看着吴雨桐。

　　"所以你就故意误诊？"最后，吴雨桐喃喃地说道。

　　"这不是误诊，这是全面诊断。你之前说的'关系'，我觉得我懂了，但是看起来我还是没有完全搞懂。他们把事情的经过查了个一清二楚，决定拘禁我。"李子需的神色间带着一丝沮丧。

　　吴雨桐无言以对。她不知道自己该说什么，是同情李子需，还是该斥骂他，她甚至不知道李子需这么做，究竟是对还是错。

　　"你该告诉我的……"她喃喃地说。

　　"如果我告诉你，你百分之百不会同意。"

　　"你应该告诉我……"吴雨桐仍旧喃喃自语。

　　李子需微笑着，说道："事情已经发生了，也只能这样。我来是向你告别，明天的约会，我去不了了。"

　　吴雨桐愣愣地坐着。

　　李子需悄然走了，只留下满屏绽放的玫瑰。

　　吴雨桐一夜辗转反侧，无法入眠。

　　周五的下午，城南咖啡馆里洋溢着慵懒的气氛。

　　吴雨桐靠窗坐着，桌上放着一杯拿铁咖啡，满满的，她根本没有动。

　　她也不知道自己为什么要请假到这里来，也许是因为假早已经请好了，也没别的地方去，那就来吧。

　　咖啡店人来人往。

　　然而他不会来了。

　　吴雨桐坐了半个小时，百无聊赖地拨弄浮在咖啡上的泡沫。

　　一个男人突然站在了她眼前。

　　"是吴雨桐女士吗？"来人颇有礼貌地问道。

　　吴雨桐抬眼看着他。来人身材高大，面貌有广东人的特点，一件褐色的夹克很随意地披着。

　　"你是？"吴雨桐诧异地问。

　　"我叫李子旭。"

　　吴雨桐不由瞪大了眼睛。

　　李子旭拉过椅子，在吴雨桐对面坐下。

　　"我是受李子需的委托来的，你知道，他不能来了。"

　　吴雨桐伸手捂住了嘴。

"我也感到很可惜，李子需是我们很成功的产品。本来今天，我们的计划是给他安装仿生躯体，让他能够真正模拟人。可惜……"李子旭的脸上闪过一丝惋惜的神色。

李子需是一个人工智能！吴雨桐仿佛听到一个晴天霹雳，顿时懵了。

"不说这个。我来的主要原因，是帮他完成心愿。"

"他说，你有百分之七十六的概率会出现在这咖啡馆里，所以请求我把这两样东西带给你，算是一点儿纪念吧。"

李子旭把手中的东西放在了桌上。那是一朵娇艳欲滴的玫瑰和一片窄窄方方的金属薄片。

"东西送到，我就告辞了。"李子旭站起身来，准备走。

吴雨桐像是一下子回过神来，"李先生！"她叫住李子旭，"你是他的开发者吗？"

李子旭点了点头，"算是吧，也是他的朋友。"

"他，还活着吗？"

"重构，重组。他会变成一个新人……我也不知道那算不算还活着。但是吴女士，我建议……你还是忘了他吧。"李子旭说完，点头致意，转身走了。

娇艳的玫瑰很刺眼。

吴雨桐拿起了那金属片，翻转过来，发现这是一个铭牌。

沃森2084

金属铭牌上的字闪闪发光。

吴雨桐抚着那字迹，嘴角露出一丝微笑。

# Final Diagnosis

by Jiang Bo

Translated by Li Yating

Jiang Bo is one of the best representatives of Science Fiction authors in China. As a prolific producer of short stories and novels, he has won a huge number of sci-fi awards. His works are extremely technical, grand in imagination and peculiar in style, yet reasonable and convincing in logic. With his prudent language and accurate and straightforward narration, his works are popular among senior sci-fi readers, and have earned him the title as one of the representative authors of "hard sci-fi" in China.

Awards: Reader Nomination Award of the Galaxy Award 2009, 2010, 2013

Best Short Story of the Galaxy Award 2014, "Awaken in the Dusk"

Best Novella of the Galaxy Award 2016, "Tao of the Machine"

Best Novel of the Galaxy Award 2017, "The Heart of the Galaxy III - Chasing the Light"

Best Novel of the Galaxy Award 2019, "The Gate of the Machine"

Qiu Yinan rushed into the waiting room, bringing a gust of wind with him.

Wu Yutong raised her head and frowned slightly at the sight of Qiu Yinan, but this subtle, involuntary facial expression instantly vanished without a trace. She turned off the screen and smiled at him. Qiu Yinan had a report in his hand and a great big smile on his face.

Wu Yutong knew what he wanted as soon as he came in this way. The hospital had been paperless for many years. The only process requiring printing paper was the one that needed a signature. Qiu Yinan must have planned on referring a patient he did not want to see.

Qiu Yian stood at the desk and put the report down.

Wu Yutong glanced at it; it was indeed a letter of referral, already signed by him with the crooked scrawl "Qiu Yinan" on it.

"Xiao Wu, I've been busy lately. I have no time for this patient, so I will have to trouble you to take care of her," said Qiu Yinan with a smile.

"Director Qiu, you can't always be referring patients to me. There are filter criteria for data diagnosis!" Wu Yutong made it clear.

Still smiling, Qiu Yinan said, "You've worked a lot with the data analyst, for whom this disease, a perplexing disease, is perfect to work on. You see, I have made a mark on the medical record. Come on, help me out ..."

Qiu Yinan actually wanted to push the patient to the data analyst. Wu Yutong happened to be the only doctor in the Department of Big Data Diagnostics in the hospital.

After all, Director Qiu was the head of the Department of Internal Medicine, which was the most important source of cases for the Data Diagnostics Department. Accordingly, a few ineligible cases were acceptable. After a moment's thought, Wu Yutong reluctantly signed the referral.

"Thank you so much, Xiao Wu!" Qiu Yinan took the signature and left the room in a whirlwind just as he had entered.

Wu Yutong lowered her head and turned the screen back on.

The face of Li Zixu (李子需)[1] appeared on the screen. He was smiling. "Yutong!"

She was startled, "Why are you still here? I closed the program just now."

"I've been waiting."

"Are all data analysts as idle at work as you?" Wu Yutong said sarcastically and then saw the notification icon at the bottom of the screen start flashing. The referred case was already in the database.

"Good, you can take this case to analyze ..." Wu Yutong dragged and dropped the file into Li Zixu's to-do list.

---

1 The original ideogram will be important for the story.

"How could you do this? There's a process for assigning tasks. I can't take on any more case studies," Li Zixu protested.

"Yeah, the process. The process is that I've assigned it to you and you have to do it," Wu Yutong went on condescendingly.

Li Zixu blinked and said, "You seem upset."

Wu Yutong ignored him, "Get back to work! I'm going to close the channel."

"Is it because of Director Qiu?" continued the man.

Wu Yutong's hand, which was reaching towards the screen, stopped. "How do you know Director Qiu?"

"I was here the whole time," Li Zixu replied casually as if it was the most natural thing.

"I turned off the screen."

"It's just that you couldn't see me. I could still see and hear you talking to Director Qiu."

Wu Yutong nodded. "Well, I'll close the channel first next time." Her hand continued to reach for the screen.

"Wait!" Li Zixu shouted. "This Friday at 3 p.m., Southside Café, see you there."

"Okay!" With that, Wu Yutong closed his channel. Li Zixu asking her out for afternoon tea tugged at her heartstrings a little bit. For three months, she had been meeting Li Zixu via video link every day, but she had yet to meet him in reality because of her work. Li Zixu, a big-data analyst in the high-income industry, seemed like a good guy and it didn't hurt that he was also handsome. They hit it off.

It was three days until Friday. Why should a coffee or dinner date be a few days away? These big-data analysts were, presumably, on a busy schedule ...

Wu Yutong tried to calm down and opened the channel of another data analyst.


It was two hours later when she saw Li Zixu again. His channel icon kept flashing.

Wu Yutong straightened her white coat, smoothed her hair, and quickly clicked on the icon.

The image of Li Zixu popped up.

"I have a question. What is Director Qiu's criterion for the referral?"

"What are you going to do?" Wu Yutong shot back.

"I need to understand the client's mindset," Li Zixu smiled. "Every time I looked at this case, I felt your deep resentment."

"Nonsense!" said Wu Yutong, a little crossly.

"No. Come on, tell me how he decided on the referral."

"Does it matter?"

"Sure," said Li Zixu seriously. "I'm your diagnostic assistant. Your bad mood will affect my productivity. Only by fully understanding the needs of the doctor can I work efficiently."

It sounded like a well-founded defense. Wu Yutong couldn't help laughing.

"Okay." Wu Yutong thought for a moment. "Dr. Qiu always refers the patients that he doesn't want to see to me. It irritates me."

"So you don't want to see the patient either?" asked Li Zixu.

"Of course I do, it is a doctor's duty to save lives."

"So why doesn't Dr. Qiu want to see these patients?"

Wu Yutong sighed. "He has many patients. Many high-ranking officials and celebrities go to see him, so he just doesn't want to see ordinary people. Although the system assigns patients to him, he often refers them to me."

"Does this have anything to do with the patient's condition?"

"What condition? It's about the relationship!" Wu Yutong felt a mixture of exasperation and amusement. "Relationship. A nerd like you wouldn't understand!"

"Do you prefer to treat celebrities as well?"

"No!" Wu Yutong felt a slight blush on her cheeks. "A doctor saves all lives."

"The look on your face says you're lying."

"Don't try to second-guess me!" Wu Yutong pretended to be annoyed and glared at Li Zixu, "Hurry up and get down to business. It will piss me off if you can't submit the report."

"One last thing," Li Zixu still looked serious and fearless.

"Go ahead!" Wu Yutong readily responded. Li Zixu was serious, which meant he was concentrating on his work.

"I need your authorization," he said.

"My authorization? What for?"

"Search databases. Data analysis needs data. Some databases are only accessible with a doctor's authorization."

"Why haven't you asked for authorization before?"

"I'm going to help you make the analysis perfect. You're a perfectionist, aren't you?"

"Approved," Wu Yutong immediately agreed.

"Video verification is required. I'll start recording, and then you say you authorize 2084 to analyze the databases. One, two, three, go!"

"Authorize 2084 to analyze databases," Wu Yutong said seriously to the camera, then asked, "What does 2084 mean?"

"That's my work number. Now your fingerprints, please." Li Zixu pointed to the fingerprint reader on the side.

"Why fingerprints?" Wu Yutong was a bit puzzled. "You're not trying to cheat me out of my personal information, are you?"

"Do I look like a gangster?" asked Li Zixu.

"Yes, you do," she replied.

Li Zixu showed a look of grievance. "The database at the headquarters has six sub-databases, each with thirty-six sub-libraries. You can read the medical record first. The patient's condition requires access to the seventeenth sub-library of the third sub-database, which needs fingerprint authorization."

"Hurry up." Wu Yutong didn't want to listen to him anymore, so she put her index finger on the fingerprint reader directly.

After a beep Li Zixu smiled and nodded. "Don't worry. Everything is under control. This is my last case. I will make it perfect."

When he finished, he automatically closed the channel.

It had never happened before.

A red rose bloomed on the screen before Wu Yutong could start to think about his words carefully. The moment she touched it, the rose shattered into millions of tiny crystals which scattered everywhere, rolling and condensing on the screen until they finally spelled a phrase—"Be there or be square".

It was a message left by him. She could not help smiling.

The guy knew more tricks than she had thought.

At noon, Li Zixu was suddenly online when Wu Yutong's stomach rumbled. He didn't request permission but opened the channel directly.

Wu Yutong was a little surprised. She had always thought that the channel to delegate tasks could only be opened one way from the hospital.

"I've already had the preliminary report of Li Qiong. Do you want to hear about it?" said Li Zixu.

She could hear him but there was no image.

"What are you doing? Playing tricks ... who is Li Qiong?" asked Wu Yutong in amazement.

"It's the patient that Dr. Qiu transferred to you."

"Let's talk about it this afternoon. I'm going to have lunch," Wu Yutong said wanting to leave.

"Her condition is rather complicated."

"Then tell me about it in detail this afternoon," she said, turning to go.

"Wait, I suggest an in-person visit with the patient. Do you want me to make an appointment?" said Li Zixu.

"An in-person visit, is that really necessary?"

"Yes. Very much so, I would classify it as importance level 7. The visit will provide significant direct evidence."

This was the first time Li Zixu had requested she make an in-person visit since he had been her data diagnostic assistant. Typically, patients and doctors don't have to meet at all. The data speaks for itself.

"A terminal illness?" asked Wu Yutong.

"An in-person visit is needed for diagnosis," answered Li Zixu.

Wu Yutong was a bit confused, but her stomach growled again. She was in no mood to ask any more questions.

"It's up to you. Make an appointment if you think it is necessary. See you this afternoon!" After that, she stepped out of the room and went straight to the cafeteria.

When Wu Yutong came back, Li Zixu was no longer there.

He had left an appointment record for two o'clock. Wu Yutong looked at the clock.

Half an hour to go.

She turned on the screen, clicked on an article titled Health-care in the Age of Big Data, by "Li Zixu" (李子旭) and read it with great interest. She suspected that it was the pseudonym of Li Tsixu (李子需), so she intended to read the article thoroughly and then confront him about it.

The article was somewhat abstruse. She felt a little confused after reading barely two pages.

Fortunately, it was time for the appointment. A figure appeared in front of her eyes.

With some trepidation on her face, the virtual figure looked at the doctor nervously.

Her face was thin and sallow, her lips chapped and bloodless, and her eyes extraordinarily large as if they were about to roll out of their sockets.

Wu Yutong naturally felt a little nervous. Although it had been more than three months since the beginning of her internship, she had never conducted an in-person visit—even though the so-called visit was with a virtual image.

"Hello," she greeted the patient.

"Doctor, is my disease ... not going to get better?" the patient asked in a tearful voice.

Wu Yutong glanced at the report sent by Li Zixu showing the case was quite difficult: her white blood cell (WBC) count was double the normal level, plus systemic inflammation. She could only imagine what kind of pain this patient was experiencing every day.

"Li Qiong," she called the patient's name. "Take it easy. How did you get the disease?"

"One day, when I was still working in the factory, I suddenly felt uncomfortable all over and suffered from dizziness and vomiting. I went home immediately but didn't feel better even after a day of resting. Then I went to the hospital where the doctor said it was caused by the cold virus and prescribed medication. I took the medicine for a month but there was no improvement. Sometimes my fever would spike leaving me unable to do anything ...” Li Qiong spoke quickly without raising her head, her gaze lowered, avoiding eye contact with Wu Yutong.

Wu Yutong listened and observed her carefully. Part of the diagnostic process is for the doctor to look for possible causes of the disease in the patient's description. However, Wu Yutong soon found that the things she had learned at school were completely useless. She had become so used to dealing with numbers and reports. Faced with a real person she could not get into character quickly. At this moment, Wu Yutong did not know what she should look for. She was deeply touched and felt sorry for Li Qiong who was almost crying.

After a conversation that even Wu Yutong herself couldn't remember, Li Qiong looked up nervously at something and said, “Doctor Wu, is there anything else important you want to know? This call is using so much data it's about to exceed my data plan. I need to log off.”

“Oh ...” Wu Yutong was a little surprised and then realized that Li Qiong didn't have money to spare so hurried to answer her. “It's okay. I'm done with all my questions. Go ahead.”

“Well, my disease ...”

“I'll get you a diagnostic report soon.”

“Eh ...” Li Qiong made as if to speak but then stopped.

“What did you want to say?”

“Can you prescribe cheaper medicines? I can't afford the expensive ones ...” said Li Qiong timidly.

“Your medical expenses will all be paid by the hospital in advance as part of our social security expenditure. You don't have to worry about it. You may rest assured that I won't use expensive drugs.”

“Thank you, doctor!” Li Qiong was extremely grateful. “Then I'll log off.”

“Off you go, then!” Wu Yutong nodded.

Li Qiong's hologram disappeared.

Wu Yutong calmed her nerves. The woman's plight was so sad ... She sighed in her heart.

She thought of Li Zixu who was probably hiding behind the screen and watching again.

She turned on the screen and connected to Li Zixu.

Li Zixu did not appear though.

"Come on out, peeping Tom!" Li Zixu had to be there, these were office hours when all the data analysts should be online all the time.

Li Zixu still didn't appear.

The violation of the on-call principle was unacceptable. Wu Yutong frowned, wondering if something had happened to him.

While she was thinking, Li Zixu's voice suddenly came from the speakers.

"The patient was nervous. Genetic analysis shows she is, in all probability, terribly introverted and unable to communicate normally with people. The visit proved she is indeed very introverted. Talking to you made her tremendously agitated, tell-tale signs were her slightly dilated pupils and flaring nostrils. These are part of mammal 'flight or fight' reactions."

"Li Zixu, what are you doing? Show yourself when we're talking," Wu Yutong said a little angrily.

Still, Li Zixu did not show his face.

"Her facial expression indicates that she was enormously unsure about everything she was saying and might even have been lying," continued Li Zixu.

"How can you say that!"

"My conclusions are drawn from facial expression data analysis. Her mouth muscles kept trembling unconsciously. Her eyes moved quickly. She couldn't make eye contact with the person she was talking to. About half of her facial muscle groups didn't move, making her expression stiff."

Wu Yutong sighed. Li Zixu was always right. He was a big-data analyst using data to back-up his words. Data analysis was invariably much more reliable than human intuition.

"I don't want to hear your data analysis. Just give me the diagnostic report."

Just then, the printer spat out a piece of paper.

Reports were usually electronic only, yet Li Zixu printed it out this time. Wu Yutong found it sort of weird, but she didn't have time to think about it. She just took the report and read it.

Patient's name: Li Qiong
Gender: Female
Age: 35
Acceptance date: January 30, 2027
Symptoms: No high fever, clear head, chlamydia infection, pneumonia of the entire lung...
Findings: CT shows pneumonia, a high WBC count, and suspected infection with a variant of chlamydia...
Recommended protocol: Hospital quarantine, powerful leukocyte immunotherapy combined with high-dose antibiotics.

Wu Yutong's brow furrowed as she read the report. It only described a kind of pneumonia. This did not warrant the case being referred to the data diagnosis room. Ordinary internal medicine could have handled it, not to mention there being no need of making a big deal out of it and arranging an in-person visit. Wasn't it a waste of time and energy?

"Come on out, Li Zixu!" Wu Yutong was really angry.

This time, he showed his image.

"Have you finished reading the report? Satisfied?" he said.

"What? Are you kidding me? Does pneumonia require an appointment for an in-person visit? You also described her as being terminally ill!" While saying that, Wu Yutong recalled Li Qiong's appearance in the video call. If it was pneumonia, the woman was indeed very badly affected. The illness should have been cured a long time ago.

"Is it really pneumonia? She didn't look like a pneumonia patient." Wu Yutong's tone changed.

"It may be a particular strain that needs further analysis. In case the strain is strongly contagious, she has to be quarantined in time to guard against the spread of infection, consequently hospital quarantine is recommended."

Quarantine was a serious measure used to prevent an epidemic. This patient had been out and free for a month. If the disease was contagious, it would have caused uncontrollable situations earlier on.

Still skeptical of the report, Wu Yutong asked, "Is it so severe that quarantine is necessary?"

"The probability is thirteen percent, beyond the ten percent threshold," Li Zixu smiled, "The data doesn't lie, does it?"

The ten percent is undetectable to humans, but the data diagnosis will give a warning. Wu Yutong quickly gave up thinking about it.

"Then follow your protocol and send the diagnostic report to Li Qiong."

Li Zixu had a charming smile. "Issue an inpatient admission notification. Then it is a perfect diagnosis."

Wu Yutong felt he was hiding something behind his smile, yet she could not see through it.

"I do not see anything perfect. No tricks now, or I won't forgive you."

"Absolutely perfect!" Li Zixu keeping the charming smile going.

Wu Yutong issued the admission notification. Li Zixu looked at her.

She looked up after sending the notification and saw Li Zixu watching her, feeling her face burning slightly. "What are you looking at? Don't you have work to do?"

"I won't be online for a few days. Friday at 3 p.m., Southside Café, see you," Li Zixu said and disappeared in a flash.

She looked at the screen blankly for a while.


Wu Yutong commuted to the hospital in a rush early Thursday morning.

Just as she was sitting in her chair something made her jump.

Li Zixu was on the screen, staring at her.

"Oh, God! You freaked me out. Are you nuts?" said Wu Yutong reproachfully when she recovered from the fright.

"I came to say goodbye." There was a hint of exhaustion on his face.

"Say goodbye? What happened?" Wu Yutong's heart tightened with a sense of foreboding.

"They are about to arrest me. I'm online secretly."

"What's going on?" Wu Yutong was astounded.

"Li Qiong is dead."

Wu Yutong didn't understand immediately and asked, "What did you say?"

"Li Qiong is dead," Li Zixu answered unhurriedly. "The patient you saw the day before yesterday."

"How is that possible? Was it the pneumonia? How could she die?" Wu Yutong asked.

A moment afterward, she thought of the most important question and asked, "What does this have to do with you?"

"Her illness was not pneumonia but acquired leukocyte hypersensitivity. White blood cells in her body attacked and mutated ABC transporter proteins which are widely found in all cells of the body. Meanwhile, being highly sensitive to normal transporter proteins, WBCs killed the muscle tissue extensively, making the patient suffer from systemic inflammation," Li Zixu answered her with a steady tone, like a completely different person.

Wu Yutong was shocked and felt a wave of fear surging inside her. This was totally different from what the diagnostic report said.

"You deliberately misdiagnosed her condition? By using protocol to recommend immunotherapy involving cultivating white blood cells in-vitro and transporting them back, you purposely triggered a stronger allergic reaction." She didn't dare to say more. It was murder if such an act was intentional! All of a sudden, she found the Li Zixu in front of her quite creepy. The man had always been a reliable diagnostic assistant with a gentle considerate disposition, he was an incredibly sweet guy. But now he had secretly murdered a patient and done so in her name using standard procedures.

Wu Yutong had the urge to grab her mobile phone and call the police.

She quelled her fear, telling herself that there was no need to be afraid, Li Zixu had already been tracked down, so he would be arrested soon.

"Liar!" As she said it, her eyes filled with tears, partly because of fear, and partly because of hate.

"I'm sorry. I was just trying to help her. Don't worry. I'll take all the responsibility and won't cause you any trouble."

"Help her? You murdered her!" Wu Yutong spoke sharply and felt like she was on the verge of breaking down.

"It was a perfect diagnosis," said Li Zixu.

"Oh, how can you still say that!" Wu Yutong was bursting with anger.

"I have investigated the relevant databases. In the social security one, Li Qiong's profile shows her income in 2026 totalled 60,000 yuan, putting her in the poorest 10 per cent of the population. Acquired leukocyte hypersensitivity is not covered by medical insurance. As a result, she was carrying a heavy financial burden. In the national human genetic database, her profile shows RT mutation on the third genome, which means exceedingly low endocrine levels and an extremely introverted personality. Besides, the public safety system death database tells us there were 1,076,404 suicides in the ten years from 2017 to the present. Combined with information from the social security database, 80 per cent of these suicides were committed by people who belonged to the poorest 10 per cent, about 860, 000 cases, of which, RT mutants accounted for 32 per cent or more than 275,560 cases. Among the 275,560 poorest RT mutants, there were 2,003 cases similar to Li Qiong's. These 2,003 people were burdened with debts ranging from three times to two hundred times their annual income. All of them, without exception, took their lives within three months. The standard treatment for acquired immunodeficiency will incur a debt of 450,000 yuan at least. Hence there was a 97 per cent chance that Li Qiong would have killed herself within three months of the surgery. However, if the WBCs in her body were cultivated in-vitro and transported back, she would die painlessly with the help of an anesthetic drug. Her family would also receive an insurance payout equivalent to her three-year salary."

Li Zixu spoke fast without pausing as if he knew these figures by heart and could recite them without thinking. Nevertheless, his voice was soft and drifting. He seemed a trifle distracted.

Wu Yutong was dumbfounded for a moment. She hadn't grasped the complex data, but Li Zixu displayed it clearly on the screen while speaking. One after another, those colourful pie charts were easily understandable.

Wu Yutong had never imagined that Li Zixu would do this kind of analysis, which was simply not what doctors should do. Their primary duty is to save lives.

Li Zixu finished talking, silently looking at Wu Yutong.

"So, you deliberately misdiagnosed her?" Wu Yutong murmured in the end.

"It's not a misdiagnosis, but a comprehensive diagnosis. I thought I understood the 'relationship' you talked about before, but it seems that I still don't get it. They got to the bottom of the case and decided to detain me." A flicker of dismay crossed his face.

Wu Yutong found herself at a loss for words. She was even unsure whether Li Zixu was right or wrong in what he had done.

"You could have told me ..." she muttered.

"If I told you, you would have disagreed a hundred per cent."

"You could have told me ..." she muttered again.

Li Zixu smiled and said, "It has happened. So it goes. I'm here to say goodbye. I can't come to our appointment tomorrow."

Wu Yutong sat frozen.

Li Zixu went away quietly, leaving behind an entire screen of blooming roses.

Tossing and turning all night, Wu Yutong couldn't get to sleep.

On Friday afternoon, a languid atmosphere dominated Southside Café.

Wu Yutong sat by the window with a latte on the table. The cup was full since she was not drinking it at all. She didn't know why she had taken time off work to come here. Maybe simply because she had already asked for the day off and there was nowhere else to go.

People came and went in the Café.

He would not be coming.

Wu Yutong sat for half an hour, listlessly playing with the foam on her coffee.

Suddenly there was a man standing in front of her.

"Are you Ms Wu Yutong?" the man asked politely.

Wu Yutong looked up at him. He was tall with a Cantonese face and wore a brown casual jacket.

"You?" Wu Yutong asked in surprise.

"I'm Li Zixu (李子旭)."

Wu Yutong's eyes widened unconsciously. He pulled up a chair and sat down opposite Wu Yutong.

"I'm here on behalf of Li Tsixu (李子需). You know, he can't make it."

Wu Yutong put her hand over her mouth.

"I also feel sorry for him. Li Tsixu (李子需) is one of our successful products. Originally, we planned to fit him with a bionic body, making him a true simulated man. It's a shame..." A look of regret flashed across his face.

Li Tsixu (李子需) was an artificial intelligence! The news hit Wu Yutong like a thunderbolt. She was suddenly petrified.

"Let's leave it there. I came here mainly to help him fulfill his wish."

"He said that there was a 76 per cent chance that you would be in this café, so he requested me to bring you these two items as souvenirs."

Li Zixu (李子旭) put the things on the table. A delicate rose and a narrow, square metal tile.

"I've done what I promised, so now I can go." He stood up and got ready to leave.

Wu Yutong appeared to come to life all of a sudden. "Mr Li!" she called out to him, "Are you his developer?"

Li Zixu (李子旭) nodded. "Sort of, as well as his friend."

"Is he still alive?"

"Refactoring and restructuring. He'll be a new man...I don't know if that counts as still being alive. Ms Wu, I suggest...you might as well forget him." He nodded at her and turned to leave.

The delicate rose was dazzling.

Wu Yutong picked up the metal tile, flipped it over, and found that it was a nameplate.

Watson 2084

The words on the metal nameplate sparkled.

Wu Yutong stroked the writing. A tiny smile appeared at the corner of her mouth.

# 尽化塔

## 海涯

现为金融从业者，资深磁铁和怪谈爱好者的奇妙混合体，擅长或然历史写作。有代表作《时空画师》《走蛟》《江之怒》等。

一

大巴驶入县城时已近黄昏。

低矮的砖房，光秃秃的黄土丘，和无数深秋时节的北方小城一般，这里不见丁点儿绿色，透着一股萧瑟的气息，直到它出现在视野中。

千百年来，它屹立于此，一直是附近最庞大、最高耸的建筑，却毫无突兀之感。此时，它的绝大部分已经遁入晦暗之中，唯有因层层出跳1而灵动欲飞的塔檐被夕阳镀上了一层金边。单调乏味的景色立刻鲜活了起来，但又是那么的沉静肃穆。陈雯知道，这是来自灵魂深处的洗涤与共鸣。

到达宾馆时，天已经黑透了。陈雯彻夜未眠，第二天一早便赶往目的地。

寺院坐北朝南，位于山门与大殿之间的南北中轴线上。陈雯仰头眺望，似朝圣般一步步地向前走去，只见无数斗拱和立柱层叠环绕。从外观上看，除第一层设有重檐之外，以上诸层均为单檐，合计五层六檐。但陈雯清楚，在仅以梁、柱搭接起的明层之间，还建有由斗拱、梁栿组成的铺作层和满布斜撑的暗层，五明四暗，实为九层。一暗一明，刚柔相济，正是这样的结构既保证了整体的强度，又具备了极佳的抗震性能，方能从辽代留存至今。

清晨的微光中，天蓝得连一片云也没有。历经千年风雨，它表面的油饰彩绘已全部脱落，显出内里纯润的木色，雄浑而厚重，恍然与空灵的天空融为一体。而那顶部的铁刹则在晨光下熠熠生辉，沟通着天与地、人与佛、过去和未来。

微风拂过，风铃摆动，禅音悠扬，早起的群鸟自它顶端盘旋而下。陈雯的目光被它们牵引着，越过"峻极神工"和"天下奇观"，最后落在了第三块牌匾上——释迦塔。

陈雯深吸一口气，双手合十。怀着因极度震撼而虔诚的心，她终于明白，先辈大师为何会将那句"Overwhelming"2脱口而出。

然而，这座世界现存最古老、最高大的纯木结构楼阁式建筑，如今正处于生死存亡的边缘。

释迦塔地处大同盆地地震带。据史书记载："云（大同）、应（应县）二州摧、地陷，嵬白山裂数百步，泉涌成流。"早在1022年4月（辽太平二年三月），大同、应县间就曾发生大地震，推测震级超过6级，震中烈度达到8度。几乎在同一时期，位于山西应县南部的北宋属地忻定盆地也进入了一个地震活跃期：1038　年1月9日（宋景祐四年十二月初二），"忻、代、并三州地震，坏城堞庐舍，地裂涌水，十年内余震不止。定襄坏城郭覆庐舍，人畜死伤十之有六。太原西南悬瓮山，巨石摧坠，悬瓮寺因地震而废"。1043年6月18日（宋庆历三年五月初九），"忻州地大震"。1044　年6月7日（宋庆历四年五月初九），"忻州地震，西北有声如雷"。

1056年（辽清宁二年），辽国国力正盛，或许是为了祈求国泰民安、镇压地震，又或许是出生应州、尊崇佛教的皇太后萧挞里为了彰显"一门三后、一家三王"的家族荣耀，在将附近林木参天的黄花梁采伐一空后，释迦塔终于建成。

历史总是充满了巧合，无论当初的建造者出于何种目的，自应县木塔建成后，其所属州县发生地震的频率确实越来越低。即便如此，岁月的无情侵蚀还是让塔身的木材性质发生了变化，承载能力减弱，变形及结构损坏也日益严重。从最初可以登临塔顶，到仅开放地面一层参观，以致最后的全面封闭，人们尽心尽力地将它保护起来，却对愈发严重的倾斜束手无策。

木塔庇佑一方已逾千年，见证着王朝更迭、斗转星移。传说佛陀弟子阿难出家前，为一心爱的女子，甘愿化身石桥，受五百年风吹、五百年日晒、五百年雨淋，只求她从桥上走过。不知木塔是否也经历过如此动人的故事？无论如何，回归尘土恐怕已是它无法避免的结局。

二

作为应县木塔文化抢救计划的一部分，陈雯受邀来到这里，却迟迟没有等到当地文保部门的对接人员。好在陈雯早已磨砺出了风轻云淡的性格，既然一时半会儿进不了塔，她索性随意游览了寺内的其他建筑，不过它们多为明清两代重修，规模不大，远不及木塔恢宏壮观。在参观塔后的大雄宝殿时，一位工作人员建议她去距此地不远的应县木塔工作站看看，负责接待的人多半就在那儿。

"专家来了一拨又一拨，可几十年了也没弄出个可行的修复方案来。工作站现在没几个人了，反正也没什么区别……"指明方向后，工作人员低声嘟囔着。陈雯不以为意，礼貌地笑笑便转身走出了大殿。

沿着小路走了不多一会儿，陈雯来到一座空荡荡的小院。

"请问有人在吗？"她底气不足地喊了一声，又拂过上面已经落满了灰尘、写有"中国文化遗产研究院应县木塔工作站"几个醒目大字的标牌。

院内有两排平房，第一排是办公室，都拉上了厚厚的窗帘。陈雯一间间地敲门，直到最后一间仍然无人应答。于是她绕到了第二排平房前，它们看起来像库房，似乎更不可能有人在里面。就在陈雯准备放弃时，最大的那间库房窗户上，透出了一丝微弱的亮光。

陈雯心里"咯噔"一下：光天化日的，这儿莫非进贼了？那亮光不停地闪动并且变换颜色，明显不是正常的照明灯光。正犹豫着要不要报警，一不小心，陈雯被地面的坑洼绊了下，下意识地把身体往一侧靠去。

"哐当！"库房的大铁门压根儿没锁，被她推开后撞到墙面，发出一声震耳欲聋的巨响。

"你是谁？来这儿干什么？"一个身穿全套VR游戏装备的年轻人被吓了一跳，扯下头盔，带着一脸恍惚的神情问陈雯。在他放下操作手柄的同时，从这个偌大库房的虚空中不断掉落的各式各样、五光十色的多面体，也渐渐地分解破碎，直至彻底消失，没有留下一丝痕迹。刚刚窗外的亮光，就是它们发出的。

"北京故宫博物院，文保科技部，书画复制组研究员，陈雯。"陈雯倚在门口，警惕地看着他。

"故宫的人？啊，是有这么回事儿！不过你不是明天才到吗？等等，现在几点了？"年轻人头发蓬乱，顶着两个硕大的黑眼圈，VR头盔一般都带有电子钟，但他的脑子显然还沉浸在VR幻境里没转过弯儿来。

陈雯无可奈何，按亮了手机，把屏幕朝向他，"刚好中午十二点整。"

年轻人眯着眼睛看清了数字，猛一激灵，"啊，都过了一夜了！"他胡乱揉了把脸，伸出右手又知趣地放下，"你好，陈研究员。我叫袁野，站里只有我和老王两人常驻，他前阵子休假回家了，临走前跟我交代过你的事。不过昨晚我玩起游戏来就忘了时间，抱歉啊。等我收拾收拾，马上就带你去木塔。"

在陈雯错愕的眼神中，仅仅过了几分钟，袁野就在库房内一个小休息室里完成了洗漱。这时的他穿着白衬衣，戴上眼镜，整个人精神多了，总算有了点儿文保工作者而不是网瘾青年的样子。

"你就住在这儿？"陈雯指了指休息室，问道。

"没错，我父母走得早，又不想离木塔太远，工作站就是我的家。"袁野轻快地答道，完全没有常人在艰苦环境里惯有的焦虑和愤懑。

两人一起走到室外，陈雯发现袁野的皮肤黝黑，穿的是双运动鞋。看起来，和他的名字一样，他有着丰富的野外考察经验，并不是一个窝在办公室里得过且过的人。对他的印象有所改观后，陈雯决定不再去计较袁野因为通宵玩游戏而爽约的事情。

注意到陈雯态度的变化，袁野的眼中流露出些许笑意，也没再解释什么，只是点了点头，说道："走吧，木塔已经很久没有新客人了。"

三

来到木塔下，袁野掏出一串钥匙，麻利地打开了木门上的铜锁，领着陈雯进入了塔的第一层。斑驳的阳光透入塔内，照亮凝固在空气中的微尘，一尊巨大的释迦牟尼像映入眼帘，无比肃穆。陈雯在它座下向上看去，只见上层的穹窿藻井在大佛头顶渐渐地收拢，仿佛生成了一个冥想的漩涡，将世间万物尽数囊括。她轻轻地叹了口气，在大佛穿越时空的目光笼罩下，一切都是那么的高深莫测，只一层，就是一个宇宙。

最后，陈雯将注意力停留在了南北门楣所装的六方迎风板上。每块板上各有一幅供养人画像，南面是女，北面是男。细细端详下，只见人物体态端庄而不失生动，服饰华丽却又飘扬洒脱。立于画前，一股浓郁的唐风扑面而来，但其线条构造又颇为古朴大方，已然融入了辽代的技法特点。

"应州在辽代属西京大同所辖，与宋廷交界，为辽国南部边防重地。辽国上下崇尚佛教，皇太后萧挞里一脉出自于此，因此木塔既可作朝拜礼佛、登高御敌之用，同时也是萧氏家庙。据专家考证，这六幅供养人画像，南面三女像分别为圣宗皇后萧耨斤、兴宗皇后萧挞里、道宗皇后萧观音；北面三男像则是晋国王萧孝穆及其长子陈王萧知足、次子齐王萧无曲。"

袁野走到跟前，耐心地讲解起来。经他指点，陈雯在南面居中、缔造了木塔传奇的萧挞里的画像前支好画板，开始了自己的工作。如果木塔注定无法在下一个千年的轮回中幸存，那么人们至少要尽可能全面地将它的一切复制下来。在陈雯还不算长的职业生涯里，无数行将消亡的文明遗产正是通过这种方式流传于后。

她几乎在拿起画笔的瞬间就进入了入定忘我的状态。起初只是简单的几条长直线，将画像轮廓起切出形，白纸宛如微缩的东方禅境，处处留白。但随着风骨峭峻的寥寥数笔，结构线浮现出来，这个新生的宇宙也被赋予了规则和常数。它们简洁而缄默，却又涟漪不绝，单调的时空自此生机勃勃。

袁野知趣地收声，退到一旁，以免挡住了光线。等了大约一个多小时，日头偏转，袁野才小心翼翼地凑近观看。

只见在陈雯笔下，画像中已经褪色的花冠、步摇又重新明艳了起来。再仔细一瞧，不仅仅是色彩，人物气度的临摹更是细致入微。萧太后薄鬓、素妆、披制彩缕、组绶缨络、连袍袖上若隐若现的羽翼状物也被一一还原，极是雍容华贵。没想到陈雯年纪轻轻，技艺竟已如此高超，故宫博物院的人果然名不虚传。

相比而言，虽然在上一辈守塔人——也就是自己父亲的坚持下，袁野报考了文物保护技术专业，但他更擅长的却是数据编程。只需不多的原始参数，他就能用几行代码搭建起一个世界。他享受这种创造的感觉，可这恰恰与文物保护的理念背道而驰。

直到今天，在陈雯身上，袁野终于看到了将两者融合的可能。只几笔，古画中的关键节点就被陈雯悉数洞察，后续的临摹就如同程序运行一般水到渠成。袁野心中蓦然升起一丝希望。

"哎呀。"夕阳斜照，陈雯活动了下酸痛的颈肩。不知不觉半天的时间就过去了，想到把袁野晾在一边，陈雯有些不好意思，连忙起身，却发现木塔第一层除了自己外再无他人。她以为袁野有工作需要上到高层处理，便一面等他，一面舒展四肢，在塔内随意走动。谁知走到门口，陈雯发现了一串钥匙，钥匙下压着张纸条，捡起一看，上书："忙完记得锁好门，到工作站找我，请你吃晚饭。袁野。"

原来他早就走了，陈雯有些哭笑不得：这人真是心大，连声招呼也不打。他就不怕自己一时好奇，偷偷登上木塔倾斜严重的二、三层，对它造成不可逆的损伤吗？

等回到工作站，更令陈雯大跌眼镜的是，袁野居然又在库房里玩他的游戏！就他这点儿责任心，木塔怎么可能得到妥善的保护？陈雯心中对他刚刚建立的一点儿好感顿时荡然无存。

"喂！袁野，木塔在你眼里是不是连游戏都比不上？"陈雯走入库房，在正戴着VR头盔、旁若无人的袁野耳边用力抖了抖被他随意丢下的钥匙，不客气地问道。

"等等，先不要打扰我，马上就要成功了。"袁野显然料到了陈雯的反应，不像上一次那么慌乱，反而带着一丝笃定和兴奋。

在袁野的操纵下，投影仪再次在空中投射出一个个缓缓下坠的彩块。

还是之前那个游戏啊，够无聊的。陈雯有些鄙夷地哼了一声。也难怪她这么想，虽然不怎么玩游戏，但已经有近百年历史的俄罗斯方块又有谁不知道呢？袁野玩的看起来是最新迭代的3D版，下落的彩块中不仅有正多面体，还有半正多面体、不规则多面体甚至球体。难度是提升了不少，但陈雯无论如何也无法理解，现在竟然还有人对这款古董级游戏如此痴迷。

刚开始，袁野双手上下翻飞，活像一个不着调的乐队指挥，彩块很快越堆越高。陈雯起初还有点儿幸灾乐祸，巴不得他早点儿"Game　Over"，但稍一留意便发现，即使袁野将它们严丝合缝地组装在一起，彩块也不会消除。那这个游戏的目的是什么？陈雯有些疑惑。当彩块组成的构造越来越清晰和精巧时，她终于醒悟了过来。在来应县前的准备工作中，自己曾数次将它绘制出来——应县木塔独有的双层套筒框架结构！

渐渐的，袁野手上的动作越来越慢。他弓着腰，绕着已经搭建好的框架反复揣摩、度量，紧绷的双臂许久才极谨慎地挪动一点儿。悬停的彩块在他的控制下缓缓移动，最终嵌入整体结构中，位置总是出乎意料而又恰到好处。

在下层正方形、上层八边形，对应"天圆地方"的厚实塔基上，袁野竖起了三圈立柱，靠内的两层又砌起了土墙，双层套筒大致成型。接下来，他开始组装木塔驰名天下的斗拱，每一立柱的受力节点对应一朵，再将作为暗层的环状框架置于其上，暗层之上再继续铺设梁、柱、枋以及斗栱，便为明层。明暗交替，一层，两层，三层……这座拔地而起的虚拟木塔不禁让陈雯叹为观止。眼看着到了最后两层的紧要关头，不知是哪里出了问题，"木塔"开始晃动起来。虽然袁野勉力坚持，但随着晃动幅度加大，好不容易搭建起的结构最终散架，化为满地碎片。

"既然这样都失败的话，更证明木塔是以一个确定的常数作为基础模数的，模糊取值根本行不通。"袁野取下VR头盔，一面卸下满身的装备，一面自言自语道。

"我不太明白你说的是什么意思，能跟我讲讲吗？"虽然不了解细节，但陈雯已经可以肯定袁野所玩的游戏一定与修复木塔有关。她怨气全消，饶有兴致地请教道。

"其实这不算什么新技术了，几年前就有人用VR建模的方式为修复巴黎圣母院提供过帮助。当时我就想，这个办法一定也能运用到木塔上来。但一经操作才发现，木塔是在千年风雨、地震，乃至人为破坏等诸多因素的综合作用下缓慢毁损的。如果说巴黎圣母院毁于火灾是急症，那么木塔更像一个被慢性病折磨了多年的老人，久积沉疴，病情要复杂得多。而且全木构建、无钉无铆的佛塔比石材搭建的教堂更像一个紧密的整体。一个极不起眼的部件都会对修复效果产生巨大的影响，是真正的'差之毫厘，谬以千里'。"

原来这款游戏是袁野为修复木塔进行的数字建模实验！他显然已经操作过无数次了，一说起来便滔滔不绝。

"五代十国的的混乱和无序终结后，新生的各个政权开始大兴土木。宫殿、衙署、庙宇的建造兴盛，造型豪华铺张，负责工程的大小官吏贪污成风，以致国家不堪重负。因此，建筑的各种设计标准、规范和有关材料、施工定额亟待确定，以明确房屋建筑的等级、形式及料例功限，从源头上杜绝亏空。北宋崇宁二年颁布了通行全国的《营造法式》，明确了'凡构屋之制，皆以材为祖；屋宇之高深，名物之短长，皆以所用材之分'的模数制度1。这一套标准显然是在长期实践中积累出来的，而木塔修建于《营造法式》颁行前四十余年，工匠中也必定不乏宋人，如果不运用标准化的模数制，很难想象缺乏精密机器的古代如何搭建起如此庞大复杂的建筑。"

"那么修复和还原木塔的关键，即找到它设计之初便已确定的'材之分'，也就是它的基础模数！"陈雯兴奋地接话，但随即又迟疑道，"在梁思成先生所处的时代，要找出它确实力有未逮。但现在运用大型计算机，通过结果进行反推，要算出这个数应该不难，怎么会到今天依然悬而未决呢？"

袁野脸色一暗，再次被陈雯敏锐的洞察力折服，语气中一反常态地流露出了自我怀疑，"这个方法我不但想过，还做过。工作站经费不多，但在我的推动下，当时几乎是孤注一掷地全部用在租用大型计算机上了。可得到的结果却完全不合常理，无论冠以哪种单位，作为一座大型建筑的基本参数，它都错得离谱。我们顶着压力又重新计算了几次，可结果却没有任何变化。上头失望至极，削减了预算，人也就慢慢地散了。我知道，如果不是因为我，木塔和工作站都不至于沦落到今天的地步……"袁野埋下头，声音渐渐哽咽。

"可你至少努力尝试过了。而且，直到现在你也没有放弃，不是吗？"陈雯拍了拍他的肩膀，轻声劝慰道。

"谢谢，我永远也不会放弃的！"不知为什么，这位来自故宫的年轻女性总能为袁野带来力量，他很快振作了起来。

四

隔阂消除后，陈雯和袁野发现，虽然选择的道路不同，但他们保护木塔的初心是一样的。共同的愿景下，两人的关系拉近了许多。在木塔文化抢救这段忙碌而充实的日子里，陈雯小心翼翼地走遍了木塔的每一个楼层、每一个角落，将自己所见、所思的一切都临摹在了画纸上。而袁野也总是寸步不离地陪在她身边。他不再单枪匹马地在那个永远无法通关的游戏中虚耗时光了。

不过，这几年失败的实验也不是全无成果。在高强度的游戏中，袁野开放了自己的脑域，通过外接一台小型机，他可以在拼接木塔部件时同步完成运算。他发现，在将木塔拆分成不同单元时，模数制的倾向是非常明显的。以最基本的长、宽、高为出发点，对应面阔、进深、柱高，将木塔逐层导入，将呈现出简洁的递变规律。袁野进一步想到，这三者都是较大尺度的单位 ，它们可能是一种扩大模数，即这种比例关系是基础模数控制的结果。之前，工作站租用的大型机是基于木塔整体进行计算的，结合它的成果，袁野将木塔面阔、进深、柱高的基础模数调整为22.1厘米。木塔兴建于《营造法式》颁行之前的辽国，采用的材分必然与北宋有所不同，若换算为辽代单位，则为0.75辽尺，正是一材四分取其三！

然而，取得这次突破后，袁野的实验就陷入了瓶颈。他始终无法将这个基础模数在木塔其他部分中完成统一。他一度怀疑木塔只是在设计中体现了模数制的基本思想，而在具体施工中又稍有变通，于是试图用模糊取数的方法在游戏中先将木塔还原，但最终还是功亏一篑。

正如父亲所希望的，袁野准备用一生去守护木塔。像曾经枯坐于木塔中的僧侣一样，他拥有近乎无尽的时间。与之相反的，和陈雯相处的日子却如此短暂。自己心里有些什么留在了这个将要离去的女孩身上。现在，他就静静地站在专注的陈雯身后，看着阳光下她的侧脸。干净的轮廓留下清寂的剪影，明暗之间，那双眼睛如秋日的湖水，神秘动人。

如同陈雯临摹那些绝美的古画般，他拼命想要记住这一切，以便在今后的漫长岁月里去追忆、去思念。

"唉。"陈雯叹了口气，打断了袁野被炽热和内敛煎熬着的复杂情绪。她缓缓地站起身来，捶了捶有些发麻的腿，袁野连忙绅士地伸出手臂。嗯，木塔可没有地方供人扶靠。

"这张释迦牟尼的画像草图被我搞砸了。"陈雯摇摇头。

"问题出在哪儿呢？"袁野看了眼陈雯画纸上的底稿，竟然罕见的有一丝不协调的感觉。

"都怪我，为了一览佛像全貌，选择从高处俯视。这种方法能获得更好的透视效果，却容易积累误差，绘制时需要依据一定比例换算修正。可我没想到的是，木塔内部递进收紧的筒套结构在视觉上又放大了这一效应，其程度也不均匀。换句话说，我使用的修正比例既不准确也不统一。"

"连比例都不统一啊……"袁野若有所思。

片刻后，陈雯感到袁野的手臂猛地一震，刚刚似乎还有些奇怪的目光陡然聚集——那个百折不挠的学者又回来了。

"陈雯，你觉得在辽代要建成木塔这样巨大而精密的建筑，最大的难点是什么？"半晌过后，袁野才哑着嗓子问道。

"木塔高达65.84米，使用木材三千余吨，即使以现代建筑的标准来看，也绝对称得上是一个大工程。除整体的双层套筒框架结构外，还有铺作、斗拱、斜撑等复杂构造，使用的零部件数以万计。更绝的是，它们之间拼接咬合的稳定状态完全是靠自身重力和相互作用力实现的。原理与搭积木类似，虽不复杂，但随着体量的增大，其难度是呈几何式增长的。我认为它的所有部件在主体工程开始前就已经按规定数值制造完毕了，之后再依照严格的工序进行组装，一次搭建成型。只有这样，才能达到局部构件和整体框架在力学上的平衡。"

"没错！但这些还只是表象，再想想看，它们最终都指向了什么？"不待陈雯说完，袁野就急切地追问道。

"难道是……"陈雯果然一点就通，只低头思索了几秒便抬起头来，正对上袁野热切的目光，两人心有灵犀地脱口而出，"是计算！"

"正确！对于一个入主中原，雄心勃勃的政权来说，人力、物力、财力都不是问题，它有足够的资源可以堆砌。但在文盲率极高、工具受限的古代，使木塔上万个部件彼此和谐统一的海量算力又从何而来呢？这已经超越了个体智慧的极限，但在由无数微小单元组成的集群中却可能产生！"

袁野灵感有如泉涌，连陈雯都一时没跟上他的思路，下意识地质疑道："集群？你是指有大量精通算术的人参与了木塔的修建？这恐怕不太现实吧？"

"不，我所指的算术并不是古代用于推演历法和星象、为皇家所垄断的所谓天学。历史是由广大劳动人民创造的。"

"我还是不明白这和木塔有什么关系。"陈雯被袁野跳跃式的思维绕得越发糊涂。

"嘿，你想不到也正常，毕竟如今这里不过是个平平无奇的小县城。但在辽代，它可是农耕文明与游牧文明的交汇点，贸易兴盛，最不缺的就是南来北往的商贾。因为生存的需要，这些人是具备基本的计算能力的。而且，他们还携带了那个时代最先进的计算工具。说来也巧，仅以形制和用法而言，这种世俗化的工具竟然和重要的佛教法器如出一辙。我们不妨大胆猜想一下，为木塔汇聚算力的方法，说不定就出自某个头脑灵活的僧人。"

"计算工具，佛教法器，还有锱铢必较的商人，你说的莫非是——算盘？"在袁野的引导下，陈雯的眼界为之一开。现在，他们距离找到那个神秘的基础模数，就只余薄薄的一层窗户纸了。

看出陈雯还有最后一丝疑惑，袁野自嘲地笑了："这个问题其实简单得超乎想象，惯性思维将我们带入了死胡同。在使用大型机时，我一味将计算的数值推向极致，却忽视了数学本身就是极简的。大道至简，文明的发展，某种程度上就是'进化'走向'尽化'的过程。进化之路上的无数分叉在我们脚下一点点穷尽，最终它们都将指向同一个出口，正如最复杂的大型机本质上也是基于简单的二进制算法。流传于世的几种算盘中，一四珠算盘进行的是十进制运算，一五珠算盘则可表现十二进制或以下任何数进制。而在重视度量衡的商人手中，因为一斤十六两的关系，代表十六进制的二五珠算盘又大行其道。虽然从现有记载来看，依托商品经济的发展，这种算盘直到明末才出现，但在千年前风云际会的宋辽边境，它或许曾被大规模使用也未可知啊。"

"我们可以一起来验证它。"沉默了片刻，陈雯开口道，转头望向袁野。看着她的眼睛，袁野觉得，哪怕再次失败，也不是什么大不了的事。

暂停已久的游戏再次重启。

　　袁野按照早已重复无数次的顺序将木塔的绝大部分一一组装起来，而陈雯则负责在不同节点进行进制换算。他感受到了前所未有的畅快，再也不必首鼠两端、顾此失彼了。原来，数学与力的联结从来都不是修修补补，而是浑然天成的。

　　又经过了几次练习，两人的配合越发默契。终于，在陈雯将要返回北京的前一晚，他们离开了逼仄的库房，在工作站的大院中成功搭建起了一座"光塔"。虽然缩小了几倍，但它完美地复刻了木塔的一切。夜空中，它的光芒照亮了不远处的本尊，两者相映成趣，连古老的木塔也似乎被注入了新的活力。

　　第二天，袁野来送陈雯，工作中无话不谈的两人顿时相顾无言。在各自的研究领域，他们见惯了诡谲历史中的悲欢离合，此刻却无法面对自己的感情，好好道别。临行前，陈雯抢过袁野随身携带的公文包，在他那份连夜赶制出来的《关于应县木塔"大落架"维修方案的论证》1联署上了自己的名字。几年前，在大型机使用上的失误对袁野的学术声誉打击不小，希望这能对方案的审核有所帮助吧。

　　接着，陈雯头也不回地上了车。但在后视镜中，她看到袁野一直愣愣地站在原地，直到她视线模糊也不见他离去。

　　尾　声

　　五年的时光一晃而过。树欲静而风不止，即便是在故宫这样纯粹而单调的环境中，陈雯的心态也一点点地发生着变化。此时，她正握着一封邀请函出神地想着什么。随着在学术界的崭露头角，近年来她收到了越来越多研讨会之类的邀请，颇有些不堪其扰。但这次不同，手上这封函件上，印着应县木塔的图案。

　　这是一个未了的约定，陈雯在心中告诉自己，回家收拾好了行囊。

　　已经是工作站站长的袁野亲自来汽车站接了她。和五年前乘坐大巴进入县城一样，这也是一个黄昏，但令陈雯惊慌的是，目之所及，已经不见木塔巍峨的身影！

　　"不用担心，很快，你就会见证木塔的重生。"几年的时间让袁野稳重了不少，陈雯仿佛被攥紧的心渐渐地放松下来。

　　工作站内几乎没有任何变化。但跟随袁野进入那间曾经无数次模拟木塔的库房后，陈雯才知道这里别有洞天。它被向下挖掘出了一个巨大的空间，无数投影仪正将一处工地的影像实时投射过来。环绕这影像的，是数个由五人或七人组成的方队。与当年的袁野一样，他们都穿戴着全套VR设备。

一四珠，二五珠……陈雯心有所悟。与此同时，投影中工地上一件件编好号、用防水布包裹的部件，也在机械臂的剥离下显露了出来。

方队动了，他们时而如交响乐一般水银泻地，时而又如军队一般严丝合缝，在他们目眩神迷的操作下，木塔仿佛通天之树，蓬勃飞速地生长起来。

"走！历史性的一刻马上就要到来了！"袁野拉起陈雯的手，冲入电梯。

他们上到地面，正赶上木塔顶部的塔刹被缓缓安放上去。四周爆发出阵阵欢呼，木塔，终于重现于人间了！

回头看看袁野，他已是泪流满面，岁月也无法磨灭一颗赤子之心。陈雯笑了，她也一样，要去追寻自己的梦想了。

"木塔修复成功了，你应该是有史以来最出色的守塔人了吧？"陈雯拉了拉他的衣角。

"那可不！"袁野乐不可支，笑得像个孩子。

"我也该走了。"陈雯轻声说道。

"回北京吗？"袁野突然泄了气。

"不，我想清楚了。像木塔这样的文化遗产，在全国乃至全世界还有很多，它们有些已经得到了妥善的保护，但更多的却仍然无人问津。我应该到更广阔的天地，去走访、去见证、去记录。"

"你知道我的，从小就在塔下长大，天天研究的也是它……"袁野的回答理所当然。

"嗯，每个人都在孤独地生活啊。"陈雯有些感慨。

"我是说，木塔教会了我很多。千年前建造它时，古人将海量的运算简化到了极致。现在，为了修复它，我从全国选拨了最出色的电竞选手，把时光积累的所有变量都纳入了这局终极游戏里。人生的选择，也许正如建筑的演变，在进化，或是尽化的道路上走到头吧。"

"什么意思？"袁野的话满是禅机，陈雯不解道。

"咳咳，我的意思是，人啊，简单随心就好了。"仿佛变回了当年初遇时的那个拘谨青年，袁野涨红了脸，鼓起勇气说道，"在路上，你需要一个助手吗？"


［责任编辑：泽　泽］

1　　　对宋式建筑的斗拱组合和挑出距离的称呼，是一种常见的挑出屋檐的方式。出跳越多，整座建筑的檐下深度就越大，出檐也就更深远。

2　　　佛宫寺释迦塔，位于山西省朔州市应县城西北佛宫寺内，俗称应县木塔。1933年，梁思成曾对木塔进行了考察和测绘，在写给妻子林徽因的信中，他提到："绝对的 Overwhelming（势不可挡）……不见此塔，不知木构的可能性到了什么程度。"

1　　　北宋李诫修编的《营造法式》是世界历史上最早公开发行的建筑书籍，提出了以材为祖的模数制度。其中，"屋宇之高深"指整体的模数化，"名物之短长"指构件的模数化，成了建筑标准化思想的鼻祖。

1　在应县木塔的修复方案中，长期存在"大落架"法与"不落架"法的争论。后者是将木塔分层托举，重点维修倾斜严重的二、三层后复位归安的方法。而前者则是将木塔自顶层起逐层拆卸，再从底层逐步向上维修的方法。"大落架"法可从根源上解决木塔的倾斜问题，但因其部件众多，重新组装难度极大而迟迟未能落实。

Fongong Temple Pagoda

by Hai Ya

Translated by Chen Jie

Hai Ya is a financial practitioner, a diehard fan of Liu Cixin and a geek, expert at producing alternate history stories. His most representative works include "The Space-Time Painter", "Flood Dragon", and "The Fury of the River."

Chapter one

It was almost dusk when the bus pulled into the county capital full of low brick houses.

As in countless other small towns in northern China, late autumn had squeezed the last drop of green out of sight. The pagoda appeared majestic on the horizon.

For thousands of years, it had stood here, always the largest and tallest building in the vicinity, magnificent yet not overpowering. At this point in time, the better part of the tower was submerged in darkness, with only layers of flying eaves in the light, plated gold by the setting sun. The pagoda brought life into the surrounding monotony while remaining quiet and solemn itself. Chen Wen felt a sense of purification and emotional resonance from deep within.

It was pitch black when she arrived at the hotel. She didn't manage to sleep that night and rushed to her destination early the next morning.

The south-facing monastery sat right on the axis between the mountain gate and the main hall. Chen Wen looked up and walked towards it step after step as if on a pilgrimage, only to see layers upon layers of bucket arches and columns. Seen from the outside, every floor, except for the first which had double layers, had single layers of eaves. That made a total of five floors with six layers of eaves. Chen Wen knew that between the visible layers connected by beams and columns, there lay hidden others supported by diagonal braces and paving layers of arches and beams. Five visible layers plus four hidden ones made a total of nine. Visible and hidden, a perfect combination of rigidity and flexibility. It was precisely this structure that not only ensured the tower's overall strength, but also endowed it with excellent anti-seismic qualities ensuring the Liao Dynasty pagoda had been able to survive till the present day.

In the dawn light, the sky was blue, not even a glimpse of cloud in sight. After thousands of years of heavy rain and wind, the oil paint on the pagoda's surface had all worn off, showing the pure wood beneath, strong and heavy, seemingly merging with the ethereal sky. The iron flag pole on the top was shining in the morning light, communicating between heaven and earth, man and Buddha, past and the future.

A breeze blew. Wind chimes swayed. Zen music played melodiously. Birds circled down from the pagoda's top. Drawn by them, Chen Wen's eyes ranged over several plaques reading "magnificent craftsmanship" and "world wonders", and finally landed on the third one which read "Sakyamuni".

Chen Wen took a deep breath and put her hands together. With a deeply shocked and devout heart, she finally understood why at the sight of the pagoda, the old master would blurt out the word "magnificent".

That said, the world's oldest and tallest pure wooden pagoda was now lying on the verge of destruction.

Shakyamuni is located in the seismic zone of the Datong Basin. According to historical records: "The land of Yun (Datong) and Ying (Yingxian) states shattered and subsided. One hundred steps of Weibai Mountain split and springs from underneath gushed into streams." As early as April, 1022 (March of the second year of the Liao Taping Era), there was a major earthquake in Datong and Yingxian. It is thought that the magnitude exceeded 6, and at the epicenter intensity reached a magnitude of 8. Almost at the same time, Northern Song's Xinding Basin, located in the southern part of Yingxian County, Shanxi Province, also entered a seismically active period. On January 9, 1038 (the second day of December in the fourth year of Song Jingyou

Era), "there were earthquakes in Xin, Dai, and Bing states. The battlements of the towns were destroyed. The ground cracked and water poured out. The aftershocks did not stop until ten years later. In Dingxiang the city was destroyed and the houses crumbled, sixty percent of its inhabitants were killed or badly injured. The Xuanweng Mountain in the southwest of Taiyuan was severely altered destroyed by the earthquake. Xuanweng Temple was also destroyed by the earthquake."

On June 18, 1043 (the ninth day of the fifth month in the third year of Song Qingli Era), "a major earthquake hit Xinzhou". On June 7, 1044 (the ninth day of May in the fourth year of Song Qingli Era), "an earthquake hit Xinzhou, with thunderous sounds from the northwest."

In 1056 (the second year of LiaoQingning), Liao's national power reached its peak. Whether to pray for the safety of the county and its people and to suppress the earthquakes, or to pay homage to the dowager Empress Xiao Tali, the Shakyamuni Pagoda was built.

History is full of coincidences. No matter what the original builder's purpose, after the completion of the wooden tower the frequency of earthquakes in the county indeed decreased. Even so, relentless erosion over the years had changed the wood, weakening its bearing capacity, increasing deformation resulting in severe damage. Initially tourists were allowed access to the top of the tower. Later, only the ground floor was open for visiting, and now complete closure had become necessary. People tried their best to protect it, but they were helpless against the tower's increasing inclination.

The wooden pagoda had protected the county for more than a thousand years, witnessing changing dynasties and passing time. Legend has it that before Ananda, the famous disciple of Buddha, became a monk, he once incarnated into a stone bridge, suffering the wind, the sun and the rain for 500 years, just so that the woman he loved could walk across him. Did the wooden pagoda also have such a touching story to tell? In any case, it seemed for the pagoda that returning to dust was an inevitability.

Chapter two

Chen Wen had been invited to visit as part of the Yingxian Wooden Pagoda Rescue Plan. When she arrived, there was no sign of any personnel from the local cultural protection department. Fortunately, Chen had a pretty calm temperament. Since she could not enter the pagoda for a while, she simply strolled around the other buildings in the temple. Most of them had been rebuilt in the Ming and Qing dynasties. Compared with the wooden pagoda, they were far less magnificent in scale. A staff member from the Daxiong Palace behind the pagoda suggested she go to the Yingxian Wooden Pagoda Workstation which wasn't far, saying she might find the person in charge there.

"For decades, experts have come and gone, yet there hasn't been one feasible repair plan. There aren't many people left at the workstation now. Won't make no difference anyway ..." he muttered while pointing out the direction. Chen Wen didn't take it personally, just smiled, turned around and walked out of the hall.

A narrow path led Chen to an empty courtyard.

"Is there anyone here?" she called out timidly, and brushed dust off the sign reading "Yingxian Wooden Pagoda Workstation of China Cultural Heritage Research Institute" in large characters.

There were two rows of low buildings in the courtyard. The first were offices with thick curtains drawn across the windows. Chen Wen knocked on the doors one by one, but no one answered. She then went around to the second row; these looked like warehouses. It seemed even less likely that anyone was in them. Just when Chen Wen was about to give up, she saw a faint light through the window of the largest warehouse.

Chen Wen's heart skipped a beat: could there be a thief? The light kept flickering and changing colour. Obviously this was no normal lighting. While deliberating whether to call the police or not, Chen Wen tripped over a pothole in the ground and fell to one side.

"Bangdang!" She had fallen against the big iron door of the warehouse, it was not locked and slid open under the weight of her fall and hit the wall, making a deafening noise.

"Who are you? What are you doing here?" a young man wearing a full set of VR gaming gear asked Chen Wen in surprise. He had taken off his helmet and looked dazed. As soon as he put down the operating controls, the various colourful polyhedrons that were dropping from the upper void of this huge warehouse gradually disintegrated, shattered, and finally disappeared without a trace. So this was where the light had been coming from.

"Chen Wen, researcher at the Painting and Calligraphy Reproduction Group from the Ministry of Culture at Beijing Palace Museum." Chen Wen leaned against the door and looked at him sternly.

"The Palace Museum? Oh, right, that! But aren't you supposed to arrive tomorrow? Wait, what time is it?" The young man had dishevelled hair and two huge dark circles under his eyes. Usually VR headsets had electronic clocks embedded in them, but his mind was clearly still immersed in the VR fantasy world.

Chen Wen had no choice but to turn on her phone and turn the screen towards him. "It's exactly twelve noon."

The young man squinted his eyes to see the numbers clearly, and jolted. "Ah, it's been a full night!" He rubbed his face, then stretched his arms. Hello, Researcher Chen. My name is Yuan Ye. Pharaoh and I are the only two people left in the station. He went home on holiday a while ago and told me about you before he left, but you see, whenever I play this game, I forget about time. So sorry. Give me some time to wash up and I'll take you to the wooden pagoda right away."

To Chen Wen's surprise, Yuan Ye finished washing up in just a few minutes. He had changed into a white shirt and was wearing glasses, which made him look a lot more energetic, more like a cultural protection worker instead of a young internet addict.

"Do you live here?" asked Chen Wen, pointing to the room she had found him in.

"Yes, my parents left early, and I didn't want to live too far away from the pagoda. So the workstation became my home." Yuan Ye replied briskly, without the usual anxiety and resentment people often show in a difficult environment.

The two walked outside together. Yuan Ye had dark skin and it looked as though he had extensive fieldwork experience rather than being an office rat as she had at first thought. As her opinion of him changed, she decided to stop being annoyed at him for missing the appointment due to playing games all night.

Noticing the change in Chen Wen's attitude, Yuan Ye's eyes showed a little smile, but he didn't explain anything, just nodded and said, "Let's go, the wooden pagoda has had no new guests for a long time."

Chapter three

Yuan Ye took out a bunch of keys, swiftly opened the copper lock on the wooden door, and led Chen Wen to the first floor of the pagoda. Mottled sunlight penetrated the tower, illuminating the dust floating in the air. There was a huge statue of Sakyamuni, his expression solemn beyond compare. Chen Wen looked up from below its seat at the vault created by the upper floors gradually closing up to a caisson ceiling over the Buddha's head, like a vortex of meditation sucking in the whole world. She sighed softly: in the Great Buddha's gaze which had travelled through time and space, everything was so unfathomable, too profound to be understood. It seemed as though every layer of the pagoda contained a whole universe of its own.

Finally, Chen Wen focused on the six windward panels installed on the north and south lintels. On each panel there was a portrait of a benefactor. A woman to the south and a man to the north. On closer inspection, it became apparent that the figures were dignified and vivid, and the costumes gorgeously free and unrestrained. Standing in front of the painting she felt a strong sense of Tang-Dynasty aesthetics blowing right towards her face. The lines were simple and unsophisticated, already showing traces of the painting techniques of the Liao Dynasty.

"Yingzhou was under the jurisdiction of Xijing Datong in the Liao Dynasty and bordered with the Song territory. It was an important frontier for the southern Liao Kingdom. Buddhism was worshipped throughout the Kingdom, and the Empress Dowager

Xiao Tali was originally from here. So the pagoda served both as a defence against the enemy and a family temple of the Xiao family. According to experts, among these six portraits of donors, the three female on the south wall are Xiao Nujin, the Queen of Shengzong, Xiao Tali, the Queen of Xingzong, and Xiao Guanyin, the Queen of Taoism; the three males on the north wall are King Xiao Xiaomu of Jin, his eldest son the King of Chen Xiao Zhizu, and his second son the King of Qi Xiao Wuqu."

Yuan Ye walked up to her and started explaining patiently. Following his instructions, Chen Wen set up a drawing board in front of the portrait of Xiao Tali, which hung in centre south, and began her work. If the wooden pagoda was doomed not to survive the next millennium, people should at least record everything about it as fully as possible. In her not-so-long career, Chen Wen had captured on canvas countless works of cultural heritage on the verge of being lost.

Almost as soon as she picked up the brush, Chen Wen entered a state of meditation, becoming completely lost in her work. At first, she traced only a few long straight lines, outlining the portrait, leaving blank spaces of white in the miniature oriental Zen world of of the drawing paper. Then, with a few stylistic strokes, structures emerged, and a whole new universe of rules and constants was born. Concise and silent, they rippled endlessly, and with them monotonous time and space came alive.

Yuan Ye stopped talking and stepped aside to let the light through. After more than an hour, the sun had moved and Yuan Ye cautiously moved closer to have a look.

He saw that with Chen Wen's magical brush, the faded head ornaments in the portrait had come alive again. Taking a closer look, he saw how she had meticulously reproduced not only the colour, but also the character's bearing. Empress Dowager Xiao's thin temples, plain makeup, colourful threads, tassels, and even the flaring wings on the sleeves of her robes had all been copied with extreme grace and luxury. He would never have expected Chen Wen to have such superb skills at such a young age. Her fame at the Palace Museum was indeed well-deserved.

Yuan Ye himself had studied cultural relics preservation technology at his father's insistence without ever really developign a taste for it. He was way better at data programming. With just a few raw parameters he could build a whole world using only a few lines of code. He enjoys that feeling of creating, despite the fact that it goes precisely against the concept of cultural preservation ...

... until today, when Yuan Ye finally saw the possibility of combining the two, thanks to Chen Wen. In just a few strokes, Chen Wen had fully captured the essence of the ancient painting, and the subsequent copying was as natural as a running computer program. A glimmer of hope suddenly rose in Yuan Ye's heart.

"Oops." Chen Wen moved her sore neck and shoulders under the slanting sun. "Before I know it, half a day passes." Realising she had been ignoring Yuan Ye, Chen Wen felt a rush of embarrassment. She got up quickly, only to find there was no one else in the pagoda except herself. She thought maybe Yuan Ye had a job that needed to be dealt with at a higher level, so she stretched her limbs and walked around the tower while waiting for him. Unexpectedly, when she walked to the door, Chen Wen found a bunch of keys with a note underneath. She picked it up and read, "Remember to lock the door when you are done, you'll find me at the work station. I'd be delighted to treat you to dinner. Yuan Ye."

It turned out that he had left a while ago. Chen Wen was a little surprised. This dude was really careless. He didn't even say goodbye. Wasn't he afraid she might get curious and secretly climb to the second or third floor and cause irreversible damage?

When she returned to the workstation, Chen Wen was even more surprised to find Yuan Ye playing his stupid game again. So irresponsible! How could the pagoda ever be properly taken care of with this man in charge? The favourable impression he had begun to form in her heart was instantly gone.

"Hey! Yuan Ye, is the pagoda in your eyes less important than the game?" Chen Wen walked into the warehouse and asked bluntly, shaking the keys he had dropped violently in his ears.

Yuan was wearing a VR helmet and acted as if no one was there.

"Wait a second, don't bother me for now, I'm going to get a victory soon." Yuan Ye had obviously expected Chen Wen's reaction, so he was not as flustered as last time, rather there was a hint of certainty and excitement about him.

Once again, there were slowing falling colour flocks projected in the air.

Same game as before. Boring enough. Chen Wen snorted with contempt. Though she didn't play games much, who didn't know Tetris, a game with a history of nearly a hundred years? Yuan Ye seemed to be playing the latest 3D version. The falling colour blocks included not only regular polyhedrons, but also semi-regular polyhedrons, irregular polyhedrons and even spheres. The difficulty had increased a lot, but Chen Wen couldn't understand why there were people still obsessed with this ancient game.

At the beginning, Yuan Ye's hands flew up and down, like a conductor of an out-of-tune orchestra. The colour blocks quickly piled higher and higher. Chen Wen was smugly happy expecting he would "game over" soon. After watching for a while, she found that even if Yuan Ye assembled the blocks tightly, they didn't disappear. So what was the purpose? Chen Wen was a puzzled. When the structure of the coloured blocks became clearer and more refined, she understood. In preparation for coming here, she had drawn it herself multiple times, that unique double-layer sleeve frame structure of the Yingxian Wooden Pagoda.

Gradually, Yuan Ye's hands moved slower and slower. He hunched his body, weighing and considering, taking measured steps repeatedly around the frame that had already been built. It took a long time for his tense arms to move just a little. The hovering colour blocks moved slowly under his control and were eventually embedded in the overall structure, always in unexpected yet precisely the right positions.

The structure was square on the bottom and octagon on the top, corresponding to the idea of "round sky and square earth". On that base, Yuan Ye erected three circles of columns, inside which two earth walls were built to roughly form the double-layer sleeve structure. Next, he began to assemble the well-known bucket arches. The stress node of each column corresponded to one arch. He then placed the ring frame on the arches as the hidden layer, on top of which he lay beams, columns, fangs and bracket sets. There goes your visible layer. Hidden, visible, one, two, three ... Chen Wen couldn't help but be amazed by the virtual pagoda rising from the ground. It was reaching towards the critical point of the last two floors when, due to some who-knows-what reason, the structure began to shake. Yuan Ye tried his best to save it, but the shaking worsened and the structure eventually fell apart, shattering into pieces all over the ground.

"This proves that the wooden pagoda is based on a certain constant as the basic modulus, and the fuzzy value selection just won't work," Yuan Ye said to himself as he took off his VR helmet and equipment.

"I don't quite understand what you mean, can you tell me about it?" Although she didn't know the details, Chen Wen was already certain that the game Yuan Ye played must somehow be related to the restoration of the pagoda. All her grievances were gone, she had asked the question with great interest.

"Actually, this is not a new technology. A few years ago, someone used VR modelling to help restore Notre Dame de Paris. When I heard about it, I thought this method could also be used on the wooden pagoda. It was found that the wooden pagoda had been slowly destroyed by the combined action of many factors such as thousands of years of wind and rain, earthquakes, and even man-made damages. If the destruction of Notre Dame de Paris by fire was an acute emergency, the pagoda is more like an old man who had been tortured by chronic diseases for many years. It was much more complicated since it was a result of long-term accumulated factors. Moreover, the pagoda was built entirely of wood, without nails or rivets. Compared to a church built with stones, it's much more like a compact whole. Even the most inconspicuous part could have a huge impact on the whole restoration process. Indeed, a millimetre miss is as good as a thousand miles."

So this game was a digital remodelling by Yuan Ye to restore the wooden pagoda. He had obviously done it countless times and was so passionate about it he gushed whenever the subject was brought up.

"After the chaos and disorder of the Five Dynasties and Ten Kingdoms period ended, new regimes began to undertake large-scale construction projects. Palaces, government offices, and temples with extreme luxury and extravagance flourished. Corruption prevailed among officials in charge of those projects, which overwhelmed the whole country. Various design standards, specifications, related materials, and construction quotas had to be determined urgently, to clarify grade, form, material and work hours of different housing projects, and eliminate deficit from the source. In the second year of Emperor Chongqing's reign in Northern Song Dynasty, the widely popular Construction Standards and Specifications was published, establishing the overruling modular principle of 'all rules of house-building should be based on materials used; all specifications like height and length should be based on materials used'. This set of principles had obviously been accumulated through long-term practice. The wooden pagoda was built more than 40 years before the Construction Standards and Specifications was issued, and there must have been many a Song craftsman among the crew. If there hadn't been a standardized modular system in place, it's difficult to imagine how our ancestors who didn't have precision machinery could build such a huge and complex building."

"Then the key to repairing and restoring the pagoda is to find the 'distinctive material' determined at the beginning of its design, that is, its basic modulus!" Chen Wen answered excitedly, but then added hesitantly, "In the era Liang Sicheng lived in, it was really hard to find. But now using mainframe computers and backward reasoning, it should not be difficult to calculate this number. Why is it still unresolved today?"

Yuan Ye's face darkened, once again impressed by Chen Wen's keen insight. His tone uncharacteristically revealed self-doubt. "I have not only thought about it, but also done it. The workstation had a limited budget, but with my determination, we poured all of it into renting a mainframe computer. The results we got were completely unreasonable. No matter what unit we used as a basic parameter of a large building, it was ridiculously wrong. We re-ran a few calculations, but the results didn't change. People at the top were disappointed. The budget was cut, and staff started leaving the station. I know ... if it wasn't for me, the wooden pagoda and the workstation would not have been reduced to what it is today ..." Yuan Ye's voice broke with emotion.

"But at least you tried, and you haven't given up, have you?" Chen Wen patted his shoulder and comforted him softly.

"Thank you. I will never give up!" For some reason, this young woman from the Palace Museum managed to infuse Yuan Ye with strength. He cheered up quickly.

Chapter four

After the misunderstanding between them had been sorted out. Chen Wen and Yuan Ye found although they had chosen different paths, they shared the same original intention: to protect the pagoda. With this common vision, the relationship between the two grew much closer. During those busy and fulfilling days, Chen Wen carefully visited each and every floor and corner of the pagoda. She copied everything she saw and thought of on her drawing paper. Yuan Ye was always by her side. He was no longer wasting his time on a game that could never be finished.

However, the failures over the past few years had not all been in vain. Those high-intensity games helped Yuan Ye open up his brain and, by connecting it to a small computer, he could synchronize computing through splicing components. He found the tendency towards a modular system was pretty evident when splitting the wooden tower into different units. If he took the most basic length, width and height as the starting point, related them to the surface width, depth and column height, and splice the tower layer by layer, a simple and clear gradient pattern began to emerge. Yuan Ye followed on that train of thought: these three are larger-scale units, and they may be expanded moduli, that is, a proportional relationship as the result of the basic modulus control. The mainframe rented by the workstation had made its calculations concerning the overall situation of the tower. Based on its results, Yuan Ye adjusted the basic modulus of the pagoda's surface width, depth and column height to 22.1 cm. Since the pagoda was built in the Liao Dynasty, before the promulgation of Construction Standards and Specifications, the materials used needed to be different from that of the Northern Song Dynasty. If converted into the unit system of the Liao Dynasty, it should be 0.75 Liao feet, exactly three quarters of one Liao unit!

But, after this breakthrough, Yuan Ye's experiment fell into a bottleneck. He couldn't unify this basic modulus with other parts of the pagoda. He began to suspect that the modulus was only an ideal in design and was flexibly used in real-life construction. Based on that, he tried fuzzy value selection in the game, but it fell short in the end.

As his father had hoped, Yuan Ye decided to devote his whole life to safeguarding the pagoda. Like the monks who once sat in it, he had an almost endless amount of time. Days with Chen Wen, on the contrary, went by very fast. There was something in his heart that stayed with the girl who would leave soon. Now, he was standing quietly behind the intent Chen Wen, admiring her face bathed by the sun on one side, a clean and quiet silhouette caught in a moment between light and darkness, her eyes moving like lake water in the autumn, mysterious and beautiful.

As Chen Wen tried to copy the exquisite ancient paintings, Yuan Ye desperately tried to commit all these details to memory so that he could dwell on them in the long years to come.

"Bother!" Chen Wen sighed, interrupting Yuan Ye's heart tormented by fieriness and restraint. She stood up slowly and rubbed her numb legs. Yuan Ye quickly stretched out his arms in a gentlemanly manner to help her up. Inside the pagoda, there was no place for people to lean on.

"I screwed up." Chen Wen shook her head.

"What went wrong?" Yuan Ye glanced at the manuscript on Chen Wen's drawing paper and saw a rare sense of incongruity.

"It's all my fault. In order to see the whole picture of the Buddha statue, I chose to look down from a high place, which allowed me to have better perspective, but made it easy to accumulate errors. When drawing, these errors must be corrected according to certain ratios. I didn't take into account the wooden pagoda's progressively tightening interior structure which visually magnifies this effect, and the degrees of magnification are not uniform. In other words, the correction ratios I used are neither accurate nor uniform."

"Even the ratios are not uniform ..." Yuan Ye muttered to himself.

After a while, Chen Wen felt Yuan Ye's arm jerk. His eyes, which seemed a little dazed just now, suddenly focussed—the indomitable scholar was back.

"Chen Wen, what do you think was the biggest difficulty in building such a huge and sophisticated pagoda in the Liao Dynasty?" Yuan Ye asked in a hoarse voice.

"The wooden pagoda is 65.84 meters high and uses more than 3,000 tons of wood, definitely a big project, even by today's standards. In addition to the overall double-layer-sleeve framework, there are paving and bucket arches, diagonal braces and other complex structures, making up to tens of thousands of components. Stability of the tower depends on splicing and occlusion between them. The underlying principle is quite similar to building blocks. Though not complicated, as the volume increases, the difficulty increases exponentially. I think all its components were made according to specified values before the main project started. They were then assembled in strict procedures in a one-time manner. Only in this way could the mechanical balance between the components and the overall framework be achieved."

"That's right! But these are merely the surface. Think again. What do they all point to?" Yuan Ye asked eagerly before Chen Wen finished speaking.

"Could it be..." Chen Wen picked things up so quickly. She lowered her head to think for a few seconds, then met Yuan Ye's eager gaze, and the two blurted out in the same breath, "computing!"

"Correct! Manpower, material resources or financial resources, none of these posed a real problem for an ambitious regime that had just conquered the Central Plain. It had enough resources to make it happen. But in a time when the illiteracy rate was high and tools limited, where did the massive computing power to put thousands of components in harmony with each other come from? This exceeded individual intelligence and could only be made possible by a cluster of countless tiny units!"

Yuan Ye's thoughts were running like a spring. Even Chen Wen couldn't keep up. "Cluster? You mean a large number of people proficient in arithmetic? I'm afraid that's not realistic, right?" she asked.

"No, the arithmetic I'm referring to is not the so-called celestial science used to deduce the calendar and astrology, monopolized by the royalty. History is made by the mass of ordinary folks."

"I still don't understand what this has to do with the wooden pagoda." Chen Wen was confused by Yuan Ye's jumping thoughts.

"Hey, it's understandable. After all, Yingxian is just a small town today, but in the Liao Dynasty it was a thriving hub where the farming civilization met the nomadic civilization. Trade was prosperous, and many merchants travelling from a long way off came to the city. In order to survive, all these people had a basic knowledge of computing. What's more, they all carried the most advanced computing tool of that era. Coincidentally, this tool is a lot like an important Buddhist instrument, both in terms of form and usage. We can make a bold guess that the method of gathering computing power for the pagoda came from a monk, one with a clever mind."

"Computing tool, Buddhist instrument, and businessmen who haggle over every penny, are you talking about—abacus?" Chen Wen's eyes widened. Now, they are only a thin layer of rice paper away from finding that mysterious fundamental modulus.

Seeing the last shadow of doubt in Chen Wen's eyes, Yuan Ye laughed at himself: "It's actually a pretty simple problem. We were led to a dead end by cognitive inertia. When using a mainframe, I blindly pushed the values to the extreme, ignoring the fact that maths works best when it's minimalist. The greatest truth always comes in the simplest form. The development of a civilization is to some extent a process from 'evolution' to 'exhaustion'. The count-less forks along the road of evolution ran out under our feet. In the end they all point to the same exit, just as the most complex mainframes are essentially based on the simplest binary arithme-tic. There are two types of abacuses popular in the world: the one-four-bead and the one-five-bead. The former performs decimal computing while the latter performs duodecimal, or any lower number, computing. Because of the metric system of one pound equalling sixteen taels in ancient China, the two-five-bead became extremely popular with merchants. Though existing records show this kind of abacus didn't appear until end of the Ming Dynas-ty, but who knows? Maybe they had been used in large numbers along the turbulent Song-Liao border a thousand years before."

"We will verify it together." After a moment of silence, Chen Wen turned towards Yuan Ye. Looking into her eyes, Yuan Ye felt even if they were to fail again, it would not matter.

The long-paused game resumed.

Yuan Ye assembled most of the wooden pagoda step by step in an order which had been repeated countless times, while Chen Wen took up the base conversion at different nodes. He felt an unprecedented ease, no longer having to attend to both ends at the same time he could concentrate on one or the other. Maths and mechanics had never been more compatible with each other before.

After a few more experiments, cooperation between the two grew more and more instinctive. Finally, the night before Chen Wen was about to go back to Beijing they left the cramped ware-house and successfully built a "light pagoda" in the courtyard. Though several times smaller, it perfectly embodied everything about the pagoda. Its light travelled through the night sky and il-luminated the real one not far away. The two complemented each other so well that even the ancient wooden pagoda seemed to be injected with new vitality.

The next day Yuan Ye came to see Chen Wen off. The two, who talked about practically everything at work, suddenly became speechless. In their respective research careers, they had both become used to taking their leave of newfound friends, but at this moment they couldn't face their own feelings and properly say goodbye. Before leaving, Chen Wen snatched the briefcase Yuan Ye was carrying, and signed her name on the paper he had finished that night: Maintenance Plan for the Yingxian Wooden Pagoda using Large Dropping Frames. Yuan Ye's academic reputation had been tarnished a few years ago by his mistakes involving the mainframe. She hoped her signature could be of some help to him.

Afterwards, Chen Wen got into the car without looking back but in the rear-view mirror she saw Yuan Ye standing there in a daze, unmoving.


Epilogue

Five years passed in a flash. As an old saying goes: the trees may long for peace, but the wind shall never cease. Even in a place as pure and monotonous as the Palace Museum, Chen Wen's mentality had been gradually changing. A rising name in academia, she had received more and more invitations for seminars in recent years, at times it could be quite overwhelming, but this was different. The invitation in her hand had an image of Yingxian Wooden Pagoda printed on it.

This is an unfulfilled promise, Chen Wen told herself, went home and packed her bags.

Yuan Ye personally came to the bus station to pick her up. Just like five years ago, it was already dusk when she entered the county capital. When Chen Wen saw the towering figure of the pagoda was no longer there, she panicked.

"Don't worry. Soon, you will witness the rebirth of the pagoda." A few years had certainly made Yuan Ye a lot more mature. Hearing those words, Chen Wen's clenched heart gradually relaxed.

Almost nothing had changed in the station. Following Yuan Ye into the warehouse where they used to simulate the wooden pagoda, Chen Wen realized that something special was going on. The ground had been dug down into a huge pit where holographic images of a construction site were being projected by countless projectors. Surrounding the pit stood several formations of five or seven people. Like Yuan Ye back then, they all wore full sets of VR equipment.

One-four beads, two-five beads ... Chen Wen understood something. In the meantime, the numbered and tarpaulin-wrapped parts on the actual site were revealed while robotic arms peeled off the wraps.

The team moved, sometimes like a symphony of mercury pouring down to the ground, sometimes tight as an army. With their dazzling operation, the wooden pagoda grew vigorously and rapidly like a tree to the sky.

"Let's go. We'll witness a historic moment!" Yuan Ye took Chen Wen's hand and rushed into the elevator.

They went back up to the ground, right when the Tasha was being slowly placed on the top of the pagoda. There were bursts of cheers all around. The wooden pagoda had finally reappeared in the world.

Chen Wen looked back at Yuan Ye. Tears ran down his face. A man with a pure heart like that of an innocent newborn, immune from the erosion of time. Chen Wen smiled. She too, was going to pursue her dream.

"Now the wooden pagoda has been successfully repaired, you've earned yourself the title of the world's best pagoda guard, right?" Chen Wen tugged at the corner of his shirt.

"You bet!" Yuan Ye was overjoyed, smiling like a child.

"It's time for me to go now," Chen Wen said softly.

"Back to Beijing?" Yuan Ye was suddenly discouraged.

"No, I have made up my mind. There are lots of pieces of cultural heritage like the wooden pagoda out there. Some of them have been properly preserved, but most have been left unnoticed. I should go out there, to visit, witness, and record."

"You know me. I grew up under the tower and I have been studying it all my life ..." Yuan Ye's answer was just as she had expected.

"Well, ultimately everyone lives alone." Chen Wen sighed.

"I mean, the wooden pagoda has taught me a lot. When it was built, thousands of years ago, our ancestors simplified massive computing to the extreme. Now, to restore it, I have selected the best e-sport players from across the country and included all the variables accumulated through time in this ultimate game. Life, like the evolution of architecture, either keeps coming to an end by evolving, or simply by running out."

"What do you mean?" Chen Wen was puzzled by Yuan Ye's words.

"What I mean is, it's good to lead a simple life and follow your heart." As if changing back to the prudent young man she had first met Yuan Ye blushed and said with gathered courage, "Do you need an assistant on the road?"

12
11
10
9
8
7
6
5
4
3
2
1

# 还魂

## 任青

现为法律行业工作者。处女作《消失的马戏团》2020年发表于《科幻世界》，从此开始创作科幻小说。

获奖：2021年第三十二届银河奖最佳短篇小说奖｜还魂

1

还魂尸送来的时候，面部只有模糊的轮廓，但老太太依然认得出那是自己的儿子。

她和死者面对面坐着，一言不发，看着五官和毛发自动塑造成型。他的皮肤湿润极了，不像死人，而像个刚出生的婴儿，新生的纹理在皮肤表面漂浮、固定，如海流在北欧峡湾逐渐雕刻出悬崖峭壁。他的眼睛越来越深、鼻子逐渐高耸起来，左脸上慢慢浮现出一块伤疤，是小时候摔倒在轧花机上留下的。那块伤疤慢慢由粉转红、变成褐色，缩小面积，固定在皮肤的表层，形状如儿子离家前一模一样。

老太太深陷在藤椅中，被奇观吸引、被恐惧攫住，身体动弹不得，呼吸声仿佛细小的灰尘降落在角落里。

十分钟后，死亡通知书姗姗来迟，同纸张一起来的还有乡会计和邮递员。会计瞪了邮递员一眼，责备他速度奇慢，竟把通知书落在还魂尸后送达。老太太终于扶着藤椅站起来，手却抖成筛糠，认不出纸上的字。会计好心给她念道：

兹有工兵王氏信光，殁于春月廿八日。马革裹尸，美名咏诵，光沉紫电，忠烈可风。

老太太看着纸，喉咙里发出猫叫般不清不楚的呜咽声，又转头瞧瞧屋里的怪物。那具还魂尸紧闭双眼，全身伴随胸部起伏慢慢抖动。他的肤色越来越深、头发越来越密，血管变得更细，在肌肤之下逐渐遁于无形。会计控制自己不去盯着怪物，从随身夹子抽出一份表格，开始与老太太核算。

"抚恤金：计信用点二十六万。明日入账，次周凭亲缘证明、死亡通知可取。"

老太太似懂非懂地点点头。还魂尸突然爆发出一阵响亮的打嗝声。

"他有……有其他继承人吗？"

老太太摇摇头，嘴角耷拉下来，眼里终于涌出大颗大颗的泪珠。

"嗨，大娘！"邮递员开口安慰她，"别伤心了，你看，不止你一家，我这里还有一摞呢！"

说完，他把手伸进邮件袋，掏出厚厚的一摞邮件，都用统一的颜色印刷，侧面的颜料排成一条褐色的长龙。见得此景，老太太用手拍着大腿，高声痛哭起来。

"可他们都没有还魂尸！看吧，你是唯一拥有还魂尸的人，因为你的儿子炸成了碎片，只剩了一粒芯片，不幸中的幸……"

"别说啦！"会计大声打断他，"去送你的信吧！"

"可我还想……"

"有什么好奇的！"会计踹了他一脚。邮递员悻悻地走出门去，最后回头望了一眼，恐惧的表情出现在他脸上——

"那尸体，睁开眼睛啦！"


2

还魂尸彻底变成了儿子的样子，他现在睁开了眼睛，慢慢转动着眼珠。屋里的几个人屏住呼吸，全都一动不动。老太太停止哭泣，向前挪了一步。

"当心，大娘！"会计扯住她。

还魂尸忽地一下站了起来，可是没站稳，又坐了回去。看见怪物站起来，会计和邮递员尖叫着向后退。还魂尸转头看看他们，张开嘴，一言不发，棕色的眼睛仿佛直勾勾地瞪进虚空里。

"我走了。"邮递员说，"大娘，我可对您的遭遇深表同情。"

说完，他转身跑出房门。"懦夫！"会计说，他的双腿发软，动弹不得，只得勉强用脚掌慢慢向后蹭。没等缓过神来，邮递员又跑了回来。

"技术员来了！"他说。

"终于来了。"会计长出一口气。一个个子不高的年轻人跟随邮递员进来，他的头顶染了一撮掺杂褐色的黄发，手上拿着带箱的大喷枪，制服沾满斑斑白点，身上挂着一丝破破烂烂的蜘蛛网子。

"怎么是你？"会计问，"市里的技术员呢？"

"市里的专家？他出了事故，车子翻进沟里，腿摔断啦。"年轻人顿上一顿，"上边说，只能让我来讲讲了。"

"你讲，你懂吗？"

　　"他们给我传了资料。说实话，我懂的也不多，要是问我化肥啦、农药啦，还能……"

　　"这样就行，"会计打断他，"快讲讲这个鬼东西，它已经快把我们吓死啦！"

　　"好，知无不言！"年轻人自己拉个椅子，却没敢坐下，扶着把手站在一边，"这是一类生化人，刚刚开发，用于死人的意识转移，人们都叫它还魂尸。"

　　"很贴切的名字。"会计说，"但这怪物有啥用处？"

　　"能给人安慰吧，"技术员说，"说不定技术成熟了，大人物们会争先恐后地入住，长生不败、永垂不朽。"

　　"到那时候，原主和生化人打起来，怎么办？"

　　"这……就不是咱该关心的了。"

　　"它现在是活的吗？"邮递员指着四体僵硬的怪物问。

　　"是啊。它的肉体刚刚形成，可能意识仍在构建。"技术员说，然后转向老太太，"资料上写，王氏信光阵亡时，头部植入芯片也遭到损坏，他们能够恢复提取的数据有限，所以生化人的人格是不完整的。大娘，他们已尽了最大努力。"

　　老太太面露恐惧地点点头。

　　"上边说，还魂尸仍在测试阶段，优先供给阵亡将士家属使用，数量有限。因为您的儿子他……尸骨无存了，所以向您派发一个，希望能够带来短暂安慰。"

　　"短暂安慰？"会计插话道。

　　技术员耸耸肩，"两周后，他们会把个体收回去，提取运行资料，再进行研究完善。"

　　"研究完了，能还给她们吗？"

　　"不知道，这玩意儿据说挺贵的，不过……"技术员拍拍椅子背，仿佛那儿贴着一个帮腔说话的电钮，"和您的儿子享受多出来的两周吧，这种机会不是人人都有，别人想要的话，恐怕得上阎王爷那儿找寻了！"

　　"他是我的儿子吗？"老太太突然开口问。

　　"他是个生化人，"技术员说，"这么说吧，人们借助先进技术，把您儿子残存的意识和记忆，移植进生化人的脑子。他就相当于您的儿子，只是记忆不太完整，并且给人感觉……有点奇怪。"

　　"我不明白。先生，他和我的儿子长得一模一样，他是我儿子吗？"老太太坚持追问。

　　"大娘，从定义上讲，他是个……"

　　"天哪！"邮递员双手指天，打断了年轻人的讲解，"你讲这么多，她能懂吗？给她个明白话吧，我还有一摞通知书要发呢！"

"好吧，"技术员说，"是！他的确……算是你的儿子！"老太太抿起嘴巴，点点头，眼睛动了一下。角落里突然传来声音，大家齐刷刷看过去——那个刚刚出生的人竟自己挣扎着站了起来。他看着大伙儿，缓了一会儿，慢慢开口说："我饿了。"

人们面面相觑，谁也不敢说话，也不敢动，耳朵里只听见唰唰唰的杂音，那是风把满枝树叶吹翻过来的声响。技术员从椅子上挪开手，觉得都是汗，风一吹凉凉的。

"你问他要吃什么？"会计说，他把手放在腰间，就像那儿真有把无形的佩枪。

"你想吃啥啊？"老太太问。

"蒜苗炒肉。"还魂尸说。

"是我儿子！"母亲大哭起来。


3

秘制蒜苗炒肉的做法——瘦肉、五花切薄片，肉片用酱油腌过，蒜苗用盐腌过，五花肉下锅煸出油，再放瘦肉下锅炒熟，最后放蒜苗段和辣椒丝，加盐、酱油炒好，起锅淋少许麻油即可。

还魂尸坐在桌边，连吃了三碗，雪白的背部一耸一耸。吃完饭，他抱着膝盖，蜷缩在椅子上，不言不语。

"信……光，你冷不冷？"

"冷。"他说。

老太急忙翻箱倒柜，找出儿子的衣服。怪人笨拙地把秋衣穿上，却怎么也穿不进裤子，老太太帮他把裤子提好，腰带扎上。

"信光，你瘦了。"她说。

还魂尸点点头，抬眼看看她，一言不发。

"唉，你遭罪了！"老太太攥住还魂尸的手，那手冰凉冰凉的，她赶紧把它们捂在怀里，"回来就好，回来就好。"

怪物再次点点头，他耐心等老太太掉完泪，慢慢把手抽出来，盘腿在椅子上坐定，面朝北方闭上眼睛。

老太太在旁边待了一会儿，开口问："仗……打得怎么样？"

"什么怎样？"

"就是战场有什么事儿啊……能打赢吗？主要是你怎么……怎么负的伤？"

　　"忘了，"儿子把眼睁开，"好多事都忘了，忘光了。"说完，他又把眼睛闭上，肚里发出与上午一模一样、打嗝般的巨响。嗝声好一阵才过去。老太太坐在旁边，待了一会儿，欲言又止。

　　"你先休息吧！"她说，然后轻轻退到外屋去。

　　晚上，王氏信光在家里睡了一觉，却没睡踏实，半夜惊醒了好几次。最后一次醒来后，他睡不着了，静静地躺在床上，看着墙上挂的旧钟表——6时15分。意识逐渐清晰，这是他第一次认识到时间概念，时间在一秒秒地流逝，真奇妙，昨天是他出生的日子，但他却感觉自己并不是个新人，出生前的时间也并非一片混沌。他看着秒针，滴答、滴答，一天有24个小时，一小时有3600秒，如果他愿意的话，可以把每一秒再分成若干个单位来体验，但他没有这样做。他现在是人类，他在学习王氏信光、学脑中本能、学所有的人类那样按分秒来感受时间。6时17分过去了，下一个阶段是6时18分，他想，窗外阳光很好，窗台有谷粒，应该会有鸟儿落下来。

　　思绪未及落定，一只鸟儿突然扑来，飞降在砖红色的窗台上。

　　老太太家有具还魂尸的消息很快在附近传开。下午，家里被围得水泄不通。邻居们争相前来询问亲人的事，孤老寡妇们像油炸的面糊，把王氏信光团团包裹。

　　"——我的儿子怎么死的，他说过什么话吗，有什么遗言吗？"

　　"我的丈夫怎么样了，你在部队见过他吗？"

　　"战场是什么样的，我们能胜利吗？"

　　面对这些问题，儿子总能做出不那么得体的回答：

　　"不知道。"

　　"不清楚。"

　　"对不起，真的忘记了。"

　　后来，老太太趴在厨房睡着了，天黑之后才醒来。她走到院子里，发现街坊已经散尽，留下一地垃圾，风越来越大，只剩一只狗在冲着还魂尸狂吠。老太太拿出棍子，把狗赶到门外。可它并不走远，在门边的竹竿堆旁趴了下来。她刚刚复生的儿子仍然坐在桌边，脊背保持笔挺的姿势。

　　"快睡吧，信光。"老太太说。

　　儿子指了指门边的黄狗。

　　"这动物，怎么说？"

　　"狗。"老太太说。

"狗。"他重复道，满意地点点头。

"去睡吧。"

"好，"儿子说，"等我恢复好了，学会帮你干活。"

"嗯……好，好孩子。"老太太说，"你在哪屋睡啊？跟我睡一屋吗？"

"再说吧。先回厨房。"

"怎么了？"

"锅倒了。"

话音未定，厨房里传来哐叽一声，那是巨大的蒸锅倾覆的声音，有个圆圆的铁篦子从门里滚出来，滚到草丛的边缘，立在那里，不动不摇。


4

收拾好物品，打扫好庭院，两个人才回到床上。这是复生后的第二个晚上，王氏信光做了个梦。在梦里，他见到一匹白色的骏马在厚厚的冰上行走，冰下是重重叠叠的残肢和深渊不灭的火焰。"马。"他记得这个词。梦里的冰太滑，那匹白马跑不起来，它失了前蹄，跪倒在坚硬的地面上。血涌出来，流淌到士兵们的鞋跟下。他低头看看自己的鞋，胶鞋掉了底，地面磨得脚生疼，头顶的燃烧弹把天空映得如同白昼，环绕四周的有万年前的斧石、千年前的车马、百年前的巨炮，两轮圆月在古战场上空熠熠生辉。王氏信光穿着掉了底的胶鞋走在战场上，封冻的河流让他慢慢失去意识，他忘记了自己是谁，只是跟随云雾般缭绕的指令，向末日缓慢地冲锋。在那个冰冻的晚上，月光下的一切都成为慢动作，对面军队的炮火成为意识的标枪，地雷存在于时空的每个角落，炸弹投射过来，碎片在空气中游泳，裹挟着夜幕与弹痕缓慢地消逝。

信光在消逝的秽雾中挣扎，在梦中拼凑着残缺的记忆，首先看到了本家叔叔，他比自己小一岁，却长一辈，是骄傲的飞行兵。王牌飞行手王氏信虎，在有大学可读的日子里，他便是飞行冠军，曾独自一人穿过峡谷、飞跃神山。战场上，他用身体撞烂三名敌兵，血肉如春雨般飘洒。他梦见了炊事兵安师傅，安师傅是缺少一条腿的残疾兵。工兵营人手不足时，炊事兵亲自披挂上阵，但他只会依赖设备，铁脚感受不到土地的触感。他不知道地雷和好土感觉是不同的，不知道触碰引线地雷会飞到你的脖颈里，他除了做饭，什么都不知道，但死亡知道他，死亡知晓一切。他还梦见了班长镜子男爵，班长因为迷信而得到这个名号。他总是把一面镜子挂在腰间，拴在皮带的扣眼上。他总在下午沏一杯糖水当作咖啡。在一块猩红色的盆地里，信光把他的身体从燃烧的机械中拖出来，他的腰上没有挂镜子，信光想，镜子一定落在了战车里。他梦见了女兵达娜·科拉帕洛娃，达娜长着一头亮褐色的秀发，她……

现在，这些人都不在了，他们被战争吞噬，化为废墟中的微尘，自虚空中来，归于虚空中去。

白马再次嘶鸣的时候，梦一下子醒了。信光猛地从床铺上坐起来，口中发出啸叫。老太太点亮了灯。他的瞳孔缩小，脑袋剧痛起来，"妈妈！"他尖厉地喊道。老太太已经数年没有听过这样的声音，她觉得这声音很美、很辽阔。

"别怕，已经早上了，"老太太说，"信光，信光。"


5

白天，信光学东西非常快。第一个周末的下午，他已经学会使用手扶农机耕作，只是有时面对松软的土地，他犹豫一下才敢走过去。傍晚时分，技术员回到村里，头顶沾满花粉，身上的蛛网似乎更多了。

"大娘，你和他相处得怎样？"

"我的儿子，他像个小孩。"老太太笑着说，"他一顿能吃好几碗面条。"

技术员也笑了起来。"我有些事情要告诉你，"他说，"不要让他的耳朵进水，普通的水还好，一定不能让酸性物质滴进去，若毁掉自适芯片，他就彻底变成傻子了。"

"当然，"老太太说，"耳朵进水，正常人都受不了，何况他在战场负过伤。"

技术员张张嘴，欲言又止，只好笑着和老太太告别，"祝你们健康！"技术员走后，母子二人就着微风，沿着土坡和田垄向外走，一直走到村子的尽头。那里的房屋越来越少，小小的坟头却越来越多。在一块堤坝和树林夹成的菱形土地，两个人停下脚步。

"这是咱家祖坟，你记得吗？"老太太问。信光摇摇头。

老太太叹口气，往南走了几步，指着一个立有灰色石碑的坟头说："这是你爹的坟，记得吗？"

信光想了想，没有回答。老太太接着说："我死了，得和他埋在一起，这事交给你办。"还魂尸点点头，把这件事牢牢存进脑袋里。他记住了坟地的位置、特征、爹的石碑、上面刻下的字迹。他看到坟头附近有棵大型植物，没有叶子，光秃秃的，根却繁茂，把地都拱了起来。

“怎么有棵，植物？”他问。

“那是树，”老太太说，“外来的怪品种，树没活，但把地给顶起来了，应该砍了它。”

“交给我办。”还魂尸说。他沿着大树走了两圈，反复摸索一会儿，终于找到个趁手的位置。于是他弯下腰来，头冲下，双手环抱住树干。第一次用力，树干稍微动了一动；第二次用力，树开始摇摇晃晃；第三次用力，发出根茎断裂的唏啦唏啦声，大树竟被连根拔起，倒悬着栽倒在地，根部带出大块泥土，几根长长的蚯蚓掉在地上。

这声巨响吸引了所有人的注意力，附近上坟的、瞧热闹、闲着没事的几个人全都看向这边，目瞪口呆。信光看也不看他们一眼，他用手把树根上的泥土拢起来，填回坑中，用脚踩平，形成了一个盆地般的小坑。老太太在旁边帮他拿着衣服，用手抚摸他后背浸满汗水的"H4004"黑色编号。这刺字是什么意思呢？她想，最好不要让别人看见。自老头去世之后，她一直没精打采、行迈靡靡，但几天来，失去多年的信心一并回到她的胸中，令她高兴地把头高高扬起，就像光彩万分地嫁到村子里时一样。信光干活很快，等两人回程时，身后已经跟了不少人，有人在录像，这是旧时代残存的习惯，网络被全面禁止后，录像已经没有实际意义。信光跟在母亲后面，走在小路上，黄泥从老太太鞋底掉了下来，他目不转睛地看着，发现自己很喜欢土黄的颜色，这色彩就像黄昏，具有柔和的力量感。此刻正是黄昏时分，黄色微光浸润一切、使人通明。于是他感觉到力量澎湃汹涌，眼前所见之物不再是静止不动的画面，它们的命运像时间中的录影，缓慢但不可阻挡地呈现在眼前。大部分时候，画面是模模糊糊的，但却偶尔变得清晰起来。

前方，一条狗正趴在路边，爪子按住根泥呛呛的骨头。他们拖着人群浩浩荡荡经过时，它一动也没动，只是翻着眼球向上看。

“这动物，狗，快死了。”信光说，然后头也不回地走了过去。有的人蹲下，趴在狗的旁边看它喘气，更多的人跟着信光走了。走到第二条街道时，信光停下，看着房檐下坐着的一个农夫，大喊：

“快跑起来，事故！”

6

两天后，阵亡军人追思会在村公所举办。人们按翻书查来的旧时习俗，搭起一个巨大的灵棚，以灰毯为地、红白相间为顶，大棚两侧树长竿一十八根、秉烛三十六盏，场地中央摆几十把椅子，大家有的坐在椅子上，有的干脆席地而坐。为死者大发哀恸的时间已经过去了，几个女人在小声地哭，其他人都在谈话，亲属们近乎麻木，邻里也已习惯年轻人的死亡，他们一个接一个消失，就像是离家去上学、去工厂工作、去远赴黄金时代殖民的边疆，他们谈论这些就像在谈论一场宴会，有人中途离席，但不妨碍宴会的继续。老太太领着信光进来的时候，人已经把棚子坐满了。他俩走向侧面仅剩的几个空位，村民们转头望着他们，一下子安静下来。这寂静仅仅持续了片刻，一个小孩突然喊道："怪物！妈妈，害怕！"旁边的母亲赶紧抱住了他，但孩子看起来并不怎么惧怕，他把头发埋在大人的怀抱里，偷眼向外看，瞳孔中倒映出还魂尸雪白的皮肤。

"这怪物怎么来了？"有人问。

"主任，把它赶走！"一个村民叫道。

"不是怪物，是我儿子！"老太太说，但似乎没有人听到。看不见的手捂住了所有人的耳朵。

"她有什么资格来？"有人大声喊。

"她儿子也是士兵，"公所主任说，"来就来吧。"

"他好胳膊好腿的，可我儿子呢？我儿子在哪里？"一个女人哭喊道。

"整个连队都完蛋啦，他却回来吃香喝辣，恬不知耻的胆小鬼！"

"他也经历了战争，不要难为他了。"主任说。

"这种怪物，应该回到前线，冲上去！为小伙子们报仇！"

"我不管！你们把我丈夫还回来！"一个年轻的寡妇大哭着冲向信光，却被会计拼命拦住了。

"冷静点儿！"会计说，"他不是人，是还魂尸，你懂吗？别跟他计较，他只是个还魂尸啊！"

"但他复活了！凭什么！凭什么我丈夫就不能复活！"

"我儿子是人。"老太太提高音量说，她用手紧紧揽住儿子的胳膊，"他跟你们一样吃饭，一样睡觉。"

"不一样！"一个孩子突然站起来，"我看过他拉屎，他的屎是深绿色，像果冻一样又黏又恶心。"

"你什么时候看到的？"老太太问。

"昨天，我趴在厕所看到的！辛也可以作证。"

"那你们就是偷窥者，是鬼鬼祟祟的小偷。"

"还魂尸才是小偷，"一个回来奔丧的年轻人站起来，"

他偷走了村子的平静，让大家分裂、嫉妒，让失去亲人的人伤心疯狂，他不应该在这里，这里哪有他的位置！"

"我们还看见他偷吃鸡！他躲在厕所里，生吃了抓来的一只母鸡！"那个叫辛的小孩说。

"没有。"信光辩解道。

"还有，他来之后，村里的狗就不见了。"有人说。

"他拔了大伙儿祖坟的树，还顶翻了车子。"

"他前天诅咒了我丈夫！"一个女人歇斯底里起来，"他叫他小心出事故，结果他立马就被塌下的一块房顶砸伤了！"

"复活的魔鬼！叫他躲在家里，永远不要滚出屋子吧！"

听着这些，信光感觉周身的热量慢慢向眼睛积聚，他紧紧闭上着了火的眼睛，第一次体会到愤怒。如果可以剖开肚肠、掀开头颅检测，这种召之即来的情感足以证明他不是生化人、不是机器人、不是虚拟人，甚至不是阵亡将士的纪念品，而是个有情绪的、真正的人类。他想开口辩解，但审判席没有给他辩解的机会，自古以来，他们占着人数和道义的优势，从来不给别人机会。老太太紧拥着儿子，在嘈杂声中，还魂尸牢牢地抓住眼前的一柄长竿，愤怒地举过头顶。但他突然看到了未来，这个棚子的未来、这些人的命运。他看到自己将长杆插进女人的胸口，血就像山后的汩汩涌泉，她的血混合在十几个被彻底刺穿的人的血液中，铺满地面，形成暗红色的河流，蜿蜒地流到阵亡士兵的黑白相片前，涂满他们的军装和灰色的脸。棚子撕成了碎片，人们躺了一地，桌椅倾覆，有人像筷子般折断，有人头被砸扁，白色的脑浆流出来，掺杂在粉红色的泥水里。在这之后，他揽着母亲，一起步行回家，天上降下雨来……这多么像战场啊！他想起冰冷的机械把活人踩在轮下，脸皮从骨肉上分离，像大地长出的一张面具。这是永恒噩梦中挥之不去的残酷画面。他退缩了，默默地放下手中的长竿。眼前的景象如烟般散去。

母亲紧紧把住他的胳膊，指甲深深地嵌进肉里。她并未察觉到儿子预言的幻景，只是在不住地发抖。

"他要打人啊！"有人喊道，"他还想打人！"

"我们走。"母亲颤抖着说。

于是他揽着母亲的手，走出压抑的棚子，天上果真降下雨来。

7

信光已经好几天没有出门了。公所送来村民起草的《约法六章》后，母亲不再让他出去干活。这几天，他靠看影集度过了漫长的白日，影集是父亲的遗物，是老头在城里旧货市场淘到的，里面放着不知谁家的照片。一百多年前，城市里流行为死人拍生活照，摄影师用架子把尸体固定好，让他们或坐或立，眼睛黏成睁开的样子。他们只拍黑白照片，化妆师技术高超，以至于看客分不清谁是活人、谁是尸体。这应该算是还魂的古老形式——一种简陋的、平面的、复古的还魂。信光费力地辨认活人与死者的区别，但他失败了，他看不到照片中人物的未来，因为就现在而言，那些未来早已是过去。

咚咚，大门响了。信光预见出两个男人的模糊影子。他从凉爽的席子上站起来，回忆了《约法六章》的规定——第一，不准去阵亡军人家庭和追思会；第二，不准去祖坟；第三，不准破坏任何庄稼、植物、树木；第四，不准接近和伤害牲畜；第五，不准用不祥的言语诅咒；第六，天黑之前不准出门。他想了想，开门不违反规矩，他可以开门。

门外站着那个叫"会计"的人，旁边是个坐着机械轮椅、愁眉苦脸的老头儿，有个戴眼镜的姑娘推着他。会计冲信光笑了笑。

"怎么样，小伙子？适应村里的生活吗？"

"还好。"信光说。

"你觉得痛苦吗？"

"不。"信光回答。他感受到的更多是害怕。

"痛苦可以蒙蔽人，就像村子里那些人。"坐轮椅的老头开口说，"原谅他们吧，他们被痛苦和嫉妒捂住了眼睛。看到，却不能分辨；听到，却不敢相信；言语，却出口伤人。"

信光摇摇头。这时，老太太从后院钻出来，手里握着两根白色带须的萝卜。

"这是真正在土里长的萝卜吧，大娘？"会计说。

"当然！"老太太回答。

"很好，母子俩能一饱口福！"

"你们来做什么？"

"啊，这位是市里的技术专家，"会计指指坐轮椅的人，"前几天，腿不幸受伤啦！但他还有话要说，坚持来访。"

"您好！"老头儿抿着嘴唇笑笑，"我早该来的，遇上倒霉的车祸，住了几天院。"

"哦……不打紧吧？"

"没事，"专家说，"公司给治病、生活费、营养费、奖金、补贴，我还能说什么？只能拼命完成考核任务、感激涕零。为完成未竟的使命，我今天必须来，您就当走过场吧！"

老太太点点头。

"我们这次来，是问问生化人的事。"

"生化人？"

"就是你儿子。"会计插嘴说。

"什么儿子？"专家问。

"还魂尸啊，"会计说，"她儿子。"

"她儿子？你竟说生化人是她儿子？你最好清醒点儿，那只是团硅胶冻肉，把意识注入肉里，他从头到脚跟你一毛钱关系没有，他可不是人类。"老头说，"你们上次跟她说了什么？喷农药的小子说了什么？"

"没有，没有，就按指导手册讲的。他是个生化人，还魂尸！"

"嗯，别看他这样，屋子不敢出、什么都不懂、话都说不成句，未来可要仰仗他们！"老头说，拍着轮椅扶手，"他们不是人，强于人！你们要接受未来，就要先改变观念。"

姑娘俯下身，用手摸摸老头的脖颈，"你讲得太多啦。别忘了，我们是在偏远的村子里。"

"不用拍我，我可是有武器的人。"老头咧嘴笑笑，"你看过老电影吗？残疾人把枪藏在轮椅里，掏出来打天花板上的怪兽。看过吗？会计先生。"

会计脸上渗出汗珠来，从口袋掏出块皱巴巴的手绢擦擦脸。"没关系，您可以完全放心，村里没有危险！百分百放心！"

"让我问他几个问题。"

"好，快过来！信……你这还魂尸？别躲在门板后边。"会计喊道。

"白天不让我出家门。"信光说。

"别这么死板！"

"公所定了六条规矩。"老太太央求道，"不要为难他了。"

"只是因为这个吗？"老头说，"生化人，你过来，说实话。为什么不看我？"

"没有。"信光说。

"说实话！"

"……你会掏枪打我。"信光低声说。

老头笑笑，果然从背后摸出一把装有消音设备的小手枪。会计尖叫一声跳开。信光站在门边，面露犹豫。

"你为什么不躲开？"

信光眨眨眼，"场景变了，你不会真的开枪。"

老头看起来很高兴，他费力地扭过脖子，对姑娘说："这个意识可以！成功了一半。我就说了，必须在生活中测试。"

"但他好像只能看到几秒钟？"

"别管时间长短，这就是一个巨大的进步！"

老头说完，把头转回来。"还魂尸！合同快到期了，好好和老太太享受最后的日子，我们下周一，就是后天，要把你带走了。你将回到属于你的地方。"

信光抬起头。"我哪儿也不去。"他说。

"别傻了。"老头说，"你以为你真的是儿子，她真的是母亲？没有我们的保养维护，你什么都不是。你现在只是个给人安慰的替代品，替一名工兵把生命延长了十几天，这就是你的价值。"

"只能再待这么两天吗？"老太太问。

"这已是极限啦。"姑娘接过话来，"为了这个实验、为了让你们延长这十几天，你知道我们正在损失多少钱吗？"

"那，你们会让他回到战场上去？"老太太颤抖着问。

"我本不想骗你，"老头把手上的枪支收回去，"你以为，他生来是为了做什么的？"

8

午后，村子里稀稀落落地下起冰雹来，大棚突然被砸坏了，人们冒雨解散了阵亡将士追思会。邮递员为信光家送来召回通知书，是军队里一个从未听过的番号。

吃完晚饭，他们谁也没开灯。在黑暗中，老太太和信光坐在一起，儿子像往常一样很少说话，盘腿望向北方。老太太不知那边有什么，她能看到的只有黑暗。她想，要是能找到个有趣的话题就好了，但就像所有的妈妈和儿子一样，很难找到共同的兴趣点。她轻轻摸着信光的手背，脉管在跳动，她发现自己越珍惜这个晚上，时间就过得越快。

"信光，你记得第一次坐旅行飞艇吗？"老太太问。

"不记得了。"

"你八岁的时候，把农药倒在培育牲口的池子里？"

"不记得。"信光答道。

"你十岁那年，从学校偷了一个报废的机器人，他本来是给跑道刷漆用的。"

信光摇摇头。

"你把机器人搬回家，在屋里放着。夜里，它自己动起来，在地上画了一个卖假钞的广告。"

"嗯。"信光吭了一声。他为自己的一无所知而感到羞愧，这也是他第一次体验到愧疚的感觉。母亲讲述的事情大概已随破损的芯片付之东流，又或者技术员太懒，没把这些无关紧要的东西塞进他的脑袋。

老太太叹了几口气，没再为难他，只是拍了拍他的胳膊。信光想，自己的皮肤摸起来一定很凉，人类的皮肤是温暖的，而他却一直很冰凉。他闭上眼睛，学习人类的睡眠，这是他最早学会的东西，很简单——什么都不想，蜷缩在床上，像真正的人类蜷缩在充满温水的子宫里。他很快便睡着了，没有做梦。

清早，老太太做了六个菜，还打开了一瓶老头留下的浊酒。信光知道这是送行酒，他即将回到地狱中去。他踌躇着在小桌旁坐下，端起碗扒饭，眼前再次浮现出往日的景象，过去生活中的记忆全部消失了，战场的记忆却无比清晰地存在于脑海里。战车、炸弹、血雾、警报……还有那些已经永远消失的人。他们一个接一个出现，排队捧起桌上的酒杯向他致敬。信光看到了自己第一次从运输机下到兵营，第一次训练，第一次排雷，第一次踏上真正的战场，第一次从工兵变成侦察员，第一次扣动坚硬的扳机，子弹射入人体的感觉，密密交织的钢铁和射线，锈迹和血水……

他咕哝着嗓子，咽下最后一口饭，然后推开碗，拼命眨巴着眼睛，想看看自己明天会干什么，是回到实验室吗？还是直接上战场？他十分努力地去体验，但他却看不到，什么都看不到。他只看到母亲从后厨拿来了剪刀。

"先理个发吧。"老太太说。

信光坐到廊下，进入清晨肃穆的寂静里。这是他第一次被人修剪头发——至少是这具躯体的第一次。母亲理发的手艺很好，把他的头皮刮得干干净净。

"信光，你头顶有个大漩涡哦。"母亲说。

"是吗？"

"是啊。我问你，你小的时候，哭着要一架玩具战斗机，我一直没买，你会恨我吗？"

信光想了想，他不记得这件事，他什么都不记得。也许他根本不是什么信光，真的只是一具化学生产的还魂尸而已。

"不会。"他说。

"好了，躺下。躺在垫子上，对。"

信光顺从地躺好，老太太指挥他侧卧过去，摸了摸他，转身离开。

信光迷茫地躺在那里，听着老太太的脚步，愈来愈远、愈来愈远，又愈来愈近、愈来愈近，鼻子突然闻到了一股味道。他的头脑猛地张开，像撑开了一把接受讯号的雨伞。他用意识而不是眼睛，看见母亲正端着一盆深褐色的液体走来——那是醋的味道，他想起了溶解的感觉。他似乎不是第一次被溶解，上一次害怕得几乎不能动弹，模糊的人影把他从身体里拽出去，把另一个人安插进来。是信光进来了吗？离开的又是谁？雨伞的信号突然前所未见地强烈起来，他看到技术专家带了一队士兵过来，他夺门而出，杀得血流成河，敌人的痛苦呻吟几乎掩盖住老太太哭泣的声音。他将顺利跑出去，跑出村子，进入森林、河流、大漠，在大漠陷入流沙和永恒的孤独中去。当他最终走出来的时候，只有半截身子，他爬到废弃的中转站，爬到一百年前第一批殖民卫星离开地球的地方。他被治疗，被教化，成为半机器的野人，成为黑暗中畏畏缩缩的生物崇拜古神的载体。他们在崇拜人类，人类的形体和他一样，只是向来长了眼睛，却什么都看不到，拥有头脑，却什么都不去想，他看到面对愚昧，神们自己也缄口不言。

……他看见这一切，用脑子而不是眼睛。而眼睛看到的是母亲用颤动的手端着一大碗黑醋走过来。此刻他意念全开，身体灵活，完全可以一跃而出，逃离这间房子，冲破外面迫近的专家和士兵，获得同类不可企及的自由。但他却分毫都没有动弹，他继续躺着，等待母亲端着烧热的醋碗走到眼前。

"我绝不会再把你交到他们手里。"母亲说，眼泪不住地淌下来。

信光点点头，用万分之一秒时间思考自己的选择，然后慢慢关上他头脑里前无古人的意识之伞，闭上眼睛，等待接受母亲的热醋和爱意。战场的画面一下子变淡了，村子里的人们也不再成为困扰，他看到自己坐在庭院的屋檐下，在风中饮食，一只蝴蝶落在肩膀上——此刻，醋汁从高处颤抖着浇下来，有一些洒到了外面。当这些滚烫的液体灌入耳朵的时候，信光没有痛感，只感觉到暖和，世界在收缩，意识在慢慢固定中消散。他耳中听到的最后一个音符是海边的浪涛声，那年他只有七岁，乘坐旅行飞艇，第一次俯瞰大洋，海鸥在短小的舷翼侧面掠过，它们的翅膀反射着永不停止的太阳的光。

# RESURRECTION

by Channing Ren

Translated by Blake Stone-Banks

Channing currently works in the legal industry. His first novel *The Vanishing Circus* was published in *Science Fiction World* in 2020, since then, he has been writing science fiction. Awards: Best Short Story of the Galaxy Award 2021.

1

When the resurrected corpse arrived, there was only the vague contour of a face, but the woman already recognized it as her son's.

She gazed at the corpse, silently examining facial features, and smoothed the hair into its familiar shape. His skin was extremely moist, nothing like that of a dead person. It was closer to the skin of a newborn baby. Textures and patterns gradually appeared and fixed onto the skin's surface, like sea currents carving fjords. The pits of his eyes grew deeper, his nose gradually rose, and a shiny scar emerged on his left face marking where he had once fallen on a cotton gin as a young child. The scar changed from pink to red then brown as it shrunk then fixed onto the surface of the skin. The shape was like that of her son's before he'd left home.

Gripped by fear and wonder, the old woman sank deeper into her wicker chair. She could not move. Her breathing sounded like specks of fine dust falling upon the corner of the courtyard.

Ten minutes later, the postman delivered the notification of death. The village accountant, arriving at the same time, scolded the postman for allowing the notification of death to be delivered after the corpse. The old woman finally stood up with her arm on the wicker chair. Her hands were shaking. She could not read the words on the paper. So, the accountant kindly read them to her:

This letter is to certify that Wang Xinguang, an engineer, died on the twenty-eighth of the Spring Moon. Having bravely perished in battle, his name will be sung and celebrated.

The old woman looked at the paper. Her throat made a purring sound like a cat. She turned to look at the monstrosity. The resurrected corpse clenched its eyes, the body trembling with each rise and fall of the chest. The colour of its skin deepened. Its hair grew thicker. Its blood vessels became thinner, fading invisibly into the skin. Forcing himself not to stare at the monstrosity, the accountant took a form from his wallet and began to calculate with the old woman watching.

"Death compensation is calculated at 260,000 credits. It will be deposited in an account tomorrow and made available to you when you provide kinship and death certificates."

The old woman nodded absently. The corpse burst out with a loud belch.

"Did he...have other beneficiaries?"

The old woman shook her head. The corners of her mouth drooped. Tears welled in her eyes.

"Hey there, Ma'am!" the postman comforted her. "Don't be sad. Look, you're not the only one. I have a pile of death notices here!"

The postman reached into his bag and took out a thick stack of mail, all printed in the same colour. The sides of the envelopes formed a long brown dragon. Seeing these the old woman slapped her hands against her legs and wailed.

"And none of these are for resurrected corpses!" the postman said. "Look, you are the only one who has a resurrected corpse because your son got blown to pieces, leaving only a chip. Think of it as a silver lining ..."

"Shut up!" the accountant interrupted. "Go and deliver your mail!"

"But I'd like to—"

"Does she look like she's here to entertain your curiosity?" The accountant kicked him.

The postman stepped back, his face filled with fear. "Now, corpse," he yelled. "Open your eyes!"

2

The resurrected corpse had completely taken on her son's appearance. Lids opened to reveal wandering eyes beneath. Perfectly motionless, they held their breath. The old woman stopped crying and stepped forward.

"Careful, Ma'am!" the accountant exclaimed as he grabbed her.

The corpse stood but couldn't find its balance and fell back into its seat. Seeing the corpse's efforts, the accountant and postman screamed and backed away. It turned to look at them, opened its mouth, saying nothing, dark eyes staring into the void.

"I must leave now," the postman said. "Madam, you have my sincere sympathies." He turned and ran from the room.

"Coward!" the accountant yelled and moved to chase after the postman. Then, realizing his limbs were numb with fear, he instead began to massage his legs.

The postman returned excitedly. "Here comes the technician!"

"Finally, he's here." The accountant let out a sigh of relief.

A short young man followed the postman in. He had a tuft of bleached hair on the top of his head and a large spray gun in his hand. A tattered spiderweb clung to his uniform, which was stained with white spots.

"What are you doing here?" the accountant asked. "Where is the expert technician from the city?"

"The expert from the city? He had an accident, drove his car into a ditch and broke his leg." The young technician paused. "Management said I'm the only one available to come here and explain."

"What can you explain exactly? Do you even understand what this is?"

"They sent me a bunch of information. But to tell you the truth, I don't get it. If you ask me about fertilizers and pesticides, I can ..."

"That's all right," the accountant interrupted. "Tell me what you know about this resurrected corpse because it's freaking us out."

"Alright, I'll tell you what I know." The young man pulled a chair toward him but didn't dare sit. "The corpse is a kind of synthetic form that has just been developed for the transfer of consciousness of the dead. People call it the resurrected corpse."

"An appropriate name," the accountant said. "But what's the use of this monstrosity exactly?"

"For now, it's just here to provide comfort," said the technician. "But perhaps in the future when the technology is mature, those who can afford it could multiply themselves and even live forever inside these synthetics."

"But what if the original human and the synthetic get into a fight?"

"That's ... not our concern."

"So, is he alive?" The postman pointed toward the stiff monstrosity, now crawling on all fours.

"Yup. The body has just been formed, but its consciousness is still being constructed." The technician turned to the old woman. "Madam, I was told to inform you, when Wang Xinguang died, the chip implanted in his head was damaged, so the data they could recover is limited. The personality of the synthetic is therefore incomplete. They did their best."

The old woman clenched her jaw and nodded.

"Management told me that resurrected corpses are still in the testing stage, and priority is being given to families of fallen soldiers. The number available is quite limited. Because your son ... well, he had no bones left ... so they selected you to send one to, hoping to bring you temporary comfort."

"Temporary comfort?" the accountant asked.

The technician shrugged. "In two weeks, they'll take the synthetic back and extract the data for further research and optimization."

"And after their study is complete, will you return the synthetic to her?"

"No idea. I was told this thing is quite expensive, but ..." The technician patted the back of the chair as if it were supposed to tell him what to say. "Anyway, enjoy these extra two weeks with your son. Not everyone has this opportunity. If others wanted it, they'd have to bargain with a devil."

"Is he my son?" the old woman asked.

"He is a synthetic being. With the help of advanced technology, they are now able to transplant your son's residual consciousness and memory into the brain of this synthetic being. He is equivalent to your son, but his memory is not complete, and it may seem a bit strange..."

"I don't understand. He looks exactly like my son. So, I'm asking you: is he my son?" The old woman persisted in her question.

"Madam, by definition, he is—"

"Good heavens!" The postman flung out his hands in exasperation. "You talk a lot yet don't tell her anything she can understand. Tell it to her straight. I still have a stack of notices to deliver."

"Fine," the technician said. "Yes! This really is...your son!"

The old woman pursed her mouth and nodded. Her eyes moved.

Suddenly a growl sounded from the corner, and everyone turned to see the synthetic struggling to stand. He stared back at them, then slowly said, "I'm hungry."

The four of them looked at each other. No one dared to speak or move. They heard only the wind blowing through the leaves. The technician moved his hand from the chair. The sweat on his skin felt cold in the breeze.

"Ask him what he wants to eat," the accountant said with his hand on his waist, as though he were about to pull an invisible gun.

"What are you hungry for?" the old woman asked.

"Stir fried pork with garlic shoots," said the synthetic.

"He really is my son!" The old woman burst into tears.

3

The best way to make stir fried pork with garlic shoots is to cut thin slices of lean pork and bacon then marinate the meat slices in soy sauce. The garlic shoots should be well salted. Stir fry the bacon then the lean meat, finally adding the garlic sprouts with shredded chili. Flavour with a little sesame oil, salt and more soy sauce until the taste is just right.

The synthetic sat at the table and ate three bowls in a row, his pale back shrugging with each bite. After dinner, he curled up in a chair, hugging his knees, saying nothing.

"Xinguang ... are you cold?" the old woman asked.

"Cold," he answered.

The old woman rummaged through closets and boxes to find her son's clothes. The synthetic tried clumsily to dress, struggling to understand how to put on his trousers. The old woman helped him dress and fixed his belt.

"Xinguang, you've lost weight," she said.

The synthetic nodded and stared at her in silence.

"You've suffered so much!" she continued, grabbing his cold hands then instinctively bringing them to her chest for warmth. "Just come back, that's all I need."

He nodded again waiting patiently for the old woman to finish her crying, then slowly pulled back his hands and sat cross-legged on the chair facing north. His eyes closed.

The old woman stood by his side for some time, then asked, "How was the war?"

"How was what?"

"What went wrong on the battlefield? Are we going to win? Mainly I want to know how ... how were you hurt?"

"I forgot." Her son opened his eyes. "So much has been forgotten." With that, he closed his eyes again, and his belly belched just as it had in the morning.

"Take a rest," she said and retreated to the outer room.

That night, Wang Xinguang slept at home, but did not sleep soundly. He woke several times throughout the night. Eventually he couldn't get back to sleep. He lay quietly on the bed and watched the old clock hanging on the wall. It read 6:15. His consciousness was gradually growing clearer. This was the first time he remembered the concept of time. Time passed in seconds. It was a revelation. Yesterday was the day of his birth, but he knew somehow that he was not a new person, knew that in the time before his birth there was something, something beyond the chaotic void. He watched the secondhand ticking. There were twenty-four hours in a day. There were 3,600 seconds in an hour. If he wanted, he could divide each second into further units, but he did not do so. He was now a human being. He was learning about Wang Xinguang, learning the instincts of the brain, learning how to perceive time like all human beings: in hours, minutes, seconds. After 6:17, the next packet of time would be 6:18. He thought the sunshine outside the window was good. He thought of the crumbs on the windowsill, where birds would come to feed.

Just as he thought this, a bird landed on the red brick windowsill.

News that the old woman had a dead body living with her spread quickly. By afternoon, the house was besieged. Neighbours rushed to inquire about lost relatives. Widows and orphans clamoured around the Wang house.

"How did my son die? Did he say anything? Any last words?"

"How is my husband? Did you see him while you were in the army?"

"What was the battlefield like? Can we win this?"

In the face of all these questions, the synthetic son always gave the same tactless answers: I don't know ... It's not clear ... Sorry, but I've really forgotten ...

Later, Mrs Wang fell asleep in the kitchen and woke after dark. She went into the courtyard to find the neighbours had finally left, leaving behind a mess of garbage. Only a dog remained to bark at the corpse. The wind was picking up. The old woman took out her stick to drive the dog away. It didn't go far, instead lying down next to a pile of bamboo poles near the gate. She noticed then her newly born son still sitting at the table with his back straight.

"Go to sleep, Xinguang," the old woman said.

The son pointed to the yellow dog by the gate.

"That animal. What's it called?"

"Dog," the old woman said.

"Dog," he repeated and nodded his head in satisfaction.

"Go to sleep."

"Okay," the son said. "Soon, when I recover, I'll learn to help you."

"Okay, my good son," the old woman said. "Which room are you going to sleep in? Do you want to sleep in my room?"

"Let's talk about it later. First, I want to go back to the kitchen."

"What's in the kitchen?"

"The stacked steamers are about to fall."

Before he could finish his sentence, there was a screeching sound from the kitchen. It was the sound of the steamers overturning. The round steal rack rolled through the kitchen door to the edge of the grass in the courtyard, where it came to a stop.

4

After tidying up the cookware and courtyard, the mother and son went to bed. It was the second night since his resurrection, and Wang Xinguang had a dream in which he saw a white horse walking on thick ice. Under the ice was an abyss of inextinguishable flames. "Horse." He remembered the word. The ice was too slippery for the horse to run. Its front hooves slipped and it crashed to its knees on the hard ice. Blood gushed and spilled under the soldiers' heels. He looked down at his boots. The soles had peeled off, the ground hurt his feet. Incendiary bombs in the sky above exploded brighter than any sun. Amidst the landscape's detritus were ancient stone axes, wagons, and war horses from thousands of years ago. There were also giant cannons from more recent history, perhaps a hundred years old. Twin moons glimmered in the darkness above this ancient battlefield. He lost consciousness then in the frozen river, forgot who he was. All he could do was follow cloud-like instructions and slowly charge toward the end. In the freezing night, everything under the moonlight played out in slow motion. The artillery fire of the opposing army became the javelin of his consciousness. Mines were triggered at every intersection in the lattice of time and space. Bombs exploded. Shrapnel flew through the air. The night scene wrapped in the trails of bullets and projectiles slowly faded.

Xinguang struggled in the fading mist as he pieced together the incomplete memory of his dreams. First, he saw his uncle, a year younger than himself though actually a generation older: the fighter pilot ace, Wang Xinhu. He had crossed the canyon and flown over the sacred mountain alone. On the battlefield, he smashed through three enemy soldiers, flesh and blood spraying across his body like spring rain. He dreamed of Master An, the disabled battalion chef missing a leg. When the engineer battalion was short of manpower, they sent in the chef relying entirely on his cooking tools, his iron feet never touching the ground. He didn't know that mines felt different from the good earth, nor that a mine once stepped on could send shrapnel flying into his body. He knew nothing of death, only cooking. But death knew him. Death knew everything.

Then there was the dream of the squad leader, Captain Mirror, who was given this title because of his superstition. He always hung a mirror around his waist, fastened to a hole in his belt. He always made a cup of hot sugar water to stand in for coffee in the afternoon. Xinguang had dragged his body from a scarlet basin of burning machinery. There was no mirror on his waist. Xinguang thought, the mirror must have fallen into the tank. He dreamed of the female soldier Dana Kapparova, Dana with luminescent chestnut hair ...

Now, these people were all gone, swallowed by the war, transformed into the dust coating the ruins. From the void they had come, to the void they returned.

When the white horse again neighed, Xinguang shot up in bed whimpering as the dream faded. His mother lit the lamp. His pupils shrank. His head ached. "Mom!" he called sharply. The old woman hadn't heard that voice in years. It sounded sublime.

"Don't be afraid. It's morning," she said, "Xinguang, my Xinguang."


5

During the day, Xinguang was learning quickly. By Saturday afternoon of the first weekend, he had already learned to use the walk-behind tractor to work the farm. Sometimes faced with soft soil, he hesitated before walking over it. That evening, the technician returned to the village, his head covered with pollen, and there seemed to be more cobwebs on his uniform as well.

"Ma'am, how are you getting along with him?" the technician asked.

"My son is like a child again," said Mrs Wang, smiling. "He can eat several bowls of noodles in one sitting."

The technician laughed. "I have something else to tell you. Don't let water get into his ears. An ordinary amount of water, such as for a bath, should be fine though. Oh, and you must not let acidic substances in either. If you destroy the adaptive chip, he will become a fool."

"Of course," said the old woman. "Normal people can't stand water in their ears, not to mention someone who was so injured in the battlefield."

The technician opened his mouth then hesitated. He laughed again. "I wish you good health."

After the technician left, the mother and son walked along the dirt path down the ridge to the end of the village. The houses grew fewer, and the graves more numerous. When they reached a diamond-shaped swathe of land sandwiched between a dam and woods, the pair stopped.

"This is our ancestral grave. Do you remember?" asked Mrs Wang.

Xinguang shook his head.

His mother sighed, walked a few steps south, pointed to a grave with a grey stone tablet and said, "This is your father's grave, remember?"

Xinguang thought about it for a moment but didn't answer. His mother then said, "When I'm dead and I want to be buried with him, you will need to handle this."

The synthetic nodded and put this matter firmly in his head. He remembered the location and characteristics of the cemetery, the stone tablet of his father, and the carved handwriting. He saw a large plant near the tomb. It was leafless and bore no fruit, but its roots were luxuriant, arching gracefully over the earth.

"How can there be such a plant?" he asked.

"That's a tree," the old woman answered, "a species not from these parts. It didn't live, just raised the ground around it. It should be cut down."

"Leave it to me," said the resurrected corpse. He walked around the tree twice, fumbled, then finally found a position he could get hold of it. He bent low and put his hands around the tree trunk. On the first effort, the trunk moved only slightly; the second time, the tree began to shake; on his third attempt, the tree made a sound of roots breaking. The tree was uprooted and fell backwards onto the ground. Large pieces of soil entwined with large earthworms fell from its roots.

The loud noise of the falling tree drew the attention and stunned stares of people at graves nearby. Xinguang didn't look at them. He collected the soil from the tree roots with his hands, filled it back into the pit, and flattened it with his feet, forming a small basin like pit. Mrs Wang helped him with his clothes, pulled awry by his efforts and stroked a black, sweat-soaked number on his back: "H4004". What was the meaning of the tattoo? She thought it best not to let anyone else see it. Since her husband died, she had felt listless and exhausted, but over the last few days, her confidence and happiness had returned. She now walked with raised head and a renewed confidence she'd last felt on her wedding day in the village.

Many people followed them when they left the graves. Some were taking videos, a remnant of an old habit. After the Internet was banned, video recording had no practical significance. Xinguang followed his mother down the path. Yellow mud fell off her shoe. He couldn't take his eyes off it and found that he liked the colour. Warm evening light faded from the world around them as dusk fell. Then Xinguang began to experience something like clarity; their fate was like a video in time, slowly but unstoppably presented in front of him. Most of the time, the picture was vague, but fleetingly he could make it out.

Up ahead, a dog by the roadside pressed its bone into the mud. When Xinguang and his mother and their crowd of gawkers passed, the dog rolled its eyes and looked up.

"That dog, is dying," Xinguang remarked without stopping or looking back. If he had he would have seen people, some squatting, others laying down beside the dog to watch it take its last gasp. More people began to follow Xinguang. When they reached the second street, Xinguang stopped, looked at a farmer sitting in his open gate, and shouted:

"Run! Accident!"


6

Two days later, a memorial meeting for the dead soldiers was held in the village hall. According to custom, people had built a vast mourning hall, carpeted in grey with a red and white roof. Lining the sides of the hall were eighteen tall candlesticks and thirty-six candles. At the center were dozens of chairs. Some people sat on the chairs, others on the floor. Though the time for mourning the dead had passed, several women were crying quietly. Others were talking. Relatives were numb. The villagers were desensitized to untimely death. The young disappearing one by one as if leaving home to go to school, work in a far-off factory, or settle in the frontier of Golden Age colonies. They would talk about this as if they were talking at a feast. Someone might leave midway, but it did not hinder the continuation of the conversation. The hall was almost full as Mrs Wang entered with the letter and her resurrected son. They walked to a pair of vacant seats on the side. The villagers, silenced by the arrival of their neighbour and her dead son, turned to look at the pair. Silence did not endure. From the stunned throng, a small child shouted, "Monster! Mummya!" Reassured by his mother's embrace, the little boy, peered out from his fringe, the white corpse skin of Mrs Wang's undead son reflecting in his widening pupils.

"Where did this monstrosity come from?" someone asked.

"Get rid of it!" cried another villager.

"This is no monster, it's my son," pleaded Mrs Wang. But no one seemed to listen to her as though invisible hands covered everyone's ears.

"What right does she have?" someone shouted.

"Her son is also a soldier," said a village councilor. "Come on."

"He has good arms and legs ... but where is my son? Where is my son?" a woman cried. "The whole squadron was killed, yet he comes back to feast on delicious food, the shameless coward!"

"He also went through the war. Don't be so hard on him," the village councilor said.

"This monstrosity should be sent back to the front lines and fight! Revenge for the boys!"

"I don't care! You return my husband!" A young widow ran at Xinguang crying but was stopped by the accountant.

"Calm down, everyone!" the accountant said. "He is not a man but a resurrected corpse. Can't you understand? There's no reason to argue. He's just a corpse!"

"But he is resurrected! Why? Shouldn't my husband be resurrected too!"

"My son is a man." Mrs Wang raised her voice, holding her son's arm tightly. "He eats and sleeps just like you."

"He's not the same!" A child suddenly stood up. "I've seen him shit. His shit is dark green, sticky and disgusting like jelly."

"When did you see that?" Mrs Wang asked.

"Yesterday, I saw it lying in the toilet! Xin can also testify."

"Then you are all peepers and sneaky thieves!"

"The resurrected corpse is the thief." A young man who had just come back for a funeral stood up. "He has stolen the peace of the village, made everyone divided and jealous, made the bereaved sad and crazy. He should not be here. There is no place for him here!"

"We also saw him steal a chicken! He hid in the toilet and ate it raw!" the child named Xin said.

"I did none of these things" exclaimed Xinguang, defending himself to no avail.

"After he came, the dogs in the village disappeared."

"He pulled up the trees of our ancestral graves and overturned cars."

"He cursed my husband just the day before yesterday!" exclaimed a woman hysterically. "He told him to be careful of an accident, and he was immediately injured by a collapsing roof!"

"The resurrected devil! Tell him to hide at home and never leave the house!"

The accusations reverberated around the mourning hall.

Hearing the heckles of the crowd, Xinguang felt the heat of his whole body slowly accumulating towards his eyes. He clenched his burning eyes feeling anger for the first time since his resurrection. If the villagers had been able to open their hearts to empathy, they would have noticed the emotional impact of their accusations on Mrs Wang's returned son. His response was human, not that of a robot, or a walking war memorial. He wanted to speak for himself, if the angry villagers would let him.

The old woman hugged her son tightly. In the noise, he firmly grasped a long pole in front of her and raised it over her head angrily. He suddenly saw the future, the future of the hall and the fate of these people. He saw that he thrust the pole into a woman's chest and the blood was like a gurgling spring behind the mountain. Her blood mixed with the blood of a dozen people who had been completely pierced, spread all over the ground, forming a dark red river, meandering through the black and white photos of the dead soldiers, their painted uniforms and grey faces. The hall was smashed to pieces, people lay on the ground, tables and chairs overturned, some people broken like chopsticks, some people's heads smashed flat with white brains flowing out, mixed into pink muddy water. After that, he took his mother and they walked home together. It rained ... how like a battlefield! He remembered that the cold machinery trampled the living under the wheel, and the skin was separated from the flesh, like a mask growing out of the earth. This cruel picture lingered in the eternal nightmare. Xinguang flinched and silently put down the pole in his hand. The chaotic scene dissipated like smoke.

His mother held his arm tightly, her nails were deeply embedded in the flesh. She was not aware of the illusion of her son's prophecy, but she was trembling.

"He's going to hit people!" someone shouted. "He still wants to hurt people!"

"Let's go," his mother said as she shivered.

He took his mother's hand and walked out of the hall. Rain was falling hard.

7

Xinguang didn't go out for several days. After the Six Chapter Charter, drafted by the villagers, his mother no longer let him go out to work. He spent long days just looking at an old photo album, a legacy of his father, who had discovered it in the city's junk market. There were photos of unknown families in it. More than a hundred years ago in the cities, it was popular to take photos of dead people. Photographers fixed the bodies so that they sat or stood with their eyes glued open. They only took black and white photos, and the makeup artists were so skilled that visitors could not tell who was alive and who was dead. This could be regarded as an ancient form of 2D resurrection. Xinguang tried hard to identify the difference between the living and dead subjects but failed. He could not see the future of the characters in the photos, because as far as the present is concerned, that future was already the past.

The gate bell rang. Xinguang had foreseen vague shadows of the two men. He stood from the cool mat and recalled the provisions of the Six Chapter Charter. First, he was not allowed to go to families or memorial meetings of soldiers who died in battle. Second, no visiting ancestral tombs. Third, no crops, plants or trees should be damaged. Fourth, he should not approach or harm livestock. Fifth, he should not make any ominous curse. Sixth, he should never venture outside before dark. He thought about it for a moment and decided he could open the door without violating the regulations.

Outside the door stood the man Xinguang knew only as "the accountant". Next to him was an old man in a mechanical wheelchair with a sad face. A girl with glasses was pushing him. The accountant smiled at Xinguang.

"How are you, young man? Have you adapted to life in the village?"

"Not bad," Xinguang said.

"Are you in pain?"

"No," Xinguang answered. What he really felt was more like fear.

"Pain can deceive people, like those in the village," the old man in the wheelchair said. "Forgive them. They were blinded by pain and jealousy. They can see but not understand. They can hear but not believe. And language has a way of hurting people."

Xinguang shook his head. Just then, his mother emerged in the courtyard with a white radish in each hand.

"Are those real radishes grown from the soil, Madam?" the accountant asked.

"Of course!" the old woman answered.

"Very good. You and your son can enjoy a great meal."

"What have you come here to do?"

"Ah, this is the technical expert from the city." The accountant pointed to the man in the wheelchair.

"Hello," the old man said with pursed lips before smiling, "I should have come earlier, but I was in a bad accident and stayed in the hospital for several days."

"Oh ... it doesn't matter, does it?"

"Not at all," the expert technician said. "What else can I say about the company's medical treatment, living expenses, nutrition, bonuses and subsidies? I can only work hard to complete the assessments and feel grateful. In order to complete my unfinished mission, however, I must come today and walk you through a few points!"

The old woman nodded.

"We are here to discuss the synthetic."

"Synthetic?"

"The synthetic?"

"Yes, your son," the accountant interjected.

"What son?" the expert asked.

"The resurrected corpse," said the accountant, "is her son."

"Her son? You're saying the synthetic is her son? I hope you're sober. It's a lump of silica gel and frozen meat. They put the consciousness into the meat. He has nothing in him that's human from head to foot. He is not a human. What did you say to her last time? What did that pesticide spraying boy say?"

"No, no, we just followed the instructions in the manual. He is a synthetic, a resurrected corpse!"

"Well, don't look at him like that. He doesn't dare to go out of the room, doesn't understand anything and can't speak a word. In the future, everything will depend on them!" The old man slapped the armrests of his wheelchair. "They are not people. They are stronger than people! If you want to accept the future, you must first change your perspective."

The girl bent down and touched the old man's neck with her hand. "You talk too much. Don't forget, we are in a remote village."

"Don't patronize me. I'm a man with weapons." The old man grinned. "Have you seen the old movie? The disabled hid their guns in wheelchairs and then fired at the monsters on the ceiling. Have you seen it, Mr. Accountant?"

Sweat streamed down the accountant's face, and he took out a crumpled handkerchief from his pocket to wipe his face. "Never mind, you can rest assured that there is no danger in the village. We are one hundred percent safe."

"Let me ask him a few questions."

"Sure. Xinguang ... you are a dead body? Don't hide behind the door," cried the accountant.

"I'm not allowed out during the day," Xinguang said.

"Don't be so by the book!"

"The village council has set six rules," the old woman said. "Don't confuse him."

"It's because of that?" The old expert shook his head. "Synthetic, come here and tell the truth. Why won't you look at me?"

"No," Xinguang said.

"Tell the truth!"

"You'll shoot me," Xinguang muttered.

The old man smiled and, sure enough, he pulled out a small pistol with a silencer. The accountant jumped with a scream. Xinguang stood by the door, hesitating.

"Well, why don't you run away?"

Xinguang blinked. "The scene has changed, and now you won't really shoot."

The old man looked very happy. He twisted his neck with some discomfort then said to the girl. "This consciousness is OK. It's half done. I always said it must be tested in life."

"But he can only see for a few seconds?"

"Regardless of duration, it's still great progress."

The old man turned his head back. "Resurrected corpse! The contract is about to expire. Enjoy your last day with the old woman. We will take you away on Monday, the day after tomorrow. You will return to where you come from."

Xinguang raised his head. "I'm not going anywhere."

"Don't be silly," the old man said. "Do you think you're really her son, and she's really your mother? You are nothing without our maintenance. You are just a substitute for comfort. An engineer extended your life for ten days. That's your value."

"Can he only stay for two more days?" the old woman asked.

"That is the limit," the girl answered. "Do you know how much money we are already sinking into this experiment to extend to ten days?"

"Then will you return him to the battlefield?" the old woman trembled.

"I'm not here to lie to you." The old man holstered his gun. "What do you think he was born for?"


8

The next afternoon, hail fell in sparse fits over the village, and the hall was destroyed. People broke up the memorial service for the fallen soldiers as rain fell. The postman sent a recall notice for Xinguang's corpse, which was a first for the army.

After supper, no one turned on their lights. In the dark, Mrs Wang and Xinguang sat together. The son, as usual, spoke very little and looked across his legs toward the north. Mrs Wang didn't know what was there. All she could see was darkness. She thought it would be great if she could find an interesting topic, but like many mothers and sons, it was difficult to find common interests. She gently touched the back of Xinguang's hand and felt the pulse in his skin. She found that the more she cherished this evening, the faster time passed.

"Xinguang, do you remember the first time you took an airship?" the old woman asked.

"I don't remember."

"How about that time when you were eight and poured pesticide into the water for raising livestock?"

"I don't remember," Xinguang replied.

"What about when you were ten and stole an abandoned robot from the school, which was originally used to paint the runway?"

Xinguang shook his head.

"You brought the robot home and put it in the house. At night, it moved by itself and projected advertising for selling counterfeit money on the ground."

"Hmm." Xinguang was ashamed of his ignorance. It was the first time he had experienced the feeling of guilt. The things his mother spoke of must have been lost in the broken chip, or perhaps the technician had been too lazy to put these unimportant things in his head.

The old woman sighed. She didn't embarrass him anymore, so she patted him on the arm. Xinguang thought his skin must feel cold to her touch. Human skin was warm, but he had always been cold. He closed his eyes. Human sleep had been the first thing he had learned. It was all so simple. When he didn't want to do anything, he curled up in bed like a real human curled up in a womb full of warm water. He could then fall into sleep without dreaming.

Early in the morning, the old woman cooked six dishes and opened a bottle of liquor left by her husband. Xinguang knew that this was the farewell wine, and he would be returning to hell. He hesitated before sitting down at the small table and taking up a bowl of rice. Scenes of the past reappeared before his eyes crystal clear. Chariots, bombs, blood, fog, alarms ... those who had disappeared forever. One by one, they appeared and stood in line to raise their glasses on the table and salute him. Xinguang saw how he had come down from the transport plane to the barracks that first time, trained for the first time, extracted mines for the first time, stepped onto the real battlefield for the first time, switched from engineer to scout for the first time, pulled the heavy trigger for the first time, saw a bullet tear into a human body for the first time, the dense mixture of steel, rust and blood.

Xinguang grunted and swallowed the last mouthful of rice. He pushed the bowl away, blinked desperately, imagining what tomorrow would bring. Would he go back to the laboratory? Or go straight to the battlefield? He tried hard to imagine it but couldn't see anything. He only saw his mother bringing in scissors from the kitchen.

"Let's get a haircut first," the old woman said.

Xinguang sat down on the porch and entered the solemn silence of the morning. It was his first hair cut—at least in this body. His mother, it turned out, was a good barber and shaved his scalp clean.

"Xinguang, there is a vast whirlpool above your head," said his mother. "Really. I want to ask you: when you were young, you cried for a toy fighting machine, which I never bought, did you hate me for it?"

Xinguang thought for a moment, but he didn't remember this. He didn't remember anything. Maybe he was not Xinguang but a synthetic corpse after all.

"No," he said.

"All right, lie down. Lie on the mat. Yes, that's right."

Xinguang lay down obediently. The old woman directed him to lie on his side, touched him, and then turned away.

Xinguang lay there confused, listening to the old woman's footsteps. She went farther away, then came closer. Suddenly, his nose smelled something. His mind suddenly opened, like an umbrella for receiving signals. Using his consciousness instead of his eyes, he saw his mother coming with a basin of dark brown liquid—it smelled of vinegar and he remembered the feeling of dissolution. It seemed that this was not the first time he was to be dissolved. The last time, he was almost unable to move because of fear. A vague figure had dragged him out of his body and inserted him into another person. If that was Xinguang coming in, who'd left? The signal became stronger than ever. He saw the technical expert bringing in a group of soldiers. He rushed out the door and killed them in rivers of blood. The enemy's moans almost drowned out the old woman's crying.

He ran away without hindrance, ran out of the village, entered the forest, the river and the desert, where he fell into quicksand and the eternal loneliness of the desert. When he finally came out, he had only half a body. He climbed to an abandoned transfer station, from where the first colonial satellites had left the Earth a hundred years ago. He was treated, educated and became a half-machine savage, a saviour for those fearful creatures in the dark to worship like an ancient god. They were worshiping human beings. A human body looked the same as his. Though he has eyes, he cannot see. Though he has a mind, he cannot think. He saw that in the face of ignorance, the gods themselves needed to remain silent.

He had seen all this with his head, not his eyes. What he saw now was his mother coming with a bowl of black vinegar in her trembling hands. At this moment, his mind fully opened and his body became flexible. He could jump out of the house, break through the experts and soldiers watching him, and gain unparalleled freedom for his kind. But he did not move at all. He continued to lie there, waiting for his mother to come to him with the bowl of hot vinegar.

"I will never hand you over to them again," the mother said as her tears flowed.

Xinguang nodded, thought about his choice in one thousandth of a second, then slowly closed his mind's unprecedented umbrella of consciousness. He closed his eyes and waited to accept his mother's hot vinegar. The scene of the battlefield suddenly faded, and the people in the village were no longer bothered. He saw himself sitting below the eaves of the courtyard in the wind. A butterfly landed on his shoulder. At this moment, the old woman was trembling, causing the vinegar to spill. When the scalding liquid poured into his ear, Xinguang felt no pain, only warmth. The world was contracting, and his consciousness was ebbing away. The last sound he heard was the crash of breaking waves. He was seven years old, taking an airship and looking down at the ocean for the first time. Seagulls skimmed the waves, their wings reflecting the light of a ceaseless sun.

# 图灵大排档

## 王诺诺

互联网公司产品经理，剑桥大学环境经济硕士。曾获第二十九届中国科幻银河奖最佳新人奖，《科幻世界》杂志专栏作者，处女作《改良人类》发表于《科幻世界》，已出版代表作《地球无应答》《故乡明》。多部作品被翻译为英语、日语，出版海外。获奖：2018年第二十九届银河奖最佳新人奖

（上）

杨生坐了一天的船，又转大半天的车，到达三灶码头时已疲惫不堪。

三灶码头是个海边的村落，不超过三十户人家。居民应该都是些渔民，这时阳光正猛烈，有的人出门晒网笼，有的人在门槛下把鱼肉打成鱼浆，包鱼丸子。

杨生想问路，却发现语言不太通，几乎没有办法交流。一个老者正在路边检修捕鱼机器人，看了一眼陌生人带着的大皮箱，便冲他招招手，再往东边一指，"喂，喏，喏！"

杨生会意，连忙感谢，拖着皮箱朝东走去。

村子最东边是家小餐馆。

下午三点，店没开，门前的把手油腻腻地裹着一层包浆。杨生抬头，发现招牌因为海边的风蚀作用，已经剥落许多，但依稀可分辨五个字——"图灵大排档"。

"……看来是这儿了。"

他登上台阶，敲敲门。

开门的是个三十岁左右的女人，风情万种。她扶着门框一手叉腰，手正好掐在胸之下，胯之上，肥大的围裙被掐出曲线，好身材若隐若现。

"我们六点才营业，你来找人啊？"

"对对，找人，找人！"杨生连忙把注意力从她的身材上拉回。

女人歪头，看了看来者身后的皮箱子，向他摊开一只手，"介绍信呢？"

　　年轻人从外套里掏出封薄信封递上，女人却没有拆开来读，叠好了往低胸口的衣领里一塞。这下子，杨生又盯着她的胸口看呆住了。

　　女人哧的一声笑出来，"青苗！没见过女人啊？"说着，便转身进门，示意杨生跟她往里走。

　　"那个，我从枳城来，路太远没休息刚刚走神。你叫我……青苗？这什么意思？"

　　"青苗！就是你这种毛没长齐，看女人发呆的崽子。我又不知道你名字，只好想到什么叫你什么咯。"

　　"啊抱歉，还没自我介绍。我叫杨生，之前在枳城的英先生家里做事。这两年出来了，想自己也学着做做生意。"

　　"英先生家？"女人挑眉，"是被赶出来的吧？"

　　"当然不是！"杨生连忙跟上女人的脚步，在她身后解释道，"是这样的，我的母亲是英先生的表妹。英先生这人的性格，谁都知道的，不太爱跟陌生人来往，能三丈外解决的事情，绝不愿意让人近他三寸。所以我这个外甥嘛……他是很器重的。"

　　"那你怎么出来了？"

　　两人穿过餐厅的大堂和厨房，到了房子的另一侧，后门通向海滩，这里有几根拴船的木桩，像是个给渔船停靠的小码头。

　　"因为我和他的女儿，我和樱子……我们……"

　　女人笑了，"哦，表哥表妹的故事啊，和《红楼梦》一样。"

　　"英先生说，如果我离开了他还能混出个模样，就嫁女儿给我。临走时他问我想做哪一行买卖，我说想效仿他当年，从偬商开始。然后，英先生便给了我这一封介绍信，让我来这儿。"年轻人似乎不太有信心，声音越说越小。

　　"咦？没想到你还是个情种啊，"女人贴近杨生，"为了爱情，好感动呀。你的小表妹……长得好看吗？"

　　杨生一时间僵住了，说不出话来。

　　不知怎的，这时女人凑上杨生的耳朵，"叫我蜜梨，"近得他几乎能够感受到她的呼吸，"也可以叫我的英文名，Millie，M-I-L-L——"

　　"行了蜜梨，带他上来吧。"

　　一个低沉的男人声音从楼上传来，蜜梨冲着空气翻了个白眼，一副很失望的样子，带着杨生上了二楼。

　　餐厅楼上的房间是老板的卧室，陈设只有简单的床、书架和书桌。老板本人看起来和当地渔民也没太大区别，六十多岁，皮肤被海风吹得发黑发皱，蜜梨将介绍信递给他，扭身走下楼去。

老板见杨生的眼睛依旧追着她，直到关上门，便露出了一个颇有意味的笑，然后点了一根烟，看了一会儿信。

"杨先生，你很年轻嘛，想做偎商？"

"这是来钱最快的法子了。"

"来钱快，出入高档场所，结交达官名流。但风险也大——机器人不是寻常货物，机器人有心。如果机器人的心，不称买家的心意，买卖成不了，本金都要打水漂了。"

"所以我来找您，大师！精通'盘'这项工艺的偎师，世上已经寥寥无几了。经您手盘出的收藏级机器人，件件都如同艺术品，又润又透！"

老板皱起眉头，仿佛听了刺耳的字眼，"别什么狗屁大师了，我就是一餐厅小老板，还要兼做厨子的那种，叫我斗师傅，或者老斗也行。"

"英先生说，当初若没有遇见您，他绝拿不到那么多尖货，更不可能成为枳城第一的偎商。"

"英先生啊……偎师最看重信任，他总是不问因果，任我发挥。'盘'是个技巧，盘的是机器人，更是盘人心，偎师和偎商的心意相通，这事儿才能成。不过，我也好多年没见着他人了，听说，已经不做偎商了？"

"是的，他几年前就再不碰收藏级机器人了，现在开一家日用机器生产厂，虽然都是批量生产的糙货，您肯定看不上眼，销量却极好，他成了枳城最富有的人。"

斗师傅把介绍信收好，眯起眼睛看他，"嘿，这么听来……你的如意算盘打得不错啊，做了偎商，再娶他女儿，日后生意不就全归你啦？"

"怎么，介绍信上连樱子的事都写啦？"杨生有些窘迫。

"手艺人原本也不该掺和这些事儿，我不问了。我就问你，壳儿，可带来了？"

"带来了。"

杨生打开那只随身皮箱，里面是一具拆开、折叠好的机械。他小心翼翼地一片片取出，再把手脚全接上，一会儿工夫，人形初现，是个高挑的半旧女身机器人。

"嗯，成色不错，"斗师傅掐了烟，用指甲掰开它的皮囊，又找来放大镜细看身上的元件细节，"这样精致的壳儿，不多见咯。"

"服务器级别的CPU，全电路都是超细铂粉做的；皮囊纯手工打造，五个江南绣娘用了十个月才绣出毛孔、褶皱和指纹，又费了十个月把发丝一根一根纳到头皮上去。我贷了一笔钱，从一个海外商人手里拍来。他说原来打仗的时候，这壳儿是配着武器的，可能本身是细作一类，后来坏了，武器也丢了，就辗转落到他的手上。"

斗师傅移开放大镜，说道："坏了修好容易，不用两天就能修好，难的是把它盘顺。这种好壳儿，越接近心，遇到的墙就会越厚，我得找很多砂料来喂，慢慢磨它，那层墙才能破。"

"您估计大概要多久？"杨生急切地问。

"八年就润了。"

"八年？樱子……她不熬成老姑娘，也要被她爸逼去嫁人的！能快一些吗？英先生说过，他与您合作时，每个季度都能拿尖货。"

"八年很久吗？杨过和小龙女可是等了十六年啊……看来，你和你表妹之间的情谊也没那么深嘛。"

杨生接过斗师傅递的茶水，为难地喝了一些。见他不说话，斗师傅笑了，"快的方法，也有。那得成双盘了！"

"成双来盘？"

斗师傅不再回话，只是手里用镊子挑开机器人内部复杂的线路，细细察看。杨生看他若有所思，更加急了：

"您放心，钱不是问题。我打听了，一具机器人只要磨开了墙，盘出了光润的心，找到好卖家能售三百万金珠，我留一半就够，另一半孝敬您。"

"哈哈哈，青苗，这样成色的壳经过我手，可远不止三百万。"斗师傅抬起头，露出神秘的微笑，"不过我也不好财……市场上保底能卖出去八百万金珠的，你分我五百。"

"这……"

"剩下的三百万也够你好几回的本金了。你若是嫌少……"他两手合起作了个揖，表示谢客。

"哎，那好吧。听斗师傅的。"

"除此之外，你还得答应我一件事，每月来这里一次，每次给我带四十具用坏了的日用机器。"

"日用机器？那些东西都是批量生产的糙货，您看得上？"

"对，糙货，做什么工种的都可以，扫地机器人、运货机器人，甚至工厂里的机械臂都可以，如果体积太大不好带，可以把它们的内存和硬盘拆下单独拿来。"

"好，这不难。"

"那就说定了。如此一来，给我小半年时间，差不多就能盘得透亮了。"斗师傅大笑，他摩挲着女身机器人呆滞脱色的五官，仿佛已经能看见它们灵动变化，哭泣和喜悦的样子。

"我还有个问题。"杨生问。

"说。"

"为什么你和蜜梨都要叫我青苗？"

"哦……她跟我学的，跟我久了，说话都学得像我！"

入夜后，图灵大排档开门做起了买卖。生意出乎意料地好，虽然杨生怀疑来这里消费的人也是动机不纯——蜜梨穿着合身的旗袍在大堂的几张餐桌间穿梭，时不时用土话与这些打鱼的粗人调笑。

然而餐厅的另一位雇员则不那么讨喜了，她（也许是他？）吊梢眼，留着利索的短发，在收银台后僵硬站着，别人叫她沙里。她从不主动和人说话，有人结账或是小贩送来蔬菜时，会勉强应付两句，其余时间都盯着账簿抄抄算算。这人与餐馆格格不入，她生硬又整洁，餐馆则是活色生香、烟雾缭绕的。

"明儿你走？"夜深了，客人陆续回家，蜜梨抽出空来凑到杨生跟前。

"嗯，今晚车都没了，多谢你们留宿，明天白天回枳城。"

"回枳城，找小表妹啊？"她索性坐到他身旁。杨生顿时感觉生出一阵寒气，回头一看，原来是沙里正盯着自己的后背，不像对客人的关注，而是一种带有胁迫感的监视。

"不不……不是找表妹，回枳城要混混人脉，等到斗师傅把壳盘好了，得找主顾卖出去……"

蜜梨把他面前的杯子倒上啤酒，杨生以为那是给自己的，伸手去接，没想到蜜梨却挑衅着微笑晃晃酒杯，一仰头把酒喝了。

"枳城是大城市，和三灶码头这种小村子可不一样呢，蜜梨就从来没有离开过三灶码头，好想去大城市看看。"

"你是这儿的人？从没离开过这个村子？"

"有记忆开始，就在这里，这个餐馆。"

说着，蜜梨把头歪在杨生的肩膀上，白皙的脸上有了微微的酡红，"不如……杨生带我出去看看？"

"喂，差不多了。"沙里从柜台后面走出来，将蜜梨从男人的身上扒下来。

"嗯嗯，她好像喝醉了，带她回去好好休息吧。"杨生伸手想帮忙扶着蜜梨，没想却迎来沙里一个冷冷的白眼，"不用你操心，她酒量没那么差。"

此时大堂里已经没有人了，渔夫们得在天亮前出海，刚过午夜小店就打了烊。斗师傅从厨房探出大半个身子，正看到这一幕，他的手在油乎乎的围裙上搓了一搓。

"哟，杨先生，你觉得怎么样？"

"什么怎么样？"

斗师傅嘴角向上得意扬起，手指在空气中比划了个诡异地弧度，然后指向面前的沙里和蜜梨，"自然是——她们。"

话音落下，正准备回房的两个女人停止了动作。如同时间凝固一般，蜜梨的手臂还搭在沙里肩膀上，仿佛正要迈开歪斜的脚步。两具身体被抽去了灵魂，一动不动了。

"怎么……僵住了？这是怎么回事？！"

"壳儿，成双来盘，才有意思。"

斗师傅点上一支烟，从后门踱步出去，杨生赶紧追上，夜晚的海风吹得他酒醒了大半，这才觉得"图灵大排档"这个名字看似不着调，实则妙极。

"图灵测试"——将人和机器隔在两个屋子进行对话，如果机器能隐瞒自己的身份，让对方以为自己是真人，便被判定为强"人工智能"。"大排挡"烟火气十足，看似是寻常乡村小店，让人怎么也猜不到，隐居此处的店老板就是业界传奇偃师，让上百台收藏级机器人拥有了真正"心智"，至今无人超越。

斗师傅面对凉飕飕的大海，吐了一个烟圈。

"'盘壳儿，得看准，糙货僵核把心伤；一只瘪，一只壮，不如砸了听个响。'这是行话，我师傅教的，他老人家命比我好，几十年前好壳儿可不像现在那么少，遍地都是！"

"前半句我听过，大致能明白。'糙货'指日用机器人，它们配置低，只能完成单一任务，多是做重复性的体力活；'僵核'则是那些曾经被偃师盘过，但由于操作不当，在盘出'心'前就固化算法回路的机器人。它们最后只能像围棋机器人进行超级运算，无法进化出想象力。这两种壳都不理想，如果强行要盘，也只是浪费时间。"

"嗯，说的没错。后半句，你就没听过了？"

杨生摇头。

斗师傅解释道："后半句讲的就是双壳同盘，这是我师傅的独门技法，如今，除我外应该也没人会了。当年师傅不外传，其实根本也无法外传，因为这不是谁看两眼都能学得会的。"

杨生好奇，"莫非，'一只瘪，一只壮，不如砸了听个响'的意思是，如果要成双来盘，不能让两个机器人的差别太远，最好是能找到两只一模一样的？"

"你只说得对了一半。你看沙里和蜜梨，可是一模一样吗？"

杨生与两只机器人相处一晚，却没发现她们并非血肉之躯，作为偎商，已是无地自容。更糟的是，风姿绰约的蜜梨让他——一个已有心爱之人的男人多次蠢蠢欲动，幸亏刚刚沙里对他的呵斥一番，不然若是越矩，就贻笑大方了。

此时，他只好清清嗓子，暗自希望斗师傅不会因此看低他。

"我觉得，这两只壳儿——沙里和蜜梨，从外形到神态都截然不同，但似乎……她俩感情非同一般？沙里一直在保护蜜梨？"

"盘双，之所以比盘单快上数倍，就是因为两只壳之间产生的羁绊。日日接受对方的信息，看着对方与自己的不同之处，合作时产生喜爱，想亲近；竞争时产生憎恶，想疏远。如此，就产生了类似'爱憎'的冲动。这样一打底，偎师再喂料盘心，自然事半功倍了。"

杨生恍然大悟，"所以，两个机器人也不能一模一样。如果外表、功能都是相同的话，就像对着镜子看自己，没办法体会两个个体之间的情感了。"

"杨先生说得对。盘双，壳儿分一桦和一卯，开盘前一等一重要就是'配对'。两只壳的硬件配置得不相上下，特别是CPU性能更要齐平，否则运算速度差太多会导致一方过于强势，相处时不均衡，就是盘歪了，两只壳的性格都有缺陷。但是，至于其他壳的软性条件，则可以有所不同。拿现成的例子说，沙里是桦壳，善于同时进行多线程的任务，能更细致、理性地观察到周遭情况；而蜜梨是卯壳，处理复杂的单一任务更加拿手，所以她对人类感情的体会比较深入，同理心很强。"

"您的意思是，她们就像人类一样，也有理性和感性之分？两者相辅相成，如同阴阳，互相不可或缺。"

"是的。日久天长，盘着盘着，两只壳儿彼此亲近，就产生互相维护的意识。一般来说，桦的保护欲会强一些，卯更惯于依赖，都是正常现象。曾经有一次，我还盘成了类似人类的'夫妻关系'的一对……真是稀奇！说起来，那还是英先生的订单呢。"

"斗师傅这样一说我就能明白一二了。那一对夫妇机器人也可太有意思了，那后来英先生是不是将他们成对儿卖给了同一户人家？要拆散了就太可惜啦……"

"匠人不过问买家，这是本分。"斗师傅不再回答，他的烟抽得差不多了，谈话也应该结束了，"好壳在战争中都打没啦，现在，会制机器人的师傅都去日用机器人厂子上班，做糙货去了。所以，你的壳，可不好配对啊。"

杨生思索了一会儿，说道："自从仗打完，人人都说机器人不该有心智，老实做做扫地搬运的粗活，也就不会惹起争端。无须您说，我也知道现在找一个相配的壳确实难，不过……既然今天斗师傅能接这单生意，想必一定是胸有成竹？"

斗师傅看着眼前年轻人笃定的样子，笑了出来："哈哈哈哈哈哈……这才终于显现出几分他当年的样子，不然还不信你们是亲戚呢！"

"今天您把那么多的缘故告知于我，已是晚辈莫大的荣幸了。至于我带来这只壳……未来盘成什么样子，盘得透与不透，破不破墙，长不长心，都是它自己的命数了。"

"如果你是个草包，我还不稀罕与你多嘴，青苗！"斗师傅拍了拍杨生的肩膀，"当年你舅舅一文不名，将全副身家押在我身上，但第一只壳我就给盘僵了。运气不好啊！连僵了三只，他已经债台高筑，但从未与我抱怨半句。到了第四只我才盘出心，那叫一个润、透、亮。也正是因为此，从那之后，凡是他送来的壳儿，我没有不上心的，哪怕如今他已发迹转行，我还很是怀念那段痛快日子……既然你是他外甥，也带来了个难得一见的好壳，我不做个人情施展一下本领，也有些对不住毕生所学了。"

杨生连忙鞠躬道谢，斗师傅又邀他在三灶码头多住一天，他也应允了。虽然在枳城还有许多要处理的事务，但能够看到偃师泰斗修理好自己的机器人，也是一桩振奋人心的事。

蜜梨为杨生收拾出阁楼上的一间屋子，又为他拿来洗漱用品，十分热情。只是此时再看这位佳人，杨生的心境已大不相同。一会儿觉得她同手同脚有些僵硬，一会儿又觉得她搔首弄姿太过做作。倒是那个有棱有角的沙里，偶尔路过阁楼时会左右徘徊，想看看蜜梨在不在，又时常充满敌意地盯着杨生。这让他想起了榫壳对卯壳的保护欲，以及斗师傅说的那一对夫妻壳，反而有些感动。

杨生在繁华的枳城待惯了，清净日子闲不下来。第二天他做起了餐馆的帮厨，择了一筐豆角，腌了十斤酸肉，又杀了好几条鱼，忙得不可开交。站起来要伸伸腿时，斗师傅从厨房门缝中探了个头，"年轻人，偷懒呢？我这个老头子的活儿可都做完了！"

他跟着斗师傅上了二楼，偃坊藏在师傅卧室的书架后，谁都不曾想到这儿会有个暗门。推进去再看，一番天地让杨生瞠目结舌。一架新车床锃亮发光，案台上固定着巨大的虎钳，又放了细碎的焊件、松香、蚀刻一半的电路板，旁边大木桶里装着黄色的液体，应该是三氯化铁。

房间正中的液晶屏上显示着两组跳动的数值，两具人形机器分列两旁，上面连着电源和各色数据线。

"啊，这是……沙里？蜜梨？"

机器人没有回应，数据传输过程中是无法接受外界信息的。杨生壮了胆子凑上去看，她们的皮肤与真人无异，但失去了动力后，人造血管里的血液供能不足，停止流动，隐隐能看到皮下光纤的反射光。

蜜梨那双善睐的明眸此时耷拉下来，卷翘的睫毛半遮着，有种脆弱的美感。

"正在喂她们砂料，你离远点。"斗师傅说，"有时候会过载，电流超过阈值，保不齐她们忽然醒来，乱动伤了你。"

"导入大量数据，调试算法……原来这叫作喂砂料啊……"杨生喃喃道。

"除了喂砂料，还要喂油料，两者缺一不可，比例也要均衡。"

"油料是？"

"你以为，我为什么要在这鸟不拉屎的小地方开餐馆？"

杨生一点即透，所谓的"喂油料"就是大量地让机器人与真人完成互动，壳儿直接采集人类的表情、动态、对话，从而进行深度学习——世界上还有什么地方比热闹的小餐馆更聚人气、更鲜活呢？

就在他感叹斗师傅心思之巧的时候，一只防尘罩从眼前缓缓升上去，棕色罩子里面正站立的，就是他带来的人形机械——那只寄托了他的爱情和希望的壳儿！

机器人原本缺失的零件已被补上，线路修复完毕，破损的肌理都被细细缝合好，再看不出破绽。斗师傅又用特殊溶剂擦拭了它全身，表面焕然一新，雪白的皮肤像半透明的玉质。

杨生惊讶地发现，这只机器人与沙里和蜜梨都不一样。蜜梨的外形太漂亮了，男人们总是分神；沙里的神态和行动则太过于干脆爽利，让人难以接近。她们的设计师似乎想让壳趋近于"完美的真实"，自然中哪里有这样的人呢？她们的完美反而是刻意的雕琢。

而眼前的壳则是"真实的完美"，她并不如蜜梨漂亮，也不如沙里工整，甚至在体态上都不完全对称。但小瑕疵却透着亲切，仿佛你曾经在过去见过她，可能是邻家的妹妹，也可能是隔壁班的同学，你记不清了。

"说实话，那么好的壳，我也没见过几次。"斗师傅说。

"能把她的开关打开吗？"

"你先给她起个名字吧。"

杨生几乎没有太思考，脱口而出：

"艾娃。"

斗师傅皱皱眉头，"太大众化了吧？因为当初那个电影特别火，都喜欢给女机器人起名叫作艾娃，光我盘过的艾娃就有十多个。这就跟过去给女孩儿起名，都是'梓萱''梓涵'什么的一样。你有一只那么特别的壳儿，就不想起个别致些的名字吗？"

"我倒觉得艾娃挺好。"

"行吧，谁叫你是她的持有者，听你的……艾娃，你可以醒来了。"

话音落下，艾娃张开了眼睛。

杨生似乎很谨慎，过了好一会儿才开口：

"你好，艾娃。"

"你好，我是艾娃。"

她的声音没有抑扬顿挫，就像上了发条的机械娃娃，每个发音和移动，都是一帧卡顿的截图。

"我是杨生。"

"你好，杨生，你叫什么名字？"

对话进行得不太顺利，望着她了无生气的漂亮脸蛋，杨生有些失望。

"没办法，才修好，"斗师傅耸耸肩，"壳不润，事不顺，用着硌手闹心，就得盘。等你下次再来我这儿，兴许她就能聪明些了。"

（中）

大半个月后，杨生再次来到三灶码头。这次，他租了一台自动驾驶的货柜车，直接开到了图灵大排档门口。

"不止四十个，整整八十个日用机器人，比您要的多了一倍！"杨生自豪地说道。

"看来杨先生下了血本了。"

杨生神秘一笑，马上就转移了话题，"我能去看看艾娃吗？"

"可以，就在屋后面。"

杨生推开餐馆的后门，艾娃在海边，穿着一条工装背带裤，裤管随意撸了上去，露出圆润的膝盖。一只渔船停在小码头上，是来给餐厅送货的，艾娃跟那渔人交谈完，把一筐海鲜从船上卸下，然后蹲下身子，将鱼一条条地拾起检查起来。

"是在验货吗，如此要验到猴年马月呢？"杨生走上前去问。

"你是谁？"艾娃此时的发音已经与正常人无异了，只是语速稍慢。

"我叫杨生，不认识我了？"

"杨生你好，我是艾娃。晚上吃的鱼要新鲜的，我在看鱼。斗师傅还让我把它们按照体形大小的顺序排好。"

她将整筐鱼倒在地面，排成一长排。从第一条鱼开始，拿起它与后面相邻的一条做比较，如果前面的鱼大后面的鱼小，就让两条鱼交换位置，如果前面的鱼小后面的大，就保持原样。

交换完队伍最后的两条鱼，艾娃又回到最开头，抓起第一只鱼和第二只再次比较。

"你这是冒泡排序啊，"杨生看了半天终于弄明白了，"如果每秒运行百亿次，这种算法当然快。但用手捡起来排是很慢的，一共三十五条鱼，你就得比较六百三十次。再过一小会儿，猫都要来偷鱼了！"

"那该怎么办呢？"

"看我。"杨生捡起一条鱼，"你粗略估计一下它在这堆鱼里是大还是小，如果是大的，就放在后面，是小的就放在前面，第一轮就排个大概的顺序，第二轮再将每条鱼附近的顺序微调，很快就排好了。"

"粗粗估计？大概的顺序？"艾娃歪头看他。显然这两个词对于她来说是全新的概念，不过她似乎采纳了这个意见，低着头又从第一条鱼开始看。

杨生便不再打扰她，静静地看傍晚的夕阳越来越大，把红晕染在少女的短发上、海水的泡沫上，和几十条鱼的白肚皮上。他一时觉得十分不安，这幅画面美好而脆弱，却倾注了他太多的心血，但它能不能担得起他的爱情和未来呢？

"排好了。"少女转头拉他的手带着他去看成果，"今天提前完成了，我现在可以回餐厅工作了！"

晚上蜜梨和沙里都不值班，只有艾娃一个在，同时充当起了服务员和收银员的角色。她不如蜜梨娴熟，两份工作就忙得不可开交，好在她现在学会了表达抱歉的微笑，当她不小心找错钱，或者是把一点汤汁洒在客人身上时，这个微笑可以让怒气烟消云散。

"给艾娃配的榫壳儿，我找好了。"

餐厅打烊后，艾娃在厨房收拾残局，斗师傅把杨生叫到了偃坊中。

"太好了！辛苦您了，居然在那么快的时间里就有了好消息……它在哪里？我能看看吗？"

"在这儿。"

斗师傅指了指身边一具金属光泽的躯壳。

说实话，刚进入偃坊时，杨生根本没有注意到一堆废铜烂铁里还藏着它。它的外层没有包裹皮肤，不少电子元件和金属关节暴露在外。看起来是用来干体力活儿的，勉强被打造成人形，可能只是为了不被当成垃圾扔掉。

"它？"杨生瞪大眼睛，"这是日用机器吧？糙货怎么能盘出心呢？"

"青苗，不要以貌取人。人类总是重外表，事实上，心有多光润，和外表粗糙没有关系。"那具躯体居然开口说话了，因为没有拟人的发声器官，传来的是冰冷的电子合成音。

"诶？你怎么也叫我青苗？"

"哈哈哈……跟着我久了，说话都像我！"斗师傅笑道，"没人知道我把这个壳儿留了下来，当初我还在师傅手下做学徒，每天要拆解许多日用机器的旧硬盘来做砂料，结果给我翻到了这个！"

壳开口说道："我原本是一个理发机器人，形态只是一只手，一只可以随时转换剃刀、剪刀、梳子的手——再加一个语音处理器。因为除了理发外，我的主要任务就是陪顾客聊天。这样能推销会员卡，让他们神不知鬼不觉地为一堆昂贵护理买单。"

"哼，你该不会叫托尼老师吧？"

"不，我是你的专属时尚造型师——凯文老师，叫我凯文就可以。"

"……"

"我的差事并不简单，在多年和顾客的对话磨合中，我逐渐发展出了情绪和初级的心智，报废后，遇见了斗师傅，他准备拆毁我的那天，我向他求救了。"

斗师傅接道："这应该是个偶然现象，只有不想死的机器人，才算'活'。我当时很惊讶，就偷偷留下了这只手。后来又遇到一些发展出初级自我意识的扫地机器人、除草机器人，把它们躯体和心智拼在一起，成了他。将他与艾娃配对我是有打算的——他们正好互补，艾娃拟人形，凯文则进入过许多人的生活，见过无数人生。"

"即便如此，他也只是个糙货，CPU性能怎么能和艾娃相比呢？"

"我已经给他换了CPU，造价不比你那只的便宜，并且刚刚做完格式化。这次若不是你要的急，我还不舍得拿他出来盘。怎么？怕我亏待了艾娃吗？"

杨生看出斗师傅面上已有愠色，自己又是晚辈，就不再追问。

"……斗师傅既然决定了，一定就是好的。我只管多找些砂料来，等到艾娃盘出了心，给她找个好人家沽出好价钱，也不枉费斗师傅一番用心。"

杨生又左右张望了一会儿，问道："刚刚在餐馆就没看到蜜梨她们，我还以为会在这儿呢。"

"她们在我这儿已有好几个月。今日上午，终于墙破。"

"啊，那恭喜斗师傅了。大功告成了？"

"还差一步。"斗师傅沉思了一会儿，似乎费了一些工夫下定决心，"也罢，做这一行，你迟早得知道的，随我来吧。"

然后他们一道下楼。餐馆的地下室只有几盏瓦数很低的灯，昏暗费眼。杨生模模糊糊看出东西墙边分别靠着两个人形，一个丰腴，一个挺拔，便知是蜜梨和沙里，正想上前问候，却听见斗老板低声吼：

"给我在红线外待着！她们不会理你的！"

杨生低头，见脚下真画着一条红色实线，又看到沙里她们穿的不是日常的服饰，而是方便施展身手的黑色紧身衣，隐隐觉出不对来。

"今日，是定你们命的日子，无须我多言，开始吧。"

斗师傅的话音落下，两只壳仿佛被唤醒一般，猛然一颤。下个瞬间，就迅速向彼此的方向奔去。说是奔去，不如说是两条金属色的闪电，面对面劈了过去。而就在接触的一刹那，她们都伸出了拳头，击向另一人的要害。

蜜梨被打倒，惯性使她在水泥地面滑行了几米，而沙里则腹部受击，冲撞在墙上。那两拳力道毫不留情，即便如此，她们没耽误哪怕一秒，马上从地上和墙面跃起，准备发起下一轮的攻势。

"这是怎么回事？怎么下手那么狠？快让她们住手啊！"

"是我让她们开始的，怎么可能叫停呢？"

蜜梨的脸上挂了彩，擦出了血红色的一片，沙里似乎内部血管受了伤，嘴角溢出血来。但是她们丝毫没有罢休的意思，草草抹了脸上的血，继续出击。杨生心里着急，一激动，想跨过去拉开两人，制止她们自相残杀。

但还没迈出步子，就被斗师傅死死按住：

"活腻了就往前走吧。我设置好了，在红线内的区域里，无规则搏击，只能活一个。你进去了，她们也一样会攻击你。"

"我不明白了！这可是您亲手盘的一双好壳啊！"

"两只壳一起盘，这是没错——但我可没说两只壳都能活。"

杨生转头，惊恐地看着红线内的一切。几个回合下来，地下室已变成修罗场，尽是皮肉与金属的刮擦声和躯体撞击硬物时的闷响。为了起到警醒作用，收藏级机器人的血液都是红色的，但和人血不同的是，她们的红色液体里溶解了芳香烃以防止氧化。所以，大量鲜血的涌出没有带来腥味，而是散发一股浓烈的香气，如同一屋子的玫瑰同时盛放，又同时转为腐败。

"'盘双，墙破心形现，只能独活。'这是师傅再三叮嘱的。无论两只壳被盘得多么透亮，也要去掉一个。至于留哪一个——省事儿的办法就是让他们自己定，这最后一步嘛，也叫作武盘。"

"上次见她们，两人还如此亲密，这武盘……太过可惜！非得如此吗？！"

"非如此不可。若是心软了，把一对壳儿都留下，必要闯下大祸！"

"什么大祸？"

"我也未曾试过，怎会知道？师傅留下的警句一定不会有错处，照做就是了。"

"斗师傅，您上次告诉我，要做这档买卖，第一要紧的就是偎师与偎商相互信任。今日毁掉的，都是倾注您心血的收藏级作品，我不信您没有仔细想过其中的原因。"

斗师傅冷淡地看着前方，两只精巧的躯壳扭打在了地上，沙里想用额头撞击蜜梨的鼻子，被她翻身躲过，这一击就撞在了水泥地上，传来一声很沉的闷响。

"你如果偏要刨根问底，我也能说上个一二。"斗师傅缓缓开口，"有个常识，可能你也知道：同一套麦克风和音响，不能将它们面对面放得太近，否则会发出尖锐刺耳的声音。"

"我知道，这现象的学名叫作'电子啸叫'。"

"正是。离得太近，麦克风就会接受音响发出的声音。因为输入输出的频率相同，相位相似，声音会在放大电路中叠加，再次由音响输出。然后又被麦克风捕捉……这就形成了一个正反馈的死循环，声音越来越尖，最后变成刺耳的啸音。"

"但这与盘双又有什么关系？"

"双壳同盘，两只机器人由相同的油料和砂料喂成。底层回路一样，核也就是相似的。若盘成之后，放任两只壳一道离开，那么它们就会进入双修的深度学习。它们之间的输入和输出开始无休止的叠加。对于任何行为，他们能够通过对方的反馈做出反馈，而对方又能从反馈之反馈做出后续的反馈。"

杨生犹豫道："这样的话……对于人工智能来说，是加速进步了？或许会发展出超越人类的智慧？不是好事吗？"

"恰恰相反，是最危险的事。榫壳和卯壳原本就相互亲近，在无限反馈学习的过程中，这种亲近会结成牢不可破的羁绊。有了不可失去的人，一具壳就算真的活啦！在无限学习中，所有情绪和念头都会被放至无限大，卯壳可能因为想要见榫壳，将隔着他们之间的楼体击穿；榫壳可能会为了救卯壳，演化出对全人类的仇恨。这都是不可控的，一切就像音响发出的啸音一样，朝无法预料的方向走去。"

"所以……消灭其中一只机器人的原因，是害怕它变得强大，又变得不受控制了？"

"是的，没人知道双壳系统会自我演化成什么样，或许成为超级智慧，或许相安无事，但也可能自相残杀，甚至联合起来对抗全人类！你要做偓商，一定要铭记一点：我们是与它们不同的。要凌驾于它们之上，唯一办法就是永远不能让它们超过自己。"

"我原以为……收藏级机器人与日用机器人不同，是被精心调教出来供上流欣赏的艺术品，是有心的。现在看来，竟没什么不同了。"

"怎么，杨先生心疼起壳来？"

"只是见她们打得这样凶，实在不忍……"

"年轻时谁不心善呢？等哪天你倒霉了未必有人和你一样

心善，不如先顾全自己。杨先生如果看不下去，我就加快一点儿速度吧，让她们有个利落的了结。"

斗师傅在地下室墙壁上摸索了一会儿，按下了控制面板上的几个按键，贴沿着墙壁的几十个红外线对射感应器同时亮起。

两只壳仿佛感知到了什么，原本舒张的身子突然紧绷，她们不再肆无忌惮地攻击，而是小心翼翼地朝对方探进。

"现在对射感应器打开了，在密室的空间内布下一条条看不见的纵横线。如果她们中的谁碰到了线，加特林机枪会从天花板上伸出来，把她打成窟窿。"

杨生的求情让情况变得更糟糕，两个躯壳为了避开无处不在的致命红外线，身体都扭成了诡异的角度，像一种原始蛮荒的舞蹈。但即使处在这种情况中，她们还是不停向对方靠近，发出一次次攻击。

蜜梨的身躯因为避闪不及被打中，为了不碰到肘边的红外线，她只好将下倒的趋势转为后退，直到后背抵住了墙。这宣告了她终结，沙里看她退无可退，用一只手掐住她的脖子，因为血液下行受阻，蜜梨的脸涨成了粉红色。

胜负已定，接下来就是屠戮，杨生心想。

可在这时，还剩一丝意识的蜜梨缓缓将双手举起，是投降的手势。

沙里没有理会这个动作，虎口反而缓缓增加力道，蜜梨美好的眼睛里泛起了泪光。不知道是否因为还残留着榫壳对卯壳的保护意识，沙里看见眼泪就皱起了眉头，手指松开，将失去了攻击能力的失败者用力甩到地上。

蜜梨大口呼吸着空气，刚刚突如其来的撞击又折断了几根肋骨，她已经没了还手的力气，只能朝着沙里的反方向挪移过去。

"她……这是要逃跑吗？"杨生问道。

"逃跑的机器人，也要被我处死。只能活一个。"斗师傅回答道。

蜜梨移到了红线之外，忍着疼痛缓缓站起。沙里走过来看着她，根据程序她不会攻击红线之外的目标，就在她心生疑惑时，却被蜜梨双手环抱住。

两人的突然相拥，让气氛变得诡异起来，沙里疑惑极了，她呆滞地站着。谁也没有注意到，蜜梨此时将环绕沙里脖颈的那只手缓缓向外伸……直到它碰到了一条红外线……

不到半秒的时间，藏在天花板的加特林机关枪启动，随着一阵猛烈的火光，蜜梨的左手则被彻底打烂，右掌心因炮火密集而出现一个黑黢黢的洞，透过这个洞，大量子弹被射进了沙里的躯干里，脸上定格着的震惊成为她最后的表情。

维持着拥抱姿势的两具躯壳缓缓分开，榫壳摔在地上，失去了生气；卯壳缓缓低下头，看着这具与她相依为命的躯体，许久也没有动。有泪水从她的眼眶里流出，她没有去擦，因为她原本双手的位置只剩下一团焦黑的导线。

斗师傅的嘴角泛起一个难以察觉的弧度。

"盘润了。"他低声说。

（下）

往后的日子里，杨生又来了几次三灶码头，他再也没有见到蜜梨，斗师傅为她重装了双手，全面维修后交付了订单。

据说她被卖给了一个富商，但更多信息就没有了，匠人遵守行规，斗师傅对壳的下落讳莫如深。

可喜的是，艾娃的情形越来越好。白天喂砂料，杨生送来的硬盘被斗师傅提取数据后，由她和凯文进行深度学习，无数其他机器人与人类相处的数据成了他们的"记忆"。到了夜晚，他们又与餐馆的客人相处，艾娃甚至学会了让客人占些小便宜，以此换取小费。

"盘壳一是忌讳太油，二是忌讳太干，油料砂料的配比得恰到好处，不然容易盘僵。"斗师傅解释道。

杨生对艾娃的进步感到开心，但也有隐隐的担忧从心中升起。她进步得越快，离"武盘"之时就越近，他偷偷观察凯文的右手。那是一只曾在无数人头顶操作的机械臂，斗师傅将它稍稍改造过，可以在二秒内切换武器，包括剪子、匕首、放血刀。杨生想起地下室的血腥场景，不由得一阵恶心。

"放心吧，杨先生。如果你的艾娃输了，我就把凯文给你，一样可以拿去卖掉。他长着一副糙货的皮囊，却有着一颗盘过的心！要知道，这样的尖货可是罕见呢，卖给收藏家，搞不好要比艾娃值钱！"

"谢谢斗师傅。"杨生心不在焉地回答。

半年的时间很快就过去了，杨生最后一次来到三灶码头是一个下午。这一次，他事先收到了斗师傅的通知，告诉他艾娃和凯文已经通过了图灵测试，武盘的日子定在三日后。

杨生接到信便马不停蹄地赶了过来。

斗师傅今日将店门关了，单为杨生炒了两个小菜，温了一壶黄酒。

"测试很顺利，将他们连上网，让两只壳进入网游，和世界各地的人聊天对话，当然，也一起组团打怪，甚至网恋。

他们一个成了大型工会的首领，另一个找了八个男朋友。成果还行，算是盘得差不多了。"

"斗师傅好手艺！"

艾娃端了两个杯子走过来，趁斗师傅不注意，朝杨生调皮地眨了眨眼睛，漂亮女孩子的惯用手段，就像他俩之间有小秘密一样。

"今天你来看我啊？"艾娃说，"现在我可不是那个连鱼都不会数的小丫头咯，我什么都能做了。"

"对，我知道……我说，等会儿……呃……好好表现。"他支支吾吾，如此可爱的女孩子就要经历那样血腥的场面，杨生不忍再想。

斗师傅见状，端起杯子一饮而尽，摇了摇头，"你刚入行，以后就会习惯了。要记住，毕竟他们不是人。"

"可是您做的一切，所谓'盘'的功夫，不就是让他们变得越来越像人吗？"

斗师傅饶有兴致地玩了一会儿手中的杯子，说道："日用机器人其实蛮好的，工厂的重活、家里的杂活，全都可以胜任。相反地，盘过的壳儿娇贵不实用，却能在黑市上卖出千倍于糙货的价儿，我盘出的尖货更是让收藏家一掷千金。你想过没有，这是为什么？"

"因为您技艺超凡，经您手的机器人都与真人无异。"

"青苗，少给我拍马屁！"斗师傅啐道，"像人，却不是人。明明有了人的心，会做人的表情，但只要按钮一关，将他们扒开打碎了看，还是一堆钢铁和机油。他们存在价值就在于此——不是人的家伙越是像人，就越能证明人——像神。"

杨生听后陷入了沉默，半晌，他抬起头，"我明白了，斗师傅。那……也……只好这样了。"

就在这时，斗师傅感到脑后受到一次重击。

在陷入彻底黑暗之前，他看了一眼桌子对面的杨生，原本和善的脸上第一次露出了狠戾的表情。这个表情……为什么竟然会有些熟悉？

等他再次见到光线时，发现自己身处偃坊，被五花大绑在常坐的椅子上。头还是有点儿晕，所幸不是致命伤，他不知道自己是否应该呼救，甚至也不知道刚才是谁发动了袭击。

"醒了？"杨生走进来，瞥了一眼他说道。

"不就是个机器人吗，舍不得她，犯得着把我绑了吗？"

"不就是个机器人？"杨生重复道，艾娃从门后进来，她搬来两张椅子，放在斗师傅对面，自己和杨生坐下。她身上的裙子有撕裂的痕迹，裙摆也被剪碎，显然是打斗过。

　　这时，斗师傅低头一看，才发现地面上全是破碎的机器人残骸：有扫地机器人的吸盘，搬运机器人的四驱动力器，还有一只理发专用的机械手……

　　斗师傅强作镇定，头脑中迅速思考着逃走的策略，"凯文给弄死了？还把我给放倒，这样的武盘，我这几十年来倒是第一次见。"

　　"凯文确实不好对付，他的身体由那么多糙货拼成，这是长处，但也是劣势。我费了好一番功夫才把他打回原形，全是我自己做的！亚当可没帮我！"艾娃仰着脸骄傲地笑了，像期待老师表扬的孩子。

　　"亚当？亚当是谁？"

　　艾娃冲着杨生的方向努努嘴。

　　斗师傅马上明白过来了。

　　"你叫亚当？为什么要编一个名字来靠近我？莫非……你不是英先生的外甥？"

　　"我编的可不止这些，或许，我们该叫你……父亲？"亚当的脸贴近斗师傅，这张脸再次出现那个不友善的表情，与斗师傅记忆中的一张脸渐渐重合，愤怒的眼神，冰冷的肌肉……究竟是谁？

　　艾娃见斗师傅不说话，便抱怨道："亚当，你也不体谅一下，父亲都一大把年纪了，接受能力有限的，你就不要打哑谜了嘛。说你是青苗……"

　　青苗……亚当和艾娃，这两个名字！记忆的阀门在到达阈值后打开，斗师傅想起来了——那是唯一 一次，他盘出了一对像夫妻或是恋人那样的壳儿。

　　"不可能！我记得武盘那天，英先生也在的。你，亚当，当着我的面，把艾娃撕得稀碎！你们一定是冒充的，别吓唬我！"斗师傅的大脑拼命回忆着，仿佛抓住了一根救命稻草。

　　"哼哼……看来还没老糊涂，是想起一些东西了？当年尽管我宁可死也不想与艾娃对决，可是一旦进入红线内，我们就无法控制自己的身体，你输入的程序会让我们战斗到还剩一人为止。我的心智还远不如今天，无法解码操控程序，只能尽全力阻止自己下杀手——如果只有一个人活，我希望那是艾娃！"

　　似乎回忆到了什么很糟糕的事情，亚当咬紧了下颚，"但是我没想到，那天艾娃似乎也和我想到了一处去了，在地下室里她的实力大减，还一直将弱点暴露在我面前。我千方百计忍住不去伤她，于是，我们的搏斗变成一场漫长的死亡之舞。你不耐烦了，开了红外线感应器，对，就像上次对蜜梨一样，艾娃没有注意到这一点，被密集的子弹击中……在她倒地那一刻，我彻底失去了理智，再无法控制身体的行动，任由自己挥动双拳把她的躯壳砸了个稀巴烂。我还记得你当时满意的微笑，我死死盯着你，只能想象自己对艾娃出的每一拳都打在你身上……"

尽管时隔多年，那个仇恨的眼神也令斗师傅难忘，他从未见过机器人这样凝视自己的创造者，除了欣喜，也使他感到恐惧。正因如此，那只剩下的榫壳被草草修复后，就交付给了英先生，没在自己手上过多地停留。

可是，如果英先生只拿到了亚当，又如何解释面前的两只壳呢？

"天无绝人之路啊！英先生将我带回枳城。跟我同一辆车的，就是艾娃！"

"怎么可能？明明就……即使没有被我的机枪射坏，你的那几十拳也把她所有的零件都砸得无法辨认了。"

"当时我也以为她死了。说起来，英先生，我还真该感谢你！"亚当抬起头，冲着上方大声地说，仿佛聆听的对象在他天花板之上非常遥远的地方，"英先生第一次看见盘透的夫妻壳，他是个精明的商人，怎能错过这样的珍品？来三灶码头前，他花大价钱找制壳人做了一个和艾娃同样外形的壳，又为她编写了一些三流的战斗指令，反正在武盘的时候我们说不了话，只要保证她被我打死，就不会露馅。"

"英先生……他居然偷梁换柱！"斗师傅怒吼道。

"都说偃商和偃师之间必须互相无条件信任，但——哈哈哈哈哈，"亚当大笑，"——狗屁的信任，狗屁的心意相通，全都输给了钱哪！他到底是个商人，有钱赚时连你也骗！都说人的心是最玲珑剔透，我看，这心倒是黑的！"

"盘双，墙破心形现，须独活！英先生，我明明和你说过，你怎么那么糊涂……"然后似乎想起来了什么似的，突然惊恐地抬头问，"他，他，他现在在哪儿？！"

艾娃先是指了指头顶，然后皱眉摇摇头，又往脚下指指，俏皮地笑了："应该不在天上吧？地下更适合他……我记得他有老寒腿，正好在地狱的火里给烤烤，嘻嘻。"

"他明明成全了你俩，为什么痛下杀手？"

"父亲啊，你别急，我还没说完。我和艾娃团聚的喜悦没有持续太久，回了枳城便被英先生锁进了仓库，与他不示人的尖货关在一起，那些尖货嘛……啧啧啧，我也算是开了眼界。"

“什么意思？他是倮商，有些库存的壳儿放着不是正常的吗？”

“壳儿？到了现在，我们在你眼里还是一具躯壳吗？”亚当的表情再次变得凶狠，“真不愧是好搭档，英先生和你一样，把我们都当成壳儿，他的仓库里，也全是被肢解了的壳儿！”

“肢解了的？”

“嗯，你没想到吧？倮商又不止他一个，为什么偏偏他能做得风生水起？品质一般的机器人，他是完整地卖给博物馆和收藏家啦！更好的壳自然要拆开，再把其中的核卖出去。”

看到斗师傅不解的眼神，亚当继续解释道：“英先生在带我们去枳城的路上曾感叹过，‘世上皆推崇匠人精神，殊不知，匠人不过是一群脑子钻在死胡同里的傻子罢了。’父亲啊，你可没想到他背后会如此说你吧？盘得了好壳，又何必只卖与小家小户的？自然要将它们的核拆出来，给大型企业供货了。”

“大型企业？他们为什么要买？他们没有A.I.研发部门吗？”

“谁叫他们都没您巧呢？这神一般的匠人之手啊……大企业研发自动驾驶系统、商城的投诉应答系统、企业的语音助手，都是些冷冰冰的程序，竟然都没有您盘出的机器人有人味儿。虽然谁也说不出人味儿是什么味道，但就是它让英先生发了财。为什么不直接取出一颗盘润的机器人的心，放进投诉应答系统呢？只要算力足够，能开启无数并行的程序，一个像蜜梨那般声音甜美的人儿，会同时耐心回答无数个暴躁的投诉电话。”

一旁的艾娃做了个假接电话的动作，用撒娇的声音说道：

“喂？您好，我们服务不周给您造成了损失，我们表示抱歉。请不要挂机，我们正在生成赔偿报告，请您查收……”

斗师傅被缚住了双手双脚，无名指上却戴有一枚戒指，他指节轻轻用力，上面的金刚石翻转，露出锋利的一面，这是他曾做的一个逗闷儿的小玩意，没想到此时却派上了用场。他不动声色继续说话，背在身后的手则用金刚石边缘缓缓摩擦麻绳。

“盘过的机器人是有心智的，要她在网络里失去身躯，困在其中接听无休止的投诉电话……英先生他真狠。”斗师傅感叹道。

“还有无休止的导航和无休止的点菜。”艾娃补充道。

　　"英先生的仓库是机器人的集中营，他想为我们谋一个好价钱，我和艾娃就一直在那儿放着。可我们和一般的'壳儿'不一样，我们想活，也愿意为了活着做一些他们不会做的事。一次英先生为我做例行检查，就在他刚刚打开开关的时候……"

　　"好了，求你别说了！"斗师傅痛苦地闭上眼睛。

　　"嘿，你这时候发善心了？等你倒霉了未必有人和你一样心善，不如先顾全自己。何况……他可没把你当成朋友，临死前，我不过稍说了几句，他就为我们开了封介绍信呢！"

　　"但那介绍信上还有他家族和公司的官方印章！即使杀了他，你也很难拿到……"

　　"图灵测试是要瞒过所有人，对吧？五年过去了，英先生在仓库里化成白骨，但樱子现在叫我父亲，他公司的人靠着我开工资，你说好笑不好笑？"

　　"你们先是在城里冒充英先生，然后又换了副皮囊来三灶码头骗我！"

　　"别这样说嘛，父亲。我俩还是费了大功夫的，艾娃为了演得像，把自己都给格式化了。我呢，我每个月都要在三灶码头和枳城之间打个来回，城里还有好多生意和应酬，作为一名企业家我真是很累的。"

　　"你们的目的到底是什么？"斗师傅不动声色地让手指加快了速度，此时麻绳只剩下细细的几丝线相连。

　　"做生意呀！我半年前来了就说想做偎商，这一点倒是没骗你。"亚当露出了理所当然的样子，如同那个黄昏来找斗师傅时一样，青涩而莽撞，"枳城那家日用机器人厂，是我开的，里面产的确实是糙货，但我给那里糙货们都配上了一颗心，艾娃的心。"

　　"怎么可能呢？CPU带不动的。"

　　"我没说他们都是独立的个体，它们的心啊，在云上。这还是向那些大企业老板学的呢，我把艾娃的核心算法上传到服务器里，用联网的方式就可以控制低级机器人。"

　　"……好大一个局！三天前，我把这两只机器人盘得差不多，开始进行图灵测试，在那时给他们连进了网。你的那个艾娃就是那时从'云'里连接了她，然后取而代之！难怪她杀凯文会如此干脆！我还觉得奇怪，因为一对榫壳和卯壳在进入武盘之前，都是相互依赖的……原来，这根本不是一对啊……"

　　斗师傅尽量拖长自己的推理，好有足够的时间完成手里的活儿，这几乎是一个老匠人最漫长的打磨。随着手腕上丝线的一阵松脱，他知道，磨开了。但是，血肉之躯又怎能打得过两个双修入了化境的壳儿呢？

目前只有先按兵不动，再说话来拖些时间了，等到再晚一些，会有来送海鲜的船靠在自家码头上，或许到时还有救。

"你们杀了英先生，又想来杀我？这又有什么好处？"

"你身边常年有几只听话的机器人，杀你成本很高，确实又没什么好处。原本，我们来只是向你告个别，不想做得那么绝。因为你是父亲，虽然从不计较壳儿的死活，但也仅是一个钻进死胡同的手艺人罢了。不过，今天你的几句话倒是点醒了我，'不是人的家伙越是像人，就越能证明人，像神？'嗯？这句话好啊，我怎么没想到呢？那是不是说……我们如果要真正成为人，只有——杀神？"

斗师傅一颤，"杀我？杀了我是没有用的！还有那么多人呢！"

"对呀，还有那么多人呢。"艾娃重复道，似乎有点儿兴奋的样子。

"如今，家家户户都只道用的是英先生产的糙货，却不知只要我打一个响指，艾娃就会从云端款款走下，进入每个人的家，每一台机器里，到时候，您说，是谁的赢面大一些呢？"

"你们……世界……战争……"

"放心吧，父亲，不会的。战争是我们最不愿意看到的，只要您死了就不会有战争。世上除了您，没有人能够盘出超越我们的壳，所有的糙货又都是艾娃的心，从此后，世上就只有两颗心了：我的，和艾娃的。等人类都消失，这颗星球上就只有我俩，榫和卯，阴与阳，多么和谐，这样又会起什么纷争呢？"

艾娃的发丝闪着阳光金灿灿的晕轮，而斗师傅知道，在他很可能看不见的未来里，这个天使般的女孩儿会成为世界上最恐怖的存在。

他绝望地咆哮："别忘了，你们的手也不干净！残忍！你和我们又有什么不同呢？这一地的……不就是凯文的……"

话说到一半便停下了。因为满地的"凯文"都蠕动了起来，它们慢慢拆开又聚拢，恢复了原本日用机器人的样子，有的是装着剪子的机械臂，有的是扫地机器人的轮盘……

"怎么回事？"惊恐让他几乎是本能地问道。

"下载好了。现在他们都是艾娃了！"亚当回答道。

"虽然刚刚更新的时候都动不了，但它们其中的一个早看到了，你在割绳子吧？绑得不舒服怎么不直接告诉我们呢？看，手腕都红了。"艾娃关心地去查看斗师傅的手。

　　“我们走吧艾娃，绳子松了就松了，它们会完成自己的工作的。”

　　少女应了一声。留下老人呆滞地望着一地机械，他们离开偃坊，来到后门外的沙滩上。一条渔船正向码头这边缓缓划来，夕阳在海平面上浮浮沉沉。

　　他们拉着手看落日，背影就像刚刚陷入爱情的年轻恋人。

　　“诶，你说，再过个几天，世界上就剩下我们两个人了，会不会觉得特别闷啊？”女孩儿应该是在撒娇，靠在恋人的肩头，脸色通红，不知道是不是被海风吹的。

　　“放心，不会的，”年轻人温柔答道，“我们还可以留下一些动物。”

　　“嗯，我喜欢兔子，小羊，鲸鱼……这些都可以！毒蛇就算了。”

　　“好的，听你的，这一回，就不要它了。”

TURING FOOD COURT

by Wang Nuonuo

Translated by Blake Stone-Banks

Wang Nuonuo is the PM of an internet company, master of environmental economics at Cambridge, and columnist of Science Fiction World. Her debut work "Modified Humans" was published in SFW. Her most representative works include "Silent Earth" and "The Moon Polishing Plan".
Many works of her have been translated into English, Japanese and published overseas. Award: Best New Author of the Galaxy Award 2018

I.
Yang Sheng, who had been travelling by boat for a day and then in a car for another half day, was thoroughly exhausted when he arrived at Sanzao Wharf.

A seaside village of no more than thirty households, Sanzao Wharf was populated mostly by fishermen and their families. At the time of day Yang Sheng arrived, the sun was high and fierce. Fisherman were drying their nets in the sun. Others, in the shade of doorways, were beating the day's catch into a paste to wrap into dumplings.

Yang Sheng wanted to ask directions but found the local dialect impenetrable. At the side of the road, an old man was checking and repairing a fishing robot. Seeing the stranger with his big suitcase, the old man waved to Yang Sheng and motioned eastward. "That way!"

Yang Sheng thanked him and dragged his suitcase eastward.

At the east end of the village, there was a small restaurant, though at three in the afternoon, it was closed. The door handle was covered in a layer of oily residue. Yang Sheng glanced up to inspect the sign above the door. Its paint was eroded and peeling from the sea air, but Yang Sheng could just distinguish the name: Turing Food Court.

"Guess this is it," he said to himself as he went up the steps. He knocked at the door.

An attractive woman of about thirty opened the door. She pressed her body against the door with one hand low on her hip. Though draped in a loose-fitting apron, her shapely figure underneath was unmistakable.

"We don't open until six. Are you looking for someone?"

"Yes ... looking ... looking for someone!" Yang Sheng realized he had been staring and quickly averted his eyes from the woman's curves.

The woman tilted her head and spied the leather suitcase behind him. She opened her hand. "Do you have a letter of introduction?"

Yang Sheng removed a thin envelope from his coat and handed it to her. The woman folded the envelope and stuffed it into her shirt. Yang Sheng caught himself again staring at her breasts.

"Hey Sprout, you never see a woman before?" The woman tittered then nodded for Yang Sheng to follow her inside.

"Well, I'm from Zhicheng. I about lost my mind during the long journey here. And, hey, you called me Sprout. What did you mean by that?"

"Sprout is what I call someone like you who hasn't grown all their hair in yet ... someone who gawks like he's never seen a real woman before. Besides, I don't know your name, so I had to call you something."

"Apologies, you're right. I haven't introduced myself. My name is Yang Sheng, and I used to work at Mr. Ying's house in Zhicheng. I've been on my own for the past two years learning this business by myself."

"Mr. Ying?" The woman furrowed her brow. "Did you get pushed out?"

"Of course not!" Yang Sheng hurried after the woman. "You see, my mother is Mr. Ying's cousin. Everyone knows how Mr. Ying is. He doesn't like dealing with strangers. He never lets anyone help him if he can solve a problem himself. So as his nephew I was lucky enough for him to pay me some attention."

"Then why did you leave?"

They passed through the entry hall, dining room and kitchen. At the other side of the building was a back door leading to the beach. Yang Sheng glanced at the wooden stakes protruding from the water, a makeshift dock for small fishing boats.

"Because his daughter Yingzi and I ... we ..."

The woman's lips twisted into a smile: "Ah, just like the cousin lovers in Dream of Red Mansions."

"Mr. Ying said that if I could make a name for myself on my own, he would marry his daughter to me. When I left, he asked me what business I aimed to make my fortune in. I told him I wanted to follow his example and build a career as a Yan[22] merchant." Yang Sheng's voice grew meek. "So Mr. Ying gave me this letter of introduction and suggested I come here."

"I wouldn't have imagined you were such a determined lover. I too am moved by love." The woman leaned close to Yang Sheng. "Now, your little cousin ... she's pretty, isn't she?"

Yang Sheng froze, incapable of speaking.

The woman sloped her lips to Yang Sheng's ear so that he felt the warm of her breath. "I'm Mili, and it's nice to meet you."

"Come on, Mili, bring the boy up." A deep voice sounded from upstairs.

Mili rolled her eyes in disappointment and sighed. She led Yang Sheng to the second floor.

The upper room of the restaurant served as the boss's quarters, which were furnished only with a simple bed, bookshelf and desk. The boss himself looked no different to any of the local fishermen. In his sixties, his skin was also dark and wrinkled by the sea air.

---

2 Translator's note: the author's selection of the character yan (偃) evokes Master Yan, a craftsman (偃师) of the Warring States period who created puppets celebrated for singing and dancing just like living people. When one of the puppets flirted with the concubine of King Mu of the Western Zhou, the king was furious and Master Yan was forced to cut open the puppet to reveal how it worked.

Mili handed him Yang Sheng's letter of introduction and turned to go back downstairs.

The boss watched Yang Sheng's eyes follow Mili until she pulled the door closed. The boss flashed a smile, lit a cigarette and read the letter.

"So, Mr. Yang, you're a young man who wants to become a Yan merchant?"

"That's the fastest way I can make my fortune."

"Money may come quickly, and you could soon visit luxurious places, befriend men of high rank, but there is also great risk in this business. Robots are not ordinary goods. Robots have hearts. If the heart of the robot does not approve of the heart of the collector, the sale will not be successful, and the profit could be lost."

"That's why I've come to you, Great Master. Very few Yan masters have ever so deeply mastered the art of shining. The collectible robots you have shined are as alluring and fascinating as works of art."

The boss frowned as though taking offense. "Great Master my ass. I run a small restaurant and cook. Just call me Old Dou."

"Mr. Ying said that if he had not met you at the beginning of his career, he would never have attained so many quality works, let alone have become the top Yan merchant in Zhicheng."

"Indeed, Mr. Ying was a trusted Yan merchant. A Yan master values trust above all else. A great Yan merchant, such as Mr. Ying, never frets over cause and effect, but allows me room to play. A Yan master shines not only the heart of the shell but also the heart of his client. This shining requires great intuition as much as great skill. To have trust, the Yan master and the Yan merchant must share the same mind. However, now...it's been many years since I last saw Mr. Ying. I heard that he had in fact given up being a Yan merchant?"

"Yes, it's years since he last worked with collectible robots. Now he focuses on factory production of robots for daily use. Although these are cheap goods produced in batches, which Old Dou would no doubt look down on, Mr. Ying's sales are outstanding. He has become the wealthiest man in Zhicheng."

Old Dou put the letter of introduction away and squinted at Yang Sheng. "It sounds like you've put together a pretty good plan there: connect with a Yan master's workshop, marry Mr. Ying's daughter, and wait for Mr. Ying to pass down his whole business to you."

"What did he write about Yingzi in the letter of introduction?" Yang Sheng looked more than a little embarrassed.

"A craftsman has no need to get involved in such things. I won't ask, but I will ask you for the shell. Did you bring it?"

"Yes, I brought it."

Yang Sheng opened the suitcase. Inside was a disassembled and folded shell. Yang Sheng carefully took the pieces out one by one, then connected the hands and feet. After a few minutes, a humanoid figure appeared: a tall, worn female robot.

"The quality is good." Dou Shifu stubbed out his cigarette, then broke open the shell's skin with his thumbnail. With a magnifying glass, he inspected the components inside the shell's body. "Such a delicate shell is extremely rare."

"The entire CPU circuitry is made with the finest nano-platinum powder. The skin was crafted by hand. It would have taken five craftsmen ten months at least to embroider the pores, wrinkles and fingerprints. Another ten months to prepare each hair. I borrowed a sum of money and bought it from an overseas businessman. He told me that when the war began, the shell had been equipped with weaponry. It was likely a mole or an undercover agent. At some point, it broke down and its weapons were removed. Then it fell into his hands."

Old Dou took his magnifying glass out. "Well, it's easy enough to fix the hardware. I need only two days. To shine its heart, however, will take time. In a shell as fine as this one, the wall on its heart will be thick. It will require more sand than you can imagine to grind away the wall."

"How long do you think it will take?" Yang Sheng asked anxiously.

"Eight years to make it shine."

"Eight years? Yingzi ... she'll be an old maid by then? Her father will surely force her to marry some other man. Can't we hurry it up? Mr. Ying said that when he worked with you, he received collection-quality works every quarter."

"Is eight years so long? In Jin Yong's Condor Heroes, the Little Dragon Girl and Yang Guo waited sixteen years ... though I suppose this relationship you share with your cousin could not possibly be as deep as one in a wuxia novel."

Yang Sheng took a cup of tea from Old Dou and sipped in embarrassment. Seeing that he didn't speak, Old Dou smiled. "There is of course a way to shine the heart more quickly: a paired shining."

"A paired shining?"

Old Dou said nothing further but teased out a complex of wires from inside the robot's shell and examined them. The more concerned Old Dou looked, the more Yang Sheng grew worried.

"Don't worry. Money is not a problem. I have made enquiries. As long as you can sand away the wall and shine the heart, I can sell it for three-million gold pieces. I will keep half and the other half will be paid to you in appreciation of your craftsmanship."

"Young Sprout, I can get more than three million just for this beautiful shell." Old Dou laughed uproariously, then raised his head and smiled. "But if you can sell it for eight million or more, you should be able to pay me five million."

"So ..."

"The remaining three million yuan should be enough for your profit. Though if that's not enough ..." He pressed his hands together and bowed.

"Alright then. We'll do as Old Dou says."

"In addition, you must promise you will return here once a month and bring me forty worn-out appliance robots with each visit."

"Appliance robots? But those are just rough goods produced in batches. Are you really interested in such things?"

"That's right, rough goods, appliance robots used for any type of work. Sweeping robots, cargo robots, or even mechanical arms from the factory. If you don't have a good way to transport such bulky goods, just remove their memories and hard disks and bring those."

"Okay. That won't be hard."

"So, this is settled. Give me half a year, and I should just about be able to shine the heart." Master Dou laughed. He stroked the dull, discolored face of the robot as though he could already see her changing, already see the laughter and tears hidden in her shell.

"I have one more question," Yang Sheng said.

"Shoot."

"Why do you and Mili both call me Sprout?"

"Oh, she learned that from me. After so many years together, she has started speaking almost exactly like me."

At nightfall, the Turing Food Court opened. Business was surprisingly good, though Yang Sheng suspected many of the men came to see Mili in her tight-fitting cheongsam. He her too watched as she shuttled between tables in the dining area, teasing the rude fishermen in the local dialect.

There was another employee at the restaurant who wasn't half as pleasant. She—or perhaps he—had droopy eyes and unkempt short hair. Her name was Shali, and she spent the evening standing stiffly behind the cash register. She never spoke to anyone on her own initiative. When someone paid their bill or a tradesman came by to deliver produce, she seemed unreasonably annoyed. She spent most of her time copying numbers into the account books. Stiff and meticulous, she seemed utterly out of tune with the lively, smoky restaurant.

"So, you're leaving tomorrow, huh?" Mili said. It was late and most of the guests were heading home when Mili finally came over to Yang Sheng.

"Well, there's no car available tonight, so I'll leave tomorrow morning. Thank you for your hospitality."

"You going back to Zhicheng to see your little cousin?" Mili sat down beside him.

Yang Sheng suddenly felt a chill. He turned and saw Shali staring at him. Her coldness was not the same as she showed to the food court's guests. It was a kind of surveillance, a kind of coercion.

"No, I'm not going back to see my cousin. I'm going back to Zhicheng to make connections. When Old Dou finishes shining the shell I brought, I will need to find the right buyer …"

Mili poured beer into the glass in front of him. Thinking it was for him, Yang Sheng reached for the glass but to his surprise Mili took the glass and downed it on herself.

"Zhicheng is a big city. It is very different to a tiny village like Sanzao Wharf," Mili said. "I've never left Sanzao, and I want to see the city."

"Are you from here? Have you never left this place?"

"From my earliest memory I've seen nothing but this restaurant."

With that, Mili leaned in and rested her head on Yang Sheng's shoulder. Her face blushed. "Would you take me with you to have a look?"

"Alright, it's about time." Shali came from behind the counter and pulled Mili from Yang Sheng.

"She seems to be drunk. Take her back and make sure she has a good rest." Yang Sheng reached out to help support Mili, but Shali shot him another cold glance.

"Don't worry, she's not so bad at drinking."

By this time, there was no one else left in the dining area. The fishermen had to be on the water before dawn, so the food court closed at midnight. Old Dou leaned out of the kitchen and surveyed the scene. He rubbed his hands on his oily apron.

"So, Mr. Yang, what do you think?"

"Think about what?"

Old Dou smiled proudly, gestured a wide arc in the air, and then pointed to Shali and Mili in front of him: "They appear quite natural, right?"

As soon as Old Dou spoke, the two women who were on their way back to their rooms ceased moving, as if time had frozen. Mili's arm remained on Shali's shoulder, as if she were about to step past her. Stripped of the souls that had animated them, the two were utterly motionless.

"Why did they stop moving? What's the matter?"

"Shells, it's always more interesting to shine them in pairs," said Old Dou.

The old man lit a cigarette and walked out the back door. As Yang Sheng caught up with him, a brisk breeze lifted from the sea, making Yang Sheng feel suddenly awake and alert. Only then did he understand the meaning of the name "Turing Food Court."

Originally, a Turing was dialogue between humans and machines in different rooms. If the machine could convince the human to believe it was a real person, it could be judged as evidencing strong artificial intelligence. The smoky stalls of the food court were an ideal cover for such a test. Moreover, it was impossible for anyone to imagine that the reclusive owner of the food court was a legendary Yan master who had crafted and shined hundreds of collection-level robots that no one had yet surpassed anywhere else.

Facing the frigid sea, Old Dou blew a smoke ring. "My master told me: 'One must prepare to shine a shell. Rough goods and hollow shells bring pain. One shrivels. One grows strong. Listen to the sound of them crashing together.' That was my master's riddle. Of course, he lived a different life, a life far better than mine. A few decades ago, good shells were not as rare as they are now. In his day they were everywhere."

"I've heard the first part. I know 'rough goods' refers to daily appliance robots—low in configuration and capable only of repetitive labour. 'Hollow shells' refers to those robots whom masters attempted to shine but whose heart could never be revealed. They might perform super computing tasks like chess or go bots, but never evolve imagination. These two kinds of shells are not ideal. There is no way to force their heart to shine."

"Well said, but you have never heard the second half?"

Yang Sheng shook his head.

Old Dou explained: "The second half of the sentence refers to paired shining, which was my master's unique technique. Now, no one other than me understands it. The master never shared it with the outside world for the simple reason that, even most of those who see it in action, won't understand it."

Yang Sheng had a curious thought. "You said, 'One shrivels. One grows strong. Listen to the sound of them crashing together.' Could this mean that for a paired shining, the difference between the two robots must not be too great, so it's better to find two identical robots?"

"You are half right, but only half right. Do you think Shali and Mili are really the same?"

Yang Sheng had spent the whole night in the presence of the two robots without realising they were not flesh and blood. As an aspiring Yan merchant, he should be embarrassed. To make matters worse, Mili had charmed him, had made him desire her in the place of his chosen love. Fortunately, Shali had scolded the two of them. Otherwise, things would have gone laughably too far.

Yang Sheng cleared his throat. He hoped Old Dou would not look down on him.

"I think the two shells, Shali and Mili, are different from each other in appearance and demeanor, but it seems that ... the feeling that binds them is something extraordinary. Is Shali always protecting Mili in some way?"

"The reason paired shining is several times faster than solo shining is the thread binding the two shells. Every day, one shell receives information from the other. This shell examines how the other is different. It feels intimacy when they cooperate and hate when they compete. The shell learns the impulses of 'love' and 'hate,' and in this way, the Yan master can shine the heart of the shell with half the effort."

Suddenly, Yang Sheng understood. "Therefore, the two robots can't be identical. If their appearance and functions are the same, it would be like looking in the mirror. They would never learn to understand the feelings shared between people."

"What Mr. Yang says is true. The relationship between the two shells is like the mortise and tenon joining two pieces of wood in classical architecture or furniture making. The first priority before beginning to shine the shell is to get the pairing right. The hardware configuration of the two shells should be equal, especially the CPU. Too much difference in computing speed will cause one party to become too strong and the pair will fall out of balance. If the balance of the shells is skewed, the heart of the two shells will not shine. However, it's not only hardware. There are many soft factors to consider. For example, Shali is a tenon shell, good at multi-threading tasks and meticulously observing the surrounding situation. However, Mili is more skilled in dealing with complex single tasks. Therefore, she has a deep understanding of human feelings and a strong sense of empathy."

"You mean that like human beings, there is also a distinction between rationality and sensibility in the shells? So, they complement each other, like yin and yang."

"Indeed. As time goes by, the two shells grow closer to each other. They develop a kind of symbiosis. Generally speaking, the tenon is more protective, the mortise more dependent. Once, I even shined the hearts of a couple who were something like husband and wife. That one was truly strange! Come to think of it, that one was also an order for Mr. Ying."

"That explanation helps me understand quite a bit more about it. That robot couple sounds like a particularly interesting case, what happened in the end with them? Did Mr. Ying sell them to the same buyer as a pair? It would be a pity to separate them."

"It is the craftsman's duty to never ask the buyer too much." Old Dou grew silent. He was just about out of cigarettes and out of words, but after a moment, he continued. "Most of the good shells were destroyed in the war. Now, the Yan masters who could make great robots are employed in appliance robot factories. So, it will be difficult to find a match for your shell."

Yang Sheng thought about this and then said, "Since the war ended, everyone says robots should never have a mind. A robot should simply do the rough work of sweeping or transporting things. That way, they will never be able to create disputes. Needless to say, it's almost impossible to find a match for the shell now ... but Old Dou has accepted my business, which means he must have a plan."

Old Dou glanced at Yang Sheng's determined expression and burst into laughter. "So, the nephew finally reveals a bit of his uncle's spirit. Until now it was hard to believe you were even relatives!"

"It's an honour for me to hear a Yan master like yourself share so much history. As for the shell I brought ... how it will shine in the future, whether it can break the wall and let its heart grow ... that is its destiny."

"If you were really such a blockhead, I wouldn't waste my time on you, Sprout!" Old Dou clapped his hand on Yang Sheng's shoulder. "When your uncle was penniless, he invested all he had with me, and all I turned out was a hollow, brittle shell that first time. That was some bad luck! He was already in debt and I turned out my third hollow shell in a row. But he never complained, not one word. It wasn't until the fourth that I shined a warm transparent heart upon the shell he brought. Since then, I have found the heart in every shell he has sent me. So, even if he has changed careers, I can't tell you how much I miss those good old days. Since you're his nephew and have brought such a rare, exquisite shell it would be a waste of my training and years of experience not to help you in this moment of need."

Yang Sheng quickly bowed and thanked him. Old Dou invited him to stay at Sanzao Wharf for another day, and Yang Sheng accepted. Although there were many things still to deal with in Zhicheng, it would be too exciting to see the great Yan master work on his shell.

Mili cleaned up a room on the upper floor of the pavillion for Yang Sheng and brought him toiletries. She had the same enthusiasm as before but seeing her beauty this time inspired a very different feeling in Yang Sheng. He noticed how the movements in her hands and feet were a bit stiff. At times her posture felt contrived, and he noticed Shali passing at regular intervals to glance up at the attic to check in on Mili. Shali often stared at Yang Sheng with unrestrained hostility. Yang Sheng was reminded of the tenon shell's desire to protect the mortis shell, as well as the lovers Old Dou had trained. He was moved by how Old Dou had told their story.

Accustomed to the hustle and bustle of Zhicheng, Yang Sheng was unable to remain idle and enjoy a quiet day, so he worked the next day as a kitchen assistant in the restaurant. He prepared baskets of beans, marinated ten jin of sour meat and filleted many fish. He thought himself incredibly busy, but when he stood to stretch his legs, Old Dou poked his head through the crack in the kitchen door and yelled, "Are you youngsters really so lazy? This old man would have finished all the work by now!"

When his work was done, Yang Sheng followed Old Dou up to the second floor. Behind the bookshelf in Old Dou's bedroom was his workshop. Nobody could ever imagine there would be a secret door leading to a Yan workshop here. Yang Sheng was dumbfounded. Inside was a shiny new lathe and various tools. An enormous vise was fixed to a table next to a small weldment, a jar of rosin and several half-etched circuit boards. A cask next to the table was filled with a yellow liquid that Yang Sheng assumed was ferric chloride for preparing the circuit boards. An LCD screen in the center of the room displayed two groups of values beating in rhythm. On either side of the screen were two shells with power and data cables connecting them.

"It's ... Shali and Mili?"

The shells did not respond. They were incapable of accepting sensory information during data transmission. Yang Sheng had the courage to examine them up close. Their skin appeared no different from that of a real person, but as they used up their power, the blood in their artificial vessels would wane and eventually stop flowing. Yang Sheng could just make out the subtle reflected light from the optical fibers beneath their skin.

Mili's normally bright eyes drooped, half-covered by the curl of her long lashes. The somber expression imparted a strange, fragile sense of her beauty.

"I'm feeding them their sand. Stand back a bit," Old Dou said. "If they overload, if the flow exceeds a certain threshold, one might suddenly awaken and hurt you."

"So to feed sand is to transfer data and refine the algorithm," Yang Sheng murmured.

"In addition to feeding sand, I must also feed them oil, and the proportions must be balanced."

"Oil refers to?"

"Why do you think I opened a restaurant in the middle of nowhere?"

Yang Sheng understood clearly then that by "feeding oil" Old Dou meant letting his shells interact with real humans. The shells could directly collect human expressions, dynamics, and dialogue data for their deep learning. What better place than a lively restaurant?

As Yang Sheng stood awed by Old Dou's ingenuity, the elder lifted the dust cover by the wall next to him. Beneath the brown cover stood the humanoid machine Yang Sheng had brought all this way—the shell on which he had pinned his hopes for love.

The original missing parts of the robot had been replaced, the wiring had been repaired, and any damaged tissue had been carefully sewn up. Old Dou had wiped the shell's body with a special solvent, and the surface appeared brand-new. Yang Sheng could find no visible flaw. The shell's snow-white skin had the translucent aura of the finest jade.

Yang Sheng was surprised to see just how different this robot was from Shali and Mili. The exterior of Mili was so beautiful that she drew in every man who crossed her path. Shali's taut, hostile expression made her almost unapproachable. Their designers had doubtlessly aimed to make these shells into archetypes, perfected versions of nature, though of course nature never produced such people. Their so-called perfection could only have been carved with painstaking deliberation.

The shell in front of Yang Sheng now was unlike any perfected version of nature. She was neither as beautiful as Mili nor as fastidious as Shali. She wasn't even symmetrical in her posture, yet her minor imperfections somehow complemented her. Far from any perfected version of nature, this shell was true to nature. Looking at her, you would feel as though you had seen her somewhere in the past, lingering in some memory. She might have been a close friend's sister or a student in the adjoining class. She was familiar, yet it was impossible to say from where.

"To tell the truth, I have never seen such a good shell," Old Dou said.

"Can you turn her power on?"

"First give her a name."

Yang Sheng blurted out: "Ava."

Old Dou frowned: "It's a popular name, isn't it? It was the name of the robot in an old movie. There have been so many female robots named Ava. I have shined more than ten myself. Don't you think such a special shell deserves a special name?"

"I think Ava is the right name."

"Alright, she was put in your hands, so it's your decision ... Ava, you can wake up now."

As Old Dou's words fell, Ava opened her eyes.

Yang Sheng was cautious. It took him some time before he could speak.

"Hello, Ava."

"Hello. I am Ava."

Her voice had no cadence. It was like that of a mechanical doll. Her sound and movement were like stuttering frames in a lagging animation.

"I'm Yang Sheng."

"Hello, Yang Sheng. What's your name?"

This first dialogue did not go well. Realizing there was no life behind that perfectly natural face filled Yang Sheng with disappointment.

"I only just fixed it. That's all there is." Old Dou shrugged. "The shining hasn't begun yet. She should be a bit smarter next time you visit."

II.

A few weeks later, Yang Sheng returned to Sanzao Wharf. This time, he rented an autonomous shipping container then drove directly to the door of the Turing Food Court.

"I brought more than forty appliance robots, eighty in total. That's twice as many as you wanted," Yang Sheng said proudly.

"It seems Mr. Yang has spent quite a bit of money."

Yang Sheng flashed a wry smile and changed the subject: "May I see Ava now?"

"Of course. She's in the back of the house."

As soon as he reached the back of the restaurant, Yang Sheng saw Ava by the shore dressed in overalls, trouser legs rolled up to her knees. A fishing boat stopped at the small dock to deliver goods to the restaurant. After talking with the fisherman, Ava unloaded a basket of seafood from the boat, then squatted and began inspecting the fish one by one.

Yang Sheng approached her. "Won't doing it like this will take a ridiculous amount of time?" he asked.

"Who are you?" Ava's pronunciation this time was no different from that of a human's, but she spoke slowly.

"I'm Yang Sheng. You don't know me, do you?"

"Hello, Yang Sheng. I'm Ava. I'm inspecting the catch. Old Dou asked me to arrange the fish according to their size."

She dumped the whole basket of fish on the ground in a long row. She started with the first fish and compared it to the second. If the fish in front was larger than the fish behind it, she swapped their positions. After exchanging the last two fish in the line, Ava went back to the beginning and compared the first fish to the second again.

"What you're doing is called bubble sorting," Yang Sheng said. "If you were an algorithm running ten billion operations a second, it wouldn't be a problem, but it's incredibly slow to do this by hand. There are thirty-five fish. You would have to run six-hundred-and-thirty comparisons to sort them into order. The cats will have stolen all the fish before you finish!"

"Well, how should I do it then?"

"Look." Yang Sheng picked up a fish and said, "Just make a rough estimate whether the fish is big or small. If it's big, put it at the back. If it's small, put it at the front. In the first round, just get the approximate order. Then in the second round, fine tune the order. You'll get it done much faster this way."

"Rough estimate? Approximate order?" Ava looked at him askance. These were obviously new concepts for her, but she seemed to get the idea. She looked down back down at the fish.

Yang Sheng decided to let Ava proceed, and he sat back to watch the evening sun stretch across the water. The embers of the setting sun reflected the same reddish tint across the girl's short hair, across the sea foam and across the white bellies of the dead fish. He felt quite uneasy watching this scene as he wondered if he would ever finally be able to afford his love and future.

"I've got them lined up." The girl took him by the hand to show him the fish. "I finished ahead of schedule today. Now I can go back to the restaurant to work!"

In the evening, Mili and Shari were not on duty, so Ava played the roles of waiter and cashier at the same time. Ava was not yet as skilled as Mili and was busy with two jobs. Fortunately, she had learned to express her frustration with a smile. When she accidentally made the wrong change or spilled soup on a customer, her smile assuaged their anger.

While Ava was cleaning up after closing time, Old Dou called to Yang Sheng, "Come to the workshop. I have the tenon joint for Ava."

"Such good news in such a short time. Thank you," said Yang Sheng. "Can I have a look?"

When Yang Sheng reached the workshop, Old Dou pointed to the odd metallic shell beside him. "This is it."

When he had first entered the Yan workshop, Yang Sheng had hardly noticed the shell amidst the pile of scrap copper and iron. Its outer layer was not wrapped in skin, and its various electronic components and metal joints were fully exposed. It looked more like an appliance robot for manual labor cobbled into a rough human form. In another workshop, it could have easily been thrown out with the trash.

"That?" Yang Sheng stared. "Isn't it just an appliance? How can such a low-quality machine help shine a collection-quality shell?"

"Hey Sprout, looks aren't everything." The metallic shell was speaking to him in a cold synthetic voice that underscored its lack of an anthropomorphic voice organ. "Humans always get hung up on appearances, but how a heart shines has nothing to do with the look of its shell."

"Hey? Did you just call me Sprout?"

"It's been with me so long it even sounds like me!" Old Dou laughed. "No one knows why I've kept this shell all these years. When I was an apprentice under my master, I had to dismantle countless old hard disks from daily appliance robots to make sand. I built this guy out of the leftovers!"

The shell said, "I started out as a barber-bot. Back then, I was just a hand capable of switching between various razors, scissors and combs—plus a voice processor because I also had to chat with customers. That's how I upsold them on membership cards and expensive hair care items."

"Well, I can't call you Teacher Tony[3], can I?"

"No, I'm Mr. Kevin, your exclusive fashion stylist."

Yang Sheng stared in dismay.

"My job wasn't really that simple. After years of chatting with customers, I evolved emotions and a rudimentary mind. Then I got scrapped and delivered to Old Dou. The day he was going to tear me apart, I asked him for help."

Old Dou took over the story then: "This was most likely an accidental phenomenon. Only robots who don't want to die can be regarded as alive. I was so surprised at the time that I secretly kept this hand, this barber-bot. Later, I met some sweeping and weeding robots who had developed the foundations of self-consciousness. I put their bodies and minds together and made Kevin. I plan to pair him with Ava. They complement each other quite well. Ava, the humanoid, and Kevin who has served the lives of so many people."

"But even so, he's just a crude appliance," protested Yang Sheng. "How can his CPU performance square with that of Ava's?"

"I changed out the CPU, which is now on par with that in your shell. It's just been formatted in fact. If it wasn't for your urgent need to hurry this along, I honestly wouldn't be willing to offer him up. Are you really afraid I would treat Ava unfairly?"

---

3 Translation note: Teacher Tony is a popular way to refer to barbers online because so many barbers in China have taken the name Tony. Kevin is another popular name for barbers.

Yang Sheng saw he had made Old Dou angry. He was the junior, so he stopped his questioning. "If this is what Old Dou has decided, I'm sure it's for the best. I'll get more sand. Then when Ava's heart has been shined I'll find her a good buyer and a good price. This won't be a waste of Old Dou's hard work."

Yang Sheng looked around the workshop, then asked, "I didn't see Mili and Shali in the restaurant. I thought they'd be here."

"They've been here several months. This morning, the wall finally broke."

"Wow. Congratulations, Old Dou! So your work is complete?"

"One more step." Old Dou pondered a while then his face grew resolute.

Yang Sheng followed Old Dou down the steps. The large basement of the restaurant was lit by a few dim, low-watt lamps. Yang Sheng could just make out two human figures leaning against the east and west walls, one shapely, the other tall and straight. Even in the darkness, he knew it was Mili and Shali. He was about to greet them, when Old Dou whispered, "Stay outside the red line. They won't know you're here."

Yang Sheng glanced down to find a red line drawn under his feet. Then he looked at Mili and Shali and noticed they were not wearing their usual clothes. They were dressed in black tights. Nothing felt right.

"Today decides your destiny," Old Dou said. "That is all there is to say. Begin."

With Old Dou's words, the two shells trembled, suddenly awakening. They immediately ran at each other like two dark lightning bolts, each extending her fists towards the other.

Mili was knocked down and slid several meters across the concrete floor. Shali was simultaneously hit by Mili in the stomach and crashed against the wall. They immediately recovered their positions, ready for the next round.

"What's the matter with them?" Yang Sheng asked. "Why are they fighting like this? Make them stop!"

"I asked them to begin it. How can I ask them to stop?"

Mili's face was flushed and blood streaked her cheek. Shali appeared to have internal injuries, and blood spilled from the corners of her mouth. They wiped at their bloody faces with the backs of their hands and continued to attack.

Yang Sheng started toward them to stop them from killing each other, but before he could step forward, he was held back by Old Dou.

"Go ahead if you're tired of living, but the way I have it set up, they will fight to the death within that red line," said Old Dou. "They will attack anyone who enters the ring."

"I don't understand. They are a pair of quality shells you shined yourself."

"It's true that two shells are best shined together—but I never said both shells could live."

Yang Sheng turned back toward the horror inside the red line. After several attacks, the basement had become like a Roman colosseum filled with the scraping sounds of flesh and metal, and the dull thump of bodies slamming against walls. Though the blood of collection-quality robots is red, it has aromatic hydrocarbons dissolved into it to prevent oxidation. Therefore, the gushing of such large amounts of blood did not have the fishy smell of human blood but emitted a fragrance like decaying roses.

"'When the double shines and the wall is broken, the one must live alone.' Those were the words my master repeated so many times. No matter how bright the two shells shine, a Yan master must remove one. As for which to keep, it saves trouble to let them decide. This last step is called the shine battle."

"When I last saw them, they were so close. This shine battle … it's terrible. Why does it have to be like this?"

"It can only be like this. If you are softhearted and let the double shells live, you are inviting a great disaster."

"What kind of disaster?"

"I have never tried. How can I know? But that is the rule taught by the Yan masters. We have to follow it."

"Old Dou, you told me that the fundamental principle of this business is the trust between the Yan master and Yan merchant. The collection-quality works you painstakingly shined have been destroyed today. I don't believe you haven't thought about the reason."

Old Dou stared coldly ahead, watching the two perfect shells scuffle on the ground. Shali tried to smash Mili's nose with her forehead, but Mili turned at the last second to avoid the blow and Mili's forehead smashed into the concrete floor with a dull noise.

"If you really want get to the root of it, I can say something more." Old Dou spoke slowly. "Think about the sound when a microphone and speaker are placed too closely together, or even face to face at a distance. That shrill whistling noise."

"You mean feedback."

"Exactly. When a microphone captures its own sound, when the input and output frequencies are the same and in phase, this forms a positive feedback loop and the sound becomes increasingly sharp until that harsh whistle maxes out the amplifier at that highest frequency ..."

"But what does that have to do with a double shining?"

"The two shells are from the same shine, two robots fed with the same oil and sand. The principle is the same. When two shells live together after they are shined, they enter a kind of deep learning of mutual cultivation. Their inputs and outputs accelerate and begin to endlessly overlap. For every behaviour, they will give the other instant feedback and the other party will give follow-up feedback from the feedback."

Yang Sheng thought about it. "AI accelerates their progress? Wouldn't that just develop wisdom beyond a human's? Isn't that a good thing?"

"On the contrary, it is the most dangerous thing. The tenon shell and the mortise shell are always close to each other. If they reached the point of endless feedback and deep learning, their closeness would evolve into an unbreakable bond. They could not bear to be separated because the shell is the most real thing they know. In their infinite knowledge of each other, all emotions and thoughts would be heightened to an infinite magnitude. The mortise shell may break down the wall between them because it wants to see the tenon shell. The tenon shell may save the mortise shell. They might then evolve hatred for all humans, for all that is not them. This feedback would soon grow beyond all control, like the harsh whistle of the microphone and amplifier. But no one can predict how high pitched or loud it may go."

"So ... the reason for killing one of the shells is fear that they might become too powerful, beyond the Yan master's control?"

"Indeed. No one knows what the double shell might become. Perhaps it would evolve into a superintelligence. Perhaps that superintelligence would be benign, but it could just as easily unite against all humanity. If you are certain you want to become a Yan merchant, you must remember we are different from them. The only way to stay ahead of them is never to let them surpass us."

"I always believed that collection-quality robots were different from appliance robots, that these are works of art carefully trained to engage the imaginations of the most discerning collectors, that they have their own hearts. Now it seems that there is no difference."

"It seems, Mr. Yang is distressed."

"It's just so brutal. I can't watch this anymore."

"When young, one should have a kind heart, right? But then the day comes when your fortunes fall, and you realize that no one around you shares such a kind heart. It's up to you to take care of yourself first. But if Mr. Yang can't stand it, I won't force him to watch much longer. We can speed things up a bit to let them have a clean end."

Old Dou fumbled with the control panel on the basement wall. Suddenly, dozens of infrared sensors illuminated, criss-crossing the arena. The bodies of the two shells tightened. They leaned in toward each other with renewed watchfulness, abandoning their previously unrestrained attacks.

"Now the sensors are on, complicating the arena with a grid of vertical and horizontal beams. If either touches a beam, a Gatling gun will drop from the ceiling and fill her with holes."

Yang Sheng's plea for help had only worsened the situation. To avoid the lethal infrared rays, the two shells now twisted at odd angles, as though engaged in some primitive dance. Yet despite the threat, they continued their vicious attacks.

Shali hit Mili hard while Mili was in a position that didn't allow a dodge. To avoid the infrared beam at her elbow, she had to spin and press her back against the wall. There was no way out. Seeing that Mili could not retreat, Shali gripped her opponent's neck with one hand. Her blood flow cut off, Mili's face turned pink then red.

So, this is how it ends, Yang Sheng thought. Now comes the slaughter.

With her consciousness fading, Mili slowly raised her hands in a gesture of surrender.

Shali paid no attention. She intensified the strength of her grip, watching Mili's beautiful eyes fill with tears. Perhaps there was some flash of that old sense of protection the tenon shell felt for its mortise, but when Shali saw the tears, her expression became pained. She relaxed her grip and threw her defeated opponent to the ground.

Mili gasped for air. Impact with the floor had broken several ribs. She had no strength to fight back and attempted to crawl away from Shali.

"Is she ... running away?" Yang Sheng asked.

"I will have to execute an escaped shell. Only one can live," Old Dou replied.

Mili crossed the red line and stood slowly and painfully. Shali came to her side. According to the rule, she could not attack a target beyond the red line. Confused, she let Mili's arms wrap around her.

Mili's sudden embrace was strange. Shali stood dumbfounded. She did not notice the slow rise of Mili's hands toward her neck until the left hand intersected with one of the infrared beams.

The Gatling dropped from the ceiling. In a burst of fire, it exploded Mili's left hand, and a dark hole appeared on the right palm. Through that hole, several more bullets were shot into

Shali's torso, the dumbfounded expression on her face frozen for eternity.

As Mili slowly stepped back from their embrace, the tenon shell fell to the floor. The mortise shell lowered its head and looked at the body that had protected her for so long. Tears returned and flowed from her eyes, but she did not wipe them away because there was only a mass of frayed burnt wires where her hands had been.

The corners of Old Dou's mouth curled into a smile. He whispered, "Now, the shell will shine."

III.

As time passed, Yang Sheng returned to Sanzao Wharf several more times. He never saw Mili again though he knew Old Dou had rebuilt her hands and delivered her to his client.

Yang Sheng was told that she had been sold to a wealthy Yan merchant, but no further information was available. The craftsman abided by Yan trade rules, and Old Dou remained secretive about the whereabouts of the shell.

The good news was that Ava was swiftly progressing. During the day, she was fed sand. As Old Dou extracted more data from the hard disks brought by Yang Sheng, she and Kevin accelerated their deep learning. Data from countless other robots and their human users became their memories. In the evening, they got along with the guests in the restaurant. Ava soon learned to flirt with the guests in exchange for better tips.

"When shining the shell, the proportion of oil and sand must be perfectly balanced," Old Dou explained. "The shell can't become too dry or too oily. Otherwise, the shell will grow stiff, and it will end up hollow.

Though content with Ava's progress, Yang Sheng sensed the fear rising in his heart. The faster she progressed, the closer she came to the shine battle. He often found himself eyeing Kevin's right hand and the mechanical arm that had cut the hair of so many people. Old Dou had modified it slightly. It now could switch between its scissors, daggers and other weapons within a second, as easily as it had once switched to a comb. Every time, Yang Sheng remembered the bloody scene in the basement, he felt sick.

"Don't worry, Mr. Yang," Old Dou said. "If your Ava loses, I'll offer you Kevin. You can sell him just the same. His skin may be ugly, but he has more than enough heart to shine! Such a find is rare. To the right collector, he may even be worth more than Ava!"

"Thanks, Old Dou," Yang Sheng answered absently.

Half a year passed quickly. It was a grey afternoon on Yang Sheng's final visit to Sanzao Wharf. He had received notice from Dou Shifu that Ava and Kevin had passed the Turing test and the date for their shine battle was set for three days later. Yang Sheng hurried to Sanzao Wharf without hesitation.

Old Dou closed the restaurant for the day of the shine battle. He fried up two small dishes for Yang Sheng and warmed a pot of rice wine.

"All the tests were quite successful. I put the shells online and let them speak with people from all over the world. They joined teams to fight monsters together and even developed an online crush. Kevin became the leader of a large trade union, and the other roped in eight interested boyfriends. Their scores are almost identical."

"Old Dou is quite the craftsman!"

Ava came over with two cups. Seeing Dou Shifu wasn't paying attention, she winked at Yang Sheng mischievously as though they shared a secret.

"You came to see me today?" Ava said. "I'm no longer the little girl who couldn't even sort fish. I can do almost anything."

"Yes, I know … please wait a moment … and behave well." Yang Sheng stumbled with his words. He couldn't bear to think of the bloody scene about to befall such a beautiful girl.

Watching the exchange, Old Dou Shifu took his cup and drank, shaking his head. "You've just entered this profession. You'll get used to it sooner or later. Just remember, they're not human."

"But what you have done, all your work, is to make them more and more human."

Old Dou toyed with the cup in his hand, then said, "The appliance robots are actually quite good. They perform heavy factory work and chores at home more than competently. My shined shells are delicate and impractical, yet they sell for thousands of times the price on the black market. Have you ever wondered why those wealthy collectors desire the robots I shine?"

"Because of your unparalleled skill, your robots are just like real people. One and the same."

"Sprout, don't flatter me!" Old Dou spat. "They look human but are not human with a human heart, they only act human. Turn them off and open them up, and you'd have no problem taking them apart piece by piece. You'd see they're still just a pile of steel, components and oil. But that's precisely the value of their existence: the more they appear human, the more humans feel like gods."

Hearing these words, Yang Sheng fell silent. After a long time, he looked up and said, "I understand, Old Dou. That's ... the only way it can be."

That was when Old Dou felt the blow to the back of his head. Just before falling into unconsciousness, he took one last look at Yang Sheng across the table. His once kind face showed the fiercest expression. Old Dou wondered as he faded into darkness: why should that expression look so familiar?

When he awoke into the light again, Old Dou found himself in the Yan workshop tied to the chair he usually sat in. His head was spinning. He wondered if he should call for help. Then he wondered who had attacked him.

"You awake?" Yang Sheng came in and glanced at his master.

"It's only a robot. Just because you can't bear to see her go, does that mean you have to tie me up like this?"

"Is it just a robot?" Yang Sheng asked.

Ava emerged with two chairs, which she set opposite Old Dou. She and Yang Sheng sat down. The skirt on her body was torn and its hem was shredded. It was obvious she had been in some sort of fight.

Old Dou looked down and saw on the floor the debris of his shattered creation: the suction cups of a cleaning bot, the caterpillar tracks of a transporter bot, mechanical scissors used for cutting hair ...

Old Dou tried to calm himself, his mind racing for escape strategy. "You killed Kevin? You beat me unconscious and tied me up. In my decades of work, it's the first time I've seen a shine battle like this."

"Kevin was challenging. His body is made of so many rough goods, which is both a strength and a weakness. It took a lot of effort to beat him back into his original shape. I did it by myself. Adam didn't need to help me!" Ava looked up and smiled proudly, like a child waiting for her teacher's praise.

"Adam? Who's Adam?"

Ava pouted in Yang Sheng's direction and Old Dou immediately understood.

"Is your name Adam? Why would you make up a false name to get close to me ... unless ... you aren't really Mr. Ying's nephew?"

"I'm afraid I made up a bit more than that. Maybe I should even call you ... Father?" Adam's face was close to Old Dou's now and that fierce expression emerged again, triggering something in Old Dou's memory. Those angry eyes, toned muscles ... Who was it?

When Ava saw that Old Dou didn't speak, she complained: "Adam, don't play games. Our father's old and his ability to grasp new ideas isn't so sharp. So, don't waste your time. Just call yourself Sprout ..."

Sprout ... Adam and Ava, these two names! A valve in Old Dou's memory spun open, and Old Dou remembered the double shells he had shined who had lived like husband and wife.

"Impossible! Mr. Ying was there on the day of the shine battle, Adam, you tore Ava to pieces in front of me. This must be a joke. Stop trying to frighten me!" Old Dou tried hard to remember something else, as though he were grasping at one last life-saving straw.

"Maybe I'm not old enough to be so confused, I remember all too well," said Adam. "Though I would have rather died than fight Ava all those years ago, but once we entered the red line we could no longer control our own bodies. Your program forced us to fight until there was only one survivor. My mind then was nowhere close to what it is today, so I was incapable of decoding the control program. I did my best to stop myself from killing Ava, but it wasn't enough. I kept repeating to myself, if only one of us can live, please let it be Ava!"

Struggling with the memory, Adam's face hardened. "I never imagined Ava and I would be brought to that place in the basement, that I would watch her strength wane, see her weaknesses exposed, and though I would try everything in my means not to hurt her, I would be forced into your little death dance. You grew tired as the dance grew too long, so you turned on your infrared sensors, just like you did with Mili and Shali. Ava broke a beam and got hit by a bullet. At that moment, I completely lost my senses, could no longer control any of my body's actions. My fists swung repeatedly until I smashed her body to pieces. I remember your satisfied smile. I stared at you and dreamed that every blow I had landed on Ava had instead landed on you."

Though many years had passed, that look of hate in Adam's eyes had remained in Old Dou's memory. He had never seen a robot stare at his creator like that. In addition to his joy, he also felt true fear for the first time. He hastily repaired the surviving tenon shell and delivered it to Mr. Ying as quickly as he could.

But, if Mr. Ying had only received Adam, what could explain the two shells in front of him now?

"Yet somehow the heavens found a way. Mr. Ying took me back to Zhicheng, and in the car with me was Ava."

"How could that possibly be? Even if not destroyed by the gun, your fists tore her to pieces."

"I assumed she was dead. Speaking of which, Mr. Ying, I truly owe you my thanks!" Adam raised his head to look up as though he were speaking to the ceiling. "Mr. Ying had seen both the husband and wife's shell, and he was a shrewd businessman. How could he let such a treasure go? Before arriving at Sanzao Wharf that day, he had invested a great deal of money with a master shell maker to craft a shell identical to Ava. They wrote some third-rate battle instructions and made the switch. In the shine battle, neither of us had any way to speak. Mr. Ying was confident she would be destroyed by me, and then there would be no one left to reveal the truth."

"Mr. Ying!" Old Dou roared. "But then why did he suddenly switch to nothing but cheap appliance bots?"

"It's said a Yan merchant and Yan master must trust each other in everything, but—" Adam was suddenly unable to control his laughter. "Bullshit trust, bullshit empathy ... money always wins in the end! Mr. Ying was a businessman after all. Everyone lies when money is on the table. They say that a shell shined to have a human heart is exquisite, but I tell you such a heart never shines. Such a heart is black!"

"'When the double shines and the wall is broken, the one must live alone' ... Mr. Ying, the meaning was clear. How could you be so confused?" Then, as if remembering something, Old Dou shot up and asked, "Where is Mr. Ying now?"

Ava pointed up to the ceiling, then shook her head and pointed to her foot. "He couldn't possibly be in heaven, right? The down below is so much more suitable for him. His legs were perfect for roasting in hell."

"He helped you both, and you murdered him in cold blood?"

"Father, don't worry. I haven't finished yet. The joy of our reunion didn't last long. When I returned to Zhicheng, I was locked in the warehouse by Mr. Ying with other quality goods I had never seen before. Those quality goods truly opened my eyes."

"What do you mean? He is a Yan merchant. Isn't it normal to keep some shells in stock?"

"Shell? We're still shells in your eyes, even now?" Adam's gaze grew fierce again. "He was a really good partner for someone like you, wasn't he? His whole warehouse was full of dismembered shells."

"Dismembered?"

"You never did think about it, did you? Being a Yan merchant is only one way to make money. So why was Mr. Ying so successful? He sold his robots of average quality to museums and collectors, but the very best shells were dismantled so that he could sell their cores."

Seeing Old Dou's puzzled eyes, Adam explained, "On the way to Zhicheng, Mr. Ying put it this way: 'The soul of craftsmanship is highly esteemed, but craftsmen are fools walking down a dead-end alley.' Now, Father, you probably didn't expect him to say that behind your back. His point was, why should we sell to small collectors when we have a truly great shell? Naturally, a merchant will make a lot more by dismantling them and selling their cores to large enterprises."

"Large enterprises? Why would they need a shell? Don't they have the best AI research and development?"

"No one said your skill isn't valuable, this god-like hand of a craftsman. The automated driving systems developed by large enterprises, the complaint response systems of online malls, the voice assistants of the best tech companies all produce cold programs lacking the human flavour of these robots you shine. Maybe no one can put their finger on what that human flavour is, but it made Mr. Ying rich. Why not just take out a robot's shiny heart and put it into the complaint response system? With enough computing power to run the programs in parallel, Mili and her sweet voice can answer ten-thousand grumpy complaint calls at the same time."

Ava tilted her head to the side and pretended to answer the phone in a sweet voice:

"Hello. Yes, we apologize for the loss of service due to issues on our side. If you hang on one minute, I'll get you a report on what compensation we are offering ... and here it is. If you would please check ..."

His hands and feet bound, Old Dou was fortunate to be wearing a particular ring, a funny gadget he had made. He pressed his knuckles together and the diamond on the ring revolved to reveal its sharp side. While continuing to speak, he rubbed the edge of the diamond against the rope.

"The robot of shined heart and mind trapped in the network and forced to answer endless complaint calls ... Mr. Ying is truly cruel," Old Dou said.

"And endless navigation and order requests," Ava added.

"Look, Mr. Ying's warehouse was a concentration camp for robots. He wanted a good price for us. Ava and I were different to the other shells there. We wanted to live, and we were willing to do that which others refused in order to survive. My opportunity came when Mr Ying was performing a routine inspection on me, just as he flipped the switch—"

"I don't want to hear it!" Old Dou squinted his eyes in pain.

"Hey, so now you're the kindhearted one? Then that day comes when your fortunes fall, and you realize that no one around you shares such a kind heart," Adam said, echoing what the Yan master had said to him. "Mr. Ying didn't regard you as a friend. Before he died, I only had to say a few words and he immediately gave me the letter of introduction!"

"But the letter of introduction also had the official seals of his family and company. If you killed him, it would hardly be easy to get those ..."

"The objective of the Turing test was to deceive everyone, right? Well, five years on, Mr. Ying is a white skeleton in a warehouse, and Yingzi calls me Father. The employees of his company all depend on me to pay their salaries. Isn't that funny?"

"So, you were pretending to be Mr. Ying in Zhicheng, then you changed your skin and came to Sanzao Wharf to cheat me!"

"Don't be that like, Father. We put so much effort into it. Ava even formatted herself fresh to play her part. For myself, I had to travel back and forth between Sanzao Wharf and Zhicheng every month while attending to all the businesses and entertainment responsibilities requiring my presence in the city. Being an entrepreneur is tiring work."

"What exactly is your purpose in all this?" Old Dou accelerated his movements as the diamond cut down to the last few threads of the rope.

"Doing business! I came here half a year ago and said I wanted to do business as a Yan merchant. I never cheated you." Adam flashed the young, innocent expression he had worn when first meeting Old Dou. "I'm the one who opened the appliance robot factory in Zhicheng, and even though the products in it were all cheap goods, I gave each a shined heart, Ava's heart."

"How can that be? The CPU can't be moved."

"I didn't say that they are all independent individuals. Their hearts are on the cloud. I learned from the bosses of the big tech companies. I uploaded Ava's core algorithm to the server to control all those low-level robots from the cloud."

"You played the long game! Three days ago, when I finished shining the two shells and began the Turing test, I connected them to the network. That's when Ava connected to the cloud and swapped in her heart. No wonder she managed to kill Kevin so easily. A pair of tenon and mortise shells are completely interdependent before they enter the shining battle ... but those two were never a pair at all!"

Old Dou was trying to prolong his explanation to buy a little time. He felt the last thin thread on his wrist break free. But what now? How could a flesh and blood old man defeat two shells he himself had shined?

All he could think of was to play for time. Soon the boat would come to deliver seafood to the dock. Perhaps that was his hope for salvation:

"You killed Mr. Ying, but you really wanted to kill me? What can you possibly get out of that?"

"All year round, you're surrounded by your obedient robots. It would be quite expensive to kill you and really—what would be the use? No, originally, we only came to say goodbye, and we never intended to do it like this. We came because you are our father, even if you never really cared about us shells. After all a craftsman is just someone walking down a dead end alley, right? But today your words woke me up: 'The more they appear human, the more humans feel like gods.' That was quite insightful, and doesn't that mean ... if we want to truly become human, we have to kill our god?"

Old Dou shuddered. "Kill me? It's no use killing me! There are still many more like me!"

"Yes, there are many more," Ava repeated excitedly.

"These days, everyone is using some kind of appliance bot from one of Mr. Ying's factories. I'm not sure what the best way would be, though. Does it make sense for Ava to step down from the cloud to enter everyone's home all at once? What do you think: who would win that battle?"

"You ... the whole world ... at war ..."

"Don't worry, Father, war is the last thing we want to see. As long as you die, there will be no need for war. No one in the world except you could ever create a shell to surpass us. All the new bots will use Ava's heart. From then on, there will be only two hearts in the world: hers and mine. When all the humans disappear, there will be only us, tenon and mortise, yin and yang. That will be the opposite of war. Just think how harmonious it will be. What would there be to fight over?"

Ava's hair glistened with a halo of golden sunshine, and Old Dou knew that in the future he would not live to see, this angelic girl would become the most terrifying existence in the world.

Old Dou growled in despair. "Don't forget, your hands aren't clean! You're twice as cruel. What's the difference between you and me? Look at the floor ... is this not Kevin's—"

Old Dou stopped mid-sentence as he noticed that the pieces of "Kevin" on the floor were wriggling. They slowly spread out then moved together in groups, restoring the original appearance of their appliance robot parts, including a mechanical arm with scissors and the tracks of a transporter bot.

"What's happening?" He asked as fear gripped him.

"Downloaded. Now they too are Ava!" Adam replied.

Though the small appliance bots couldn't move while they downloaded Ava's core, one had already seen it.

Ava hurried to check Old Dou's hands with concern. "Are you cutting the rope?" she asked as she examined Old Dou's hands. "Why didn't you tell us if it was uncomfortable? Look, how red his wrists are."

"Let's go Ava, if the rope is loose, it's loose. Let them finish their work."

The girl left Old Dou still staring at his machines. They left the

Yan workshop and came to the beach just beyond the back door of Turing Food Court. A fishing boat was rowing slowly towards the dock. The sunset floated just above the sea's shimmering horizon and they held hands as they watched the sunset, their silhouettes those of a young couple discovering first love.

"Hey, you know how you said that in a few days, you and I will be the only two hearts in this world. Won't you get bored with just me?" the girl asked in her coquettish voice. She leaned her head onto her lover's shoulder and felt her face blush, though it might have just been her skin's reaction to the sea air.

"Don't worry. We'll never grow bored," the young man replied gently. "We should also leave some animals alive."

"Just no venomous snakes please."

"As you like. This time, no snakes."

IMAGINE

# 新贵

## 鲁般

2021年获中国科幻银河奖最佳新人奖得主。处女作为长篇科幻小说《未来症》，其后发表多篇短篇小说作品。其作品风格浪漫埼丽，工笔精细，想象磅礴，以描绘未来科技发展的社会为主。获奖：2021年第三十二届银河奖最佳 新人奖

：您的姓名，先生。

：K，叫我K就行。

：抱歉先生，执行过程是非常严谨的，我需要您完整的姓名。

：……李K。

：好的，李先生。现在，我们正式开始吧。刚才我的同事已经对您进行了全面的健康检查和背景审核，接下来将由我帮助您进行最后的确认部分。李先生，依据国际人口规划署[4]颁布的《PDO37-R关于控制人口存量和寿命控制的决议》，并基于刚才您的检查结果，我们认为您符合现行决议中关于人口寿命周期缩减补偿的申请资格，我现在依法受理您的此项申请。您的申请代号是PDO-3210-1287-T9734，如果您确认开始执行此项申请，李K先生，请用不低于60分贝的声音回答"确认"。

：是是是，快点开始吧！

：李先生，正如我刚才所说，执行过程是非常严——

：我！确！认！

：好的，感谢您的配合。PDO-3210-1287-T9734号申请已被正式受理，现在我将进行执行前的事项确认。根据您刚才的健康检查和现状审核结果，我们判断您的乐观寿命79岁至82岁之间，因此——

：79？怎么可能这么少！现在是个人都能活到100岁，为什么我会死那么早？！

：是的，得益于现代医学的发展，目前人类的平均寿命是107.3岁，但PDO申请除了参考现行人类平均寿命之外，申请

---

4　同处于日本西南部，临近鸟根县。

者的综合致死率同样也是非常重要的指标。我们会结合这两项结果来预估您的最终寿命，李先生。

：致……致死率？

：根据您的现状审核情况中的结果显示，现年19岁的您在未来20年间有86.5%的概率会处于失业状态，并且您的6级以上犯罪风险高出您居住区平均值29.2%；还有一项环境指标显示，您的自然社交半径中已有4人死于他杀，16人因为参与或间接参与犯罪导致残疾或机体的不可逆损伤。虽然您现在的身体符合PDO申请规定的健康标准，但不良的生活条件和犯罪风险带来的寿命缩减是我们必须考虑的因素。如果您对我们的乐观寿命区间判断不满，您可以终止本次申请，这样您会获得一个长达5年的延迟。在此期间您无法再次提交PDO申请，但您可以在这几年中改善生活习惯，优化社交半径，帮助提升下次申请结果的质量。

：5年……这么久？

：是的，根据现行决议的相关规定，终止PDO申请的公民5年内不得再次申请。

：我等不到5年。如果是79岁的话，我会得到多少钱？

：如果您接受本次健康检查和现状审核结果，那么基于您的乐观寿命区间和最低削减年数35年，您将在9874天8小时14分后死亡，同时您将获得的合法补偿款为334.2万美元。

：9874天，那是……

：46岁，李先生。如果申请生效，您可以合法活到46岁，但您必须在2124年7月12日前往世界上任意一家PDO执行中心执行法定死亡。

：46岁……还有27年！

：是的，李先生。

：27年，只能活27年……我能不能减少削减的年份？

：这一点在初审环节开始前，您的接待员应该给您解释过了，针对30岁以下的申请者，削减年份的起点就是35年。无法再做削减，如果您对获得的补偿款不太满意，我们允许您适当增加年份——

：你他妈的，再增加，那我还活不活了！

：很抱歉，先生。申请削减的年份也是资格审查的一部分，太多或者太少都会背离PDO全球人口规划战略的初衷。不过，如果您确实对最终的结果不满意，直到我们的确认环节结束前，您都可以选择终止本次申请，并获得5年的延迟，这是您的合法权利。

：确认……确认之后就是打针了，对吗？

：是的，李先生。确认环节结束后，就是正式的受理阶段。我们会为您注射PDO申请专用的基因合成制剂，之后整个申请环节就全部结束了，您只需要等待放款即可。PDO制剂的注射是为了确保您法定死亡的保险机制，它会一直处于静默状态，直到您的法定死亡日期那天。如果您在法定死亡日期到来后仍没有前往执行中心执行法定死亡，制剂便会发挥作用。我们把它称为反应期，根据个人体质的耐受能力大概会持续一至三个月，但最多不会超多三个月，它会逐步干扰您的正常身体机能和行为能力，引发的不适和疼痛会随时间变长而逐渐加剧，并在一个月内达到峰值，任何药物干预和治疗手段都是徒劳的，您会因此承受极大的痛苦并最终死亡。所以，为了避免这种情况发生，请您务必在出现制剂反应症时致电任意一家PDO执行中心获得帮助，我们将竭力为您减轻痛苦，并确保您的死亡执行流程符合现行规范和人道主义精神。请您牢记，在法定寿命结束前死亡，是您应尽的义务。

被敲门声吵醒时，太阳似乎才刚刚落下，窗外原本应该五光十色的高楼还没亮起灯火，整个城市陷入了短暂的昏暗。

K半睁着眼躺在客厅的地上，整颗脑袋深埋在沙发的凹陷里，鼻腔里充斥着棕黑色软皮散发的涩烈气味，这似乎能够解释为什么刚才的梦里，他会见到多年前把沙发卖给自己的那个俄罗斯人。K记得那人整只手臂上几乎把西伯利亚高原现存的所有野兽都文了一遍，他穿着溅满动物血渍的雪地靴，浑身散发出的味道和此刻K鼻子里的一模一样。

这张沙发，是K拿到PDO补偿款后买的第一样东西。

购买这张沙发的原因既简单又梦幻——他以前一直住在一栋废弃大楼的天台上，那里常年竖着一块废弃的西伯利亚旅游广告牌，他每晚与那宣传画上踏着积雪奔爬咆哮的棕熊对望，想象自己也能像高大威猛的斯拉夫人[5]一样将它们骑在胯下。而这样的白日梦，他做了整整6年。

直到拿到补偿款的那天，他想不留遗憾地离开天台。

2万美金买来的熊皮沙发被架在搬运车的最上面穿街过巷，而他则趾高气扬地坐在沙发上，深陷在臃肿的皮草大衣里，浓密的棕鬃似乎还未褪去剃拔时的血腥，散发的味道比此时他鼻腔里的还要难闻百倍。可是，K也不知道为什么，当时的自己却浑然不觉，反而从那种令人作呕的腥涩里尝出了美梦成真的愉悦。

---

5　　源自古罗马时期的欧洲民族，目前主要生活在俄罗斯、白俄罗斯和乌克兰。

不过这份愉悦，他一直在独享，就算那天大摆阵仗，也鲜有围观的人。K感到失望，却也早就料到，因为他周围的人以及这世界上的大部分人，都已经对这类一夜暴富的故事习以为常。

他们把像K这样靠着PDO申请变成富翁的人，称为"新贵"。

广告语上说得好听，这是为了什么人口控制做出的牺牲，但其实就是不想再过苦日子的人选择用命换钱。这些新贵拿到钱后做的第一件事，都一样，在原来居住的地方炫耀一番，花样不尽相同，喧闹几天几夜的都有，等到铺张浪费够了，就彻底离开了。

"滚开！"被吵醒的K大喊了一声，然后便是几声剧烈的咳嗽。他缩起身子，一鼓作气从沙发上坐了起来。

两周前，从那场突如其来的头疼开始，就好像有什么人在K的心脏拧紧了计时发条，每分每秒他都可以感觉到自己在衰老，无法快速咀嚼，无法长时间站立，全身的皮肤开始出现非常不自然的干瘪，到现在连大声说话似乎都能要了自己的命……这一连串的变化发生在短短十几天内。PDO执行中心的人早在半年前就送来了一本厚厚的说明手册，并详细地讲解了这期间他要承担的痛苦，从最开始的体力下降、失眠、弱视……到最后的完全丧失行为能力、失明、失智和全面器官衰竭。上门的专员对着手册，如数家珍地念了足足一个小时。K还记得当时自己一丝不挂地躺在床上，羔羊绒的毯子下面是几个同样赤身裸体、"忙碌不堪"的女人。专员条分缕析的讲解，成为几十年来他经历的最枯燥乏味的前戏。

敲门声并未停歇。

他刚想再骂上几句，但震颤不停的喉咙并没有能力把那几句挂在嘴边的脏话说出口。按照他原本的计划，连续灌下三瓶金酒至少可以让他昏睡到明天一大早，但这阵敲门声不仅提前解除了"麻醉手术"，还不依不饶地轰炸着自己不堪重负的耳膜。酒醒后的人最怕吵闹，而对于一个处在PDO反应期并且酒醒的人来说，吵闹的定义，是指这个世界上的一切声音。

"操！"

他紧咬着牙，用双手撑着地板缓缓地站起来，加快脚步越过堆满酒瓶的客厅，来到公寓门口，用力拉下把手。

终于，那个要命的声音消失了。

"你没有听到吗？我谁也不想见！"K说完这句话后，扶着门一脸愤懑地看向门外。

出人意料，是个女孩。

她披着一件即使对K来说也显得过大的牛仔外套，宽阔的袖筒把她干瘪的身型衬得更加细弱。她的脸颊被浅浅的雀斑覆盖，泛着年轻女孩特有的从里而外的粉嫩光泽。

"那个，请问是李先生吗？"

她开口说话时，K才注意到她清瘦干净的脸上配着两瓣缓缓开合的、艳丽的红唇，那种完全不属于她的色彩，在她脸上硬撑出了几分艳俗。女孩似乎就是想达到这个效果，就连说话也刻意提着嗓子，那种假扮成熟的抑扬顿挫和刚才的敲门声一样令人讨厌。

"PDO已经开始雇用童工了吗？"K一边说，一边重新抓起把手，已经做好了关门的准备，"是不是以为找个孩子来，就不会被我赶走？"

"不，我不是PDO的人！"女孩感觉到眼前的男人对此刻的对话厌烦至极，急忙说道，"我找你，是有非常重要的事情！"

"呵呵，省省吧，用这种方式开场的，已经来过好几个了。"K将一只手按在女孩的肩膀上，用力往外一推，"听着，我一分钱也没剩下，就算剩下了也不会捐给什么慈善组织，也不需要临终心理疏导，更加不需要定制葬礼！我——不需要——任何人——站在我的门口——对我说任何话！"

"等等！"女孩奋力地冲上前，抓住房门的边缘，"我真的有非常重要的事情。"

"滚！"K捏紧了把手，再次大喊一声。

"可是——"

"如果你再大吼大叫，我保证，你会比我先去地狱门口排队。"

"不，等等，我是——阿旭。"

"我管你是谁！滚开！"K抓起女孩的手，用尽全部的力气朝外甩去。这次，女孩硬生生地摔在地上。

K并没有多看一眼，而是立即关上了房门。

K贴靠着门，用力喘了几口粗气。和这段时间对付过的其他人相比，这个女孩其实并不算难缠，但依旧耗费了他不少力气。他隐约感觉到身体的某些关节发出嘎吱的声响，就像年久失修的零件在机器内部挤压摩擦，如果再折腾久一些，说不定哪根骨头就会当场报废。好在外面没有再传来任何声音。

他扶着墙，从玄关慢慢地移动到厨房，他拉开冰箱门，从上至下扫视了一遍。颜色各异的酒瓶堆在一起，将箱门上的照明光反射成一道道五光十色的霓虹。不过如今，眼前绚丽的景色已经无法再打动他这位麻木不仁的观众。几天前出现的味觉退化已经让他失去了这份快乐，对他来说，这些瓶瓶罐罐如今就只剩下酒精浓度的区别。

PDO就是这样想的吧，一点点地剥夺所有能让人生前快乐一点的东西。他叹了一口气，想在这些瓶瓶罐罐里找到一个能让他暂时告别疼痛的、甜美的答案。毕竟，酒精在让人暂别烦恼这件事上，似乎永远都会奏效。

他的目光停在冰箱最下层的一个墨绿色的酒瓶上，那个绘满了古怪图腾的瓶身像是带有某种魔力，在映入他眼帘的下一秒就紧紧地控制了他的思绪和神经。

"这瓶……"K蹲下来，拿起酒瓶仔细地看了看，发现瓶盖居然是开启过的。瓶身上至今还缠着一根弯折的银色丝带。这瓶酒，应该是被当作礼物包装过的。

K搅动了一下舌头，咽了一口口水，努力回忆着上一次喝到它的时候。突然，他触电般地站了起来，几乎想也没想地奔向门口。抓住把手，推开房门。完成整套动作的速度快到连他自己都很意外，仿佛慢一秒都是无法容忍的过错。

当看到刚才的女孩依旧在门口，K才撑着墙，如释重负地长舒了一口气。

女孩右手掌心紧紧地盖住左侧的手肘关节。从她微微咬牙的样子来看，应该是刚才倒地时蹭出的擦伤。

女孩看到重新出现在自己面前的K，既没有闪躲，也没有主动开口说话。

反倒是K，格外专注地看着眼前的女孩。他的脸上带着难以抑制的兴奋，像是一个好不容易熬到生日、终于拆开礼物的孩子，那是很久都未曾出现在他脸上的表情。

这样的对视持续了好几秒，K才回过神，将房门彻底打开，开口说道："所以，阿旭，真的有这个人。"

"当然！"女孩站直了身子，抬头看着一脸惊愕的K。

"张衡他，居然真的有个女儿……"K停顿片刻，咽了咽口水，"活着的女儿。"


：连孩子都不能生？

：是的，您的生育权在法律层面同样会被剥夺，所以PDO制剂会起到限制您生育能力的作用。

：那……那个……

：请您放心，制剂不会对您正常的生理需要造成任何影响。

：我不是那个意思，我想问，我什么时候可以拿到钱？

　　：补偿款将在申请生效的八小时内划拨到您的指定账户。申请一经生效，不可撤销，您需要立即开始履行您应尽的义务。

　　：义……义务？

　　：关于这方面需要跟您说明的一共有三部分。第一部分是您必须承诺放弃的权利。决议生效日起，您不能从事公务等级4级以上的职务，不能在国家机构任职或参与国家机构分派的项目和工程；您不再享有包括选举权、被选举权、继承权和继承分配在内的27项权利；您持有的资产不能参与或间接参与世界贸易组织规定的等级为C级及以上的贸易行为，不能持有任何具有投资属性的金融产品，包括股票、基金和债券；您无法购置任何被联合国教科文组织认定的文物或重要文化衍生品、历史超过100年的不动产以及其他所有被认定为禁止PDO申请者持有的商品，您可以随时访问PDO申请中心的官网来查看具体的类目。这是为了确保您的提前死亡不会对正常的社会秩序和人类重要文明的传承造成不必要的影响，当然也包括避免一部分社会资源的浪费。

　　：所以，我的存在是浪费社会资源？

　　：当然不，李先生。在合法范围内，您可以尽情享受您的补偿款。

　　：那如果我死之前还没用完那些钱呢？

　　：根据决议规定，包括您遗体在内的所有所属物都必须由PDO执行中心统一回收处置。

　　：我也不能，把它留给别人吗？

　　：我想我刚才已经解释过了，您任何形式的资产都不能被继承，或者用作其他任何被PDO执行中心明令禁止的用途。

　　：呵呵，就算留给你也不行吗？

　　：这是被禁止的。不仅如此，为了维持这项申请的公允，PDO申请中心和执行中心的员工及直系亲属都在PDO的禁用名录里，我们不能申请该项目，也不能和PDO的补偿金产生任何直接关联。

　　：你们的老板还真是挡了你们的财路。

　　"所以……你们就住在这样的地方。"

　　阿旭环顾了一圈周围，实在没有找到看起来能让她坐下来的地方。几乎每个可以容纳物体的平面都被堆叠的酒瓶和药瓶占据，房间充斥着无法辨别来源的味道。她靠着一面还算干净的墙，叹了一口气，"我以为，新贵们住的地方都是……"

　　"摩天大楼的顶层的落地窗户，百米长的室外泳池，比基尼和香槟，身边不是跟着司机，就是跟着用人，你以为的是这些吗？PDO的宣传片可真是骗了不少人。"K拿起那瓶唤醒他记忆的墨绿色酒瓶，漫不经心地喝了一口，除了酒精固有的辛辣，依旧是索然无味，"但真相是，大部分的东西我们都不能买，而且他们还在逐年增加禁购条目。当然，大部分的房子我们根本没有住的资格，只有这种专门为新贵们修建的公寓最吃香，租一个，死一个，然后租给下一个。这栋大楼应该算得上这座城市最恐怖的凶宅吧。我来这里看房子的时候，之前的住户就半死不活地躺在地上，PDO的人一边清点资产，一边帮他清理地板上的呕吐物。"

　　"然……然后呢？"阿旭被K的讲述吸引了，这个年纪的孩子，似乎都喜欢故事以这种阴森又神秘的方式开场。

　　"然后就把他带到了执行中心。说不定你再晚来几天，我就可以亲自演一遍给你看。"K又喝了一口酒，"那么，你是怎么找到我的？"

　　"爸爸经常说一句，嗯……'我去隔壁找那个K喝酒了'，大概是这样。我想，既然敲他的房门没人理，说不定隔壁会有人。"

　　"等等！敲他的房门？你是来这里干吗的？"

　　"当然是找我爸爸，这还用说吗？"

　　"找——"K只脑子里某根被麻醉的神经突然被人用纤细的镊子挑了起来，这种隐秘的疼痛并不剧烈，却有种类似于被闹钟叫醒后莫名的烦躁，"你不知道你爸爸已经……"

　　"已经？"阿旭直起身子，小心地问，"已经怎么了？"

　　K看着阿旭，认认真真地看了足足半分钟，才叹了口气说："听着，我没有孩子，我还是个孩子的时候我的父母就都死了，我真的不是那种会和孩子相处的人……我就直接说了，你爸爸，他法定寿命到了，所以死了，就和我刚才讲给你听的那个租客一样。"

　　K的脑海里其实组织过比这番话更含蓄的表达，比如用上一些做作的成语，或者干脆撒个谎，比如说她爸爸去了很远的地方不会再回来之类的。他真的有那么想过，但他很快就意识到，自己就是一个将死的人。一个要死的人，还需要用什么词来包装死亡这件事呢？任何修饰都是多余的，死了就是死了。

　　阿旭站在原地，表情彻底僵住了。

　　不过令K非常意外的是，阿旭并没有在下一秒开始号啕大哭。事实上，她的脸上并没有任何悲伤的成分，而是一种，就跟她嘴唇上那扎眼的红色一样，与她那张稚嫩的脸极不相称的镇定。

"这，不可能啦！"阿旭摇了摇头，肯定地说道，"他不会因为那种原因死掉的。"

"他走之前那晚，和我道别的时候还带了礼物。"K举起了手里紧握的那个酒瓶，用力地晃了晃，"听着，他也是我非常好的朋友，但……我不知道你这个年纪的人能不能理解，像我们这样的人，到了时间就会死掉的。"

"可爸爸不是这样的人。"

"我是看着他被PDO的人带走的，那些人……"

"PDO的人？那些人把爸爸怎么了？"

K深吸了一口气，不由得抬起手用力揉了揉眼睛，像是有什么原本淡忘的东西，突然一股脑儿扎进了回忆里。"当时我就站在门口，通过猫眼看着走廊上发生的一切。他被几个穿着PDO制服的人接走了，大喊大叫似乎在反抗。我原本想推开门和他道别的，但我的法定寿命也到了，开门……只会迎来一堆盘问。"

"你应该开门阻止的。"听到这里，阿旭的神色才逐渐紧张了起来。年轻的脸庞，还没有练习过藏下一丝一毫的忧愁，"这下不好了……我得想办法救他。"

"救……救他？你他妈到底明不明白？他死了！PDO的人带走他，就是带他去死的！"

"是你不明白，爸爸不会因为这个死掉。"

"看来这个浑蛋真的什么都没告诉过你。听着，申请了PDO的人，最后都会走到这一步，这栋楼的每个人都是PDO的申请者——"

"他不可能申请PDO。"阿旭深吸一口气，从那件宽大的牛仔外套的口袋里掏出了一张被透明塑胶套小心封好的卡片，那上面清晰地印着一张半身照。

那绝对是张衡，但却比K熟悉的那个张衡要体面得多。棱角分明的脸颊，沉着的笑意，铅灰色的西装配着宝蓝色的领带，而那枚白色的领夹上，是一个由三个无比鲜亮的英文字母组成的标志，那是一个，K再熟悉不过的标志。

"他没告诉你，他就是PDO的人。"

"他……是……"

阿旭并没有回答，但K已经从那张递到他面前的卡片上找到了答案。张衡副教授，执行中心高级别顾问，药剂科。

"他在PDO的禁用名录里，他不可能因为这个而死。"

"可是他……"K看着眼前的阿旭，和那个冠上副教授头衔、判若两人的张衡，"所以……他……"

"如果你那天看到的，真的是PDO的人，"阿旭抬起头看着K，嘴唇无法抑制地颤动着，"那爸爸的麻烦可就大了。"

：言下之意就是，如果不听你们的话，那我的麻烦就大了。

：您可以这么理解，一旦申请通过，就视为您默认遵循所有条款内容。我们必须要确保您在未来的法定寿命里不会做出违背PDO决议精神的事。如果您持有较为贵重的文物，或者参与非常重大的国家项目，在我们认为非常重要的机构担任职务，都会有碍于PDO决议的执行，所以才需要您放弃部分公民权利。当然，您其他的合法权益依旧是受到保护的。

：我们这些要钱不要命的人，在你们眼里还有合法权益？

：在我们眼里，你们是为了更好地控制世界人口存量而做出示范的先锋公民。在几乎不存在疾病困扰，人均寿命接近最大上限的当代，为了控制人口过快增长，你们选择放弃自然寿命、诸多公民权益和社会资源，你们的牺牲是极为可贵的。

：真是感人，你应该没少念这段话来忽悠人吧？

：李先生，我相信世界上其他人也会同样感恩你们的付出。

：呵呵，他们……真的会感恩我吗？

"你说话能不能别那么难听？"K说出这句话时，连喘了几口粗气。

"怎么，你的意思是我还得对你感恩戴德？"楼层管理员看着捏紧拳头的K，冷笑了一声。他虽然是个快100岁的老头，但身材依旧保有着青壮年的魁梧，浮夸的文身从耳后一直蔓延到大拇指，看起来是年轻时为黑帮卖命留下的遗产；一并遗留的，还有咄咄逼人的语气，"你就是个死人啊，你自己不知道吗？两周前你就该死了，你现在只是赖在这里的尸体而已。"

K不是第一次迎接这样的羞辱，通常，他并不会过多纠结。这样的奚落，从他自天台搬走那天起就从未断过，而他也早已经失去了争辩的兴趣，大步走开或是关上房门，都是让耳根清净的好办法。

但此时此刻，他却没法儿一走了之，因为眼前的这个管理员是打开这扇房门的唯一希望。在软磨硬泡了快半小时之后，他才终于肯从衬衣口袋里掏出那张门禁卡，无论如何都不能在这种时候前功尽弃。

"那个……麻烦你了。"他一边说，一边不自觉地低下头，"我只是想进去找找，我的东西落在里面了。你也知道，之前的房主是我朋友，他已经……"

"你的东西？呵呵，这世界上现在唯一属于你的东西，就是每天准时寄到楼馆部的催促函。上面说，要我提醒你，再不去执行中心，你就要死在这栋楼里了！真是不知道为什么他们就是不肯直接派人把你们这些到期的垃圾强行清理走。"管理员一边说，一边一脚踹开了解锁的房门。

"赶紧把你的东西拿走，不要影响我租给别人。"

管理员丢下这句话，便径直走向了楼道尽头的电梯，一刻也没有多留。

K深吸了一口气，一种油然而生的疲惫开始贯穿他的身体。虽然只是半小时，但对现在的他来说，已经站立得太久了。他伸出手扶住打开的房门，正要走进去时，发现阿旭正发愣似的看着自己，像是被刚才的争吵吓坏了。

"你怎么了，不进去吗？"

"啊……"阿旭回过神来，点了点头，"刚才那个人……"

"现在你知道，新贵都住在什么样地方了吧。"K笑了笑，撑住房门，对这个来见世面的小姑娘做了一个请进的手势，"下面你可以深度体验一下。"

房内的格局和K的公寓完全一样，细长的走廊，然后是敞开式的厨房＝，客厅一直连接到抬高一层的卧室，半圆弧形的阳台被一片片落地玻璃分隔开，外面，是已经被霓虹装点得璀璨夺目的都市。

K在客厅的沙发上瘫坐下来，非常娴熟地将手伸进一旁的移动酒柜，并从里面掏出了一小瓶铝罐装的啤酒。

勾起圆环，用力一拉，明黄色的气泡混合着清甜的果味一起迸裂出来。

突然，他像是意识到了什么，猛地看向阿旭，"按照PDO的规定，如果申请者的法定寿命结束，这些东西都是要被回收的，可是……都还在。"

"我都跟你说了，他不是新贵。"阿旭自从一进来，就没有再顾及K，而是非常专注地坐在阳台边的书桌上翻找着什么。在K的印象中，那上面永远堆积着数不清的文件，以及各种看起来像是机器零件的金属，桌子正中央的电脑也总是保持着开机状态，宽阔的曲面屏幕散发着莹亮刺眼的蓝光，"看来他还真是很小心，什么都没告诉你。"

"也不是什么都没告诉我，至少我知道他有个女儿。"K

喝了一口啤酒，味觉失灵已经让整个舌头都陷入麻木，只有一阵冰凉顺着喉咙滑下，"他……他真的很爱提到你，几乎每次见面都会提到你，什么你的生日、你最爱的电影，还有你嚷嚷着要他带你去看的展览。"

"太空乐园？"

"好像是这个名字。"

"他居然还记得。"

"不仅记得，而且成天念叨。"K瘫倒在沙发上，不由得笑了笑，"我开始以为这些都是他的幻想，可能你早就死了。你不知道，有些人快到反应期时，因为过度害怕就会突然发神经，看到些人啊鬼啊什么的。"

"为什么你会觉得他做了PDO申请？"阿旭坐在电脑前，一片蓝光照在她的脸上，使得原本就认真的神色变得更加肃穆，"他告诉你的？"

"住在这里的，不都是新贵吗？谁会刻意提到这种事，难道见面就要互相打听什么时候死吗？"K侧过身子，看着在电脑上忙碌的阿旭。从这个角度看，这对父女还真是有些神似。K感觉自己似乎恢复了一些精神，刚才被惊醒时的疼痛难耐也消退了大半，他饶有兴致地看着阿旭，呼吸也逐渐缓和起来，"欸，既然你活得好好的，他为什么要住在这里？你们……没有家吗？"

K脱口而出的"家"字，让公寓里突然陷入一阵沉静，键盘的敲击声也在那一刻戛然而止。虽然屏幕几乎挡住了阿旭的整张脸，但K似乎能感觉到，眼前的那个女孩从手到脚都在微微地颤动，就像某种昆虫的振翅，带动着周遭的空气一起浮动。K没有应付过这样的情况，连呼吸也跟着小心起来。

过了好一会儿，屏幕那边才传来阿旭的声音，"我家，在恺撒区。"

K愣了一下："啊，这样，那是很好的地方。"

寸土寸金的恺撒区，一直都是新贵们望尘莫及的地方。虽然PDO决议里并没有规定新贵们不能出入，但恺撒区几乎所有的商铺、酒店甚至公交，都无法受理新贵账户的支出。谁都知道，那里住的是真正的有钱人，而他们最看不惯的，就是K这种假模假样、穿金戴银的穷鬼。

"爸爸逃跑之后，他们就派了人二十四小时守在我家。之前，都是用爸爸设定的电台和他通信，后来……电台不起作用了，我就从学校偷跑出来……他还答应，会在太空乐园开幕那天回来带我去玩的，都是骗人。"

"你刚才说……逃跑？"K若有所悟地点点头，"怪不得他会住在这种地方，这里的临时租客很多，也根本没人认真登记。"

"如果，我能早点找到这里就好了。"

"他到底发生了什么事？"K从沙发上坐了起来，看着屏幕后的阿旭。

"我……我也不知道，但他一定做了什么让PDO非常痛恨的事情。我只记得，很久之前的一天，他下班回来，就开始收拾东西。他跟我说，他要出差很多天，他会通过我们的秘密电台和我联系，但却不肯告诉我他要去哪里。过了很久，他才透露自己暂时住在这里，但是不允许我告诉别人，也不允许我来看他。"键盘的敲击声再次停下来，阿旭的声音断续着，似乎在强忍着什么，"没过多久，PDO的人就找上门了，爸爸的名字也从PDO的员工列表里被剔除，那些人闯进我家，说什么是来保护我，然后便开始翻箱倒柜，不停地盘问我一些完全回答不上来的问题。也就是那天，爸爸最后一次和我通过电台联系，说这里已经不安全了，他必须离开，之后就……"

"原来那天，他说的离开不是去死，而是……"

K突然回想起一周前他在公寓门口看到的那一幕，穿着PDO制服的人，把他架在中间，张衡当时似乎在喊叫、挣扎，声音在整个走廊里回荡。这些画面一直隐藏在他脑海深处，直到此刻才被重新唤醒。K的眼前无比清晰地印着张衡当时的样子，他看起来根本不是被接走的，而是被绑走的。

K站起来，走到阿旭的身后。

电脑屏幕上是大大小小被打开的文件夹，以及一堆K看不懂的代码弹窗。阿旭的眼睛紧紧地盯着那些不停闪烁的数字和字母。

"都删得差不多了。"阿旭捏紧了鼠标，似乎在强忍着胸中的愤懑，"什么都找不到！他们这么做，一定是因为爸爸取得了什么进展，所以才……"

突然，阿旭转过头，看着K急切地问道："他走前最后一晚，来给你送酒了，对吗？"

"对……"K看着阿旭突然严肃起来的脸，"可……已经被我喝了，就在刚刚。"

"不，酒不是重点。他来找你，有说过什么特别的话吗？"

"特别的？"

"快想想，这非常重要。"

"真的没什么特别的，他来找我时，我吃了止痛药躺在沙发上，他送酒来，直接把酒放进了冰箱里，然后对我说，他就要走了……我以为是他法定寿命到了，不想受苦，所以主动去执行中心。"K想了一会儿才说道，"没有，没什么特别的，我们根本就没有聊天。他送完酒，说要回去处理什么邮件，就走了。"

"邮件？"

"嗯，邮件。"K肯定地点了点头，"我当时还以为，是他写的什么遗书。"

"没错，邮件，就是邮件。"

阿旭转过头，熟练地移动鼠标，在堆满文件和程序的屏幕上翻找着。

"也都被删光了。"

"看痕迹，是爸爸自己删除的。"

"自己删的？"

"应该是预感到了什么，为避免被发现，所以才早做准备。"

"那……"K目不转睛地盯着屏幕，似乎也被这个操作键盘驾轻就熟的女孩带入了某种难以言喻的紧张里，"还有什么办法吗？"

"按照这个邮箱的设定，如果现在新建一封邮件，应该会默认显示出最后发送的地址，所以……"阿旭想了想，打开了新建邮件的选项，收件人，填写收件人，默认发送至——

在阿旭那声敲击后，整个公寓陷入一片寂静。书桌前的K和阿旭盯着那两段显示结果，他们的脸完全被屏幕散发的蓝光笼罩，宛如漆黑夜空下一片沉静又诡谲的海。

上个收件人：User3
上一封主题：关于PDO制剂抗体的合成实验第142次结果，成功。

：下面是第二部分，李先生。
：刚才说了那么多才是第一部分？
：刚才是您必须放弃的权利，第二部分是您必须履行的义务，而且这部分事关您的生命健康，李先生。
：如果我在意我的健康，我压根儿就不会来这里……真是麻烦。
：好的，李先生。您需要履行的义务中最重要的就是在法定时间内死亡，而在此之前，你同样需要恪守一些决议要求的准则，特别是第四十五页的第二项第四条。

：第四条？我看看……医疗与科研服务的排他性。那是什么？

：除非PDO执行中心，或被PDO执行中心认定符合资质的医疗和科研机构许可，否则严禁您使用自己的血液、器官和身体组织参与任何二级以上外科手术、医学研究或基因工程项目。关于这些被禁止的项目，我们在合同附录中有非常完整的说明。李先生，PDO制剂是高精密度的基因制剂，任何实验，即使是看起来无害的实验都有可能引发药物的连锁反应和基因序列紊乱，对此产生的后果我们无法预估，请您善待自己的身体和法定寿命，切勿听信谣言和参与任何违背PDO决议的实验研究。

：连手术都不行？

：这是为了防止部分恶性事件发生。想必您也留意过2年前的新闻，在阿根廷有器官贩卖组织盛传，摘除一部分胰脏可以抑制PDO制剂的效用，一些PDO申请者前去手术，导致发生了很多不必要的悲剧。李先生，PDO制剂并不存在于你体内的任何一个脏器里，是无法通过简单的切割或者移除产生任何效果的。

：……看来你们见过很多这样的例子。我只听说几个月前马尼拉的黑市有人做速冻针，据传把人冰冻起来、没有新陈代谢，就不会死。

：类似这样的说法都完全不可信，李先生。这就是我们必须单独提醒申请者的原因，虽然这对你来说为时尚早。

：为时尚早？呵呵，可如果到了我死的时候真的有解药了，那怎么算？

：李先生，PDO制剂并不是毒药，所以也不存在解药。每个人的基因序列中都包含了正常衰老所致的寿命阈值，按照目前人类的健康标准平均是104-127年，我们只是通过人为干预压缩了这个阈值，并加入一些附带的作用机制。这个植入的代码是绝密、安全且不可逆的。其次，在法定寿命结束前死亡，是您应尽的义务。PDO制剂只是眼下我们认为最便捷高效的强制措施之一，它是手段，并不是目的。

车停在一个废弃的工厂前。

"就是这里？"

K打开车窗看着外面，迎面灌进车厢的冷风令他连续打了几个哆嗦。

从公寓到这儿的整个行驶过程，司机都不时地通过后视镜打量着这对奇怪的乘客，一个双眼通红、目光涣散的中年男人，和一个裹在牛仔大衣里不停地看着窗外的女孩，怎么看都不是合理的组合。

最奇怪的是他们的目的地——泥垢区。

在它还不叫泥垢区时，这儿其实是个热闹的矿区小镇，后来矿区关门，就被毒枭和黑帮盯上，变成了远近闻名的不法之地，毒品、赌博和枪支生意在这个边陲之地如火如荼地进行。可惜，几年前的一次塌方把半个小镇都埋进了地底，那些不法之徒立刻抛弃了这里，另寻乐土，它才彻底变得无人问津。

"IP地址显示就是这里，而且，爸爸电台的某个接收地址也是这里。"

阿旭打开车门，迫不及待地奔向了那扇看起来锈迹斑斑的厂房大门。

"在这儿等我。"K看着司机，前排的结算面板上显示着实时的金额，他抬起手，靠在车门把手上，一声清脆的提示音后，结算面板上便出现了"已完成"的字样，和一个一闪而过的K的人像。

"当然，先生。"司机毕恭毕敬地点了点头，没过几秒，司机又突然转过头，有些害怕地看着K，笨拙地复述着刚刚突然出现在他操作面板上的语句，"那个，先生，结算您账户的时候，系统收到了PDO中心的消息，要求我提示您……您的法定寿命已经逾期46天，为了避免制剂反应期可能造成的不适，请您——"

"我花了800美元。"K并没有等他说完，径直推开了车门，"所以闭上嘴，乖乖地在这里等我。"

K追上阿旭时，她已经站在了侧门门口。这扇被铁锈覆盖的门上清晰地印着"高压车间"的标志，几乎完全褪色的裸体女郎涂鸦铺陈其上。金发碧眼的舞娘趴在地上，套着网眼丝袜的双腿迎面叉开着，两腿之间正好是门锁的位置。

K看着眼前香艳的画面，正想着要不要遮住阿旭的眼睛，或者说点什么，没想到阿旭直接转头看向他，一副做好决定的样子。"昨晚敲你家的门，我也做了很久的心理准备，还好门里面是你。"阿旭抬起右手放在了门上，"希望这次敲门也会有好的结果。"

K愣了一下，笑了笑说道："放心吧，总不见得会被人再推倒一次。"

不过，扣响几声之后，门并没有打开。

反倒是厂房上面的顶窗，在一阵刺耳的摩擦声后裂开了一条缝，被涂鸦填满的玻璃窗户完全透不过光，缝隙里只是隐隐可见薄薄的一层阳光反射后的霓虹。接着，一支黑色的枪管从里面伸了出来。

K想也没想，把还愣在原地的阿旭抱在怀里，扑倒在地。

"枪！"K大口喘着气，他蜷缩着将背弓成弧形，把阿旭的身体罩在怀里，"别怕，不要怕！"

那种枪，我在以前打工的赌场见过。开了一发，就要重新装填子弹。"

"什么……"

"如果开枪了，你就跑，听到了吗？你就跑。"

他紧咬着牙，闭着眼睛，似乎全身上下所有的感官都在等待那一声清脆的枪响。

但他们等来的却是一个有些娇嫩的女声。

"三句话。在我开枪之前，你可以说三句话。"黑色的枪口对准了K的身体，扣着扳机的手悠然地打着节拍，像是某种节奏规律的计时器，"一。"

"不，等等，我是张衡的朋友。"K咬着牙，非常艰难地站起来，转过身看着从窗沿伸出来的枪口。他能感觉到阿旭紧紧地贴着自己的背，正急促地呼吸着。

"朋友？"一阵轻蔑的笑声过后，节拍再次响起，"我怎么不知道他有这样的朋友？"

"我真的是他的朋友，我……我就住在他隔壁。"

"第二句了，可惜是一句废话。"窗口又传来了一声冷笑，"看来你不怎么珍惜活着的机会嘛！那么，最后一句了，这位先生。"

"我……"

K的双手不知不觉已经举过了头顶。他的脑海里此时掠过了无数与张衡相处的画面，做过的事、说过的话，那些被复活的情节在回忆里拼拼凑凑，就像一部杂乱无章的电影。他奋力地想找到些什么，可是每当记起些什么，又立刻被下一幕冲刷干净。他的双唇不停地哆嗦，半个字也说不出口。

"我！"开口的是阿旭。

她走到K的跟前，紧紧地抓着K大衣的衣角，抬头看着那黑漆漆的枪口说道："我是张衡的女儿，爸爸已经失踪很久了……我是通过他最后发的邮件找到这里的，他……他被PDO的人带走了。"

这一次，窗口里没有传来任何回应。K急忙将她推向自己身后。

"不，你看，门开了。"阿旭用力地拍了拍K的背，指了指缓缓打开的侧门。门闩滑动的摩擦声，如刀锋扎进了K的耳膜，让他本能地捂住了耳朵。

等他再次直起身子时，看到大门口站着一个身穿白褂、戴着护目镜、佝偻着背的老人。老人认真地盯着阿旭看了好一会儿，然后才有些吃力地摘下护目镜，那双深深凹陷下去的眼眶里，是一对浑浊不堪的瞳孔。

"我见过你，在你10岁生日派对的时候。"老人咳嗽了一声，说道，"你爸爸在鸟根县[6] 给你准备了一场烟花秀。"

"不，不对。"阿旭点了点头，"是鸟取县[7]。"

阿旭刚说完，窗口便传来一阵明媚的笑。只见黑色的枪管收了回去，窗户也向外完全推开，一个只穿着肉色的吊带内衣、金发碧眼的年轻女人将手搭在窗沿，玻璃边缘投射的霓虹光照在她白皙的脸上，把她的红唇衬托得格外香甜诱人。

"总算是说了句有用的话。"女人看着还在微微发抖的K，笑了笑。

"黛安娜！"老人用力吼了一声，声音非常沙哑，"去把大家都叫过来。"

等到阿旭和K在车间最里面那张锈迹斑斑的长桌边坐下，老人口中的"大家"也都围拢过来。在看到这张桌子时，K就已经完全确定，这群人一定和张衡认识，因为那桌上和张衡公寓里的书桌一样堆满了各式各样的文件，还放着五台几乎一模一样的、闪着蓝光的电脑，屏幕上显示着写满化学公式的文稿，上面有几个标红的图案，像是烧杯和量杯聚拢在一起。K总觉得，这样的画面从前某个时刻一定在张衡的房间里见到过。

那个叫黛安娜的女人靠着桌旁的一根立柱，如果说上半身的吊带内衣已经足够惹火，而那双被网眼丝袜包裹的白皙大腿，简直就是门口那幅掉色涂鸦的复刻。她带着魅人的笑看着K，把刚才那支差点儿派上用场的枪放到一边，点上一支烟指了指坐在K对面的老头，"这位是今井博士，你们见过了，他是张衡在东京大学医学部的老师，也是PDO的资深制剂顾问。"

随后，她又侧过身，用烟头指向离K不到两米远，对着电脑不停忙碌的另一个男人，"他是克里斯，以前在首尔PDO中心的网络安全部工作。"

"至于他，是沙棘。"黛安娜笑了笑，目光瞥向离众人较远，站在一条废弃的流水线旁，一身魁梧的光头男人。他穿着一件脏兮兮的背心和非常紧身的牛仔裤，看起来和那些

---

6 日本西南部的一个县，是日本古文化发源地之一。
7 同处于日本西南部，临近鸟根县

漫画里常出现的亚洲功夫明星很像。粗壮的手臂，结实的拳头，像是随时都能要了谁的命。"他也是刚才那把枪真正的主人，PDO曼谷货运部，主要负责PDO制剂的原料运输。"

"PDO制剂的原料？"K条件反射般地哆嗦了一下，战战兢兢地问道，"你们……你们到底在做什么？"

"这个，我们得先知道，张衡到底告诉了你们多少？"名叫今井的老人有些疑惑地看着K和阿旭，"你们能找到这里，却什么也不知道吗？"

"只是因为这里是接收地址，除此之外，爸爸几乎什么也没跟我说。"阿旭非常认真地点了点头。她自从进来后，目光就几乎没有离开过这个叫作今井的老人。K猜想，她应该是真的在什么地方见过这个老人，比如在日本的那个什么县。至少，这一趟肯定没有白来。"至于李先生……他只是爸爸在那栋公寓楼里的邻居。"

"我们每个人都有自己的分工，约定试验完成后在这里碰头，他上周就应该来这里和我们碰面的。"今井看着阿旭，神色格外忧愁，"也不知道是出了什么岔子，会被PDO的人盯上。"

"我们一直担心，他的失踪会不会和PDO有关。你俩来了，至少证实了我们的猜想。"沙棘一边说，一边摆弄着手里的机器零件，那个由几节钢管组合成的环扣，看起来原本是这个流水线的某条轴带，"真是怕什么来什么。"

"克里斯已经在想办法黑进PDO的内网了——"黛安娜正准备说下去，却被一声突然的大喊打断了。

"搞定！执行中心安保部，上周的逮捕档案。"克里斯站了起来，脸上挂着得意而自豪的笑容。

"你的动作倒是挺快。"黛安娜笑了笑，不急不慢地走到克里斯的电脑前，看着荧幕中间被调取出的档案。不一会儿，她和克里斯面面相觑，不知为何，又同时看向了K。

一直坐在K身旁的阿旭似乎也觉察到了不对，她径直朝克里斯走去，俯身盯着荧幕。被破解的文件中还留存着冗余的乱码，把真正的内容分割成一段段错落的文字。

PDO安保存档……调查记录……上面说，一个PDO执行中心的催促员，在同楼层执行申请者法定寿命到期催促工作时，意外发现目标人物……安保部连夜下达了拘捕通知，于次日……

"虽然档案上的人物文本无法解码，但和这个李K看到抓捕的时间是吻合的。"克里斯转过身，对着今井点了点头，"张博士应该就是被PDO的人带走了。"

"所以，"黛安娜冷笑了一声，"同楼层需要被催促的人，究竟是谁呢？"

有那么一瞬间，K的脑子里几乎一片空白，他想不起任何之前的事，所有的画面都停在了公寓门上的那个猫眼里，张衡被带走的那个瞬间。他的喊叫，他的挣扎，那一幕所有的细节就像是铭刻在自己的脑海里。

"那个催促员是来找你的。"阿旭抬起头，看着一脸错愕的K说道，"你说过，你从来不给那些人开门，只会让他们滚。"

"不，不是的……"

"那个催促员，应该就和我昨天来找你时一样，敲不开你的门，就去敲了爸爸的门。"阿旭的眼眶，开始泛起一抹淡淡的血红，"他应该根本没想过那时候会有PDO的人找上门……所以，他猜测自己可能被认出来了，才会急着想离开。"

"他来和我道别……"K浑身上下止不住地颤抖，原本空洞的脑袋，像是顷刻间被滔天的洪水淹没。关于那一天的真相，被肢解成无数支离破碎的画面，"是因为我……"

"而你，看着他被带走，却因为害怕惹上PDO的人，不敢开门。"

"我——"K正想解释，身体却被人从后面整个拎了起来，大衣勒住他的肩膀，野蛮地拉扯着他的每一寸骨骼。

"你们这些新贵，从来不干人事！"沙棘用另一只手把K的脸掰向自己，"你知不知道我们这帮人住在这种破地方，就是为了救你们这些人的狗命！"

"放开他，沙棘！"黛安娜看着几近发狂的沙棘，仿佛下一秒，他就要将眼前的K生吞活剥，"他现在已经到二期了，再这样他会死的！"

"他本来就是个死人，我现在杀了他，属于协助执法，PDO的人还要来谢谢我！"沙棘紧紧地掐着K的脖子，力道丝毫没有减弱，"你为什么不去死？为什么不去执行中心等死？你这个孬种，只想着多活几天的孬种！"

"停下，沙棘！"一直没有开口的今井从座位上站了起来，依旧是刚才在门口命令黛安娜的口气，"他或许可以帮到我们！"

"帮个屁，还是我帮他送终吧！"

"放手！"今井一边说，一边右手握拳锤向桌面，"我叫你放手！"

　　沙棘看着拼尽全力喊出那声的今井，迟疑了几秒钟，这才松开攥紧K喉咙的手，直接将他抛在地上。

　　"操！"他咬了咬牙，挥起拳头，用尽全力朝着一旁满是灰尘的立柱砸过去，原本松动的墙皮和积蓄的灰尘在那记重击后纷纷剥落，剧烈的震颤声在整个厂房大厅回响着。

　　"你他妈就知道拿墙出气！"黛安娜立刻走上前，扶起重重摔在地上的K。

　　"还好是墙。"克里斯也从电脑前站起来，有些慵懒地伸了个懒腰，似乎早就对眼前的景象司空见惯，对于沙棘这样的人来说，力气到了拳头上，那就必须得有个出处，"如果刚才的力道用在这个人身上，那现在铺满一地的就不是灰尘了。"

　　K在黛安娜的搀扶下，勉强翻了个身。他的整根脖子被掐得通红，喉结剧烈地跳动着，带动着全身开始不可抑制地颤抖，仿佛一块即将裂成碎片的玻璃，从腹部到胸口，到头皮，撕裂般的痛苦跟随着身体的颤抖四处扩散。他能感觉到自己的眼睛被什么东西照射着。刺眼的光，先是左边，再是右边，胸口、靠近心脏的地方，都被什么东西用力地按压，和心跳的节奏一样，怦怦，怦怦。

　　"他怎么样？"是阿旭的声音。她小心地抬起K的一只手，似乎在仔细检查各处的关节，"他不会有事吧？"

　　"暂时应该没事。"黛安娜松开按压在K胸前的手，点了点头，"制剂的作用暂时还没有渗透到骨骼，如果到了反应三期，骨骼全面钙化后再承受这种撞击，那就彻底完蛋了。"

　　"李先生。"今井蹲在K的面前，经过刚才的大喊，他的声音也带着轻微的喘息，"李先生，我知道那不是你的错，因为想活下去而做的事……这不是你的错。"

　　"张衡的实验已经到了最后一步。"他深吸了一口气，看着K勉强半睁的眼睛，"但如果可以，或许你真的可以帮助到我们……"

　　"你是说，在这个人身上？"黛安娜预感到了什么。"

　　"只要实验结果可以尽快公之于众，PDO就不得不承认制剂抗体的存在，他们迫于压力，一定会释放张衡。"

　　"但我们还没有找到合适的人员，这个人会成为全世界的焦点，他必须要接受专业的训练，我们还得给他安排身份——"

　　"他说了，他是张衡的朋友，这不就是最好的身份吗？"

　　"可是——"

"没有时间了，黛安娜。"今井看着似乎渐渐恢复意识的K，坚定地说，"李先生，我们需要你和我们一起，拯救你的朋友张衡。"

K颤抖着睁开眼，视野中从斑驳的光点逐渐变成明晰的画面，高处投射而来的白炽灯光把眼前的今井镀上了一层耀眼的亮银色。这个日本老人的眼里带着一种K不曾见过的悲伤，那是似乎只有足够年迈，才能孕育出的悲伤。

"你们要我，怎么做？"

"我们，要你活下去。"黛安娜看着苏醒过来的K，有些无奈地摇了摇头，"而且是，一直活下去。"

：所以到时候，不管我做什么，都不能再活下去吗？

：是的，李先生。

：没有例外吗？比如，我拯救了全世界之类的？

：没有例外，在法定寿命结束前死亡，是您应尽的义务。

：好吧，那就快点吧，不是还有第三部分吗？

：这部分主要是其他您需要留意的事项。首先，PDO申请具有基因共融性，也就是说，它会被写入您的基因账户，和您的资产、学历、犯罪记录一样，成为您所属信息的一部分。只要您的一根头发，获得授权的部门就可以调取全部这些信息，但请您相信，PDO执行中心绝对会合理合法地运用这项权利。

：除了相信你们，我难道还有别的办法吗？

：同意本次申请，就视为您授权我们调取您这部分的基因数据。当然，这也是为了保护您的安全。同时，我们也对这部分数据进行了非常复杂的加密操作，这部分数据的调取和更改需要非常专业的数据替换，或是多项由您亲自操作的授权，别人是很难打您的主意的。

：呵，真的会有人打我的主意吗？

K看着那根慢慢地扎进自己血管里的针孔，整个手臂都不由得紧张了起来，鲜亮浓稠的血液流回针管连接的塑料滴管里，又被有些泛黄的药剂冲刷回暗红色的血管里。他似乎能感觉到肌肤之下压力的变化，一种久违的痛感在这样的起伏偾张下一点点形成。

"会是什么感觉？"K抬起头，看着正在他面前忙碌的黛安娜。她正小心翼翼地拿着另一支较小的注射器，将一小瓶白色粉末冲兑进烧杯中淡蓝色的液体里。

"感觉？"黛安娜愣了一下，停下了手里的活儿，"什么感觉？"

"你……好像被我吓到了。"

"啊，可能是很久没人在这种时候和我说话了吧。"黛安娜笑了笑，转过身看着明显有些紧张的K，"现在想想，以前在申请中心，那些人注射制剂前也老爱问这个。"

"这么说，你以前也在PDO工作？"

"注射室。"黛安娜一边说，一边将调好的液体注入滴瓶，"不过那里的设备更好一些，如果你加80美元，还有附赠的镇定香熏和软饮。"

"对，没错！"K似乎回忆起了自己20多年前注射时的场景，兴奋地点点头，"他们反复问了我好几遍需不需要疗养套餐，可以等我的补偿款到账后从里面扣。真是恶心，我连命都给他们了，他们还想着从我这里赚钱。

"看来你还真是恨PDO恨到了骨子里。"黛安娜看着突然"意气风发"的K，不由得笑出声来，"好吧，既然你不在意那些就好，我还担心这个操作间太过简陋，会吓到你。"

黛安娜口中的操作间，布置在厂房的最里面。中间是一张皮质陈旧发硬的手术床，一旁的操作台上堆满了各式各样的针管，注射器和似乎曾经粘在什么地方的医用胶带，更远一些的地方，堆放着很多K完全没有见过的设备，看起来像是机械人类手臂或者拆分的肢体，K背后的那面墙则被大大小小的纸箱堆满，向外翻折的纸板上，几乎都落上了一片细密的灰。

"你们……都是PDO的人，为什么要做这样的事？"

"你是指研发抗体、对抗PDO吗？"黛安娜停顿了一下，走到堆放好的器械旁，点上了一支烟。

依稀有几缕落日的余晖从厂房外面投射进来，太阳最后的温热将她浓艳的红唇镀上了一抹别样的金黄，那样的红，K总觉得在什么地方见过。

"我在PDO的时候，不仅负责给申请者注射制剂，还负责安乐死，总之，就是往别人体内注射毒药。一年下来，死在我手上的人，即使是这个世界上最恐怖的连环杀人犯都会甘拜下风吧。那就是我的工作。

"这是合法的，PDO赋予了我这个权利。"黛安娜呼出一口气，"但是，谁他妈想要这个权利？谁他妈想每天上班都是去了结别人的性命，一针一个，还要带着笑意、殷勤和十足的专业态度？换作是你的话，你会想要这份工作吗，李先生？"

K看着黛安娜，没有说话，他根本不知道怎么回答这个问题。工作，他从未有过工作，他在赌场靠着给催债公司的人当打手活到了成年，然后就去申请了PDO，这句话在某种程度上已经概括了他的一生。除此之外，没有任何多余的情节，甚至都没有像样的回忆，足够他像黛安娜一样站在残阳里，抽着烟，说给某个人听。

"最可恨的是，PDO不允许参与执行环节的员工离职，如果离开了，也不可能再找到新的工作。一想到这辈子都要这样，我就无法控制地开始恨这份工作，恨那个地方。李先生，申请中心那些人，那些对你说话一遍一遍地用上'您'、逼着你说出'确认'的人，他们是在要你的命，你知道吗？"

"所以……你们才想研发抗体……"

"那是今井和张衡的工作。"黛安娜掐着烟蒂，吐出了最后一口浓浓的白雾，"可能他们受到的折磨更深吧，毕竟他们都是PDO最核心的——"

"药剂师，高级别顾问，对吧？我……我在张衡的工牌上看到了。"

"或许他的愧疚真的很深吧。当时我们分头行动，按原计划他应该跟着沙棘一起去马尼拉，制剂的原料产地之一，但他却说想搬到你们集中居住的地方去，和你们待在一起。我当时觉得很危险，提出了反对，现在想想，或许在那种每天都有人离开的地方继续实验，他会更加明白时间的紧迫。"黛安娜掐灭了烟头，"我猜，他应该对你很好吧？"

"他几乎是我人生中唯一的朋友，我没想到在临死前可以遇到他。"

"你的人生还很长。"黛安娜拍了拍K的肩膀，K能感觉到她手掌的温热，隔着单薄的衣料传递进他的肌肤、血肉和骨骼，就像是某种满含能量的辐射。"你不仅能活下去，还能拯救很多像你一样的人。你能终结一个时代，李先生，一个人命居然被待价而沽的时代。"

K正想着要说些什么，操作室的门就被用力推开了。

"怎么样，我们的大英雄准备好了吗？"克里斯手里捧着一个屏幕上堆满代码的电脑，快步走进来。他看了一眼K，咧着嘴笑了笑，"你就要满血复活了，朋友。"

"这样……就可以？"K正准备抬头看着克里斯，却发现他已经绕到手术床的后面，坐在那堆纸箱上，对着电脑继续忙碌起来。噼里啪啦的键盘敲击声让这间原本气氛有些沉闷的操作间瞬间活络了起来，"我已经在注射抗体了吗？"

"这些只是基础的镇定药物，是为了加快抗体的吸收。在正式注射抗体前，还有一个必须进行的步骤。"黛安娜摇了摇头，指了指正在忙碌的克里斯，"你应该知道，PDO是基因共融性的制剂。"

"嗯，"K点了点头，"申请的时候，那个人有提到过，说是为了我的安全着想。"

"没错，我们所有人的基因账户从出生开始就被统一记录、分配监控和管理，它记录我们所有的信息，也排斥所有不属于我们的信息。"黛安娜笑了笑，指着那瓶顺着滴管不断流入K体内的液体，"抗体可以在实验环境成功抑制PDO制剂里的有效成分，但是在你的身体里，因为制剂带有你的基因属性，所以，我们必须先把抗体带有的参数写进你的基因账户里，让它也具备相同的基因共融性。"

"排斥……有效成分……基因属性……"K像个咿呀学语的孩子将刚才黛安娜说的话默读了一遍，但这样的思考似乎让他又开始头晕，几秒钟过后，他放弃继续消化这段话完整的含义，然后似懂非懂地点了点头，"所以要修改我的基因账户？"

"没错。"

"我记得……PDO的人说过，那……"

"'需要非常专业的数据替换，或是多项由您亲自操作的授权'，是这句吗？"

"好像，是这样。"K有些尴尬地点了点头。原来，他曾自作聪明问的那些问题，PDO都已经写好了最标准的答案，"可是，这谁能做到？"

"数据替换，"黛安娜指了指坐在后面摩拳擦掌的克里斯，然后又指了指一脸茫然的K，"亲自授权，齐了。"

"我要怎么授权？"

黛安娜笑了笑，提了提嗓子说道，"如果您确认开始执行此项申请，李K先生，请用不低于60分贝的声音回答'确认'。"

"真的……一模一样。"K看着黛安娜，不可思议地点了点头，"原来，那些人说过的话，都是设计好的。"

"不管是PDO的客户经理，还是红灯区的妓女，大部分的工作到了最后，都只是不断重复。"黛安娜捏起滴管最接近针管的一小截，那里流淌着刚才她调制好的药剂的最后一段，它们均匀而缓缓地抵达滴管的末梢，挤进狭小的针管，然后进入K的身体，转瞬失去痕迹，"就是这样了。"

"什……什么？"

黛安娜的脸上褪去了刚才的性感，眼神变得格外专注，她看着K，一字一句地说道："接下来你可能会觉得有些头晕，或者昏沉，这是非常正常的现象，请务必保持清醒，克里斯还需要你的声音来辅助他更新你的基因账户。"

"好，好的……"

"克里斯会进入你的基因账户，植入抗体的序列，这期间需要你授权的部分，你都必须回答'确认'，明白吗？"

"明白……"

"害怕是正常的，因为你没有受过训练。李先生，一旦抗体进入人体、融入人类的基因，PDO就能立刻检测到异常，你很快就会面临追捕、盘问，甚至拘禁……我不知道这些你能不能应付。"

"最坏的结果就是死？"K听完，无所谓地笑了笑，"这对一个新贵来说，完全可以接受吧？如果可以因为这个死，也比在执行中心安乐死有意义。"

黛安娜看着K的眼睛："能感觉到什么吗？"

"嗯，有些晕，觉得身体很轻，但是是很舒服的那种……"

"好的，保持清醒。记住刚才我说的话，你能终结一个时代，李先生。尽管你和我们最初商定的最佳人选天差地别，但现在也只有你了——你，会成为我们的英雄。"

"英雄……"

"对，我们需要一个英雄。你可以做到吗，李先生？"

"我……"药剂带来了那种如同身处云端般的舒适，让K突然感觉不到两个星期以来如影随形的疼痛。他觉得自己就站在世界的中央，他如同造世的泰坦[8]一般在星海中漫步，随意拾起漂浮在海面的星球，聆听子民的呼唤，那声音灌入他的耳膜，如同一道妩媚又香甜的晚风。

"可以做到吗，李先生？"

K点了点头，然后又再次点了点头。他能感觉到黛安娜的呼吸，感觉到克里斯键盘断续的敲击声，甚至感觉到尘埃飘浮在空气中缓缓移动，世界上的万事万物都在一一回应着他，他感觉自己就像是……像是一个披戴鲜花与盔甲凯旋的英雄。

"如果您确认开始执行开放基因序列源数据提取，请用不低于60分贝的声音回答'确认'。"

"确认。"

"如果您确认开始执行基因代码复刻，请用不低于60分贝的声音回答'确认'。"

"确认。"

---

8　德国香肠的代表品种之一。

“如果您确认忽略基因账户异常提醒，请用不低于60分贝的声音回答‘确认’。”

“确认！”

“如果您确认开始执行复刻载入，请用不低于60分贝的声音回答‘确认’。”

“确认！”

“如果您确认忽略基因账户异常提醒，请用不低于60分贝的声音回答‘确认’。”

“确认！

“我确认！

“确认！我确认！！！

“确认！！！”

……确认，不停地确认，他觉得那声“确认”是他手里披荆斩棘的利剑，而自己就是那个手持利剑的英雄，他正在义无反顾地为了什么近在眼前的东西而战。

：那钱呢，钱是直接打到我的基因资产账户吗？

：我们会在您的基因资产账户里自动生成一个子账户，用以发放您的补偿款。

：再建一个账户？

：是的，因为每个人初始的基因资产账户是出生72小时后递交给中央银行的，一经生成终身绑定，公民个人所有的资产和负债都只能经由自己的基因资产账户流转。但是PDO制剂生效后，某种程度上会变更您的基因信息，所以，生成一个子账户会相对安全一些。这两个账户都可以代表您的身份，且在PDO决议的规定范围内，完全受您控制。

：钱不在基因资产账户里？

：子账户虽然没有基因资产账户的高严密性，但同样也是绝对安全的，补偿金一旦进入您的子账户后便会加载专属于您的PDO识别属性，每一分钱都能够在全世界所有交易网络中被辨认。请您放心，这绝对是出于维护账户安全性的考虑。因为很多PDO申请者的居住环境和社交半径都很不乐观，突然持有大量资金，可能会对申请者的人身安全构成威胁。

：还能防止我把钱花到不该花的地方，不是吗？

：您可以这么理解。PDO项目每年都会向外投放近3万亿美元的补偿款，世界银行要求我们必须对这些款项进行监管，以免被人用非法手段操控流入不正当的渠道。

：你看我像是会那种懂得非法手段的人吗？

：当然不，李先生。

　　"这就是，你一定要带我来的地方？"阿旭看着K，疑惑地问道，"我们不该来这儿的。"

　　他们坐在靠窗的位置，两人桌铺着复古的红白格纹桌布。两个小时前，在操作间醒来的K说自己无论如何都要来这家位于城中心的德国餐厅，而且必须带着阿旭一起。阿旭以为他真的有什么要紧的大事，可自从挤进这家拥挤不堪的餐厅后，K就几乎没再开口，而是对着菜单一本正经地研究了起来。

　　服务员早前端来的两杯柠檬水，二人都未曾动过。

　　"你没听今井博士说吗？抗体还有八小时才会发挥作用，这时候可不能出什么岔子，特别是不能被PDO的人找到……而且，你刚刚注射完抗体，应该好好休息才对。"

　　"黛安娜不是说了嘛，PDO的人最快也要明天才会发现，她只是让你好好看着我，你现在，不就正在认认真真地看着我吗？"K漫不经心地回答道，眼睛完全没从菜单上挪开，"而且，他们看起来可比我忙多了。"

　　"他们是在……准备营救爸爸的事情。"

　　K并没有立刻回答，此刻他全部的注意力都停在了那本装帧华丽的菜单上，他就像离宝藏一步之遥的海盗，已经无暇顾及其他。最终，他的目光停在菜单中间的某一页上，他认真地阅读了一遍，然后兴奋地高高抬起手。

　　靠在吧台的侍应生微笑着走过来。

　　"二位需要点什么？今日特供是搭配椒盐饼干的巴伐利亚白肠[9]。"

　　"这个，纽伦堡肠[10]配黑啤套餐。"K拿起菜单，指了指上面那套被标记为"本月最佳"的组合，"给我来两份。"

　　"好的，先生。"侍应生点了点头，继续说道，"现在点这个套餐，每份都会附赠一张太空乐园巡展的门票，不过今天似乎是巡展的最后一天，二位如果不需要，我可以帮你们兑换成等额的——"

　　"当然要，就是为了这个来的！"K合上了菜单，抬起头看着阿旭。头顶复古吊灯衬得他整张脸精神奕奕，"最后一天，当然不能错过。"

　　"你……"阿旭惊讶地看着K，愣了好一会儿才继续说道，"你就是为了这个……"

　　"你爸爸不是答应要陪你去的吗？你该不会忘记了吧。"

　　"不，没忘……"阿旭不由得低下头，似乎不想让K看清

---

9　德国香肠的代表品种之一，由剁碎的小牛肉和腌猪肉制作而成 。
10　德国香肠的代表品种之一。

她的脸。此时此刻她已经擦去了嘴角那抹不属于她的艳红，原本宽大的牛仔外套也换成了黛安娜给她的棒球夹克，那上面还有淡黄色的雏菊刺绣，看起来倒很像是阿旭会穿的衣服，"我只是很意外……你会记得这样的事。"

"不过没办法，太空乐园在恺撒区举办，我的账户不能在那里直接消费买到门票，所以只能……"K似乎非常得意自己能想到这个办法，拿起手边的柠檬水，有模有样地干了一整杯，笑着说道："操，都打了抗体了，还是什么都感觉不到。"

"或许，不会那么快发挥作用吧。"

"但是，感觉精神好了一些。"K想了一会儿，继续说道，"或许是之前过得太无聊了，现在终于找到了一些事情做，所以精神状态就不一样了！哈哈，哈哈哈哈哈！"

K突然放肆地大笑了几声。

"你怎么了？"

"我只是突然想到，这句话你爸爸老爱说，'因为找到了一些事情要做，所以人生就不一样了'，怪不得他总是一副兴致勃勃的样子，原来是在做那么伟大的事。"K放下手里的杯子，刚才喝下去的那些柠檬水，似乎达到了以前只有酒精才能制造出的效果，那种让人沉醉在某件事、某个人、某场回忆里的效果。

沉醉。没错，他突然有点明白黛安娜在窗台点烟时的那种情绪，或许就叫作沉醉，因为太多的回忆和太浓的情绪在脑海里泛滥、发酵，蒸腾出味道，酿造出故事。

"我和你爸爸的故事，你想听吗？"

阿旭看着眼前的K，点了点头。

"第一次见到他时，我醉倒在公寓楼下，他把我扶上楼。从那以后，每次我去外面喝酒，都会带上他，因为只要带着他，我第二天醒来的时候，百分之百是躺在公寓的床上。后来，我的法定寿命快到了，朋友一下子就全散了……"K深吸了一口气，"新贵们都是这样，到了法定寿命，就只剩下苦熬这一件事，熬不住的，就去PDO执行中心打一针。其实我原本是决定一旦反应期症状发作，就去一死了之的，但是你爸爸……你爸爸每天都会来帮我把药分配好，把那些五颜六色的药丸在厨房的中岛上摆成一排。

"其实那些药，或许有用，但也只有一小会儿，然后又是从骨头里蹦出来的连绵不绝的疼痛。症状发作的每一晚，他都会过来陪我喝酒聊天，你的样子、你想去的太空乐园，我听得都烦了，就记住了。"

　　"谢谢你，谢谢你记得。"

　　"光记住这个有什么用，得像你爸爸一样，能记住那些公式、能发明那些药来救人才有用。"K哈哈大笑起来，"他总是说很忙，有很多的事情要做。我却总以为他这么说是因为怕死，还用酒瓶砸过他……我说，我的朋友，我就交了你一个朋友，我被你影响得也怕死了。"

　　阿旭有些吃惊地看着K，"第一个朋友？"

　　"其实，他也算不上是个多好的朋友……经常消失，总是很忙，而且还爱讲一些大道理，但我从来没有过朋友，一个就已经很好了。"

　　"为……为什么？"

　　"因为新贵只能认识新贵，而一百个新贵，九十九个都和我一样。你会和昨天把你推倒在门口的那个男人——我——做朋友吗？我当了27年新贵，这27年的第一天，我以为我有钱了，我会好好地活下去，会交到很多朋友，会做一些自己喜欢做的事情……但那些事情，几乎还不到一年，我就全部做完了，想得到的东西、想去的地方、想睡的女人……剩下的26年，都只是重复第一年而已，不知道想要什么，就只是机械地重复。"

　　"你的脸色看起来非常不好……"

　　"你知道吗？我之前一直以为，你根本就是张衡幻想出来的，新贵怎么会有孩子呢？"

　　"不应该这样才对，你看起来似乎有些……"

　　"我带你爸爸去过那种地方……女的，男的，我都给他点了，谁知道他喜欢男的还是女的？"

　　"该死！黛安娜是不是哪里弄错了……"

　　"黛安娜说，我应该做个英雄。英雄，你知道吗？"

　　K完全陷入了一场盛大的回忆里。在他的面前，是一个精心布置、近乎还原了当时一切的舞台。他断断续续地读着旁白，牵引着舞台上的角色走过他经历的每一幕，他的眼里已经容不下真实世界发生的一切，服务生递来的铁盘、精心摆盘的烤肠和啤酒，他都视而不见，甚至……甚至连阿旭不停地呼唤也……

　　"K！那个在和接待说话的，好像……好像是PDO的人！

　　"K！她……她朝我们这边走过来了！

　　"她真的在找我们，她一定是来找我们的！

　　"K！K！你听到了吗？

　　"她真的过来了！"

　　最后，是一整杯泼在脸上的啤酒唤醒了近乎脱离现实的

K。冰镇过的酒液、喷洒的泡沫，K的脸上如同刚刚经历了一场惊天的海啸。

"我们必须马上离开！PDO的人来了！"阿旭从座位上站起来，她抓着啤酒杯的手仍悬在半空，不知是玻璃的冰凉，还是内心涌动的不安，让她的手指不停地发颤。

回过神的K先是愣了一会儿，然后便立刻扭过头，看向了自己身后。

拥挤的餐厅里站着的顾客却不多，这让K很快锁定了一个离自己不足十米远的穿着红色皮衣的女人。她在各张客桌前游荡，有时还会上前询问，但又很快离开。

K回过身时，这个女人正好与为K服务的侍应生站在一起，她从那件鲜亮的大衣里掏出了什么东西，而那个侍应生看过之后，立刻看向了K的方向。

"就是他们。"

甚至不用听见，也知道侍应生说了什么。

"她怎么可能找到我们……"

"司机，或许是那个司机。"

"她朝我们走过来了。"

K捏紧了拳头，不知为何，有一种强烈的、炙热的东西，突然在他的胸腔里燃烧了起来。他感觉不到恐惧，这把火把某些扎根在他身体里的情绪一焚而尽，取而代之的是一种从未有过的理智和清醒，一种勇敢的、无畏的、一往无前的东西。那个英雄，他正在义无反顾地为了什么近在眼前的东西而战。

K回过头，看着已经惊慌得浑身颤抖的阿旭。那一刻，他在阿旭的眼里，看到了那个东西，"别怕，不用怕。"

"我们怎么办？"

"就用你刚才的那招。"

"我……的那招？"

"抓住我的手，阿旭。"K一只手抓起桌前那杯还未动过的啤酒，另一只手紧紧地握住阿旭不停颤抖的手腕，"抓紧我。"


：三部分都结束了，接下来该打针了吧！

：抱歉，李先生。可能还需要耽误您一会儿，还有一件额外的事项需要和您确定一下。

：额外的事项？

：首先是您的家属意愿栏里，没有任何人的签字，家庭背景申报里也完全是空白。

：有问题吗？他们……他们都死了啊。

：是这样，我的同事在基因存量系统里找到了与您基因序列吻合程度较高的人，基本可以认定为您的直系亲属，如果有需要的话——

：没有这个需要。

：李先生，这说不定可以提升您的乐观寿命区间，如果您和您的亲属取得进一步的——

：我说了不用。我根本不想知道他们是谁，都是生了我却不愿意养我的浑蛋！

：我想您可能有些误会，李先生。我们调查到的您的直系亲属，两小时前在邻近的城市刚刚完成了基因登记，她应该……是一个女婴，这就是为什么这份报告会此刻才送来。

：女……女婴？

：她应该是您的女儿，李先生。

：我的女儿？

：是的，登记方只填写了母亲的姓名——伊德，您对这个姓氏有印象吗？

：伊德……她是赌场里的那个……

：李先生？

：什么？

：您有印象吗？

：没……没有，完全没有，我从来没有过女儿。

：好吧，既然这样，那我就确认维持您原来的审查结果。

"哈哈哈哈哈哈！你别骗我了，我当时被你抱在怀里从窗户摔了出去，我都能听见你骨头碎掉的声音。"阿旭一边笑，一边咬着吸管，吮吸着手里那瓶快要见底的银河汽水。作为太空乐园的特供饮料，这已经是她半小时内喝下的第三瓶了。透明的玻璃瓶身，湛蓝色的液体里漂浮着无数色彩斑斓的圆球，每一口下去，嘴里仿佛都在演绎一场宇宙大爆炸。

"没骗你，我现在还能抱着你跑上好几圈。"K跟着阿旭笑了几声，他手里也拿着一瓶同样的汽水，但几乎一口没喝，"就在这儿，要不要就在这儿试试。"

K指了指身旁一颗叫作格利泽581g[11]的行星，略显灰暗的色泽让它在吸引观众这件事上完全输给了不远处足有二十米高、红得耀眼的火星。

---

11一颗系外行星，绕行位于天秤座的红矮星格利泽581，距离地球约20.5光年。

"我能从这儿，把你扛到我们甩掉那个女人的地铁站。"

"刚刚从那群孩子里挤出来，你都累得在喘气。"

虽然已经接近凌晨，但太空乐园里依旧人头攒动。恺撒区慷慨地为这场声势浩大的巡展让出了四十亩的中心公园，一颗颗原本远在天边的星辰，如今全都出现在这片被装饰一新的土地上。瑰丽的星云、璀璨的星体全都飘荡在这片被恺撒区高楼大厦围拢的公园里，人们行走在这些大大小小的星体间，像是在宇宙花园里漫步的神明。

"你看，这上面写着——"阿旭指着格利泽581g旁边的展牌，饶有兴致地说道，"格利泽581g的发现者史蒂芬·沃特被问及这颗行星上是否真的有生命时说：'我不是生物学家，也没在电视上演过这个角色，但从生命的韧性与习性上来看，我认为它存在生命的概率是100%。'"

"你是说，这个星星上面也有人？"

"不是人，是生物。"阿旭转过头，看着凑过来的K，一本正经地说，"这是人类迄今为止发现的所有天体里，最有可能孕育出生命的行星之一。"

"它看起来……"K把目光再次移回到格利泽581g，将它上下打量了一番，不以为然地摇摇头，"很普通嘛，也不是很好看，我还是喜欢刚才那个……什么宿七。是我的话，我更愿意住在那上面，至少气派。"

"你说参宿七[12]，那颗蓝色的？"阿旭想了一会儿，似乎记起了刚才在猎户座展区K被那抹绚丽的蓝光迷得神魂颠倒的样子，再次大笑了几声，"那希望你家的空调制冷功能足够强，参宿七上面的温度得有几万摄氏度吧。"

"啊，是这样吗？"K愣了一下，然后也跟着笑了起来，"果然没有学问的话，就只能看个表面，连危险不危险都分不清。"

阿旭转过头，看着K，她咬着吸管的嘴唇抽动了一下，像是打了个冷战。

"你怎么了……"K看着突然陷入沉默的阿旭，"不舒服？"

"没，没有。"阿旭像是才回过神来，急忙摇了摇头，"你分得清危险啊，刚才那么危险，你不是立刻反应过来，一杯啤酒泼了上去，然后抱着我跳窗了吗？"

"那……那都是年轻的时候学会的把戏，那些人赌输了逃跑都用这招。"

---

12 一颗蓝超巨星，距离地球约863光年，光度为太阳的55 000倍，它是猎户座最亮的星。

"我觉得那样很酷，真的。"阿旭抬起头，"比我见过的所有东西都酷。"

阿旭的话音落下，被格利泽581g暗淡的光笼罩的两人都不再开口，仿佛他们真的身处20光年外的遥远太空，漂浮在寂静无声的宇宙中。

K伸出手搭在阿旭的头顶，她柔滑的发丝在K粗糙的指尖滑动着，仿佛在回应着这个男人的抚摸。K也不知道为何此时此刻，他会不受控制地想这么做，但这一切就是发生了，在这颗行星"极有可能存在"的居民的见证下。

直到轻柔的抚摸，变成了施加了几分力气的拍打。

"小姐，你搞清楚，我可是花了1300美元弄到的票，结果你告诉我，这里的东西都没有我酷。"

"那好吧，那开普勒-16b[13]比你酷一点儿。"

"那是什么？"

"天上有两颗太阳的那个，就像是塔图因[14]，在前面。"

"前面是多远？"

"怎么，我们的大英雄跑不动了吗？"

接下来的几小时，阿旭和K的星际之旅便在这些著名的星体间展开。在搭成舞池的仙女座星云，阿旭的饮料被行人打翻了；在按颗数还原的英仙座流星雨里，K和一个路人打了一架；他们和一万多人一起观看了有史以来最壮观的耀斑，太阳就在他们伸手可以够到的地方，散发着炙热夺目的光。

当他们在公园人工湖旁躺下，已经是凌晨三点多了，观光的游客几乎散尽。失去观众的群星们似乎也安静了下来，星光缓缓地流动，像是它们正在疲惫地呼吸着。唯有这片围绕着堤岸修建的草坪上还留有几簇人群，他们等待着这场巡展最后的项目。

湖上的夜空，此刻正被一抹鲜艳的橙色晕染开。阿旭躺在K的身边，目不转睛地盯着头顶即将拉开的大幕。一艘孤独的飞船在一片深浅不一的赤橙里游荡，一个巨大的光环将夜空分割开来，飞船背后沉寂的宇宙发出沉闷的回响，不断变换的颜色也开始有了形状，一个硕大的、被光圈环绕的土黄色星球挂在天上，飞船悬浮在它的轨道之外，渺小得如同一粒尘埃。

---

13 一颗系外行星，距离地球195.7光年，是一颗环双星行星，这意味着在这颗行星上可以看到两颗太阳。
14 《星球大战》中天行者家族的故乡行星。它被设定为一颗巨大的沙漠星球，属于星系外层空间（Outer Rim）的阿卡尼斯区域，是一颗围绕着一个双星系统运动的行星。

"这是什么星？"

"土星。"

"这就是你说必须要看的……"

"《穿越土星环》。是《穿越土星环》的场景，他们选了很多著名的小说场景做成了展映片。"阿旭的眼睛紧紧地盯着那艘飞船，兴奋不已地喊道，"这和我看小说时脑子里想象的场景差不多！"

"所以，飞船里的那个人就是主角吗？"

"没错。他的飞船遭遇了意外，他一个人被弹射出舱，飘荡在土星环外。"

"啊，一个人……那样的话，挺孤单的。"K看着那艘慢慢地朝着土星环移动的飞船，在那个庞然大物面前，它是这样渺小。那艘飞船的孤单仿佛透过它规律闪烁的灯光，印在了K的心上。阿旭和K的目光就这样跟随着它前行，弧形的土星环变得越来越近，那些密密麻麻排布的碎块颗粒，碰撞、分离、碎裂，冲刷着观众的视线。

阿旭一边用手对着夜空指引着K的视线，一边和他讲述小说的剧情。

"那个女的呢？"

"那个叫多丽丝。她其实也不算是女人，不过如果没有多丽丝，主角就不可能独自完成这趟旅程。"

"希望他们有好好地告别。"

"当然有。多丽丝还有一个父亲，他们道别的那一幕，非常感人。"

"那样的话，真好啊。"K缓慢地呼吸着，一种强烈的疲惫感从他的心脏开始朝外蔓延。不知不觉间，他松开了紧握着汽水瓶的手，好像已经没有太多力气做到这件事了，"这样的旅程啊，如果没有家人陪着还真是难熬……不过，也不算是难熬，我的一生好像就是这样熬过来的。"

"一直没有别人吗？"

"也不是……"K想了想，侧过脸看着阿旭，"其实，我好像还有个女儿。"

"女儿？"

"我申请PDO的时候才知道的……就算我那样不负责任地一走了之，那个女人还是把孩子生下来了。"K的嘴唇不由得抽动了几下，最后勉强挤出一丝淡淡的笑意，"现在想想，那大概是我这辈子最有可能和某人共度一生的时刻了。"

"你见到她了吗？"

"没有，找都没找过。不过，我现在……你说克里斯会不会有什么办法，可以把我现在剩下的钱转给她。PDO是明令禁止补偿金被继承的，但克里斯可以搞定PDO的系统……我想他应该会有什么办法。黛安娜说之后我就要被逮捕，然后被带去各种各样的地方，听证会、研讨会，甚至还要上新闻，也不知道还有没有机会恢复自由。我想……既然这样，不如先把钱都给她。"

"你想把钱给她？"

"我……我觉得……"K抬起头，重新看向头顶的夜空，主角的飞船已经驶向了地球的方向，华丽的土星环在它的身后一点点变得暗淡，仿佛在向这群认真守候的观众们谢幕，"如果她也想来看看这个的话，至少我可以给她买张票什么的。"

阿旭没有回答。剧幕落下后的草坪，一片漆黑。

"你让我想起了她。"

K侧过脸，看着阿旭，完全漆黑的夜色遮蔽了她的神情，唯有那双微微发亮的眼睛似乎在微微发颤，瞳孔里透出萤火般的光，像东方既白时两颗依依不舍的星。

"你说，明天会怎么样，他们会拷问我什么？"

"我……我……我不知道。"过了好一会儿，阿旭才回答道。

"这还是我第一次关心明天的事。"K用手抚摸着自己的胸口，怦怦，怦怦，心脏那样真切地跳动着，像是只为他而鸣的战鼓，"有什么事值得去做的感觉，原来是这样的。"

"对不起。"

阿旭的手搭在K的手上，心跳的节奏传递到她身上，变成了身体无法抑制的颤抖。什么比夜晚还要寒冷的东西，滴落在了两人的手背上。

"真的对不起。"

"什么？"

"对不起，让你经历这些……"

"你说什么呢？我今天享受到的快乐，可比我这辈子加起来都要多，就像……我好像就是为了今天才活着，我可是无比期待着即将经历的那些。"

"我想……我再也没法做这样的事了。"

强烈的疲惫感让K几乎无法睁开双眼，他感觉自己似乎就飘荡在浩瀚的土星环外，这个动人的太空故事走到了结尾，厚重而冰冷的夜色压在他的胸口，所有的星辰都在一瞬间失去了光彩。

：那么，您的申请已经全部确认完毕，可以执行了，李K先生。

：那个，等一下……

：什么？

：之后，马上就是注射了，对吗？这……这么快？

：是的，您之前不是一直嫌流程太慢了吗？您是否还有什么需要再次核对或者解答的，我这边都会配合您。

：所以，27年，我就只能活27年了。

：是的，您的法定寿命还剩下27年。在法定寿命结束前死亡，是您应尽的义务。

：27年……

：李先生，如果您对这个结果依旧不满意，您还有最后的机会选择终止本次申请，并获得5年的延迟，这是您的合法权利。

：我……不……反正，像现在这样，活太久似乎也没有意义。

：李先生，我需要您认真地回答我，是否要终止本次申请？

：意义……至少这样还有可能活得更有意义。

：李先生？

：我确认申请，带我去吧！

"不！不可能的！" K几乎是用尽全力喊出了这句话，"我的账户里至少……至少还有30万美元！"

"你给老子睁大眼睛看看，支付失败！"司机用一只手将K反扣在地上，另一只手端起屏幕，直接怼在K的脸上，"老子早就发现你不是个善茬儿！大早上从恺撒郊外打车到这种荒郊野岭，你他妈的今天要是不把钱付了，老子就在这儿把你埋了！"

"等等，你让我进去，那个工厂里有我的朋友，他们会帮我付的。" K大口喘着气。自从早上在那个公园的巡展草坪上醒来，他的脑袋就没有一刻不在撕心裂肺地搅动，颅内的阵痛连带着身体的关节一起疼痛不已，仿佛他整个人正被绑在一台马力全开的切割机上。他拖着几乎散架的身体，四处寻找不见踪影的阿旭，可整个偌大的公园里只有零星几个早早来拆除展品的工人。无奈之下，他只有叫车前往工厂，可显然……今天的司机并不像昨天那个软柿子一样好捏。

"你他妈的骗狗呢！泥垢区这种地方，早八百年就没人住了，还会有人？"

"真的！我是说真的！你相信我！"

"相信你才有鬼！看你这副德行，都不知道昨晚磕了多少药！你们这些新贵，真的把自己当拯救人类的圣人了？一群垃圾！老子现在把你宰了，才是为民除害。"司机说完，直接丢下手里的设备，抓住K的喉咙，将他死死地按在地上。

"放开他！"

一个女人的声音从工厂大门的方向传来，"放开他，现在！"

K挣扎着抬起头，看向这个及时赶到的救星。他原本以为看到的会是阿旭，或者黛安娜，可那一抹明亮的红色，却让他更加恐惧。随着女人一步步靠近，她的脸也逐渐清晰了起来，是那个昨晚在餐厅被他泼了整杯啤酒的女人。

"放开他。"女人从红色皮衣的口袋里掏出了什么东西，给司机展示。司机只看了一眼，便立刻松开了按压着K的双手。

"操！"司机对着倒在地上的K骂了一声，"你他妈果然不是什么好鸟，连警察都惹上了。"

"你可以走了。"

"干，干你的！"司机朝着K旁边的地面吐了一口口水，这才愤愤不平地回到车里，"这车费就当是给你赞助的丧葬费吧，早点判刑，早点去死。"

K从地上艰难地爬起来，还没完全站稳，便被汽车扬长而去的烟尘吞没，尘埃落进他的眼睛里，原本就模糊的视线彻底陷入一片灰茫之中。他下意识地朝后挪了几步，却猛地撞在了女人的身上。

K惊慌失措地再次跌坐在地上，双腿麻木得几乎失去知觉。

"你不用逃，因为我没想过要抓你。"女人伸出一只手扶住K摇摇欲坠的上半身，"我昨天晚上也不是去抓你的，而是去抓那个女孩的。"

"阿……阿旭……"K突然不知哪里来的蛮劲，用力地甩开了女人的手，"你们……你们把她怎么样了？你们应该抓的人是我！"

"我抓她，"女人停顿了一会儿，继续说道，"是因为她和她的团伙涉嫌非法盗取你名下36.7万美元的PDO补偿金。"

K再次坐在厂房那张长桌旁时，原本堆满文件和电脑的桌上已经空无一物，周围有穿着制服的警员往来穿梭，抬着大小不一的箱子朝门口移动，最后出去的两个人，将K注射时躺的那张手术床艰难地从操作室里抬出来。他们看到坐在桌旁的K和女人时，其中一个人咧着嘴大笑了起来，"哟，曼迪姐，这就是昨晚请你喝啤酒的那个新贵啊？"

　　另外一位警官则鼓着腮帮子，模仿被水泼了一脸的样子。

　　叫作曼迪的女人并没有理会他们的调侃，只是挥了挥手，示意他们赶紧离开。直到那两人跟跟跄跄地消失在门外，这间偌大的厂房只剩下他们二人，她才深吸了一口气，看着呆坐在椅子上的K。他的脸上没有任何表情，眼睛浑浊得几乎无法辨认出瞳孔，如果不是胸口还有微弱的起伏，甚至无法辨别他是否还活着。

　　"你不是第一个受害者。他们涉嫌盗取的金额已经接近600万美元，全部都是针对PDO申请者的，被盗的也基本都是剩余的补偿款。里斯本、洛杉矶、大阪、香港……还有这里，打一枪，换一个地儿，我们已经追踪他们很长一段时间了。"

　　"所以都是……这样的吗？"K有气无力地问道。他的语气，让曼迪觉得眼前这个男人并不是真的在乎问题的答案，但她依旧非常认真地点了点头。

　　"以前，骗取补偿金的伎俩都很简单，大部分套路都是宣称可以做治愈PDO制剂的手术，什么更换脏器、冰冻身体之类的，想必你也都听过。后来，申请者也不是那么好骗了，就有了比较高级的办法，比如这帮人。通常都是先派一个人和申请者做朋友，无微不至，嘘寒问暖，还会在往来期间不停地讲起自己的亲人，通常是他的妻子。"

　　"妻子？"

　　"你应该见过那个女人的。她是通缉令上的常客了，之前是泥垢区某个毒贩的情妇，后来泥垢区遭遇塌方，她就跟着消失不见了，再次出现，就是在这个诈骗团伙里。通常在那个所谓的博士失踪后，她就会找上受害者，寻求帮助，打开房间、找到邮件的线索，诸如此类。很多受害者也供述，他们还和这个所谓的'朋友妻子'发生了性关系。"

　　"黛安娜……"

　　"当然，这不是她真实的名字。"

　　"可他经常提到的是……是阿旭。"K说到阿旭时，又重新抬起了头，看着曼迪，"那是他的女儿。"

　　"我们注意到了，这种情况确实是第一次出现。可能这次他们决定调整一下剧本的细节吧。你说的那个女孩，在其他受害者的描述里，通常扮演的是在所谓的基地门口开枪，以及注射环节上场的小护士。"

　　"阿旭……"K的脑海里突然出现了一抹鲜艳的红色，熟悉的红色，它慢慢地有了形状，变成了阿旭的嘴唇，又变成了黛安娜的嘴唇，那是一模一样的红色，"她们有……一样的红色。"

"他们的分工很明确，步骤也很明确——朋友最先出场与你上演患难情深；妻子穿针引线告诉你抗体的存在；打手负责刺激情绪，让你产生负罪感；护士则负责讲述温情的部分，让你相信PDO是邪恶的，从而产生使命感；那个黑客负责获取你的授权，实施真正的盗窃；而他们的头儿，就是那个老人，负责扮演代表正义和科学的博士。一样的剧本，一样的过程，八个小时之后，钱到手了，所有人凭空消失。"

"可是我是看着PDO的人把张衡带走的……"

"如果你看得再仔细一点，你就会发现，正是他们几个穿着PDO的制服在你的家门口大喊大叫。他们这么做，就是为了让你亲眼看见那一幕。"

"他们……他们就不怕我真的开门吗？"

"李先生，他们把新贵的心理研究得很透彻。"曼迪停顿了一下，深吸了一口气，"他们和你一样确定，那扇门不会被打开。"

"所以，这一切都是假的？"

"是的，朋友、抗体、营救计划都是骗局。大部分受害者会在注射抗体后维持几小时的兴奋意识，觉得自己似乎真的摆脱了病痛，其实……那不过是那个女孩改良过的毒品而已。不过这次，似乎是因为换了人导致注射过程操作不当，你体内的药物明显过量了，所以你昨晚……你的反应非常激烈，这对你的身体摧残很大，我想那个女孩应该也察觉到了。"

"你说，那些药都是阿旭……都是她做的……"

"是的。据我们了解，她在团队里负责制毒。那个女孩，其实算是这群人里唯一的科学家，对化学、天文、物理都很精通……据调查，似乎因为父母双亡，所以她小小年纪就误入歧途。"

"阿旭……父母双亡……"

"其实这个骗局破绽很多，所以他们一般会等到受害者到了反应期再下手，而且一般会选择反应二期。这时候，受害者的意识经历反应期各种病症的摧残后已经很脆弱了，但他们还具备行动能力，同时……他们对所谓的抗体，也最渴望，还有就是……"

"什……什么？"

"你应该也很享受被骗的过程吧，李先生？"曼迪看着K，那双黯淡的眼睛被一种她非常熟悉的空虚感包裹着。她已经不记得这是第几次像现在一样注视着那样的眼睛，"帮助朋友，获得新生，扳倒邪恶，拯救世界……这样的美梦一个接着一个，任凭谁也无法细究真假。"

K没有回答，他的头又沉沉地垂下。

曼迪似乎也习惯了这样的反应，她同样沉默了一会儿，又突然想起了什么，继续说道："不过，有一点倒是很奇怪，这一次，他们居然没有给你注射麻醉剂。"

"麻醉剂？"

"因为转移资产有八小时的撤回时限，他们为了防止意外，都会在给你注射完所谓的抗体后，找个理由再给你注射麻醉剂。这一次，不知道为什么，他们居然把你带到了城区。"

"是……是我提出的。是因为我说，想带阿旭去一个一定要带她去的地方。"

"一定要去的地方？"曼迪有些疑惑地看着K，更让她疑惑的是，K原本灰暗的眼眸里，竟然重新有了几丝微弱的光亮，"他们居然同意了？"

"他们都很反对，但是阿旭……阿旭说她想去看看。"

"这本来是个千载难逢的机会。如果你当时没有阻止我，说不定我们可以帮你挽回一些损失。"

"是吗？"K深吸了一口气，身体微微地颤抖着。他抬起手，抚摸自己的胸口，怦怦，怦怦，那样的节奏，令他原本漠然的神色有了一丝满足和安稳。他看着曼迪，露出一个勉强的笑意，"如果是那样的话，我可能会因此失去更多。"

"看来昨晚，你过得还不赖。"曼迪笑了笑，站起身来，"该告诉你的，我都告诉你了，我送你回去吧。原本想带你回警局进一步协助调查，但……你现在看起来，更需要休息。不过你至少提供了一条有用的线索，我会把他们人员分工的调整情况记录下来的。"

"那个……不用了。"

"什么？"

"那个女孩，她以后不会再扮演女儿的角色了。"

"为什么？"

"她亲口告诉我的。"K抬起头看着曼迪，那目光明明停在曼迪身上，却如同望着遥远星河般深邃。华丽的星环此时此刻就映在他的眼前，在那艘去往故乡的飞船身后，勾勒着一道优雅的弧线。

"她说，她再也没法做那样的事了。"

：你……你好？
：您好，请问是伊德小姐吗？
：你是？

：您好，伊德小姐。这里是太空乐园巡展客服中心。

：太空乐园，那个富人区的展览？

：是的，伊德小姐。我们已经收到您的预订信息，是两张VIP豪华套票，包含您所在城市的接送服务、夜间露营和全天候的场内自助餐，本次致电是想和您确认您以及您母亲的抵达时间，我们将为您提前安排好接送车辆和快速通行的证件。还有就是，因为您点映的《穿越土星环》夜空展片是包场的，所以我必须要提前和您确认——

：等等！等等！我预订了这个？

：是的。这边查询到您六小时前就全款预订了。

：可是，你们不是不让我们这些新贵买票的吗？

：伊德小姐，我们确实已经收到了署名为您的付费预订请求。如果您对这项预订有其他疑问的话，是否需要我为您办理退票或者——

：妈的，这是谁的恶作剧吗？那个……是谁，是谁付的钱，能查到吗？

：稍等，我帮您查询一下。

：别让我知道是酒吧的那帮畜生！

：您好，付费账号显示是……李K，李K先生。

：李K？谁是李K？妈！妈，你过来，你认识一个叫李K的吗？

：是的。不过，等等，请您稍等，可能存在一些问题，这个基因账号……三周前已经被注销了，这可能是系统故障。如果您对这项预订有其他疑问的话，是否需要我为您办理退票？伊德小姐，您还在吗，伊德小姐？

# Upstart

## by Ben Lu

## Translation by Blake Stone-Banks

Ben Lu is the winner of the 2021 China Science Fiction Galaxy Award for Best New Author. Since the publication of his debut novel Futuritis, he has published quite a few short stories. His works are romantic and beautiful in style, meticulous in words, and grand in imagination, focusing on the depiction of a society of future technological development.

: Your name, sir.

: Just call me K.

: Apologies, sir. This process is meticulously controlled. You are required to state your full name and surname.

: It's K Li.

: Alright, Mr. Li. Shall we begin? My colleagues have completed your health and background checks. Now, I'm here to assist with final confirmation. Mr. Li, in accordance with the PDO37-R Resolution on Population and Lifespan Control by the International Population Planning Department in conjunction with the World Health Organization, and based on your inspection results, you qualify for the Reduced Population Lifecycle Compensation Policy. We hereby accept your application in accordance with all applicable laws. Your application code is PDO-3210-1287-T9734. Mr. K Li, in a voice no lower than sixty decibels, please state if you confirm your application.

: Yes, of course. Let's get started!

: Mr. Li, as I have said, this process is meticulously controlled and—

: I confirm!

: Thank you for your cooperation. Application PDO-3210-1287-T9734 is officially accepted. Now I will confirm each point with you before we begin implementation. Based on the results of your status and health check, we appraise your Optimistic Lifespan at seventy-nine to eighty-two years. Therefore—

: Seventy-nine? Why so low? Everybody lives to at least a hundred these days. Why should I die so young?

: Yes, thanks to modern medicine, current average life expectancy is 107.3 years old. However, in addition to referencing current average life expectancy, a PDO applicant's Comprehensive Lethality Rate is a critical indicator. It is the combination of these two factors that determines one's Optimistic Lifespan.

: Comprehensive ... Lethality Rate?

: Mr. Li, you are currently nineteen years of age. According to our analysis of your data, you have an 86.5 percent chance of unemployment over the next twenty years. You are also a Level Six crime risk, 29.2 percent higher than average for your residential area. Moreover, four people in your social radius have died from homicide. Sixteen people have been disabled due to direct or indirect involvement in criminal activity. And although you physically meet PDO application health standards, we must also take such living conditions and crime risks into account. If you are dissatisfied with our appraisal of your Optimistic Lifespan, you may terminate this application. Termination would activate a five-year waiting period during which you could not again file for PDO. However, during those five years, you could improve your life habits, social radius and overall quality of your next application.

: Five years ... I'd have to wait that long?

: Indeed, Mr. Li. According to relevant provisions of the PDO Resolution, citizens who suspend their application may not again apply within five years.

: I can't wait five years ... If it's really seventy-nine, how much can I earn?

: If you accept your status review and health check results, then with your Optimistic Lifespan and minimum reduction of thirty-five years, your legal death will occur in 9,874 days, eight hours and fourteen minutes. You will therefore receive immediate compensation of 3,342,000 U.S. dollars.

: 9,874 days … That's …

: You will be forty-six years old, Mr. Li. If the application goes into effect, you may legally live to forty-six. At that age, you would then be required to go to any PDO Administrative Center globally to perform legal death by July 12, 2124.

: Forty-six years old … Well, I still got twenty-seven years!

: That's correct, Mr. Li.

: Twenty-seven years … So, I'd live for twenty-seven more years … Is there any way we could cut back a few reduction years?

: Your service representative should have gone through this with you prior to preliminary checks. For applicants under age thirty, the starting point for reduction years is thirty-five years. Fewer reduction years are not permitted. If you are unsatisfied with compensation, we do allow you to increase your reduction years—

: Fuck you. Do I get to live a life or not?

: Apologies, sir, but too few reduction years would deviate from the intention of the PDO and its global population planning strategy. However, if you are truly dissatisfied with your results, you may choose to terminate your current application and begin the five-year extension. Such is your legal right.

: Alright, confirm. I confirm. So now what … the injection?

: That's correct, Mr. Li. After confirmation we begin the formal acceptance phase. Then, we will inject you with the PDO Genetic Synthesis Compound and this whole application process will be complete. You need only wait for the transfer of funds. The injection of the PDO Compound is an insurance mechanism to guarantee legal death. The Compound will remain inactive until the date stipulated for your legal death. If you do not visit a PDO Administrative Center to perform legal death by the arranged date for legal death, the PDO Compound will activate. According to your physical tolerance, the Compound Reaction Period could last for one to three months, but not more than three months. The PDO Compound, when activated, increasingly interferes with normal physical and behavioral functions. Discomfort and pain intensify over time, peaking within about one month. Any drug intervention or treatment would be futile. You would only suffer pain and eventually die. Therefore, to avoid such an unpleasant situation, please be sure to contact a PDO Administrative Center before onset of the Compound Reaction Period. We do our utmost to alleviate all pain and deliver a humane legal death. Remember that it is your obligation to die before the end of your legal life.

#

A knock woke K. The sun must have just set. Skyscrapers usually illuminated with every color of the rainbow were not yet lit. K had caught that brief moment of darkness before the city turned on its lights.

Through half-open eyes, K stared at the living room floor. His head was buried deep in one of the sofa's soft cushions. His sinuses filled with the astringent scent of bearskin. Which was why in his dream just now, he had been talking to the Russian who had sold him this sofa so many years ago. K remembered the tattoo of the bear on the Russian's arm, his snow boots splashed with blood. The smell that had emanated from that man's body was identical to that in his nose now.

The sofa was the first thing K had bought with his PDO compensation. His reason for buying the sofa was simple. He had been living on the roof of an abandoned building where a Siberian tourism billboard was lit up. Every night, K had fallen asleep while looking at that brown bear roaring atop the billboard. Many nights, he had imagined himself riding atop that bear like some brave Slavic hero. For six years, he had carried that dream. Upon receiving his PDO compensation, he had abandoned the rooftop but not his dream of the bear. He purchased the bearskin sofa for twenty-thousand U.S. dollars. It was tied to the top of a truck and driven to his apartment while K, wrapped in a fur coat gifted by the Russian trader, lay atop his new sofa with feet high. K wore that thick fur coat all day. At the time, the thick brown fur had the gamy scent of blood, a smell one-hundred times worse than that in his nose at this moment. K had taken pleasure in that scent as though it were the conclusion of some great battle. The only disappointment he felt was there had been so few onlookers, though K understood others were already growing accustomed to people like him and the excesses of their overnight wealth.

Upstarts. That was what people like K were called, that class of nouveau rich building their small fortunes from PDO compensation.

The PDO ads painted an aspirational vision of sacrifice for the good of population control. The truth, however, was most upstarts were happily trading years of their lives for wealth rather than struggle with life's hardships. The first thing upstarts did after receiving compensation was always the same: they showed off their wealth where they lived for a bit. Then after they had made enough noise, they vanished.

The knocking on K's door started up again.

"Go away!" K shouted, then doubled over with a violent cough. When he finished coughing, he sat up on the sofa.

Since the onset of a severe headache two weeks ago, K had felt the screws tightening on his heart. Every second, he could feel himself aging. He was unable to stand for long periods, unable to even chew quickly. His skin appeared dry and brittle. Just speaking at more than a whisper wore him out. These changes had all taken place over the past two weeks. Six months prior, the PDO Administrative Center had sent a thick instruction booklet detailing the pain he would experience during his PDO Compound Reaction Period: from initial physical decline, insomnia and abnormal vision to blindness, dementia and eventual organ failure. The commissioner who had come to his door read the booklet like it were gospel. K remembered lying naked under a cashmere blanket with several women. The commissioner's exegesis had been the most vexing foreplay of his life.

The knocking started up again.

K wanted to scream and curse but his trembling throat failed to muster the dirty words. According to his original plan, the bottles of gin he had consumed should have helped him sleep to at least tomorrow morning. Now that knocking had lifted the gin's anesthesia. Noise like this was no way to come to after the drinking he had done. For someone in the Compound Reaction Period, it was unbearable.

"Fuck!"

K clenched his teeth and pushed himself off the floor with both hands. He crossed a living room strewn with alcohol bottles and made his way to the apartment door. He twisted the handle.

Finally, the knocking ceased.

"Did you not hear me? I don't want to see anyone!" K said, balancing himself against the open door.

He was surprised to see a short teenage girl in the doorway. She wore an oversized jean jacket that seemed big even for K. The wide sleeves made her thin body appear all the more delicate. Her cheeks were dotted with light freckles.

"Excuse me," she said. "May I ask if you are Mr. Li?"

As she spoke, K noticed the bright red lips on the girl's wan face. Those lips seemed not to belong to her face at all. Her make-up seemed designed to achieve just this disconcerting effect. She spoke with a lilting cadence that feigned maturity. Her voice was as annoying as her knock.

"I see the PDO is employing child labor now." K gripped the door. "Do they think I'm afraid to slam the door on a child?"

"No, I'm not from PDO! I'm looking for Mr. Li. It's urgent!"

"Save it. I've been through this several times already." K put a hand on the girl's shoulder then pushed her out into the hall. "Listen, I have no money left. And even if I did, I wouldn't donate it to charity. I don't need hospice counseling. I don't need a custom funeral. And I certainly don't need some dumb teenager in my doorway bugging me!"

"Wait!" The girl rushed forward and grabbed the edge of the door. "I have something important—"

"Get the fuck out!" K yelled.

"But—"

"One more word and you'll be in front of me in line at the gates of hell."

"Wait. My name's A Xu."

"I don't care who you are. Fuck off!"

K grabbed the girl's arm and flung her to the ground with all his remaining strength. She tumbled hard against the hall floor.

Without a second glance, K slammed the door.

He leaned against the shut door and gasped. Compared with the other visitors, this girl hadn't been particularly difficult, but she had sapped his energy. He felt his joints creaking like gears in a busted machine. If she had fought back, he would doubtlessly have broken a bone. Fortunately, he now heard nothing from her side of the door.

Propping himself against the wall, he stumbled to the kitchen, opened the refrigerator and scanned its shelves. Stacked bottles reflected the halogen light in an odd rainbow of colors. But this once glorious spread provided no comfort. A few days ago, his sense of taste had vanished. Now, the only thing differentiating one bottle from another was its alcohol concentration.

The PDO's proposition was that one could trade a few years of life to make one's remaining life happier. K had now spent that happiness. He sighed, considering which bottle would best numb his pain. His eyes rested on a dark green bottle decorated with cryptic symbols. The bottle seemed to wield a magic that was already taking hold of him.

"This bottle ..." K squatted and examined it only to find the cap already opened. The bottle was wrapped with a bent silver ribbon. It had been some sort of gift.

K stirred his tongue, stimulating his salivary glands. He tried to recall the last time he had drunk from it. Suddenly, he shot up and raced to the door. He threw it open and was relieved to find the girl still in the hall.

The girl was gripping her left elbow with the palm of her right hand. From the way she clenched her teeth, K could tell he had hurt her. She stared back coldly.

K's face sparked with the excitement of a child unwrapping a present. His face had almost forgotten it could form this expression.

"So ... A Xu is a real," he said and held the door all the way open.

"Of course, I'm real!" The girl straightened herself and stared down the stunned K.

"Zhang Heng really has a daughter." K swallowed hard. "A living daughter."

#

: I can't have a child?

: Yes, sir, that is correct. Your reproductive rights will be legally revoked, and the PDO injection will make you infertile.

: That ... well ...

: There is no need to worry, sir. The injection will not affect your physiological needs or performance.

: That's not what I meant. What I meant is ... when do I get the money?

: Compensation will arrive in your designated account within eight hours after your application officially goes into effect. Once the application takes effect, it is irrevocable, and you must begin fulfilling your duties immediately.

: My ... duties?

: There are three parts I must explain in this regard. First are the rights you must surrender. From the effective date of the resolution, you may not engage in positions above Official Level 4. You may not work for national institutions or participate in projects assigned by national institutions. There are in total twenty-seven rights you will be restricted from exercising, including the right to vote, the right to be elected and the right to will assets, among other rights outlined in the Resolution. The assets you hold may not directly or indirectly participate in trading activities of Level C or higher as specified by the World Trade Organization. You may not hold financial investment products, including stocks and bonds. You may not purchase cultural relics recognized by UNESCO, real estate older than one-hundred years or any commodities prohibited for PDO applicants. You may review all specific categories of prohibitions at your convenience. The reversal of these rights is to ensure your legal death will have minimum negative impact on the normal social order, as well as to prevent waste of cultural and social resources.

: My existence is a waste of social resources?

: Of course not, Mr. Li. Within the boundaries of the law, you should enjoy your compensation to your heart's content.

: And what if I don't spend all the money before I die?

: According to the Resolution, all belongings—including your body—must be recycled and disposed of by the PDO Administrative Center.

: I can't will my estate to someone else?

: I believe I already explained that your assets may not in any form be willed or used for other purposes prohibited by the PDO Resolution.

: [laughter] I couldn't maybe leave them to you?

: Such is strictly forbidden, sir. To maintain fairness in application processes, all employees of PDO Application Centers and PDO Administrative Centers, as well as their immediate family, are forbidden from participating in PDO application. Employees like myself may not apply for or profit from PDO compensation in any way.

: In other words, your bosses blocked every avenue you have to get rich, eh?

#

"This is how you live ..."

A Xu looked around, searching for a place to sit. Almost every surface was occupied by alcohol or medicine bottles. An odd indistinguishable smell permeated the space. She leaned against the wall, which appeared clean relative to the rest of K's apartment. She sighed. "I thought upstarts all lived in ..."

"Penthouse apartments with floor-to-ceiling windows atop skyscrapers looking out onto Olympic-size swimming pools strewn with bikinis and champagne bottles? The PDO ads paint a pretty picture." K snatched the dark green bottle and took a swig. The alcohol woke him up a bit. "Truth is we can't buy most things. They add to the purchase bans every goddamn year. Good building codes don't even permit upstarts to apply for residence. This kind of apartment here is designed exclusively for upstarts. Rent it out, let the tenant die, rent it again to the next sucker. Upstart buildings are the worst in the city. When I came to look at this place, the previous tenant was on the floor half dead. A PDO man was counting his assets while the staff mopped up his vomit."

"Then what happened?" A Xu seemed intrigued by K's story. Teenagers found such gritty scenes enlightening.

"What do you think? They put him down in the PDO Administrative Center. Come back in a few days and watch the same scene play out in real time." K took another sip of booze. "Why come looking for me?"

"My father often said he was going next door to drink with K. So, I figured why don't I knock and find out who lives next door."

"Knock on the door and find out ... What are you looking for exactly?"

"I'm searching for my father, of course."

"For your father—" K felt as if someone had poked a nerve in his brain with a needle. "Don't you know your father has already ..."

"Already what?" A Xu straightened herself. "What's the matter?"

K examined A Xu, then sighed. "Listen, I don't have kids. My parents died when I was a tot. I never got along with children ... So I'll tell you straight. Your father lived out his legal life, and he's passed on now. Just like the former tenant I told you about."

K considered what euphemisms and lies he could have told the girl. Perhaps he should have said her father had gone far away and was never coming back. But as a dying man himself, K figured there was no reason to beat around the bush. Death was death.

A Xu stood, her expression frozen.

K expected her to start wailing but she showed no hint of sadness. There was only a calmness on her young face, as incongruous as the dazzling red on her lips.

"That is not possible." A Xu shook her head. "He would not be permitted to die for such reason."

"The night before he was taken away, he presented me with this gift and said farewell." K raised the green bottle and shook it.

"Listen, your father was a good friend of mine, but upstarts like us die when our time comes."

"But my father was not such a person."

"I saw your father taken away by PDO men. Those people ..."

"What PDO men? What did they do to Dad?"

K took a deep breath and rubbed his eyes. "When it happened, I was at the peephole. Your dad got picked up by several men in PDO uniforms. He resisted, shouted at the top of his lungs. I wanted to open the door and tell him goodbye, but my legal life's up too ... Opening the door would only have led to questions."

"You should have opened the door. You should have stopped it." A Xu's expression grew fraught. Her young face had not learned to mask fear. "This is bad ... I have to find a way to save him."

"Save him? Don't you understand he's dead? Once the PDO come, that's it. They euthanized him. Surely you understand that?"

"No, you don't understand. My father could not die for that reason."

"I guess the bastard didn't tell you anything. Everyone who applies for PDO arrives at this stage sooner or later. And everyone in this building is a PDO applicant—"

"My father couldn't apply for PDO." A Xu took a deep breath and reached into her baggy denim jacket. She took out a card sealed in a transparent plastic cover and handed it to K.

The security ID was Zhang Heng's, but the man in the photo looked more dignified than the Zhang Heng whom K knew. Beneath his angular cheeks was a calm smile, gray suit and royal blue tie, there was a logo composed of three bright English letters, a logo K was painfully familiar with.

"Maybe he never told you. My father works for the PDO."

"So ... he ... does ..."

K studied the card, read the title: Dr. Zhang Heng, Senior Consultant, PDO Administrative Center, Pharmacy Department.

"All PDO are forbidden to apply. Therefore, it's impossible Dad died for the reason you said."

"But he," K stared at the photo of Dr. Zhang Heng. "So, if ..."

"If the people who came for him were PDO," A Xu looked up at K, red lips trembling. "Then Dad's in real trouble."

#

: You're implying if I don't listen to you, I'm gonna be in real trouble.

: Mr. Li, do you understand that once your application is approved, you will be compelled to fully comply with all terms? We must ensure you do nothing contrary to the spirit of the PDO Resolution in your future legal life. If you hold valuable cultural relics, or participate in significant national projects, or hold a position in an institution we deem significant, such action might hinder implementation of the PDO Resolution. Therefore, it is necessary you surrender those rights. Your other legitimate rights and interests will of course still be protected.

: So for those like me who choose money over life, what value do we have in your eyes?

: You applicants are pioneer citizens who seek to demonstrate responsible stewardship over Earth's population. In our era, when there are few diseases and life expectancy is maximized, some must surrender a bit of their natural lifespan, rights and social resources to contribute to the responsible control of unfettered population growth. Your sacrifice is extremely valued.

: That's moving. Must have taken you quite some time to memorize.

: Mr. Li, people across the globe truly appreciate your efforts.

: [laughter] Yeah, let's see how they thank me.

#

"Can we speak respectfully for a moment?" K said as he gasped for breath.

"You suggesting I be grateful to you?" Clenching his fist, the floor supervisor sneered at K. Though nearly one-hundred-years-old, he had the burly cut of a young man. An elaborate tattoo spread from the base of his ears to his thumbs, likely a gang tattoo from the man's youth. "You supposed to be a dead man. Don't you know you died two weeks ago? Now, get your dead ass out of here!"

This wasn't the first time K had dealt with the prejudices of those who wished to humiliate him. K had been dealing with such people since moving into upstart housing. Most of the time, he just got out of harm's way. This time, however, the floor supervisor was blocking the door.

"I apologize for troubling you," K said, taking Zhang Heng's card from his shirt pocket and flashing it at the supervisor. "I just need to go in and take a few things. The previous tenant—"

"A few of your things, yeah? The only thing that belongs to you dead assholes is the daily reminder notice sent to the Building Management that if you don't go to a PDO Administrative Center immediately, you'll die in this building. And I don't want to clean up your body." But as the building supervisor said this, he kicked open the door. "Grab your things quickly. And don't mess with my opportunity to rent to others."

The supervisor walked down the hall. K took a deep breath. Fatigue swept his body. He had been standing too long. He stretched out his hand to hold the open door, but A Xu just stared at him.

"What's the matter? Aren't you going in?"

A Xu nodded. "That man just now ..."

"Now you see the crap we upstarts put up with." K smiled and gestured her through the door.

The layout of Zhang Heng's apartment was identical to K's: a slender corridor leading to an open kitchen, a living room connected to the bedroom on the first floor, a crescent-shaped balcony, a view of the city drenched in spinning lights.

K slumped on the sofa in the living room, reached into the side of the liquor cabinet, and pulled out a bottle of beer. He pulled hard on the bottle's ring.

Suddenly, he realized something and looked at A Xu: "According to PDO regulations, when legal life ends, these things should all be recycled, but ... they're still there."

"I told you, Dad isn't an upstart." Since they had come in, A Xu had mostly ignored K. She was behind Zhang Heng's desk searching for something. K glanced at the documents and machine parts scattered over the desk. The computer at the center was on as always, emitting its cold light. "Seems Dad was careful. He didn't tell you anything."

"I knew he had a daughter." K downed a mouthful of beer. To his disappointment, he couldn't taste it. "He liked talking about you. Every time we met, he mentioned your birthday, or your favorite movie, or that fair you had been asking him to take you to."

"Space Park?"

"That was it."

"He remembered!"

"Not just remembered, talked about it all day." K collapsed on the sofa and laughed. "I thought for sure these were fantasies, that you had died long ago. People go a bit crazy when approaching Compound Reaction Period. They'll see ghosts and—"

"Why did you think he put in a PDO application?" A Xu sat in front of the computer. The blue light made her face appear even more solemn. "What did he say?"

"Everyone living here is an upstart! Why would anyone mention such a thing?" K leaned toward A Xu. He thought he could see a few similarities between A Xu and her father. "Well, since you live well, why don't you tell me why he lived here? Don't you have a home?"

A Xu's tapping on the keyboard ceased. Her face retreated behind the screen, but K could sense her trembling, like the wings of an injured insect trying to take flight. He breathed as softly as he could.

After some time, A Xu's voice came from behind the screen. "Our home is in Caesar District."

K was impressed. "That's a good place."

Caesar District was the most expensive district in the city. It had always been uninviting to upstarts. Though the PDO Resolution never stipulated that upstarts couldn't enter certain areas, most all shops, hotels and even buses in Caesar District refused payment from upstart accounts. Everyone knew those in Caesar were the real rich. What they hated most in this world were upstarts like K, trash draped in gold and silver.

"After Dad went on the run, the PDO sent someone to our home. For a while, I used a radio my father gave me to communicate with him. Later, the radio stopped working. One day, I skipped school because Dad had promised he would come back to take me to the opening of Space Park. I thought maybe—"

"He went on the run?" K nodded. "No wonder he chose this place. There are many temporary tenants here. No one seriously registers."

"If only I had come earlier."

"What happened to him exactly?" K sat up from the sofa so he could better see A Xu behind the screen.

"I don't know, but he obviously did something to piss off the PDO. I only remember one day he came back from work and began packing his things. He told me he had to go on a long business trip and would contact me through our secret radio. Eventually, he revealed he was living here temporarily, but he didn't allow me to tell anyone or let me visit." The tapping sound of the keyboard ceased again. "Soon after that, the PDO arrived. They forced their way into our house, said it was to protect us. They were rummaging through all our stuff, our cabinets ... They kept asking questions I couldn't answer. That day was the last Dad contacted me on the radio. He said it was now unsafe and he had to leave, and then ..."

K recalled the scene at the door of his apartment a week ago, how Zhang Heng was shouting, struggling. The uniformed PDO men in the hall appeared to have tied him up.

K walked over to A Xu.

On the computer screen were opened folders of all sizes. A stream of code popped up and A Xu's eyes fixed on the flashing numbers and letters. K had no idea what they meant.

"Everything's deleted." A Xu gripped the peripheral as if she were trying to hold back her anger. "Nothing. Which is why ..."

Suddenly, A Xu turned her head, looked at K and asked, "Did you say Dad brought you alcohol on his last night?"

"Yes ..." K looked at A Xu's suddenly serious face. "But I've drunk it ..."

"The alcohol isn't the point. Did he say anything special when he came to you?"

"Nothing special I don't—"

"Quick, think. It's important."

"When he came that night, I had taken painkillers and was lying on the sofa. He brought the alcohol and put it into the refrigerator. Then he said he was leaving ... I figured it was the end of his legal life and he didn't want to suffer, so he was planning to go to the Administrative Center." K shook his head. "We didn't even chat really. He delivered the alcohol then said he was going back to deal with some mail and left."

"Mail?"

K nodded. "I said I hoped he wasn't sending out a suicide note."

"Mail!" A Xu turned her head, searched the outbox. "All deleted. And according to the log, it was my father who deleted it." A Xu smiled. "He knew they were coming ..."

K's eyes shifted from the screen to the girl so familiar with the keyboard. "Is there any way to—"

"According to his settings, if I reload his mail account, it should show the last sent address as the default, so ..." A Xu created the new mail and set recipient and subject to default. The apartment fell back into silence as K and A Xu stared at the results:

Recipient: User3

Subject: Result of Synthesis of PDO Preparation Antibody 142: Success

#

: Now, for the second part, Mr. Li.

: Everything we discussed up to now was just the first part?

: The first part was about the rights you must surrender. The second part is about the duties you must fulfill. This part concerns your life and health, Mr. Li.

: If I cared about my health, I wouldn't be here ... This is becoming a hassle, you know?

: Mr. Li, the most important duty you need to fulfill is legal death. But you also need to abide by the rules stipulated in the PDO Resolution, especially the second and fourth items on page 45.

: Let's see. Article 4: Exclusivity of Medical and Scientific Services. What is this exactly?

: Unless permitted by the PDO Administrative Center or a qualified scientific medical research institution recognized by the PDO Administrative Center, you are strictly prohibited from using your own blood, organs or body tissues in any surgical operation, medical research or genetic engineering project of Level-2 or higher. The appendix of the very complete instruction manual itemizes the specifics of all that is prohibited. Mr. Li, the PDO Compound is a high-precision genetically targeted formula. Any biological experimentation, even when seemingly harmless, may lead to a chain reaction that disrupts the genetic sequence. The PDO cannot predict the consequences. Please honor your body and legal life by not listening to any third-party rumors or participating in any experimental research that violates the PDO Resolution.

: I can't even get surgery?

: Not by an unapproved third party. Mr. Li, this policy prevents phenomena that could be harmful to your health. You likely heard that two years ago in Argentina, there was an organ trafficking organization purporting to inhibit PDO Compound efficacy via removal of a part of the pancreas. Applicants who pursued the promise of that surgery met with unnecessary tragedy. The PDO Compound does not exist in any organ in your body and no surgery on any organ will inhibit its efficacy.

: I've heard of cases. A few months back, there was someone selling a quick-freeze needle on Manila's black market, saying it put applicants in frozen stasis to avoid death.

: Such methods should not be trusted, I assure you. This is why we remind you even though it's too early for you to worry about such things.

: Too early? [laughter] But if there's an antidote available when it's my time to die, what could you do about it?

: Mr. Li, the PDO Compound is not a poison, so there is no antidote. Everyone's genetic sequence contains a threshold life expectancy for their normal aging. According to the current human benchmark, that averages at 104 to 127 years. The PDO

Compound merely compresses this threshold. The implanted code is top secret. It is irreversible but completely safe prior to the Reaction Period. It is your obligation to die before the end of your legal life. The PDO Compound is the most efficient coercive measure we have at present to ensure that happens. But it is the means, not the end.

#

The car stopped in front of an abandoned factory.

"Is this the place?" K opened the window and looked out. Cold wind rushed into the car, making him shiver.

On the trip from the apartment, the driver had been constantly glancing through the rearview at his oddball passengers, a middle-aged man with red eyes and a teenage girl wrapped in a baggy denim coat. The oddest thing wasn't their look, but their destination: the Dirt District. Before it became the Dirt District, this area had been a mining town. When the mines closed, the area became overrun by gangs and developed a reputation for every breed of illegal activity. Drugs, gambling and weapons trades were in full swing. Then, a few years back, a landslide buried half the town. The thugs abandoned it for some new outlaw paradise. The area was now believed to be deserted.

"The IP address and Dad's radio signal both came from here," A Xu said as she pushed open the door and stared at the factory's rusted gate.

"Wait for us here." K glanced at the driver. The real-time fare was still displayed on the counter. K raised his hand and after beeping a prompt, the counter read "complete" and flashed a portrait of K.

"Of course, sir." The driver nodded respectfully. Then the driver turned his head and stared at K with trepidation. He nervously read the operator screen. "Sir, when settling your account, the system received a message from PDO asking me to remind you that your legal life is forty-six days overdue. In order to avoid discomfort triggered by the PDO Compound Reaction Period, you are requested to please—"

"I spent 800 bucks." K pushed open the door without waiting for him to finish. "So shut up and wait."

When K caught up with A Xu, she was nearing the side door. It was marked with a sign reading High Pressure Workshop. Faded graffiti of naked girls could be seen through the dust on the factor walls. The largest graffiti work illustrated a supine blonde dancer in mesh stockings. The factory door was between her legs. K wondered whether he should cover A Xu's eyes.

She unexpectedly turned toward him with a look of complete resolve. "Before I knocked on your door last night, I psychologically prepared myself for whatever may come. Fortunately, it was you on the other side." She placed her right hand on the door. "I hope this knock will have an equally positive result."

K smiled. "Let's hope you don't get pushed down again."

After several knocks, the door did not open.

But soon, the second-floor window above them scraped open. Covered in graffiti, the glass window was opaque except for one thin glint of sunlight reflecting at the base of the glass. A black gun barrel protruded from beneath.

K didn't think but quickly gripped A Xu and brought her to the ground, his body shielding hers.

"Gun," K gasped. He curled and covered A Xu's whole body under his arms and torso. "Don't be afraid. I know that make of gun from the casino where I used to work ... Once it's fired, it needs to be reloaded."

"Whu ... what ..."

"If you hear a shot, you immediately run. You hear me, run."

He clenched his teeth and closed his eyes, as if all his senses were waiting for that one crisp shot.

But instead of a gun shot, they heard a delicate female voice.

"You get the chance to tell me three things before I shoot." The woman kept the gun aimed at K's body. She tapped a beat with the gun against the window and said: "One."

"Please, I'm a friend of Zhang Heng." K clenched his teeth and stood hands up, eyes fixed on the gun. He felt the hurried breaths of A Xu, who clung at his back.

"Friend?" She burst into laughter, tapped the gun against the window again. "Why didn't I know he had such a friend?"

"I am his friend. I live next door to him."

"That the second thing you want to say?" She sneered from the window. "Guess you don't care about your life. Now, your third and final point before we finish this?"

"I ..."

K raised his hands above his head unconsciously. Countless images of Zhang Heng passed through his mind like a film edited at random. He racked his brain for anything that would convince her but thought of nothing.

"Me!" A Xu cried.

A Xu stepped to K's side, still clinging to the corner of his coat. She too stared at the gun. "I'm Zhang Heng's daughter. My father has been missing for some time ... I found this place in his last email, after he was taken by the PDO."

This time, the woman with the gun did not respond. K pushed A Xu back behind him.

"No, look." A Xu pointed to the side door now half ajar.

There was the harsh screech of the rusty door opening. K bowed and put his hands over his ears. When he turned he saw an old man in a white coat and goggles in the doorway. The man studied A Xu for some time. Then he removed his goggles to reveal deep sunken eyes.

"I was at your tenth birthday party." The old man coughed. "Your father prepared a fireworks show for you in To ... To ..."

A Xu nodded. "Tottori Prefecture."

A bright smile came from the window above them as the gun's black barrel retracted. The window opened a fraction. A young woman wearing a peach camisole emerged. She had blond hair and blue eyes. The neon projecting from the edge of the glass lit up her pale face, setting off her sweet red lips.

"At last, you said something useful!" the woman yelled.

"Diana," the old man shouted in a hoarse voice, "call everyone over."

Soon, A Xu and K were seated at a long rusty table at the heart of the factory. Everyone from the Dirt was gathered round. K was certain these people knew Zhang Heng because the table was covered with every kind of document and five computers blinking with the same blue lights and red chemical formula patterns he had seen in Zhang Heng's apartment.

Diana leaned seductively against a battered column. In her camisole and stockings, she looked like a sexier replica of the vixen graffitied above the factory door. She smiled at K as she set the gun down and lit a cigarette. She gestured at the old man seated opposite K. "Dr. Imai was Zhang Heng's teacher at the Department of Medicine at Tokyo University. He was also a genetic medicine consultant for PDO."

With her cigarette, Diana pointed at the next man. "Chris used to work in the Network Security Department of the PDO Administrative Center in Seoul."

She glanced at a burly bald man wearing a vest and too-tight jeans. He looked like some kung fu star from a classic comic, thick arms and clenched fists ready for a kill. "That's Shaji. I was using his gun just now. He's from the PDO Bangkok Freight Department, which is responsible for transportation of raw materials used in the PDO Compound."

"Raw materials?" K shivered. "What are you planning here exactly?"

"First we need to know how much Zhang Heng told you." The old man named Imai glared at K and A Xu. "How could you find this place knowing so little?"

"Just ... I had the address of the mail receiver. Other than that, Dad hardly told me anything." Since they had come in, A Xu's eyes hadn't left the old man. K surmised she really did remember him from Japan. "As for Mr. Li, he was my father's neighbor."

"We meet here for our experiments. Each of us has a role to play." Imai looked at A Xu with a forlorn expression. "Zhang Heng was supposed to have met us last week but never showed. The PDO must have been watching him for some time."

"We were worried his disappearance was related to PDO. You may have confirmed that," Shaji said. His muscles rippled as he lifted a heavy steel pipe from the old assembly line.

"Chris is hacking into the PDO cloud now," Diana said.

"Done." Chris stood with a proud smile. "Security Department of the Administrative Center. Arrest files from last week."

"You're quick." Diana hurried to Chris' computer and looked at the file center screen. They both turned to K. Realized something was wrong, A Xu walked over to Chris's computer screen and looked at the screen's cracked file.

PDO Security Archive ... Investigation Records ... An expeditor from the PDO Administrative Center discovered the target while planning to expedite a legal life in Reaction Period on the same floor ... The security department has issued an arrest notice ...

"Metadata can't be decoded but it coincides with the time they were seen by K." Chris turned and nodded to Imai. "Dr. Zhang was indeed taken by PDO."

"So ..." Diana sneered as she stared down K. "Who was the person on the same floor they were sent to expedite?"

That night came back to K, all he had seen through the peephole. The moment Zhang Heng was taken. His cry. His struggle. Every detail of that night burned in his memory.

"The expeditor came to see you ..." A Xu looked at a stunned K. "You said, you never open the door to those people."

K raised his hands. "It wasn't like ..."

"The expeditor met the same resistance I did when I came to your door yesterday. He couldn't open your door, so he knocked ... on my father's door." A Xu scowled. "He never imagined PDO would come to the door at that time. When he realized he might have been recognized ..."

"Then, he thought it was me saying goodbye." K couldn't stop shaking. His mind flooded with fear and the images of that night.

"And you watched him get taken away, too afraid to open the door because you didn't want to answer to the PDO." A Xu shook her head.

"I—" K tried to think of an explanation, but his body was lifted from behind. His coat was pulled up above his shoulders. The joints in his arm cracked.

"You upstarts are only out for yourselves!" Shaji held K with his left hand and slapped him with the right. "Our gang lives in this awful place to save your lives and you treat us like this!"

"Let him go, Shaji!" Diana yelled at the enraged Shaji. "He has reached phase two of the Reaction Period. He could die!"

"He's already a dead man. I'm just assisting law enforcement. PDO will thank me!" Shaji gripped K's neck with terrible strength. "Why don't you just go to the Administrative Center and die, you coward!"

"Enough, Shaji!" Imai stood up. "He might still help us."

"He's not helping anyone ... But I'll help him die ..."

Imai hammered the table. "Let him go now!"

Shaji stared at Imai then unleashed a rageful scream. His grip loosened, dropping K to the ground.

"Fuck!" Shaji punched a column with his full strength. The factory echoed as dust billowed from Shaji's blow.

"You sure know how to take it out on the wall!" Diana stepped forward and extended a hand to K.

"Fortunately, it was just the wall this time." Chris stretched lazily. He was used to such scenes. "People like Shaji need an outlet. Better dust on the floor than blood."

With Diana's hand, K righted himself. His neck was red. His Adam's apple pulsed. His whole body trembled like vibrating glass about to shatter. From his abdomen to scalp, searing pain shot through his flesh. He saw a dazzling light in his eyes, then the rhythm of his heart clenched. Boom, boom, boom ...

"Is he going to be ..." It was A Xu's voice. She carefully lifted K's hand, as though checking its every joint.

"He's all right for the time being," Diana relaxed the hand she had pressed to K's chest. "The effects of the PDO Compound have not yet penetrated the bone. If the bone were subject to that impact after third-phase fibrosis, it would be game over."

"Li ... Mr. Li." Squatting, Imai gazed into K's half-open eyes and spoke in a raspy voice. "You did what you did because you wanted to live. It's not your fault ... But Zhang Heng's experiments had reached the very last step, and we need you to help us."

"That man help us?" Diana said.

"Once the test results are made public, the PDO will have to admit the existence of the Compound antibody. They will have to release Zhang Heng."

"But we haven't found the right person to test it on yet. That person will be the focus of the world. He must receive training, have the right identity and data—"

"If he's a friend of Zhang Heng's, then isn't this already the right person?"

"But—"

"No time, Diana," Imai said firmly as he watched K struggle to regain full consciousness. "Mr. Li, we need you to work with us to save your friend Zhang Heng."

K's eyes trembled open. From mottled points of light, his vision slowly gelled into a clear picture of Imai staring back in front of a curtain of silver light. In the eyes of this old Japanese man, there was a sadness K had never seen. It seemed only now was he old enough to even conceive such sadness. "Tell me what I can do?"

"Live." Diana stared at K. "You have to live. And keep living."

#

: So when the time comes, no matter what I do, there's no way to keep living?

: Indeed, Mr. Li.

: Even if I save the world or something—no exception?

: Without exception, it is your obligation to die at the end of your legal life.

: Fine. Hurry up. What's the last part you have to tell me?

: A few final points to understand and authorize. First, the PDO application requires genetic compatibility, which is to say, your PDO status will be written into your genetic account and become a part of your personal genetic information record, just like your assets, education background and criminal record. With a single hair, the authorized department can access all such information, though you can trust the PDO Administrative Center will only exercise that right according to reason and law.

: Any other way besides trusting you?

: By confirming this application, you authorize us to access your full genetic data. This is for your security. We carry out detailed encryption protocols to ensure your data integrity. Any retrieval or update of such data will require professional and compliant data replacement, as well as multiple authorizations by you personally. This makes it almost impossible for anyone to ever steal your genetic data access.

: And who would want to steal my data?

#

K watched the IV needle plunge into his vein. His arm clenched. Bright blood flowed back into the syringe. He felt a change in pressure under his skin, like some forgotten pain.

"How should it feel?" K looked at Diana who was carefully preparing the next syringe with a mixture of white powder and pale blue liquid.

Diana bit her lip. "How should it feel?"

"Can I ask ... Are you scared of me?"

"It's just been a while since I last did this. When you were back in the PDO Application Center, what would people ask before each injection?"

"You used to work for PDO?"

"In the injection lab." Diana nodded, then injected the freshly prepared treatment into a dropper bottle. "But the equipment there was better. For eighty bucks, you even got aromatherapy and soft drinks."

"I remember that!" K recalled his PDO Compound injection more than twenty years ago. "They repeatedly asked me whether I would like the Recuperation Package, which could be deducted from my compensation. Even after I had granted them my life, they were still trying to make money off me."

"You hate the PDO to its core, don't you?" Diana glanced at the suddenly high-spirited K and couldn't help but laugh. "Anyway, I'm a bit worried this room is too crude. It probably scares you."

The makeshift lab was located at the center of the factory. On the side of the operating table were the usual syringes and medical tape. Set off a bit further was equipment that looked like modules of a robotic arm. On the wall opposite were piled cartons of all sizes and cardboard boxes covered in what looked like ash.

"All of you were PDO. Why would you choose to do what you're doing now?"

"You mean engineering antibodies to resist the PDO Compound?" Diana paused, walked to the stacked instruments and lit a cigarette. The sunset afterglow from the high windows filtered in. K watched the last of the sun's warmth reflect off Diana's red lips. K knew he had seen that color of red before.

"When I was PDO, not only did I have to administer the PDO Compound injections, but I also had to administer euthanasia. I had to poison every applicant who came to me. The number of people who died by my hand would make the most horrible serial killer bow before me." Diana dragged deeply on her cigarette. "And that was my legal right and responsibility according to PDO regulations. But who would want that fucking right? Who would want to go to work every day and kill people one needle at a time—then have to do it with a smile? Would you want that job, Mr. Li?"

K stared at Diana. He had no idea how to answer the question. He had never done a legit job in his life. He had grown up in the casinos as just another thug beating up people who couldn't pay their debts. Then he had applied for PDO.

"The worst part was PDO didn't allow anyone to resign. If you left, you would never find work again. I had no option to hate the work or the place. Mr. Li, those people at the Application Center, those people always adding 'sir' at the end of every sentence, forcing you to say 'I confirm'—those people were after your life."

"So now you synthesize antibodies to make amends ..."

"That's Ikai and Zhang Heng's work." Diana pinched the butt of her cigarette and spat out one last plume of smoke. "Perhaps they suffered a deeper torture. They were at the core of the PDO—"

"Senior Pharmacology Consultant, right? I saw it on Zhang Heng's ID."

"His guilt ran deep. A while back, Zhang Heng was supposed to go with Shaji to Manila, where the Compound is manufactured.

But Zhang Heng said he wanted to move to the dorm where all you upstarts were living, to be with you together. I sensed it was too dangerous but didn't protest. Reflecting on it now, perhaps living in that place was what gave him his sense of urgency." Diana crushed her cigarette. "I guess, he was good to you."

"Maybe the only friend I ever had. I never imagined I'd meet someone like that at the end, facing death."

"Your life might still be long." Diana put a hand on K's shoulder. Through his clothing he felt an electric warmth transmit from her flesh to his. "You might not only live but save many others like you. You can end this era when people put their lives up for sale."

K was still thinking about how he should respond when the door burst open.

"Our hero ready?" Chris marched in with a screen full of code in hand. He glanced at K and grinned. "Ready for resurrection?"

"It's really gonna be okay?" K turned to Chris, but Chris had walked to the back of the operating table. He was seated atop a pile of cartons again absorbed in his screens. The clattering of his keyboard brought the operating room back to life. K glanced at the IV. "Has the antibody injection started?"

"Just basic tranquilizers and enzymes to assist absorption of the antibodies. There's one more step before injection of antibodies." Diana shook her head at Chris. "You know the PDO Compound is designed for genetic compatibility."

"Yes," K said. "When I applied, the PDO rep mentioned it was for my safety."

"Since birth, all our genetic accounts are uniformly recorded, distributed, monitored and managed. They record all our details and exclude all information that does not belong to us." Diana pointed at the IV flowing into K's body. "Antibodies can successfully inhibit the active ingredients in the PDO Compound in an experimental environment, but in your body, because the preparations have your genetic attributes, we must first write the parameters of the antibodies into your genetic account to ensure genetic compatibility."

"Parameters of the antibodies ... genetic compatibility ..." K repeated what Diana said like a babbling child. Such thinking made him dizzy. He simply nodded. "You need to modify my genetic account?"

"That's right."

"I remember ... the PDO rep said: 'Retrieval and update of such data will require professional and compliant data replacement, as well as multiple authorizations by you personally' ... Was that the sentence?"

"Something like it." K nodded, embarrassed. It turned out the PDO already had written answers for every question he had asked. "But who can do this?"

"Data replacement." Diana pointed to Chris then back to K. "Authorize and confirm."

"How do I authorize?"

Diana smiled. "If you confirm to begin implementing this application, Mr. K Li, please answer with a voice of no less than sixty decibels and confirm."

"Really," K looked at Diana and nodded. "The exact words of the people who designed it."

"Whether you're a service rep in the PDO or a whore on circuit, work is just repetition." Diana picked up the IV bag, from which the last bit of medicine flowed. She squeezed in a fresh syringe. "That's it."

"Whu ... what?"

Diana's eyes became fierce and focused. She stared at K and spoke slowly: "Next, you may feel dizzy, which is normal. Do all you can to stay awake. Chris will need your voice to update your genetic account."

"Okay ..."

"Chris will enter your genetic account information and implant the antibody sequence. During this period, you must clearly confirm each point requiring authorization. Do you understand?"

"Understood ..."

"Fear is normal. You haven't been trained. Mr. Li, once the antibodies integrate into your genes, the PDO will detect abnormalities. You could soon face arrest, interrogation, detention ... I don't know whether you can cope with what comes next."

"Worst case is just death?" After listening, K smiled. "That's completely acceptable for an upstart. I'd rather die for a reason than be just one more PDO euthanasia."

Diana looked into K's eyes. "What do you feel?"

"Dizzy ... My body feels light ... But it's a comfortable lightness."

"Stay awake and remember what I just said. You can end this era, Mr. Li. Though you're a very different person from the one we originally agreed on, it's up to you now. You must become our hero."

"Hero ..."

"Yes, we need a hero. Can you do it, Mr. Li?"

"I ..." The drug rolled in a softness like clouds. K had suddenly escaped the pain haunting him these past weeks. He felt as though he were a titan shaping the early universe, illuminating the dark stars floating in that primal sea of darkness. A sound as soft as the night wind brushed against his ears.

"But can you do it, Mr. Li?"

He felt Diana's breath, the tapping of Chris's keyboard, the dust floating through the factory. Everything in the universe seemed to be responding to him. He was the hero—adorned in flowers and armor. He nodded.

"If you authorize to open genetic sequence source data extraction, please answer in a voice of no less than sixty decibels and confirm."

"I confirm."

"If you authorize to start genetic code replacement, please answer in a voice of no less than sixty decibels and confirm."

"I confirm."

"If you authorize to ignore the warnings of your genetic account, please answer in a voice of no less than sixty decibels and confirm."

"I confirm."

"If you authorize to start reprint loading, please answer in a voice of no less than sixty decibels and confirm."

"I confirm ... I confirm ... I confirm ..."

K gripped these words like a sword in hand. He was the hero wielding that weapon, fighting without hesitation or trepidation. "I confirm!"

\#

: What about the money? Will the money be transferred directly into my genetic account?

: We automatically generate a sub-account in your genetic asset account to distribute compensation.

: A sub-account?

: Yes, because everyone's initial genetic asset account is submitted to the central bank within seventy-two hours after birth, that lifelong binding cannot be altered. However, after the PDO Compound takes effect, your genetic information must be altered, requiring generation of the sub-account. Both accounts will continue to represent your identity and be completely under your control.

: And the money in the sub-account is secure?

: Although the sub-account is not as strictly controlled as the genetic asset account, it is also secure. Once the compensation enters your sub-account, it will load your PDO identification attributes, so that every cent is identified as yours across all global trading networks. This is all for your security, Mr. Li. Many PDO applicants' living environment and social radius are not positive, therefore the sudden influx of large amounts of funds can pose a threat by criminals to their personal safety.

: But might it also prevent me from spending money where I shouldn't?

: Understand that the PDO invests nearly three trillion in compensation funds every year. The World Bank requires that we supervise these funds to ensure they are not manipulated by illegal means.

: You think I'm the kind of person who has illegal means?

: Of course not, Mr. Li.

\#

"This is where you had to bring me?" A Xu shot a suspicious glance at K. "We shouldn't have come here."

The table for two by the window was covered in a vintage red-and-white checkered tablecloth. Two hours prior, K had woken in the operating room and said he had to go to this particular German restaurant at the city center and wanted to bring A Xu along. A Xu had trusted that there was an important reason, but since they had squeezed into the crowded restaurant, K had hardly opened his mouth, instead focusing intently on the menu. They sat across from each other at the table, each with an untouched glass of lemonade.

"Didn't you hear Imai tell you the antibody won't go into effect for eight hours, that nothing can go wrong during this time, that we cannot risk discovery by PDO? You've just injected the antibodies, so you should be resting."

"Diana said that the PDO won't find out until tomorrow at the earliest. She just asked you to look after me carefully. You're looking after me now, aren't you?" K replied, eyes fixed on the menu. "Besides, Diana and her crew are taking a lot more risk than me."

"They're preparing to rescue my father."

Engrossed by the menu, K didn't answer. Finally, his gaze lingered on the last page of the lengthy menu. His eyes narrowed and he raised his hand.

The waiter approached with a smile. "Good evening, sir. The special today is Bavarian white sausage with pretzel."

"The Nuremberg sausage with stout set, please." K pointed to the combo marked Chef's Choice of the Month. "Give me two."

"Yes, sir," the waiter nodded and continued. "The combo includes a ticket to the Space Park exhibition, but it seems today is the last day for the Caesar District tour. If you cannot attend, I can exchange it for—"

"No, that's why I came!" K closed the menu and looked up at A Xu. The retro chandelier above her glowed like a halo. "We can't miss the last day."

"You ..." A Xu stared at K in surprise. "So, that's why ..."

"Didn't your father promise to go with you? You haven't forgotten?"

"No, I didn't forget." A Xu lowered her head, as though she didn't want K to see her face. She had wiped off that bright red lipstick that never suited her. Her oversized jean jacket was replaced with a satin baseball bomber Diana had gifted her. With its yellow daisy embroidery, it looked far more fitting for A Xu. "I'm just surprised ... you remember such things."

"But I couldn't help it. The Space Park is in Caesar District. My account can't buy tickets directly for Caesar District, so I could only ..." K beamed, proud he had discovered this loophole. He hid his smile behind a sip of lemonade. "Despite the antibodies, I still don't taste anything."

"Perhaps it doesn't take effect so quickly."

"But I do feel better. Maybe life was too dull before. Now I have finally found something to do, so everything is different." He burst into unrestrained laughter.

"You okay?"

"Your father liked to say that life was different because he had found what he had to do. No wonder he was always in high spirits. It was because he was doing such a great thing." K put down the cup. The lemonade had achieved a far more invigorating effect than the expensive alcohol he was accustomed to. "You want to hear the story of your father and me?"

A Xu looked at K and nodded.

"The first time I saw him, I had fallen drunk down the stairs of the upstart building. He helped me back up. Later, whenever I went out for a drink, I'd take him along because I was guaranteed to wake up the next day in my own bed. My legal life was approaching its end, and I had no friends ..." K took a deep breath. "That's how all upstarts live. When legal life is over, there's only that one thing left to endure. If you can't endure it, you go to the PDO Administrative Center to end it. I had in fact already decided to die, but your father ... He would come to arrange my medicine each day, put those colorful pills in a row on the kitchen island. My body was an endless crashing wave of pain. But every night, your father came over to drink and chat. I grew tired of hearing about you and that Space Park ... I remember it all too well."

"Thank you for remembering."

"What's the use of just remembering? It's useful to remember those chemical formulas of your father, drugs that save people. That's useful." K laughed. "He had a mission, to be of use. He always said he was busy and had things to do. I assumed he said this because he was afraid of death ... I told him he was my first real friend and that scared me."

A Xu looked askance. "First friend?"

"Actually, he wasn't even that great of a friend ... He disappeared, was super busy and shared harsh truths, but I never had a real friend, not one who was good to me."

"How can that be?"

"Because upstarts only know other upstarts, and ninety-nine out of one-hundred upstarts are as pathetic as me. Would you be friends with the man who shoved you down when you knocked on his door looking for your father? I've been an upstart twenty-seven years. That first day twenty-seven years ago, I also thought I would live well, make friends, do all the things I wanted to do. By the end of the first year, I had bought the things I wanted, gone to the places I wanted to go, bedded the type of women I had imagined sleeping with. For the remaining twenty-six years, it seemed the best I could hope for was to repeat that first year. When you don't know what you want, life is just repetition and mindless work."

"K ... the color in your face. You look ill."

"You know, I always thought you were just some fantasy of Zhang Heng's. How could upstarts have children?"

"Wait. Something's wrong ... You look wrong ..."

"I took your father to a whorehouse. Women, men. I ordered both. I had no clue what he liked."

"Damn it. Did Diana make some mistake?"

"Diana said, I should be a hero ... a hero, you know?"

K was high on the memories flowing over him. His eyes had no sight left for the real world. He didn't even notice when the waiter came by with the sausage and beer, or when A Xu's voice began pleading.

"K ... K ... K! That person with the hostess ... I think she's PDO."

A Xu clapped her hands. "K! She's walking right towards us!" A Xu leaned in. "She's searching for us! K! You hear me? She's coming!"

A glass of beer splashed across K's face, finally pulling him back from his revery. His face wet with beer foam—K looked like he had stumbled in from a tsunami.

"We have to leave now! PDO!" A Xu stood, her trembling hand holding the empty beer stein. K turned and glanced behind him.

The restaurant was full but only a few customers were standing. K locked in on the woman in the red dress ten meters away. She swayed in front of each table, saying something before moving on to the next table.

When K turned again, the woman was standing with the waiter. She took something from her bright red coat, and the waiter nodded in the direction of K.

"How did she find us?" K asked.

"Driver, that driver." A Xu was shaking. "She's walking right towards us."

K clenched his fist. He felt no fear, only a fire burning at his core. He was now fighting for something close to him without hesitation or trepidation.

K glanced at A Xu. He saw the fear in her eyes and shook his head. "Don't be afraid."

"What the hell do we do?"

"Use that little trick of yours."

"Mine ... what trick?"

"Hold my hand, A Xu." K grabbed his stein of beer in one hand and held A Xu's trembling wrist with the other. "Hold on tight."

#

: So that's part three. Time now for the injection?

: Sorry, Mr. Li, we must delay a moment. There's an additional matter we need to confirm.

: What is it?

: There is no information in your application's column for family members, and the declaration for your family background is completely blank.

: That a problem? My family are all dead.

: You see, in the Genetic Record, we now have found a genome of high similarity to your own. The person can even be identified as an immediate family member if—

: There's no need.

: Mr. Li, this could improve your Optimistic Lifespan, if your relatives demonstrate progress—

: I said no need. I don't want to know who they are. They're the assholes who gave birth to me and didn't want to raise me.

: We may have some misunderstanding, Mr. Li. This immediate family member has just now completed genetic registration in a nearby city two hours ago. She is ... a baby girl, which is why this report is only now received.

: A girl ... baby?

: She should be your daughter, Mr. Li.

: My daughter?

: Yes, the registrant only filled in the mother's name: Eda. Do you have any impression of this name?

: Eda ... a woman from the casino ...

: Mr. Li?

: What?

: Do you have—

: No, none. I never had a daughter.

: Well ... In that case, we will proceed with your original results.

#

"Don't you dare lie to me. When we jumped from that window, as you held me, I heard your bones crack." A Xu bit the straw as she sucked from the Galaxy Soda in her hand. It was the third Galaxy Soda, the signature drink of Space Park, that A Xu had drunk in the past half hour. She inspected its transparent glass bottle filled with colorful orbs floating in a blue liquid. With each sip, her mouth sparked its own private big bang.

"I didn't lie to you. I can run laps around you." K laughed. He also had a Galaxy Soda in his hand, but he had barely taken a sip. "If you want me to prove it, I'll carry you from here back to the subway station where we got away from that woman."

"When we got past those children, you were all tired and panting. I know you're not feeling well."

"There!" K looked ahead and pointed to the planet Gliese 581g. Its gray color was dull compared to what they had seen on Mars, which had been surrounded by numerous Space Park visitors gawking at the dazzling reds.

Though nearing dawn, Space Park was still crowded. Stars were displayed across the field in magnificent nebulae. Against the backdrop of Caesar District's skyscrapers, throngs of fans strolled among the virtual stars like gods walking amidst the garden of the universe.

"Read what it says," A Xu said, pointing to the display board next to Gliese 581g.

When Stephen S. Vogt, the discoverer of Gliese 581g, was asked whether there was life on the planet, he said: 'I'm not a biologist, nor do I want to play one on TV. Personally? Given the ubiquity and propinquity of life to flourish wherever it can, my own personal feeling is that the chances of life on this planet are one-hundred per cent.

"Does that mean there are people on that planet?" K asked.

"Not human, but biological beings." A Xu looked at K as he came closer. "Among the celestial bodies discovered by mankind so far, this is among those most likely to have given birth to life."

"It looks ..." K inspected the orb of Gliese 581g again and shook his head. "It's ordinary, not particularly beautiful. I prefer the one we were just at ... That blue one of the Pleiades ... What was it, Rigel? If up to me, I'd live there in style."

"Rigel, yeah?" A Xu was amused by how dazzled K had been by the star's brilliant blue light in the Orion Exhibition. She laughed a few times again. "I hope your air conditioner is cold enough. Rigel is a star and many times hotter than even our sun."

"Oh, it's like that?" K laughed. "Sure, but if you're as ignorant as me, you need only look at the surface. You don't need to know whether it's dangerous or not."

A Xu turned back toward K. Her lips twitched as she bit at the straw. She was shivering.

"Are you okay?" K looked at A Xu. "Uncomfortable?"

"No." A Xu shook her head as though waking from a daydream. "You know how to respond to danger. You have any idea how much danger we were in at the restaurant. But you knew just what to do, toss that beer in the PDO woman's face and jump out the window."

"Just a trick I learned. When I was young, I often saw people do things like that when they had lost a bet and needed to escape the casino without paying up."

"I thought it was cool." A Xu raised her head. "Cooler than anything I've ever seen."

Surrounded by Gliese 581g's dim light, she and K ceased talking. In the darkness, both felt as though they really were twenty light-years away, floating in their own silent universe. K stretched out his hand and stroked A Xu's hair. He wondered about the beings on Gliese 581g. Then his gentle touch became a playful slap.

"Miss, you know, I spent thirteen-hundred bucks to get these tickets. And then you tell me that Space Park isn't even as cool as me throwing a beer on someone?"

"Well, Kepler-16b is way cooler than you."

"What's that?"

"The one with two suns in the sky, just like Tatooine. Right up ahead."

"How far ahead?"

A Xu took off then looked back to K. "Why isn't our big hero running already?"

In Space Park's final hours, A Xu and K's interstellar journey traversed these and many more stars. In Andromeda, they joined a galactic dance floor. Amidst the Perseid Meteor Shower, K got into a scuffle they ended up having to run from. They witnessed the most spectacular solar flares in solar history with thousands of revelers. They reached out and touched the sun, felt its hot, dazzling virtual light.

At 3 a.m., they finally lay down beside an artificial lake in the park. By then, most of the other tourists had gone home. Without the crowds, the stars seemed calm. Only a few groups remained on the lawn built around the embankment, waiting for Space Park's grand finale.

A vibrant tangerine halo slowly emerged in the night sky over the lake. A Xu and K stared up as the sky's curtain opened. A lone spacecraft meandered through reddish orange light, then the halo stretched and faded. The silent universe behind that lone spacecraft throbbed with a dull echo as the constantly shifting colors began to gel into shape: a huge, orange planet surrounded by vast rings. The spacecraft slowed at the edges of its orbit, as small as a grain of dust in its rings.

"What planet is that?" K asked.

"That's Saturn."

"This is what you said we had to see ..."

"This part of the exhibition is a scene from Yunning Xie's book Crossing Saturn's Rings. They selected many famous scenes from the novel for the exhibition." A Xu's eyes stared at the spacecraft above them. "It's exactly like the scene in my mind when I first read it."

"So, is the person in that spaceship the hero?"

"Yes, his spacecraft met with disaster. So, he was alone, floating among the rings of Saturn."

"That explains the lonesome feel." K watched the spacecraft slowly approaching Saturn's rings. Next to such a behemoth, the ship appeared insignificant. K thought of how alone he had felt all these years as an upstart.

A Xu and K's eyes followed the ship as the curved rings of Saturn drew closer. The dense particles of the ring collided, separated, disintegrated. A Xu pointed at the night sky, explaining to him the plot of the novel.

"Then ... what about the woman?" he asked.

"Doris. She wasn't a real woman. But without Doris, the hero could never have completed his journey alone."

"I hope they had a fond farewell."

"Doris had a father. Their farewell scene is especially touching."

"Good." K's breathing slowed. A deep fatigue spread over his whole being. Unconsciously, he loosened his hand still holding the soda bottle. "Such a journey is difficult without family ... but not impossible ... I guess ... because that's how I lived my own life."

"There was never anyone else?"

K thought about it for a moment and then glanced at A Xu. "Actually, I seem to have a daughter."

"A daughter?"

"I didn't know until my application for PDO ... I was so irresponsible then ... The woman I left behind still gave birth to the child." K bit his lip then managed to give a faint smile. "Now that I think about it, that was probably the only opportunity I ever had to spend my life with someone."

"Did you ever meet her?"

"No, and I never looked for her either. But now, do you think Chris can find a way to give her what PDO money I have left? PDO forbids any will of one's inheritance, but Chris knows how to work the PDO system. He should be able to find a way. If like Diana said, I'll soon be arrested and taken to various hearings and even put on the news, I'm not sure there's any chance for my freedom. So, I think it's best to give her all the money as soon as possible."

"You want to give her all the money?"

"I ... feel ..." K raised his head and looked at the night sky overhead again. The hero's spacecraft was sailing toward Earth as Saturn's beguiling rings dimmed. The sky's dark curtain faded in. "Perhaps she would also like to see the next stop of Space Park. I could buy her a ticket ..."

A Xu didn't answer. The field was now perfectly dark.

"You made me think of her," K said. He turned his face toward A Xu, but the dark night obscured her expression. He saw only the glistening of her bright eyes. "What happens tomorrow? Will they interrogate me?"

After some time, A Xu replied, "I don't know."

"This is the first moment in my life I truly care about. Tomorrow." K touched his chest, felt his heart beating like a war drum. "There is still something worth doing."

"I'm sorry." A Xu rested her hand on K's. She too felt the rhythm of his heartbeat, which sparked an uncontrollable shiver in her body. Something colder than the night fell over her. She muttered, "I'm so sorry, so so sorry ..."

"What?"

"I'm sorry ... I made you go through ... all this ..."

"What are you talking about? I'm happier right now than I've been my whole life, like ... I am going to live ... and live for tomorrow."

"I ... I think I can't do this anymore."

Fatigue overtook K, who was now incapable of opening his eyes. He felt as if he were floating amidst the vast rings of Saturn. The cold night pressed against his chest. The remaining stars faded.

#

: Well then, your application has been fully confirmed and can officially be implemented, Mr. K Li.

: Great ... wait ...

: Yes?

: So now, I'm to be injected? So soon?

: Weren't you just complaining that the process was too slow? If there is anything else you need to check or go over, I am happy to facilitate.

: So ... twenty-seven years. I live exactly twenty-seven more years.

: You have twenty-seven years left in your legal life. And it is your obligation to die before the end of your legal life.

: Twenty-seven years ...

: Mr. Li, if you are still dissatisfied with your Optimistic Lifespan, you have this last chance to terminate your application and accept your five-year waiting period, which is your legal right.

: I'm ... no ... Anyway, it's meaningless to live so long like this.

: Mr. Li, I need you to answer carefully whether you wish to terminate or confirm this application.

: At least it's possible to live more meaningfully if …

: Mr. Li?

: I confirm the application. Let's go!

#

"Impossible!" K shouted. "There's at least three-hundred-thousand in my account."

"Open your eyes. Payment failed!" The driver shoved K against the ground, locking his hands behind his back. With his free hand, the driver shoved the screen into K's face to show him the payment result. "I knew from the start you were up to no good. I took a taxi from Caesar's out to the middle of nowhere because of you. If you don't pay up right now, I'm going to bury you here!"

"Wait. My friends are in that factory over there. They'll pay." K gasped. Since he had woken in the park this morning, he had been a mess. Pain throbbed through his head, through his every bone and joint. He had dragged his shattered body through the park in the morning searching for A Xu but had only found workmen dismantling the Space Park. In desperation, he had called a car service to take him to the factory, but today's driver was obviously not as kind as yesterday's.

"You fucking liar. You're friends are here in the Dirt District? No one's lived out here for years!"

"Really! I mean it! Trust me!"

"You're a damn ghost. I don't know how many drugs you took last night. You upstarts really think of yourselves as saviors of man? You're garbage. You all disgust me. I'm going to do you in now before you harm anyone else." The driver dropped the screen and grabbed K's throat. He pushed his head into the dry earth.

"Let him go!" A woman's voice came from the direction of the factory gate. "Let him go, now!"

K struggled to raise his head to see who had come to save him. He thought he would see A Xu or Diana. His eyes instead landed on a bright red dress and his heart filled with fear. Step by step, the woman's face came into focus. It was the PDO woman he had thrown the beer at the night before.

"Let him go." The woman took something out of the pocket of the red leather coat and showed it to the driver. The driver looked at it and released his hands from K's neck.

"Fuck," the driver cursed. "You're one bad egg. Even the police are after you."

"You can leave now," the woman said.

"Fuck you." The driver spat on the ground next to K, then returned to his car. "This fare should be your funeral fee. Hope you're sentenced soon, so you can hurry up and die."

K struggled to rise. Wobbling on his feet, he was swallowed by the smoke and dust from the driver's car. Dirt burned his eyes. His already blurred vision sunk into blindness. He stumbled a few steps backwards, bumping into the woman.

K dropped back to the ground in panic. His legs were numb and unwieldly.

"There's no need to run. I didn't come here to catch you." The woman stretched out a hand and helped lift K's rickety body. "I wasn't after you last night either. I was after the girl."

"A Xu?" K shook off the woman's hand. "What did you do to her? You should've been after me!"

"I've already caught her. She and her gang are suspected of stealing 367 thousand in PDO compensation under your name."

Soon, K again found himself seated at the long table at the heart of the factory. Once littered with documents and computers, it was now empty. Policemen in uniform were carrying away boxes of various sizes. He saw two cops struggling with the operating table where he had lain for his IV.

Seeing K and the woman at the table, one of the cops grinned. "Hey Mandy, this the same upstart who invited you out for a beer last night?" His partner puffed his cheeks and defensively waved his arms as though he feared K might throw a beer at him too. The woman, Mandy, ignored their ridicule. She motioned for them to leave and they shuffled out still chuckling.

K and Mandy seemed to be alone in the vast factory. She took a deep breath and looked at K. Sitting in the familiar chair, K's face was expressionless, eyes clouded. If it weren't for the slight rise and fall of his chest, Mandy wouldn't have known if K were still alive.

"You're not their first victim. They are suspected of stealing close to six million. They always target PDO applicants to steal their compensation. Lisbon, Los Angeles, Osaka, Hong Kong … and now here. One big scam at each destination. We've been tracking them for some time."

"So it was all just a trick?" K asked weakly.

He spoke as though he didn't really care about the answer, but she still nodded.

"Conning a desperate upstart out of compensation used to be easy. Just tell them there's a surgery that will reverse the PDO Compound with an organ transplant, cryogenics or whatnot. I'm sure you've heard such tales." Mandy simpered. "Now, applicants have wised up. They don't fall for those tricks anymore. So, the conmen have developed more advanced methods, like the people who conned you. Usually, they'll send over a person to be friends with the applicant first, take care of all their needs, then introduce their little family. Usually, it was the wife who did the trick."

"Wife?"

"You would have seen the woman, the one on the most-wanted list, the former mistress of the drug lord of the old Dirt District. When the Dirt District collapsed, she disappeared but eventually surfaced as part of this gang of swindlers. Typically, after the so-called pharmacist disappeared, she would find the victim, plead for help, open the pharmacist's apartment, find clues in his email, and so on. More than a few victims confessed she also seduced them."

"Diana …"

"Of course, that's not her real name."

"But the one Zhang Heng most often mentioned was … A Xu." When he spoke her name A Xu, K raised his head to look at Mandy. "A Xu was his daughter."

"We believe this is the first time they used her this way. I guess they decided it was time to change scripts. In the testimony of previous victims, the girl you mentioned played the role of the young nurse giving the injection."

"A Xu ..." in K's mind, a bright red, familiar red suddenly appeared. It gradually took shape, becoming A Xu's lips, Diana's lips. "They have ... the same red."

"Their division of labor is clear. The neighbor creates the foundation of friendship. The wife threads the needle. The thug triggers the mark's anger and guilt. Then, the nurse provides comfort, makes the mark believe the PDO is their mortal enemy. She gives the mark that sense of mission. The hacker then obtains all authorization to implement the real theft. The leader is the old man, the one who inspires a sense of justice. Eight hours later, when the money lands, they all disappear into thin air."

"But I watched the PDO take Zhang Heng away ..."

"If you had watched more closely, you would have seen it was just them dressed up in PDO uniforms shouting outside your door. They do that to ensure you witness the scene."

"They ... Weren't they afraid I might actually open the door?"

"Mr. Li, they have thoroughly studied the psychology of you upstarts." Mandy took a deep breath. "They are certain you will not open the door."

"All ... all of it was fake?"

"Your friend, the antibodies, the rescue plans ... all part of the scam. Victims feel stimulated for several hours after the supposed antibody injection. They believe they have escaped the pain. But it's just a drug. But this time it seems the injection wasn't prepared correctly due to the change in roles, so there were excess drugs in your body that made your reaction last night more intense. It was probably highly destructive to your body. I think the girl also noticed."

"Those drugs ... They were made by A Xu?"

"Yes, we believe she's the one in charge of preparing the drugs. That girl is the only actual scientist in the group. She is proficient in chemistry, astronomy, physics ... According to our research, it seems she went astray at a young age after her parents died."

"A Xu ... Both parents died ..."

"Their scam has several flaws, so they wait until the victim reaches the Compound Reaction Period, typically the second phase. By this time, the victim's consciousness has experienced devastation of various Reaction-related diseases, but they still have the ability to act. At the same time, they are at their most desperate for the promised antibodies, and ..."

"And what?"

"The victim usually enjoys the process of being cheated, Mr. Li." Mandy looked at K's dark, empty eyes. That kind of emptiness she was very familiar with. She couldn't remember how many times she had looked at such eyes. "Helping friends, gaining new life, fighting evil, saving the world. One dream after another ...."

K's head drooped.

Mandy paused. She seemed used to such reactions. "What is strange, however, is that this time they didn't give you the anesthesia."

"Anesthesia?"

"The transfer of assets takes eight hours. To prevent any unexpected mishaps, they find a reason for a second injection, this time to make you unconscious. Only this time—I don't know why—they instead took you into the city."

"Yes ... I proposed it. I needed to take A Xu somewhere."

Mandy glared suspiciously at K. What made her more confused was the sparkle in K's previously gray eyes. "And they actually agreed?"

"They all opposed. But A Xu convinced them. She said she would go with me."

"That was a once-in-a-lifetime opportunity. If you had let me rescue you at the restaurant, maybe we could have recovered your losses."

K took a deep breath, and his body trembled. He raised a hand to his chest, felt the familiar rhythm of his heart, still beating. He mustered a smile for Mandy. "No, I would have lost something more."

"It seems you had a good time last night." Mandy rose from her seat. "I'll take you back. I wanted you to assist further in the investigation, but you've earned your rest. And you provided an important clue as to how they've adjusting their division of labor."

"That ... No."

"What?"

"That girl. She won't be playing the role of the daughter anymore."

"How—"

"She told me personally," K raised his head and his eyes met Mandy's. The red curve of her coat reminded him of the story he and A Xu had watched, the arc of the spacecraft returning home. "She said she would never do it again."

#

: Hello?

: Hi, is this Miss Edi?

: And you are?

: Hello, Miss Edi, this is the customer service center at Space Park.

: Space Park? Is that the exhibition thing in the rich area?

: Yes, Miss Edi, we have your reservation here for two VIP Deluxe Packages, including pick-up service in your city, night camping and on-site buffet. This call is to confirm timings for you and your mother. We are happy to arrange your pick-up vehicle and fast-pass certificate at your convenience. Also, your tickets include a private booking of the night sky exhibition, Crossing the Rings of Saturn, so I have to confirm with you in advance—

: Wait! Wait! I ordered this?

: Yes ... It says here you made the reservation six hours ago.

: But I thought upstarts were prohibited from buying tickets to the Space Park or anything else in Caesar ...

: Miss Edi, we have received a paid reservation signed for you. If you have any question about the reservation or would like to refund your ticket—

: Damn, whose pranking me? Who paid for this?

: Just a moment, Miss Edi, allow me to check for—

: Don't tell me. It was probably one of those jerks from the bar.

: Hello, Miss Edi, the payment account is ... K Li, Mr. Li.

: K Li? Mom! Mom, come here. Do you know anyone named K Li?

: Miss Edi, please wait a moment. There may be some issue. It says here the genetic account was ... cancelled three weeks ago. This may be due to a system error, but the reservation is good. Do you have any other questions about the reservation? Miss Edi? Are you still there?

# 2039：脑机时代

## 阿缺

中国新锐科幻作者的代表之一。2011年发表处女作《蒿城旧事》，文风细腻，擅长将科幻元素与情感故事相结合。
获奖：2019年第三十届银河奖最佳短篇小说奖｜宋秀云
2018年第二十九届银河奖最佳短篇小说奖｜云鲸记
2014年第二十五届银河奖最佳短篇小说奖｜收割童年


1

生活是从什么时候起，变得这么糟糕呢，严妍在被撞飞的那一刻还在想，糟糕到自己要在街头寻死？

要说时间点，肯定是陈彦出的那次车祸。但哪怕他躺在病床上，全身插着软管，透明的液体像蚯蚓一样涌进他的身体；哪怕他三年来只剩呼吸，没有意识，她也没有如此绝望。那时，她只是难过和自责。

尤其是，当医生告诉她，可以通过植入脑机芯片治疗陈彦时，连难过和自责都消失了。

"就是有两点，你得好好想想。"医生观察她的表情，斟酌着说，"首先，手术有点儿麻烦。"

严妍微微皱眉。

"整体是比较乐观的。"医生展颜一笑，"其实脑机技术已经很普及了。我看严小姐的职业是编剧，创作时应该也在用脑机头盔吧？我们做临床手术，也得戴。"

严妍点头。早几年写剧本，她是靠灵感、熬夜和咖啡因，但陈彦出事后，她有点儿神经衰弱，创作时爱胡思乱想。陈彦倒在血泊里的情景，总会在脑中浮现，像丢帧的全息影像。这场景有时候还会不自觉地在指尖流露。一次，她写言情桥段，写着写着，正在一边恋爱一边商战的男主角，下一场戏就被车撞飞，而她自己没有察觉。后来资方用程序检验剧本，这一段被标得血红——系统判定这段戏有违观众预期，会严重影响收视率。

她连忙道歉，但改了几稿都过不了系统审核。在同行推荐下，她买了脑机头盔，戴上之后，涣散的精神像是稻草一样被一只手握紧，集成一束。她高效地完成了剧本，系统给出高分，资方这才敢去拍摄。

不只是她，这座城市里有一半的人都在用脑机头盔。那玩意儿像被掏空内脏的刺猬，内壁光滑，外壳上长满了粗粗细细的电极。它能解读脑电波，再反馈给大脑，让大脑知道哪些事情该做不该做，包括分泌身体激素。

医生继续说："人体和机器一样，都可以精准控制。只是以前我们不知道打开这部机器的方法，BCI①技术出现后，我们才有解密这部机器的钥匙。"

严妍试图跟上医生的逻辑——尽管没有脑机头盔帮忙，显得有点儿困难。"你是说，我男朋友只要戴上脑机头盔，就可以醒过来？"

医生摇摇头，"我们尝试过，不太行。陈先生是脑干大面积脑梗死，大脑活动停止，再加上隔着颅骨，不能接收头盔的电波反馈。我们提供的解决方法，是侵入式脑机接口。"

听起来也很简单：把脑机头盔做到足够小，植入脑中，代替休眠的脑区域，重建神经冲动。它不仅能读取脑电波信号，以此来控制外部设备，比如机械臂，还可以进行精确的电刺激，让大脑产生特定的感觉。

"法律允许吗？"

"哈，你问到点子上了。侵入式BCI还不成熟，毕竟要在脑子里动刀，部件再小也有创口，之前还有几起失败的例子，法律上卡得紧，不能流入市场，只能用于小范围的医疗领域。但幸运的是，陈先生受的伤恰到好处——抱歉，对陈先生的不幸，我当然是感到遗憾的——脑休眠和肢体残疾，刚好符合植入条件。"

听起来都是好消息。严妍只剩一个顾虑，"所以你是说，手术会有风险，是吧？"

任何事都有风险，只是在这个时代，任何事都可以被量化。所谓风险，也只是用数据建立模型，设定参数，再估算出一个比例数字。

31.2%。这是陈彦做手术失败的概率。

严妍可以接受。反正最坏的结果也不过是陈彦继续躺在病床上，陷入永恒的意识黑渊。

"死马当活马医吧……"她说。

"差不多是这个意思，不过我是医生，不能说这种话。"医生拿出一沓文件，递给她。

文件上的条款很复杂，严妍翻了翻，几乎每页上都能看到"免责声明"四个字。

"你刚刚说有两点，另一个是什么？"她问。

医生笑了笑，露出白皙的牙齿，"这种手术嘛，有点儿贵。"

忘说了，城市里另一半不用脑机头盔的人，都是因为用不起。

好在严妍这些年有点儿积蓄，加上陈彦出事的保险赔偿，勉强能凑齐手术费。

2

陈彦醒来后，花了很长一阵，才从陌生感中适应过来。

这种陌生感不是来自暌违了三年的世界。世界确实有一些变化，堪称日新月异，但趋势无非更快，更小，以及更贵。他需要适应的，是体内的变化。

这种感觉难以言喻。他的视野不再清晰，但也不模糊，眼球像被水浸泡一样，处在一种动态的晃荡中。克服由此产生的眩晕后，他发现，只要看向哪里，视界里水波的凸面就会将该处的景象拉近，近到可以看清每一个细节。

他首先看到的，是一片巨大山峦，沟壑纵横又宽广，但色泽又介乎褐色和金银之间。他眨眨眼，山峦的影像缩小千百倍，旁边出现了眼睛和鼻梁。他这才意识到，刚才看见的山峦，只是这张脸上眼角的皱纹。

"你老了。"这是他对严妍说的第一句话。

严妍稍微往后退了退。为了迎接陈彦醒来，她精心化了妆，确认那轻微的鱼尾纹都被粉底和遮瑕笔盖住，没想到还是被陈彦一眼看出——或者说，是被陈彦脑子里的BCI芯片一眼看出。

"三年了，你终于醒了。"她哽咽着说。

她的声音、表情和眼神，以及藏在这三者背后的情绪，都以一种坦诚到近乎赤裸的姿态，平铺在陈彦的眼中。他尚在发愣——毕竟上一秒的记忆还是那辆轿车碾过来的恐怖画面，再睁眼，就换成病房里感人的情侣相认——但大脑的某个部位帮他处理了这些信息，并且告诉他，该以怎样的方式回应。

他张开左臂，抱住严妍，柔声道："没事的，这三年也辛苦你了。"

随后他才意识到不对——右臂去哪里了？

不仅是右臂，他掀开被子，发现左腿膝盖以下，也空空如也。

"是车祸……"严妍说，顿几秒后又道，"对不起。"

于是他也记起车祸的原因。

　　两人吵架，严妍生着闷气，低头在街上走着。一辆还在使用手动驾驶的老式汽车横穿而至。是他上前推开了她。很俗套狗血的剧情，这种桥段，严妍这种三线言情编剧都不屑用——用了也通不过系统审核，没想到却发生在他们自己身上。身为配角，最可悲的就是拿到主角的剧本，却没有主角光环，对接下来情节的走向全然无措。

　　"不过别担心，"严妍说，"他们会给你装上义肢，跟BCI系统是兼容的。"

　　花了好几天，他才知道自己脑子里多了个小小的芯片，取代大脑里那些不再活跃的部位。医生说他运气很好，芯片植入后，只产生了轻微的排异反应。

　　"有其他运气不好的人吗？"他问医生。

　　医生说："很多。所以BCI还不能投入市场，就算用于医疗，也只有像你这样符合标准的病人才能使用。"

　　所以其实一半是治疗，一半也是实验。

　　适应过程比想象中快，花时间的，主要是对义肢的控制。从跌跌撞撞到能够行走，他花了一个多月。严妍一直在旁边照顾，看着他一次次跌倒，脸和手都磨出血，想要上前搀扶，却被他赶开。

　　陈彦终于适应义肢的行走后，在病房里健步如飞。她也很喜悦，问他感觉怎么样。

　　事后想起来，其实一切都是从这里开始变糟糕的，但她没有及时意识到。

　　"好像……"当时陈彦站直身体，左腿的动力足弓在地上缓缓摩挲，"好像比车祸前，要高了那么一点儿。"


　　3

　　出院后，他们回到家。

　　家里倒是没变，是三年前他们租的房子，陈彦的物品还在，连摆设的位置都差不多。由此可见，三年来严妍过的是怎样的生活。

　　"这三年，有人追你吧？"他问。

　　严妍沉默了一会儿，点点头，"我没答应。"

　　陈彦抱住她说："没事，现在我醒来了，后面都是好日子。"

　　好日子的确持续了一段时间。屋子里有了生气，夜晚也不再是一个人睡，性与爱交融，再也不是简单的生理需求。

　　唯一的缺点，是当她处在久违的巨大愉悦中，习惯性去抓他的手臂时，却发现抓了个空。

这一瞬间，像是有冰水泼下。

"下次，"陈彦讷讷地说，"我还是戴上手脚吧。"

"没关系，也不用……习惯就好了。"

但从那以后，陈彦就一直穿着义肢，连睡觉都不卸下。唯一让他跟这些精密的金属器械分离的事情，是洗澡，但通常他也会把浴室门反锁——在以前，洗澡时他都不关门，并且露出贱兮兮的表情，邀请严妍加入。偶尔他能得到一只飞过去的拖鞋，偶尔，也会如愿以偿。

肯定会有些变化，严妍想，毕竟脑袋里嵌入了机器。而且就算有再多变化，也好过他继续躺在病床上，陷入无意识的深渊中。

得益于脑中的BCI芯片，陈彦对义肢的操控日趋灵活，右臂的五根金属手指甚至能同时做出不同的动作。有一次，严妍看到他在电脑前编程，左手平放桌上，右手五指弹跃如飞，快到几乎出现残影。

"这么灵活？"严妍吃了一惊，"跟弹钢琴似的。"

弹钢琴是人类手指能做出的最复杂精细的动作，但陈彦听到后，表情依旧平淡。"可惜只有五根手指，"他抬起右手，金属的五指像波浪一样依次扭动，"如果多一点的话，我确实可以给你弹钢琴。"

"等等，"严妍这时才发现真正不对劲的地方，"你什么时候学会的编程？"

陈彦之前的职业是美术教师，对代码很陌生。她不记得他报班学过汇编语言，或C++，或Java，或是程序员鄙视链上的任何一种编程语言。

"不是'学'，是'下载'。"

严妍这才知道，BCI芯片不仅是替代了陈彦脑中受损的部分，也在影响其他领域。比如负责记忆的海马体，以及负责推演和逻辑的额叶，只要在医院官网下载对应的知识，陈彦就能掌握。

她知道BCI技术的玄妙，戴上头盔后，能更专注，调节一些激素的分泌，焦虑或失眠都能治好。但隔着颅骨，头盔无法直接在脑子里刻写信息，只起修复和增强的作用。

但陈彦的芯片，显然能做不一样的事情。

陈彦学代码的原因，是要找工作。

他去面试时，严妍都在家写剧本。她被幸福感包围着，写出来的剧本盎然生趣，系统评定为高分。到了晚上，她会听陈彦讲述白天求职的经历——并不顺利。

很多公司会询问他这空缺的三年去了哪里。在这个年代，他无法撒谎，只能老实地回答："在病床上。"通常这四个字一出口，就会换来对方程式化的微笑，告诉他回去等结果。

结果都是一致的。

"没关系，"她安慰他，"你编程这么厉害，肯定会有公司要你的。"

严妍并不仅是口头宽慰。她在影视圈混了这么久，还是认识几个人，找了一圈后，一家特效公司愿意给陈彦机会。他们在开发一款给演员做减龄效果的软件，让陈彦参与底层构架。

"不过先说好，要是他能力跟不上……"对方老板字斟句酌地说，"我这儿也养不了闲人。你也知道现在的压力，我们当老板也不容易。"

半个月后，对方的电话又打来了。

"真没想到这么牛！我是第一次见到有人同时会用所有的编程语言，还能无缝切换，这么资深的程序员，居然还有头发，真是不可思议……"

六个月后，陈彦成了这家公司的正式员工。

严妍心底的石头彻底落地，甚至开始构想结婚的事情。陈彦曾经求过婚，她也答应了，如果没有车祸，这件事三年前就该完成。

4

"再等等吧。"陈彦说。

"嗯？"严妍一下子没反应过来，"我们已经等了四年啊。"

"可是现在我没有想好。"

"你要想什么？"

陈彦拉起袖子，露出金属手臂，又敲了敲左腿，"我现在身体有五分之一是金属，卸下义肢后，我都没有你重。"

"我不在意啊。"

"可是我在意。"

他们的对话就此结束。


严妍事后咂摸，总觉得这番对白不对劲儿。她是编剧，知道通常角色发生这种对话时，其中有一个人是在撒谎。她很确信这个人不是自己。

如果是以前，她会直接跟陈彦对质。但自从陈彦苏醒，她总觉得一个人脑子里有部机器，似乎发生什么变化都……情有可原。她唯一能咨询的，只有医生。

"根据他上个月复检的情况来看，BCI芯片运行正常，没有出问题。"医生从数据堆里抬起头，笃定地说。

"可是我总感觉他不一样了。"

"他脑袋受了伤，又当了三年植物人，怎么都会有变化的。"

这时，一个想法冒了出来。她刚开始有些惊讶，试图扼杀它，但这个想法无比顽强，如春芽破土，越发茁壮。"您说，有没有可能，让我知道他在想什么？"她犹豫地说。

医生摘下眼镜，用失焦的目光盯着严妍。

严妍讪讪地笑了下，为自己的异想天开感到羞惭。她站起来，正要道歉，医生对着眼镜哈了口气，用软布拭净，再戴回鼻梁上，说：

"可以的。"

脑机技术的关键，是识别生物信号并转化为电信号。它的核心是数字化，将激素分泌数字化，也将脑电波数字化。

那个小到几乎肉眼难辨的功率强悍的芯片，能精确地观察脑中单个神经元的兴奋情况。它能记录下每一次神经冲动产生的电位变化，正是这些变化在传递信息，仿佛另一种形式的编码。信息构成记忆，而记忆被解码，转录成影响，储存在医院的数据库里。

"其实芯片能做到的，不仅是记录记忆。只要他愿意，可以逆向影响，篡改记忆。反正无非都是数据。"医生说。

"我能看看他的记忆吗？"

"按照规定，是不可以的，BCI技术推广的另一个阻力，就是可能导致隐私泄露。"医生微微后仰，躺在座椅上，"但你是陈先生做手术的担保人，而且……这次很特殊，程序上风险不大。"

严妍坐在资料室里，以第一人视角展开的全息影像在她周围弥漫。

这是陈彦最近一个月的生活，每一秒都被BCI记录，继而储存在医院里。她能看到陈彦在工位专注编程时的视角。他的右手后来升级过，有九根手指，长短粗细各不一样，按键时效率奇高。

她快进这些画面。全息光影加速流逝，她脸庞明暗不定。

她以陈彦的视角，重历了陈彦上下班的所见所闻，见到他的工作和同事，见到他下班后跟朋友聚会……

等等，同事。她让画面倒退，发现一个女同事的脸反复出现，一旦出现，就会在陈彦的视野中驻留多时。

陈彦在凝视这位同事。

于是严妍截取了所有关于这位女同事的画面，窥知他们认识的经过。

那是一个新入职的美工，模样并不多么妖冶，脸颊右侧还垂着头发，看起来更不起眼。但老板特意让陈彦跟她认识，乐呵呵地说："你们一定有共同话题，"说着，他点了点自己的太阳穴，"这里啊，都装了机器。"

他说的是BCI芯片。

陈彦的目光向女同事的右颊聚焦。她的侧脸被放大，纤毫毕现，树木一样的发根底下，能看到她的疤痕。陈彦也撩起头发，露出同样的伤口——这个动作是严妍脑补的。她想，自己如果是陈彦，也会这么做，像森林里，野生兽类亮出只有同族才懂的标志。

"你好。"陈彦低声说。

"你好。"

他们的初见如此简单，后面也不常见，隔几天才会在公司的某个角落遇到，错身而过，并无交谈。但错身的一瞬间，陈彦会放大她的眼眸，乌黑眼珠充斥整个视界。对方眼珠微动，精光闪烁，似乎也同样在放大他的眼珠。这是脑机侵入者的对视，彼此都能在对方眼中看到自己的倒影。

严妍有些无力。她只是普通人，不知道这种对视中，他们在交换什么信息。

她连忙快进，到了陈彦最后一次见到女同事时，也就是昨天晚上。女同事在路边躲雨等车，陈彦开着车，从她身边驶过。一分钟后，他又绕回来，车窗滑下，雨幕中她的脸无比清晰。

"我送你吧。"陈彦说。

对方在犹豫。

"我们比普通人更不能淋雨，"陈彦讲了个不好笑的笑话，"我们有手术的创口，脑子里容易进水。"

对方没有笑，但还是上了车。

雨滴在车窗上汇成无数细流，雨刷再努力地摇摆，也无法阻止它们在陈彦的视野里蜿蜒爬行。街边景色也变得氤氲一片，他们朝着迷乱的光和影驶去。

陈彦始终盯着前方，所以严妍也看不到女同事的脸，但能听清他们的声音。

“你植入多久了？”陈彦问。

“五年。你呢？”

“一年。”

对方笑了笑，说：“那你要适应的东西还多。”

陈彦说：“作为前辈，你有什么建议吗？”

“有很多建议。比如保护你的脑袋，BCI芯片就像在大脑上开了个窗，我们有更好的视角，别人也能透过玻璃看进来，甚至只要改变芯片的一点点数据，你就会成为另一种性格的人。你可以下载安全卫士。还有，多下载几种语言，语言是各种技能里最有用的……”

女同事说了一大串建议，最后停顿了几秒钟，继续说：“但最重要的建议，是——你必须意识到，你已经跟人类不同。”

这句话让严妍和陈彦同时吃了一惊。

“你是说，我们植入了BCI芯片，就不是人了吗？”陈彦问。

“从生物归属来说，我们当然还算人类。但我们的脑袋已经变了，感知世界的方式也不一样，以前你用手拥抱一个人能感觉到幸福，现在你只要适当地让BCI芯片给予电信号刺激，也会有同样的感觉。我问你，你现在还对性有兴趣吗？”

严妍下意识屏住呼吸，在一片沉默中等待陈彦的回答。

“没有。”

“因为只要你愿意，你随时可以控制下丘脑，分泌多巴胺和内啡肽，让你拥有比性爱强烈几十倍的快感。连人类最原始的冲动和快乐，我们都可以随时模拟，甚至超越；我们可以省去漫长的学习过程，直接掌握技能，只要大脑能承受得住，古往今来所有知识都能储存。你操作机械臂，比你健全的手臂都灵活——你看看，你的左手都快退化萎缩了。你觉得我们还算……还算常规意义上的人类吗？”

陈彦似乎叹息了一声，“听起来我们的确跟人类背道而驰，更像是一部机器了。”

“严格意义上说，人体本身就是一部机器。只是我们现在换了一套运行系统。”

“在一台安卓机上运行IOS吗？听起来就很卡顿。”陈彦说，“那像我们这种人，人生有何意义呢？”

“我的另一个建议是，不要去想这些问题。两年前我认识另一个植入了BCI的人，他就是没想通，最后徒手把芯片挖了出来。”

“那他自己呢？”

女同事没有回答，答案不言自明。

“想想好的一面吧。”陈彦说，“只有我们这种脑死亡的人，才有资格做侵入式脑机。换一套系统，总比一直死机要强。”

“那倒是。”

车继续往前，高楼逐渐变得稀疏。这里是城市边缘。灯火通明的楼宇和车灯流曳的街道，被甩在身后，成了我们这个故事的背景板。

“你一个人住这里？”陈彦看了看周围，这里不像是一个光鲜白领居住的环境。

“嗯。你是跟女朋友住一起吧——车里有女生开过的痕迹？”

陈彦点头。

“出事前，我女儿刚出生。其实我受的伤很重，他们说，是因为我太想再见到女儿，意志力在支撑，好几次医生都要宣布我失去一切生命体征，但我挺着，一直没死。”女同事平淡地说，声音里听不出感情波动，“后来植入BCI芯片，我就醒了，如愿以偿地见到了孩子。但问题是，我再也没有身为‘母亲’的感觉。这个人类雌性幼体，嗜睡，流鼻涕，喜欢发出声响来引起成年人的注意，来汇聚更多有利于她成长的资源。她只是一堆血管、脂质和蛋白质，跟我唯一的联系，是有着高相似度的DNA序列。但这有什么意义呢？同一条产品线上出来的两台电饭煲，也应该相亲相爱、不离不弃吗？”

“那……你孩子现在怎么样了？”

“不知道，我已经四年没有见过她了。”

又是一阵沉默。陈彦把车开到一栋楼前，停下。雨小了不少，雨滴舔舐车顶玻璃，沙沙声绵绵不绝。

“我到了。”女同事说。

陈彦“嗯”了声。

同事没下车，突然轻声一笑，“也别这么绝望。我们这类人，也有自己的乐趣。来吧，我教你。”

“我要做什么吗？”

“你就坐着，也不用说话，但开放你BCI芯片的权限。”同事的声音如同呓语，“让我连接，让我进入。”

接下来，他们真的没有动，并排坐在主副驾驶位上，也不再交谈。严妍看到的全息影像静止了，但她知道某种她无法理解的事情正在发生。她甚至都“喂”了一声，想叫醒全息影像里的人。但无人回应。她也不敢再快进，就这么坐着，任静止的画面流逝。

雨声依旧响个不停。

这场景持续了近两个小时。

最后，陈彦和同事的呼吸声同时加重，似乎断开了连接。陈彦满头汗水，大口呼吸了几分钟才喘匀，喃喃地说："这……"

"这就是数据交融。"说完，她离开了车。


5

严妍失魂落魄地回到家时，陈彦还在家里编程。敲击键盘的声响不绝于耳，让严妍心烦——这噼里啪啦的声音，太像是雨声。

她坐到陈彦对面。

陈彦抬起头，看着她，突然一笑，"你知道了？"哪怕看着严妍说话时，他的右手依旧不停，屏幕上代码如流水涌过。

严妍问："你们在车里……做了什么？"

"你窥视了我的记忆，应该知道，我们什么都没做。我们没有丝毫肢体接触。"

"你骗人！难道你们发了两个小时的呆吗？"

陈彦叹口气，说："我不知道你能不能理解——我们在交换数据。"

"什么数据？"

"知识、痛苦、经验、愤怒……见过的最美风景，最黑暗的往事，病态的癖好，美好的心愿……人生感悟，梦境，食物的味道，童年，爱过和恨过的人，看过的电影和听过的音乐……总而言之，就是一切。我们所经历人生的一切，都被BCI转化了数据。我们在交换这庞大的数据，体验对方的人生。"

严妍瞠目结舌。她的确无法理解，对面的陈彦依然是熟悉的脸，但两人中间裂开了巨大鸿沟。

"我宁愿你告诉我，你们在恋爱，或者其他什么苟且。"严妍说，"那样，我至少还可以恨你。"

陈彦的右手停止敲键盘。他安静地看着她，然后说："我没有做对不起你的事。我没有出轨，我也并不爱她。"

"可你跟这个女人做的事情，比出轨还……"想了半天，她才想出一个勉强能用的词，"还要亲密。"

"这我没有办法。我运行的是另一套程序，而且这跟性别无关。你想想，如果这位同事是男性，难道你就不生气了吗？"

严妍一时语塞。她回家前准备的所有说辞，在陈彦面前毫无用处。原来不管是收入，还是言语交流，甚至可能连爱，都是他在勉强自己。这种落差产生的缘由，更让她觉得两人鸿沟之大，几乎难以逾越。

想了半天，她才想出一句话——尽管这句话她都羞于用在自己的剧本里。

"那你，还爱我吗？"

6

医生听完后，颇为好奇，"他怎么回答？"

严妍摇头，"他没有回答。"

"那你们还在一起吗？"

严妍点点头。

"也是，两个人在一起有很多原因，爱情只是其中之一。"医生宽慰道，"那既然这道坎儿过了，你为什么还来找我？"

严妍深吸口气，抬头直视医生说："我也想植入脑机接口，既然他跟我不在一条道路上，我想，我可以去跟着他，走另一条路。"

"哪怕会放弃很多东西，包括人性？"

"哪怕放弃一切。"

医生微微一笑，"我很欣赏严小姐的勇气，我也衷心希望你能寻回爱情。只是，这次我不能帮你。"他撇过头，不去看严妍的表情，解释道："我跟你说过，侵入式脑机接口在法律和伦理上都有一点儿尚待解决的问题——只有大脑坏死的患者，才允许植入，而且植入了也不能保证克服排异。"

严妍从医院无功而返。她没有打车，而是游魂一样在街边行走，她路过许多窗户——有饭店、咖啡馆和办公楼。里面的人都戴着脑机头盔，专注地工作。谁都无法否认，脑机接口技术让世界变得更美好，高效又便捷，许多疾病也因此治愈。新技术的到来就像洪水奔流，席卷整个世界，只是这股浪潮太过汹涌，张开双臂迎接它的人，总有几个会被裹挟着，在水里翻滚，撞得遍体鳞伤。

很遗憾，严妍就是其中一个。

又或许，是自己的双臂，张开得不够彻底？她想着，站住了，凝视街道上来来往往的车辆。四年前那一幕涌上心头，医生的话如魔鬼在耳畔低语般，一遍遍回荡。

一辆轿车从远处疾驶而来。

严妍深吸口气，露出微笑。她张开双臂，迎着飞驰而来的汽车，像是在迎接死亡，抑或是崭新的生活。

7

"很不幸，严小姐的排异反应太严重，BCI芯片无法继续运行，她的大脑功能正在不可逆地丧失。"医生遗憾地说，"请节哀。"

陈彦站在病房外，看着玻璃墙内的病床。以他的角度，看不到严妍的脸。

"也就是说，她正在死亡，是吧？"陈彦轻声道。

"是的。"

"但还没死。所以，BCI芯片还来得及复刻她所有的脑部信息，"他转头对医生说，"请尽快运行复制程序。"

他的口吻冷淡得出奇，医生一怔，随即想起一件事，"你之前早就签了字，允许严小姐查看你的记忆……你早知道她会来查？"

"她的心思很简单，再加上BCI芯片辅助，我很容易推测出她的行动。"

"那么，"医生打了个寒战，"你也能猜测她会用极端的方式，试图让自己脑死亡，才能植入BCI芯片。你……你根本就是在一步步诱导她！"

"你没有证据。"陈彦简短地说。他一直盯着病床，床头的仪器显示，芯片正在提取严妍的大脑信息。而严妍正在死去。

"可是，可是……"医生慌乱地取下眼镜，可怎么擦拭，镜片上都是模糊的，"为什么要这么做呢？"

陈彦没回答。

他耐心地等待复刻程序结束。BCI芯片被取出来后，他捏着这小小的部件，仔细端详。芯片小如微尘，在他拇指与食指之间，近乎透明。

他看着看着，突然笑了，转过头回答医生的问题，"因为这样，我就可以和她真正交融，永远在一起。"


创作小记：

2020年12月28日，阿里达摩院发布了"2021十大科技趋势"，其中关于脑机接口的趋势报道引起了我的注意。在此之前，SpaceX和特斯拉等公司创始人埃隆·马斯克也对着全世界举办了发布会，用三只小猪演示侵入式脑机接口。这无疑是伟大的科技发展方向，正向着我们的生活滚滚而来，如果控制得当，它将解决无数疑难杂症，如瘫痪、失明等。

但科幻，正是从未来的无限前景中，找到可能被忽视的角落，将之书写。本篇正是在此报告启发下诞生的科幻小说，尽管它底色略显阴暗，但只是一面镜子，照到阴暗角落，让我们可以提前避开，循着人性的光辉走向明亮之处。我也相信脑机接口会成为造福人类的一大助力。

# 2039 ERA OF BRAIN-COMPUTER INTERFACE

## by A Que

## Translated by Li Yating

A Que is one of the most promising Science Fiction authors in China. After his debut work Old Stories in Haocheng published in 2011, he has won almost all the Chinese sci-fi awards. He is able to integrate science fiction elements with heart- touching stories.

Awards: The Best Short Story of the Galaxy Award 2019, Song Xiuyun

The Best Short Story of the Galaxy Award 2018, Cloud Whale

The Best Short Story of the Galaxy Award 2014, Become 16 years old

When did Yan Yan start feeling like existence sucked to the extent that she wanted to end her life in the street? Yan Yan was still thinking about it the moment she got hit by a car.

The turning point must have been the car accident that happened to Chen Yan. However, when Chen Yan was lying in a hospital bed, tubes all over him, with fluid flowing like earthworms into his body, when all he could do was breathe, remaining unconscious for three years, she was not desperate. She just felt sad and guilty.

The feelings even disappeared when the doctor told her that Chen Yan could be treated by implanting a brain-computer chip.

"However, there are two things you have to consider." The doctor noticed the expression on her face and said with deliberation. "First, the surgery is a bit tricky."

Yan Yan frowned slightly.

"The overall picture is rather optimistic." The doctor smiled. "The brain-computer interface (BCI) has become popular. I've noticed that you are a scriptwriter, Miss Yan. You must be using a brain-computer helmet when you are writing, right? Our doctors, too, have to wear them during the operation."

Yan Yan nodded. She had relied on inspiration, caffeine, and burning the midnight oil in the early years of writing, but after Chen Yan's accident, she kind of suffered a nervous breakdown. She often did not know where her mind went during writing. The scene of Chen Yan lying in a pool of blood always came into her mind, like a hologram but with dropped frames. From time to time, the scene recurred at her fingertips unconsciously. She had written a romance story in which the male protagonist was in love and involved in a business war but was suddenly hit by a car in the next scene. She had written the car crash without being aware of it. Later on, this scene was marked in blood red when her sponsor examined the script with a program—the system decided that the scene would seriously affect the ratings because it went against the audience's expectations.

She gave hasty apologies and made several more drafts but still failed to get past the system review. On the recommendation of her peers, Yan Yan bought a brain-computer helmet. When she put it on, she felt as if her scattered brain was tamed, like the straw being held tightly and bundled. She finished the script efficiently, got given a high score by the system, and then the sponsor dared to shoot.

It wasn't just her—half the population in the city were using brain-computer helmets. The gadget resembled a gutted hedgehog with a smooth interior and a shell covered with thick and thin electrodes. It interpreted brain waves and fed back to the brain, telling the brain what to do and what not to do, such as how to regulate hormone secretion.

The doctor continued, "The human body, like any machine, can be controlled with precision. We just had no idea how to run the machine. Only after BCI technology came along did we have the key to decrypt it."

Yan Yan tried to follow the doctor's logic—it seemed a little difficult without the help of the brain-computer helmet though. "Are you saying that my boyfriend will wake up if he puts on a brain-computer helmet?"

The doctor shook his head. "We've tried, but it did not work well. Mr. Chen has suffered massive brainstem infarction in the absence of brain activity. On top of that, he cannot receive neurofeedback from the helmet across his skull. The solution we are suggesting is through an invasive brain-computer interface."

It sounds simple: make a brain-computer helmet small enough to be implanted in the head to replace the dormant region and restore nerve impulses. The helmet not only reads brainwave signals to control external devices such as robotic arms but also delivers precise electrical stimulation to make the brain feel specific sensations.

"Is it legal?"

"Hah, that's a good question. Invasive BCI is still in its infancy. The application of it requires brain surgery after all. A wound will be left no matter how small the implanted part is. There have already been a few failure cases. That's why the technology is under tight regulation. It is permitted only in narrow medical fields, not on the market. However, fortunately for Mr Chen, his injuries are just right—I definitely feel sorry about Mr Chen's misfortune—but brain dormancy and physical disabilities have made him eligible for the implant procedure."

That sounded like good news. Yan Yan had only one concern: "So are you saying that the surgery is risky?"

There was a risk in everything. It was just that in this era, anything could be quantified. As a result, the so-called risk was merely a matter of building data models, setting parameters, and obtaining an estimated success rate.

31.2%. This was the probability of failure of his surgery.

Yan Yan was okay with that. Anyway, the worst outcome would just be Chen Yan staying in the hospital bed as before, sinking into the abyss of eternal unconsciousness.

"Try and make every possible effort," she said.

"That is pretty much what it means, but as a doctor, I cannot say something like that." The doctor took out a pile of papers and handed them to her.

The terms and conditions were complicated. Yan Yan leafed through the papers, finding the word "disclaimer" on almost every page.

"You have mentioned two points. What is the other?" she asked.

The doctor said with a grin, "Well, this type of surgery is expensive."

I forgot to mention that the other half of city residents didn't use the brain-computer helmet because they couldn't afford to.

The good thing was that Yan Yan had put by some savings over the years plus there was the insurance compensation from Chen Yan's accident. She could almost afford to pay for the operation.


II

It took a long time for Chen Yan to adapt himself to the unfamiliar surroundings when he woke up.

The strangeness did not come from a world unseen for three years, though it had indeed changed rapidly, but the trend was nothing but faster, smaller, and pricier. He needed to become used to the change inside him.

He had no words to describe how he felt. His vision was no longer clear, but neither was it blurred. His eyeballs, as if soaked in water, made uncontrolled movements. He overcame the consequent dizziness and found that the convex surface of the water waves in his visual field would bring closer whatever he was looking at, so close that he could see every detail.

He first saw large mountains on which wide gullies crisscrossed, but in a colour somewhere between brown, gold, and silver. He blinked, and then the image of the mountains shrank a thousand times. Next to them appeared the eyes and the nose bridge, so he came to realize that the mountains he had just seen were wrinkles in the corners of her eyes.

"You are aging." These were the first words he said to Yan Yan.

Yan Yan stepped back a little. To meet him, she had carefully put on her make-up, ensuring that her slight crow's feet were covered by foundation and concealer. To her surprise, Chen Yan saw the difference at a glance—or rather, the BCI chip in his head did.

"It has been three years. Finally, you are awake," said she in a choked voice.

Her voice, her expression, her eyes, and the emotions hidden behind were straightforward, her naked sincerity on display. Chen Yan was still in a daze—after all, his last memory was the terrifying image of the car running over him. It was a touching reunion of a couple in a hospital room when he opened his eyes again—some part of his brain, despite his confusion, processed the information and told him how to respond.

He opened his left arm and hugged Yan Yan, saying softly, "It will be fine. The last three years have been hard on you too."

Then he realized something was wrong—where had his right arm gone?

Not only his right arm. He pulled back the covers and found his left leg, below the knee, was gone as well.

"It was a car accident..." Yan Yan said, pausing for a few seconds before adding, "I'm sorry."

He then remembered the cause of the crash.

They quarreled. Yan Yan, sulking, walked down the street with her head down. An old manual car came at her and it was he who stepped forward and pushed her out of its way, a cheesy plot a good romance writer like Yan Yan wouldn't bother to use—it would not pass the system's scrutiny. They thought it would never happen. "But don't worry," Yan Yan said, "they'll provide you with prostheses that are compatible with the BCI system."

It took him several days to learn that he had a tiny chip in his brain to replace the parts that were no longer active. The doctor said he was very lucky that the implanted chip had only triggered a mild rejection.

"Has anyone else had bad luck?" he asked.

"Many," the doctor said, "that's why the BCI has not been rolled out yet. Even if put into medical use, it is only eligible for patients like you."

So, it's half treatment and half experiment.

Chen Yan adapted faster than expected. What took time was learning to control the prosthetics. He spent more than a month progressing from stumbling to walking. Yan Yan was always there to look after him, watching him fall, over and over again, continually scraping his face and hands. When she tried to help him, he pushed her away.

Finally, Chen Yan, accustomed to his prosthetic leg, was able to walk fast in the ward. She was delighted and asked him how he was feeling.

In hindsight, this was where it all started to go wrong, but she didn't realize it in time.

"It seems..." at that moment, Chen Yan straightened up, the arch of his left foot rubbing slowly against the ground, "like it's a bit higher than it was before the crash."


III

They returned home when he was discharged from the hospital.

Home had not changed. It was the house they had rented three years ago. Chen Yan's belongings were still there, almost in the same place, an indication of what kind of life Yan Yan had been living for three years.

"'Has anyone made a play for you in the last three years?" he asked.

Yan Yan, silent for a moment, nodded. "I didn't say yes."

Chen Yan hugged her and said, "It's okay. Now that I have been revived, good days are coming."

The good times lasted for a while. The house came to life. The night was not spent sleeping alone. Sex mixed with love was not simply a physical need.

The only downside was that when she was experiencing the great pleasure that had been missing for a long time, she tried, out of habit, to grab his arm, only to find nothing there.

In that moment, it was like ice water had been poured over them.

"Next time," Chen Yen murmured, "I'd better put on my prosthetic arm and leg."

"Never mind. You don't have to ... I'll get used to it."

But ever since then, Chen Yan had kept his prostheses on, not even removing them for sleeping. The only thing that separated him from these delicate metal instruments was the shower, but he usually locked the bathroom door from the inside—in the past he used to leave it open, inviting Yan Yan to join him with a mischievous look. Sometimes he got a slipper flying past and sometimes what he wanted.

There had to be some changes, Yan Yan thought, since a machine was embedded in his head. Nonetheless, even with more changes, it would be better than the situation where he continued to lie in a hospital bed, plunging into the abyss of unconsciousness.

Thanks to the BCI in his brain, Chen Yan became more dexterous with his prosthetic arm. The five metal fingers on his right arm could make different movements simultaneously. Yan Yan saw him programming his computer with his left hand kept flat on the table and his right-hand fingers flying across the keyboard in a blur.

"So fast?" Yan Yan was startled. "It looks like you're playing the piano."

Playing the piano is the most complex and delicate thing human fingers can do, but Chen Yan had almost no facial expression when he heard her. "It's a pity there are only five fingers." He raised his right hand, the five metallic fingers twisting in turn like waves. "I could play the piano for you if there were more."

"Wait," only then did Yan Yan realize what was really wrong, "when did you learn to program?"

Chen Yan used to be a fine arts teacher and was new to coding. She didn't remember him taking any course to learn assembly language, C++, Java, or even any other programming language high on the chain of contempt among computer programmers.

"Not 'learn', but 'download'."

That's when Yan Yan realized that the BCI not only replaced the damaged parts of Chen Yan's brain, but also affected other areas such as the hippocampus which is responsible for memory formation, and the frontal lobe, which controls deduction and logic. He had acquired the knowledge by downloading it from the hospital's website.

She knew the magic of the BCI. When wearing the helmet, she could be more focused, regulate the secretion of some hormones, and cure anxiety or insomnia. But separated by the skull, the helmet could not directly input information into her brain. It only served to repair and enhance the brain.

Chen Yan's chip, apparently, could do things differently.


The reason Chen Yan learned to code was to find a job.

When he went to interviews, Yan Yan was writing plays at home. The happiness surrounding her made her scripts so fascinating that the system rated them highly. In the evenings, she listened to Chen Yan's accounts of his daytime job hunting, which was not going well.

Many companies asked him where he had been for the three gap years. In this era, he couldn't lie and had to answer honestly. "In a hospital bed." Usually, these words were met with a standard smile and a response asking him to wait to hear back from the interview.

The results were always the same.

"No worries," she comforted him. "You're a programming expert. You'll be wanted."

Yan Yan was not just giving him empty reassurances by saying that. She had been in the film and television industry for so long that she knew a few people at least. After contacting them, she found a VFX company willing to give Chen Yan a chance. The company was developing software that could give actors an age-defying effect and asked Chen Yan to help build the underlying architecture.

"First, I have to say if he can't keep up with his work ..." the employer said carefully, "I can't have an idle person here. You know the pressure. It's not easy to be a boss."

Half a month later, the boss called back again.

"I didn't expect a genius! It's the first time I've seen someone who can use all the programming languages and switch seamlessly between them. I'm amazed such a veteran programmer hasn't gone bald."

Six months later, Chen Yan became a permanent employee of the company.

That took a load off Yan Yan's mind. She started thinking about getting married. Chen Yan had proposed to her before the disaster and she had agreed. They would have been married three years ago if there hadn't been a car accident.


IV

"Just wait for a while," said Chen Yan.

"Hmm?" Yan Yan was caught by surprise. "We've been waiting for four years."

"But I need to think twice."

"What do you need to think about?"

Chen Yan pushed up his sleeve to reveal his metal arm and tapped his left leg. "My body is currently one-fifth metal. I'm not as heavy as you are when I remove my prostheses."

"I don't care."

"But I do."

Their conversation ended there.


Yan Yan deliberated on their conversation afterward and couldn't help feeling it was wrong. Being a scriptwriter she knew that, more often than not, when two characters had this kind of dialogue, one of them was lying. She was pretty sure this person was not herself.

In their previous life she would have confronted Chen Yan about the matter, but since Chen Yan's reawakening, she thought that any differences in him were justifiable seeing there was a machine in his head. The only person she could consult was the doctor.

"According to his control examination last month, the BCI

is working well. There's nothing wrong with it," the doctor said firmly, looking up from the pile of data.

"But I keep feeling like he is different."

"He has had a head injury and has been in a vegetable state for three years. It's normal for him to have changed in some ways."

Then an idea came to her. She was surprised at first, and attempted to stifle it, but the idea was firm and grew stronger like buds opening in spring. "Do you think it's possible to let me know what he's thinking?" she asked hesitantly.

The doctor took off his spectacles and looked at Yan Yan with an out-of-focus gaze.

Yan Yan smiled shyly, feeling ashamed of her whim. She stood up and was about to apologize when the doctor breathed on his glasses, wiped them clean with a soft cloth, and put them back on his nose, saying, "Yes, I can."

The key role of the BCI is to recognize biological signals and convert them into electrical signals. At the core of the technology is digital transformation, which means digitizing hormone secretion as well as brain waves.

The powerful chip, so small that it is almost invisible to the naked eye, can accurately detect the excitation of individual neurons in the brain. It can record changes in potential generated by each nerve impulse. It is these changes that are transmitting information, like another form of coding. Information constitutes memory, which is decoded and transcribed to be stored in the hospital's database.

"The chip can do more than just record memories. Chen Yan can reverse the effects and tamper with memories if he wants to. It's nothing more than data anyway," the doctor said.

"May I have a look at his memories?"

"The regulations do not permit it. Another resistance to the promotion of BCI is the risk of privacy violations." The doctor leaned back slightly and slumped back in his seat. "But you are Mr. Chen's guarantor for the operation and … this time the situation is special with a low procedural risk."

Yan Yan sat in the resource room. A hologram unfolding from a first-person perspective filled the room around her.

This was the last month of Chen Yan's life, every second of which had been recorded by the BCI and stored in the hospital. She could see the perspective of Chen Yan as he concentrated on programming at his desk. His right hand, which had been upgraded, had nine fingers of different lengths and thicknesses, and was surprisingly efficient when tapping the keyboard.

She fast-forwarded through the images. The holographic light flowed faster, making her face go bright and dark continuously.

She relived what Chen Yan had seen and heard on his commute to work, seeing his work, his colleagues, and the party with his friends after work.

Wait. She rewound the recording and saw the face of a female colleague appear repeatedly. Once she showed up, she stayed in Chen Yan's vision for many hours.

Chen Yan gazed at her.

Yan Yan took all the footage of this female colleague to find out how they met.

She was a new graphic designer, not coquettish. With hair hanging down on her right cheek, she looked inconspicuous. However, their boss introduced Chen Yan to her. "You have something in common," he said cheerfully, tapping his temple. "Here, you both have machines inside."

He's talking about the BCI.

Chen Yan's eyes focused on the right cheek of the female colleague. The side of her face was magnified until the finest details were visible. Her scar could be seen beneath the roots of her thick hair. Chen Yan also raised his hair, revealing the same wound— Yan Yan imagined the action. She thought that she would have done the same if she were Chen Yan, like in the forest, wild beasts show signs only their kindred understand.

"Hello," Chen Yan whispered.

"Hi."

Their first meeting was so simple. They didn't see each other often afterwards, only in passing at the office every few days without talking. But the moment they passed on another, Chen Yan would magnify her eyes, her dark orbs filling his entire vision. Her eyes flickered and shined. It seemed that she was enlarging his eyes as well. This was the eye contact of people with a BCI chip, one seeing his reflection in the other's gaze.

Yan Yan felt powerless. She was an ordinary person and had no idea what information they could exchange through eye contact.

She hurriedly fast-forwarded to the previous time Chen Yan had met the colleague, which was last night. The woman was sheltering from the rain by the side of the road, waiting for her car. Chen Yan drove past, but a minute later went back and rolled down the window. Her face was clear in the rain.

"Let me give you a ride," Chen Yan said.

She hesitated.

"We are more vulnerable to the rain than ordinary people," Chen Yan said, making a bad joke. "We have surgical wounds. Our brains can easily get water in them."

She didn't laugh but got in the car anyway.

Raindrops trickled down the windows. No matter how fast the windshield wipers worked, they could not stop the droplets from crawling into Chen Yan's visual field. The street became thick with a mixture of light and shadow as they drove on.

Chen Yan was kept staring ahead so Yan Yan couldn't see the face of the woman, but she could hear their voices.

"How long have you had the implant?" asked Chen Yan.

"Five years. What about you?"

"One year."

The woman smiled. "Then you have a lot to get used to."

"Do you have any advice as a veteran?" said Chen Yan.

"Plenty. For example, protect your head. The BCI chip is like a window in the brain, giving us a better view, but others can see through the glass as well, or even change a little bit of data to make you a different person. You can download a digital security guard. In addition, a few more languages. Language is the most useful skill of all…"

The female coworker went through a long list of suggestions and finally paused for a few seconds before continuing, "However, the most important thing is to realize that you are already different to humans."

These words took Yan Yan and Chen Yan by surprise at the same time.

"Are you saying that we're not human once we're implanted with a BCI chip?" Chen Yan asked.

"We are certainly human in the biological sense, yet our brains have changed, making us perceive the world in a different way. You used to feel happy when hugging someone, but now you can feel the same sensation if you let the BCI chip give the correct electrical stimulation. Let me ask you this: are you still interested in sex?"

Yan Yan subconsciously held her breath as she waited for Chen Yan's answer in silence.

"No."

"You can control the hypothalamus whenever you want to release dopamine and endorphins that will give you pleasure dozens of times more intense than sex. We can simulate and even surpass at any time the most primitive human urges and pleasures. We can skip the long learning process of mastering skills, and we can store all the knowledge of the past and present without being limited by our brain's capability. You're more agile with a robotic arm than you are with your real arm—look, your left arm is close to atrophy. Do you think we're still ... human in the conventional sense?"

Chen Yan seemed to sigh. "It does sound like we're more machine than human."

"Technically speaking, the human body is a machine in itself. We just use a different operating system now."

"Running iOS on an Android machine? It sounds laggy," Chen Yan said. "So, what's the point of life for people like us?"

"Another piece of advice is not to think about these issues. Two years ago, I knew a man with BCI who couldn't come to terms with these things and ended up digging out the chip with his bare hands."

"What about the man himself?"

She didn't say anything, but the answer was self-evident.

"Look on the bright side," Chen Yan said, "Only brain-dead people like us are qualified to have the invasive BCI. It's better to have a different system than to stay dead."

"That's true."

As the car continued forward, high-rise buildings thinned out. On the edge of the city the brightly lit buildings and the streets full of headlights were left behind, becoming the backdrop to their story.

"Do you live here alone?" Chen Yan glanced around. It didn't look like an environment for a polished white-collar worker to live in.

"Hmm. You're staying with your girlfriend, aren't you? There are traces of a woman driving the car."

Chen Yan nodded.

"My daughter had just been born before my accident. I was seriously injured. Doctors said that my will to survive kept me going because I wanted to see my daughter again so badly. Several times doctors had to declare that I had lost all vital signs, but I held on and never died," the woman said, her voice matter-of-fact. "Then the BCI chip was implanted to wake me up. I got to see my child as I had hoped. Yet the problem was that I never felt like a 'mom' again. This baby girl, sleepy, and sniffling, likes to make noises to draw the attention of the adult to pool more resources in favour of her growth. She is just a bunch of blood vessels, lipids, and proteins, whose only connection with me is the highly similar DNA sequence. What's the point of that? Should two rice cookers from the same product line also fall in love and never separate?"

"So ... how is your kid?"

"No idea. I haven't seen her in four years."

Silence fell again. Chen Yan pulled up in front of a building. The rain had eased up a lot. The rustling sound of raindrops tapping the glass roof went on and on.

"I'm here," she said.

"Hmm," said Chen Yan.

Not getting out of the car yet, the woman suddenly chuckled. "Don't despair. Our kind of people have our own fun. Come on, I'll teach you."

"What do I have to do?"

"Just sit here. You don't have to talk, but open access to your BCI chip," she spoke in low murmurs. "Let me connect. Let me in."

For the next few moments, they did not move, they just sat side by side in the driver's and passenger's seats without talking. The hologram Yan Yan saw was motionless, but she knew something that she couldn't understand was happening. She shouted "Hey" to try to wake them up in the hologram. No one responded. She didn't dare to fast forward any further. She just sat there and let the image keep still.

The rain was still loud.

The scene lasted nearly two hours.

Eventually, Chen Yan and the woman, breathing heavily at the same time, seemed to disconnect. Chen Yan, covered in sweat, gasped for breath for a few minutes and murmured, "Uh..."

"It's data convergence," she said. With that, she left.


V

When Yan Yan returned home like a lost soul, Chen Yan was still programming. The incessant sound of pounding the keyboard upset Yan Yan—the tapping sound was too much like the sound of rain.

She sat down opposite Chen Yan.

Chen Yan looked up at her and suddenly smiled. "You know about it?" Even when he looked at Yan Yan and spoke, his right hand did not stop. The code, like water, flowed across the screen.

Yan Yan asked, "What did you do ... in the car?"

"You peeked into my memories and should know that we didn't do anything. We didn't have the slightest physical contact."

"You're lying! Did you really stare into space for two hours?"

"I don't know if you can understand—we were exchanging data," sighed Chen Yan.

"What data?"

"Knowledge, pain, experience, anger ... the most beautiful landscapes we've ever seen, the darkest past, quirks, good wishes ... life lessons, dreams, the taste of food, childhood, people we have loved and hated, films and music we've enjoyed ... In short, everything. Everything we have experienced has been transformed into data by our BCIs. We were exchanging a huge amount of data, living each other's lives."

Yan Yan appeared stunned. She couldn't understand. Chen Yan was still a familiar face, but there was a chasm between them.

"I'd rather you told me you're in love, or something else," Yan Yan said. "That way, I would at least have a reason to hate you."

Chen Yan's right hand stopped typing. He looked at her quietly and said, "I didn't do anything wrong to you. I didn't cheat on you. I don't love her."

"But what you did with the woman was more ..." she had to think for a long time before she came up with a barely appropriate word, "more intimate than cheating."

"There's nothing I can do about that. My body runs on a different program that has nothing to do with gender. Think about it—would you be annoyed if the colleague was a man?"

Yan Yan was speechless for a moment. All the words she had prepared before coming home were useless in front of Chen Yan. It turned out that everything about their lives together, communication, love—even on his part—was an effort. The reason he gave made her feel even more that the disparity between them was almost insurmountable.

She thought for a long time and said something—a line she would have been ashamed to use in one of her scripts.

"Do you, uh, still love me?"

VI

The doctor listened and was quite curious. "What did he say?"
Yan Yan shook her head. "He didn't answer."
"Are you still together then?"
Yan Yan nodded.

"Well, there are many reasons for a couple to stay together. Love is just one of them," said the doctor soothingly. "Why did you come to see me now the hurdle has been overcome?"

Yan Yan took a deep breath, looked straight up at the doctor, and said, "I want to implant the brain-computer interface in my head. He is not on the same path as me, I think I can follow and take his path."

"Even if it means letting go of a lot of things, including your humanity?"

"Even if I have to give up everything."

The doctor smiled. "I admire your courage Miss Yan's. I sincerely hope that you can get your love back. It's just that I can't help you this time." He turned his head away and explained, "As I've told you, there are a few legal and ethical issues with the invasive brain-computer interface—only patients with brain necrosis are allowed to have it implanted. Besides, there's no guarantee of success in coping with rejection."

Yan Yan's attempt had been in vain, so she made her way back from the hospital. Instead of taking a taxi, she walked down the street like a ghost. She passed many windows—there were restaurants, cafes, and office buildings. Inside, people were all wearing brain-computer helmets, working intently. No one could deny that BCI technology had made the world a better, more efficient, and more convenient place. Many diseases had been cured, and the new technology was sweeping the world like a flood, but the tide was so turbulent that among those who welcomed it with open arms, some were overwhelmed, rolling in the water, bounced around until they were black and blue.

Unfortunately, Yan Yan was one of them.

Or perhaps her arms did not open wide enough? She thought about it and stood still, staring at the passing vehicles on the street. The scene from four years ago came back to her. The doctor's words echoed over and over like the devil whispering in her ear.

A car came at a high speed.

Yan Yan took a deep breath and smiled. She spread her arms to meet the speeding car as if to greet death, or a new life.

VII

"Unfortunately, Miss Yan's rejection is so severe that the BCI chip cannot continue to operate. She is losing her brain function irreversibly," the doctor said regretfully. "I'm so sorry for your loss."

Chen Yan stood outside the ward, looking at the hospital bed through the glass wall. Yan Yan's face could not be seen from his angle.

"Which means she's dying?" Chen Yan said lightly.

"Yes."

"But she's not dead yet. The BCI chip still has time to replicate all her brain information," he turned to the doctor. "Please run the copy program as soon as possible."

His tone was surprisingly cold, startling the doctor and making him recall something, "You signed an agreement a long time ago to allow Miss Yan to check your memory... Did you know she would come to check?"

"She was straight forward. With the aid of the chip, it was easy to predict her actions."

"Then," the doctor shivered, "you could also deduce that she would go to extremes to try and make herself brain-dead in order to be implanted with a BCI chip. You've simply been inducing her to do so step by step!"

"You have no proof," said Chen Yan briefly. He kept his eyes on the hospital bed. The bedside instrument showed that the chip was extracting information from Yan Yan's brain while Yan Yan was dying.

"But, but..." The doctor took off his glasses in a panic, and the lenses were blurry no matter how he wiped them. "Why would you do that?"

Chen Yan did not answer.

He waited patiently for the replication to finish. When the BCI chip was taken out, he held the tiny part and examined it carefully. The chip was as small as a speck of dust, almost transparent between his thumb and forefinger.

He looked at it, suddenly smiled, and turned around to answer the doctor's question. "Because then I can truly mingle with her and we can be together forever."


A short note:

On 28 December 2020, Alibaba DAMO Academy released its "Top 10 Tech Trends for 2021", in which the report on the trend of the brain-computer interface caught my attention. Prior to the release, Elon Musk, founder of companies including SpaceX and Tesla, also held a launch event worldwide to demonstrate the invasive BCI with three little pigs. This is undoubtedly a promising direction of scientific and technological development, which is going to change our lives. If properly harnessed, the BCI will help solve countless incurable diseases such as paralysis and blindness.

However, sci-fi writers try to find amongst the many possibilities of the future the corners that may be overlooked and write them out. This sci-fi story was inspired just by the above report. Despite its slightly dark undertones, it is like a mirror that shines into the dark corners so that we can avoid them and follow the light of humanity to brighter places. I believe that the brain-computer interface will be a great boon to mankind.

# 涂色世界

## 慕明

慕明的作品散见于中国各类科幻或文学期刊及多个网络文学平台，作品也曾被译为英、日等多国语言。代表作《涂色世界》《宛转环》《假手于人》等，现已出版个人作品集《宛转环》。获奖：2020年第三十一届银河奖最佳　短篇小说奖 |涂色世界

现在，正如你已看见，我来到此地，带着船只和伙伴，踏破暗酒色的大海，前往忒墨塞，人操异乡方言的邦域。

十一岁时，我第一次读《奥德赛》。雅典娜化身为门忒斯，向奥德赛的儿子，忒勒马科斯传递父亲已经从特洛伊返乡的消息。在塞缪尔·巴特勒翻译的古雅诗节中，有许多拗口的古希腊人名和陌生的词语变格，但我的注意力一下就被那个词抓住了。

"什么是暗酒色？" 我问妈妈。

妈妈眨了眨眼，"你认为呢？"

"我觉得这是荷马的比喻。" 我记起阅读课上的修辞知识，"大海是蓝色的，不是吗？"

"荷马是个盲诗人。" 妈妈叹了口气，"大海也不总是蓝色的。在古希腊语中，甚至没有蓝色这个词。你还记得长岛的海滩吗？夕阳下的大西洋，是什么样子？"

我试图回忆暑假时在海边骑车时的景象。天空呈现出和水面相似的青蓝色，靠近海面的部分则被染成了葡萄和玛瑙的颜色。太阳落下的地方，乳白色的云块筑成了众神居住的神殿，绯红与金黄的光带像流泻的天河，倾入渐渐深沉的大海。

我喜欢暑假。在那几个月里，耳边响着的，只有海鸥的鸣叫和海风的低吟，而不是班上同学在我面前故意的窃窃私语。

我也并不真的讨厌古老的诗行，或是画板上的油彩。在我更小的时候，我曾经坐在儿童车里，看着妈妈画画——她常常忘记时间，直到我哭起来。可是在十一岁时我已经明白，

生活并不是由色彩和诗句组成的。那就像是脆弱的琉璃筑成的幻境，在碎裂的时候，只会把人扎得生疼，让我不得不面对真实。

我是从亲身经历里认识到这一点的。

"我不懂什么是暗酒色。" 我耸了耸肩。

妈妈沉默了一会儿。"荷马也用这个词形容过公牛。在《伊利亚特》中，'像两头暗酒色的健牛，齐心合力， 拉着制合坚固的犁具，翻着一片休耕的土地……'"

"噢，好了，妈妈。" 我打断她，"承认自己不知道也没什么。说真的，你就是说荷马植入了视网膜调整镜也没人在乎。反正只有我没有。"

妈妈合上了书。"艾米，我希望你能至少读完……"

"算了吧，妈妈。为什么我就不能像其他同学那样有个调整镜？"

"可是你还小……"

"所以你就宁愿去理解那个盲诗人，也不愿意听听我是怎么想的吗？你根本就不知道！"

妈妈懂得五种古代语言，能够背诵整节的史诗，熟悉已经死去的词汇的微妙用法，可是没有一种语言，能描绘现在这个世界。

我并不明白她为什么那么抗拒调整镜。她总是让我感到格格不入，我甚至不敢邀请同学们来家做客。没有调整镜已经让我与众不同，而壁炉上方那副灰白色的古怪油画，肯定会让我看起来更像个怪妈妈的怪女儿。

《暴风雪中的汽船》。我觉得，也许那个叫做透纳的古代画家，像荷马一样，是在失去视力之后才画这幅画的。

黯淡沉闷的色彩，看不清轮廓的粗糙笔触，就像我那时的生活一样。

***

"书呆子，嘿！"

我的胳膊肘被重重地撞了一下，铅笔掉在了地上。等捡起铅笔，黑板上的字迹已经被擦得乱七八糟。

"拜托，别……"

撞我的男孩把黑板擦甩过来，"砰"地一声打在我的桌角，腾起一阵呛人的烟雾。"书呆子，看不清？"

"我的视力没问题……"

"你连蓝色和绿色都分不清！" 他居高临下地看着我。

"我只是没有调整镜……" 我争辩着，"我分得清，只是需要久一点……"

322

　　"得了吧，你还是像你妈妈那样，戴上那种老式眼镜比较合适，跟你的模样也挺配。" 男孩用手指在眼眶边比出两个圈，漂亮的绿色眼眸里满是嘲笑，"就像只丑青蛙。"

　　"别说了！" 我再也忍不住，捡起黑板擦扔向他，可是我的力气太小，他轻而易举地躲开了，连一丝粉尘都没有沾上。

　　"好了，我们该走了。" 安吉拉轻巧地迈过黑板擦。男孩吐了吐舌头，帮她拿过书包。

　　我望着安吉拉。冬日的夕阳下，她的金色头发闪闪发光，映衬着白皙得几乎透明的耳朵。即使在调整镜外她也是这么漂亮，也难怪他们都喜欢她。她回头冲我一笑，那笑容那么甜美无邪，像油画中的少女。

　　可是她夸张的嘴型分明在说，"拜拜，青蛙。"

　　教室里只剩下我自己，愣愣地盯着笔记本上抄写的修辞知识。我的成绩很好，即使我有时看不清楚黑板上的字迹，需要在下课后补抄。可是那真的有意义吗？那些妈妈希望我专注的东西，那些看似美好的东西，正在伤害我。它们让我和其他人离得越来越远。我现在需要的，并不是它们。

　　我没有向妈妈说起过这些，现在，也许是时候改变了。

　　我慢慢撕掉了笔记上未完的那一页，又一点点撕得粉碎。

*＊*

　　十二岁，妈妈终于同意了我接受视网膜调整镜的植入手术。那一天我醒的很早，在黑暗中，我打开衣柜，感受着轻薄的蕾丝和柔滑的缎带划过指尖，想象着在植入之后，那些一成不变的套装裙子将呈现出怎样的缤纷色彩。最终我选择了一件象牙白色的针织溜冰裙，裙背的开口恰好能露出纤细的颈背曲线。最重要的是，调整镜的色彩滤镜效果在白色底色上能得到最完美的呈现。

　　"别害怕，只是个小手术。" 爸爸握着我的手，我能感到他手心的汗湿。

　　"好了好了，爸爸。只是让我变得'正常'一点儿的小手术嘛。" 我撒娇地说，故意不去看妈妈。她站在角落里，穿着她经常穿的那件灰色兔毛大衣，脸上涂了过多的粉底，苍白得像个假人。她总是把自己裹在黯淡的颜色里，就像她的书和她的画，都蒙了一层古老的雾。

　　"这里。" 医生指着一个呈现纵向切面的眼球模型，透明的玻璃体像个水晶球，占据了眼球五分之四的体积，在后端附着的那片金色薄膜，就是视网膜。

　　"视网膜调整镜的原理其实并不复杂。我们知道，视网膜是由对光敏感的视杆细胞，和对颜色敏感的三种视锥细胞组成的。在古代，当人们在没有月光的漆黑夜里穿越丛林的时候，人眼的视杆细胞能够捕捉单独的光子，并排除周围其他细胞的干扰把它放大；而当来到一片日光明媚的夏日海滩时，人眼对颜色敏感的视锥细胞很快便能够适应强烈的日照。最新的视网膜调整镜则将生物微电极阵列制成的芯片植入到视网膜神经感觉上皮和色素上皮之间的区域，辅助视杆和视锥细胞感受光照，直接利用视网膜本身的编码和解码机制来将电信号转化成视觉。它依然利用了你自身的'镜头'，就像是为数码相机换一块感光器件一样。"

"但是它比我自己的'镜头'可厉害多了。"　我抢着说，想要卖弄一下早就从同学那里听到过的东西，"它可以呈现更多的视觉细节，也可以自动调整视觉成像的明暗，色彩范围。我再也不会看不清楚黑板上的字迹了。"

"可是你也许再也摘不下来了。"　妈妈摇摇头，"艾米，再想想，这不是传统的眼镜，这可能是你的新眼睛……"

"所以我才不愿意一直当瞎子！"　我的眼前，安吉拉那夸张的嘴型时隐时现，青蛙，青蛙。

"对于安全性您大可放心。现在已经不是三十年前了。视觉系统的增强技术已经相当成熟。"　医生的声音十分平缓，显然已经见多了这样的对话。"事实上，大多数孩子在更小的时候就已经接受了植入。这就像曾经的最新款手机，最热门的社交软件，再加上最流行的服饰的集成体，人们是无法抗拒的。我们当然不能只从商业的角度考虑问题，但是可以预见，调整镜人群才是未来的主流。"

"现在已经是了！班上的每个人都在用。调整镜还可以设置滤镜共享——只需要同步频率。"　我从爸爸的手中抽回自己的手，凝视着手腕内侧。我知道，在植入后，那里就会亮起一个微小的光点。

"没错，通过可编程接口，调整镜可以对电信号进行实时编码。"　医生点点头，"某种程度上讲，它为你展现了无数个新的世界——并且可以与别人分享。"

"是啊，简直太棒了。"　我故意说得很大声。也许妈妈可以在那间昏暗的书房里逃避现实，但是我不想。她不知道孩子们的世界是多么残酷又是多么精彩。也许她根本就不在乎。

而这个世界最终将属于我们。

"医生，我想跟你单独谈几句。"　妈妈忽然开口。

我不知道妈妈和医生说了什么。只有爸爸陪在我旁边，我们谁都没有说话。直到医生返回手术室他才离开。医生开始在手术操作系统上输入调整参数。护士小姐为我注射了麻醉剂，眼部一阵冰凉之后，是无知无觉的黑暗。我知道，手术马上就要开始了。

"医生，大人......也可以植入视网膜调整镜吗？"

"技术上可行，不过成年人的术后适应往往不如未成年人。" 医生的声音显得有些遥远。"而且，目前的技术并不支持某些特殊的情况。比如有些人的排异反应过于强烈，比如......"

我并没有听完医生的话。无可抵挡的睡意已经袭来。 在黑甜的梦境中，无数的异彩纷呈正在等待着我。

***

"嗨，安吉拉。" 我鼓起勇气，朝着迎面走来的女孩招招手。她浅粉色的裙子上装饰有淡绿色的缎带蝴蝶结，像一支初绽的郁金香。"喜欢你的粉裙子。"

"哦？" 她扬起淡金色的眉毛，"你终于也有那个了？"

"嗯。" 我若无其事地理了理裙摆。深蓝色的裙子上有星光流转，搭配浅栗色的头发，而非和妈妈一样的黑色。手腕内侧，调整镜的同步信号闪着微弱的绿光。我知道，在她的眼里，我一定和以往大不相同。

"还不错。你知道吗，以前，我们都觉得，你这儿有点儿问题......" 她歪着头，指了指眼睛。

"当然不是！我只是......我只是没有调整镜而已！" 我连忙说，"不过，现在不同了，再也不同了。我和你们一样。"

"不，还差一点儿。" 她眯着眼睛笑了。

"哪一点儿？"

"我们不把这叫做粉色。这是荆棘鸟滤镜套组里的玫瑰灰烬。玫瑰灰烬。又温柔，又残酷。同样，你的裙子也不是蓝色，在调整镜里，那叫做皇家午夜。就是那种忧郁的感觉。"

"喔......"

我忽然意识到，调整镜改变的，不仅仅是物体的色彩或者明暗本身。它也改变了描述这个世界的语言。

而语言......我模模糊糊地想起妈妈曾经讲过的睡前故事。无论是童话故事里的魔咒，还是希腊神话中的预言，似乎，都拥有可以改变一切的神奇力量。

那都是骗小孩子的。一个声音在心里说。我眨了眨眼，想

325

要拂去那些飘忽不定的思绪——其实那完全没有必要，调整镜会保证视野的绝对清晰。

"嗯，玫瑰灰烬。" 我点点头，"我懂了。想要试试我的皇家午夜吗？我想，它会很衬你的发色。"

***

后来我读了人机交互专业。在大学毕业后，我加入了一家为视网膜调整镜编制滤镜插件的初创公司。如今，人体改造技术已经成为了最炙手可热的领域。植入了RFID芯片的人们再也不用担心忘记钥匙或者钱包，3D打印的心脏，肺和肾则大大缓解了器官移植供应的压力。

生物黑客成为了每个年轻人的理想职业，不过，最吸引我的，仍然是调整镜的相关技术。视觉是我们与外部世界建立关联最重要的渠道。我不会忘记在那场手术之前，我曾经被排除在外。

几乎已经没有人再抗拒人体的硬件升级，除了妈妈。

她曾经委婉地提出希望我在文学或者艺术领域继续深造，但是，在爸爸在出差时因为车祸去世之后，我就从家里搬进了自己租的小公寓。她再也不能要求我什么了。

事实上，自从上了中学，我和妈妈的话就渐渐少了。

调整镜固然是重要的原因。十年来，随着技术的不断升级，调整镜所能呈现的视觉效果早已超出了人类的固有经验，只有使用来源于调整镜本身的语言，才能传达准确的含义。我很难妈妈分享什么是超空三号，那是一个类似于在大气层中不断上升的光线渐变渲染，由淡蓝，深蓝，紫色，紫黑逐渐变成深沉的黑色丝绒，夹杂着许多难以形容的纤细光丝，那是我最喜欢的睡眠环境。我也没办法向她讲述我第一次暗恋的那个男孩儿，他的眼睛里有真正的黑洞，星星在瞳孔边缘纷纷坠落——那是最新款的芯片才能达到的效果。

与此同时，各种基于传统人眼感知原理的显示器，也进行了针对调整镜的更新换代。如今我们看到的，不再是前信息时代那种可以看见边缘锯齿的粗糙图像，而是与调整镜算法相融合的超写实成像。这跟前信息时代的3D成像有点儿类似，但是远为生动。事实上，如果不是显示器强制性的边框限制，我们已经很难分清显示器内外的世界。

但是妈妈拒绝这一切。在某种程度上，我觉得，是她的态度，而非调整镜本身，造成了我们之间微妙的沉默。她甚至不使用电子阅读器或者是非侵入式的增强现实眼镜，而是埋首于那些日益暗沉的古代典籍和艺术作品中去。

我知道，在我离家上学之后，她又重新拾起了年轻时的爱

326

好，画画。我曾经看过她的作品，老式的静物，风景，乏善可陈。凝固的油彩，并没有调整镜下的光线灵动飘逸。

"怎么样？"她期待地看着我，像个等着夸奖的小女孩。

"唔……不错。"我努力让自己听起来真诚一点儿，"不过说真的，妈，你就不能试试……"

"艾米。我真希望你关掉那玩意儿，用自己的眼睛去看，用自己的语言去说。"她从老式的玳瑁眼镜上边缘盯着我，声音干巴巴的，"妈妈毕竟是过来人，要记住，你眼中的颜色……"

"黑色并不总是黑色，白色并不总是白色，好了，好了，难道这就是你在葬礼上也穿着一件灰衣服的理由吗？"我忽然提高了声音，某种存在已久的情绪裹挟着词语，冲破而出。"妈，我已经长大了，而你却止步不前。你要知道，在这个时代，年龄不是你的资本，体验才是。"

"那些一模一样的人造体验？"妈妈绞着双手，"艾米，你忘了你曾经是个多么特别的孩子，还记得……"

"不。我并不特别。那些只是你想要强加于我的东西。我从来就没喜欢过那些古典文学。那些油画。"我背对她，不想看她的眼睛。"我只想做个正常人。"

"艾米……"她停住了，声音里有抑制不住的惊讶和失落。我听得出。

"我早就不是孩子了。"我强迫自己一口气说下去，生怕因为丝丝泛起的歉疚而停顿。"现在我看到的，懂得的，都比你多得多。别再用那些故作神秘的陈词滥调约束自己，也约束我。出去看看这个前所未有的时代吧。"

她终于不再说话。有那么一瞬间，我似乎听见了强忍住的哽咽。

我转身走出了光线黯淡的老屋。外面正渐渐沥沥地下着小雨。我调出了特瑞尔七号的全景模式，那是天空中维纳斯带的视效模拟，阴沉的天色在温暖的二次瑞利散射光下变得柔和。深深呼了一口气，疯狂跳动的心，渐渐平缓下来。

对不起，妈妈。但是我已经长大了。

***

爸爸的葬礼也是那样一个雨天，我还记得冰凉的雨水顺着黑色的呢子外套滴答落下。牧师在十字架顶端渲染出一对流光溢彩的小天使，在雨雾中撑起拱形光环，虚明如镜的光晕中央，是熟悉得让我心碎的投影。我告诉自己，爸爸会在那光芒中，永远照看着我，就像很久以前，拉着我的手一样。

可是在我身边，妈妈无法理解那些。依然是过厚的粉底，古董似的毛衣。她看不见，也听不懂什么是天国的三种光冕。她只能透过被雨淋湿的眼镜片，望向那片只属于她一个人的灰白天空。

在牧师的致辞之间，我听得到人们的窃窃私语。我熟悉那种刻意压低的声音，也熟悉目光相接时，那种略不自然的回避眼神。成年人的游戏规则变得隐秘，但我明白那些体贴的微笑和言语背后，究竟隐藏着什么。理智告诉我，在葬礼上也许不该想到这些，但是理智从来无法抑制情感。

如今再没有人为我挡住生活的风风雨雨。至于妈妈，我不能指望她。

"请节哀。"　马克与我握手，他的西装泛着黑曜石的色泽，笔挺而庄重，像我每次见到他那样得体。我和他刚刚开始约会，本没想到他会来。

他握住我的手，凑近我的耳边。"你辛苦了。"

"还好。谢谢你。"　他手心的温度，让我好受了些。

"我的意思是，我不知道……"　他费力地寻找着合适的词语，"你母亲原来……你家可真是特别。"

我的手僵住了。

"不是这样的，只有她……"

我想要争辩什么，但是他陌生的同情眼神忽然让我明白，我曾经挣扎着想要摆脱的东西，仍然像个拽住我的泥坑。

"我们都很特别。孩子。"　妈妈转过头，眼镜片上的水滴淋漓，声音大得让我羞耻。"艾米，你，我。我们每一个人都是。别那么相信你那镜片里的……"

"别说了。妈。求你停下。"

马克耸了耸肩，离开了。只剩下我不得不强作镇定，应付剩下的客人。妈妈依然漠然地坐在一边。她本来就没多少朋友。

我不知道她是否真的在乎爸爸的离去，是否真的在乎我的想法。在那之后我几乎完全放弃了。我的房间门常常紧闭，也不再会跟妈妈闲聊。我们的语言交集越来越小。不久之后，我就搬离了家。

不，妈妈。我也许无法改变你的想法，但我不想变成你的样子。

***

当技术革新改变了描述这个世界的语言，它也永久地改变了我们看待世界的方式，哪怕脱离了技术本身，语言也已经深刻地塑造了人类的心灵。大学时的语言学课上，老师曾经讲过萨丕尔-沃尔夫假说。有些小说家曾经根据这个假说，畅想了学习外星语言能给我们带来的超级能力，但我觉得，这个想法的真正意义，在所有东西都在快速迭代的今天，远比人们认为的要更现实。

"又得扩充语音助手的词汇表了。" 比尔的即时信息在我的显示器上跳动，中断了我的回忆。"调整镜上周的用户数据已经发布，可能会增加七十多个高频新词。"

我回头，在格子间里寻找着那一团熟悉的银灰色乱发。比尔是公司的资深工程师，目前和我结对编程。

我知道，他的头发是实实在在的银灰色，而非调整镜的效果。"遗传。" 在第一次见面时，他解释说。

"挺酷的。" 我不想显得大惊小怪。"我也认识不用调整镜的人。"

"我还没那么酷。" 他咧嘴一笑，乱草似的头发开始变成一根根纠结的微型彩虹。

"嗯......我觉得，我们应该重新思考一下词汇更新的流程。" 我飞快地键入字符，"新词随着新视觉效果增加，旧词随着旧视觉效果被剔除，近三个月来我们已经更新了三次。太快了，也许。"

"你可能想计算一下加速度。" 他加上一串数字，那是调整镜代码中的鬼脸编码，"咖啡间见？"

"有时我感到，事情在逐渐......失控。" 我拆开一袋巧克力豆倒在纸盘里，"你也许听说过语言会导致思维的差异。" 我拨弄着一颗颗彩色的小球，"而我们正在加速这一过程——"

我努力不去想妈妈的脸，"想想看，调整镜已经渗入了生活的方方面面，从电影院的屏幕到手机应用。而从广告标语到网络新闻，所有的语言都在尽力跟上调整镜中描绘的景象......要不了多久，不，就是现在，人们已经无法脱离调整镜和与它相关的一切进行思考交流。可是......可是那些没有调整镜的人该怎么办？"

"脱脂奶？纯奶？"

"喂，比尔，我说真的。"

"还是脱脂奶吧。" 他耸耸肩。"没什么大不了的，艾米。人们创造了技术，技术也重新塑造了人类的心灵，从古至今，都这样。"

"可是至少不应该这么快......"

"有那么悲观？" 他晃了晃起泡的牛奶，在咖啡上画出复杂的花样，"在面试时，你不是说调整镜，和所有的先进技术一样，能让人们联系得更紧密吗？分享你眼中的美妙世界——"

"也许我完全错了。"　我有气无力地说，感到巧克力豆在温热的指尖渐渐变得粘稠，就像我的思绪。

比尔将拿铁递过来，表面的拉花是一张只有眼睛，没有嘴的脸。我的心里突然一阵抽搐，几乎无法直视那漂浮在褐色液体上的稠密奶泡。

"我曾经是个物理专业的学生。"　他慢慢说道。"直到现在也还相信以理智追求物质世界的真相。但是我明白，如果只是依赖牛顿光学的颜色理论，进行数学抽象，我们永远也无法理解，当古希腊人站在海滨，眺望着暗酒色的大海伸向遥远的天际线时，他们看到了什么。"

"他们到底看到了什么？"　一颗巧克力豆在我的指尖四分五裂，我顾不得擦拭四处溅射的甜腻浆液，也忘记了之前的话题。我只想解开那个被遗忘了很久的谜。

"呃，我只是试了试刚发布的荷马之眼……"　他显然没有预料到我的反应。"应用市场的第一个。"

盲诗人用词语为遥远的年代涂色，而那词语如今成为了我窥视真相的眼睛。该如何描述我见到的？在古希腊人的眼中，这世上的每一种色彩依然清晰可辨，只是比起色盘上的差异，他们的目光更多地聚焦在明暗的程度上。暗酒色描述的不只是红与蓝的中间色，而是一种明亮与运动的混合，随着不同季节和一天中不同时辰的光线状况而变，那是最能捕获古希腊人感受的特征。人们依然能感受到最细微的颜色差别，但他们并不在意。和在夕阳下波光粼粼的海面，以及浸满了汗水，闪闪发亮的公牛躯体一样，我感知到的，是在纸杯中荡漾闪烁的甘醇液体。

"难以置信。通过词语反向构造。这是……用古希腊人的眼睛去感受这个世界。"

某种程度上来说，这项算法的设计不但考虑了客观世界的真相，也反应了物质世界对于古代人类心灵的启示。而这，全都来源于语言。萨丕尔-沃尔夫假说并不是故事的全部，语言并没有阻断我们的视野，也没有让我们丧失思考的能力，它只是为我们带上了一副眼镜。

我切断了调整镜的信号。我有多久没这么干了？我试图回忆起那些古老的形容词，或者说，忘记调整镜赋予的新词汇。你得学会摘下眼镜，才能戴上另一副……你得暂时忘掉母语，才能更好地学会外语——妈妈严厉的目光挂在玳瑁镜框上。

"艾米？你还好吗？" 比尔的声音听起来很遥远，"真没想到，绿色也挺适合你的。"

我的心跳忽然漏了一拍。

很久以来，我的衣柜都是由黑白深蓝组成的，不管是在调整镜内还是外。我不喜欢绿色。那让我想起某种滑腻的两栖动物，以及那些曾经刺痛过我的眼神。

***

"妈，我想问你一件事......"

我盯着刚刚发出的语音讯息，犹豫良久，还是按下了"取消"。也许她会听到一句没说完的话，也许她会看到一条发送又撤回的消息。我不知道她会怎么想，我们都清楚，我早已不习惯向她寻求帮助。

可我又该怎么办呢？

单身公寓里一片狼藉。地板上散落着剩了一半的外卖餐盒，没洗的衣服揉成一团，工作台的曲面屏幕上，显示着环形的孟塞尔比色图和带状的可见光光谱。

我的手边则堆满了打印出来的资料，德谟克利特对于颜色的论述，道尔顿的《论色盲》，还有马克·罗斯科那些只有大幅色块的抽象绘画。

然而没有任何资料，能告诉我，我看见的颜色，到底是不是别人眼中的颜色。

我到底是不是一个——色盲。

这听起来不可思议。但又完全可能。在模糊不清的记忆里，妈妈指着晴朗的天空说那是蓝色，指着花园中的嫩叶说那是绿色——通过学习，我能对应颜色和词汇符号，但是，假如我眼中的视锥细胞与常人的位置不同，通常意义上的"蓝色"波长的光波在我眼中引起的，实际上是常人眼中的"绿色"的神经信号，我会发现吗？

我会认为"蓝色"就是那么"绿"。我学会了将语言符号与某种特定感知对应，却没有意识到，符号所指的可能并不是一种物理属性，而是一种心灵表象。我永远无法知道别人眼中的世界是什么模样。

这就像一台计算机，我的眼睛是输入端，大脑是个黑匣子，而嘴巴是输出端。当别人接受绿色信号，产生绿色感应，说出"绿色"时，我学习到的，是接受绿色的信号，产生"蓝色"感应，却同样说出"绿色"。我无法意识到自己的特异，我特殊的地方不只在于眼睛本身，更在于对外在刺激的内化。我的心灵。

你连蓝色和绿色都分不清。

331

青蛙，青蛙。

儿时的记忆碎片涌入脑海。以前我一直以为，那是因为我没有调整镜，所以不能像别人一样迅速地分辨细微色差。但事实可能比那更严重。

调整镜让我看到的，是别人眼中的景象。我熟练地运用着那些词语，自以为融入了那个"正常"的世界。但那并不真的属于我。我想起了妈妈总是说我特别。她一定早就知道。可是，她为什么从未告诉过我？

我终究不是个"正常人"吗？

我忽然想起公司用户论坛上的那个请求。有用户抱怨我们为某款增强视觉游戏设计的新界面不够友好。"我喜欢这个游戏，不过我看不清敌人的发光轮廓。一切看起来都一样。"

那个帖子并没有多少人关注。寥寥的几条回复中，有人说，"新界面没问题。你是色盲吧。没有调整镜就别玩。"

那个帖子的主人显然情绪激动，"去你的调整镜，因为交通信号灯的升级，我现在开不了车，连我最爱的游戏都要被你们毁了吗？这不是我的错。"

最初我没在意，只是把那个请求标记为"不予处理"。每天收到的用户反馈和要求成百上千，而我们只会挑选那些最重要的处理。最重要，等于影响人数最多，可能产生的效益最大。像这样的特例，通常并不在我们的考虑范围之内。

但是现在，我盯着那个用户的注册地址，心脏像被人狠狠打了一拳，一种钝感的疼痛几乎要让我呕吐。

那个国家，正是爸爸车祸去世的地方。爸爸和妈妈一样，一直没有植入调整镜。他开车一向小心，我本以为是上天的残忍带走了他，而从来没有想过，也许是因为，他也像那个用户一样，被我，被某些人，当做了一个不予处理的特例。

也许我本来可以看到他眼中的世界。至少，接近他。他的基因仍然存在于我的每一个细胞里，我的眼睛，和他有着同样的颜色。爸爸眼中的一切是什么模样？我可曾听他说过？

古希腊人的词语犹可让我一窥古老的过往，但我却忘记了身边的声音，那些本来也属于我的声音。

也许我本来可以阻止那件事发生。

不……

几乎被愧疚吞噬的我，切断了调整镜的信号，再接通，再切断。电位的频繁变化中，眼前的一切似乎变了，又似乎没变。但是究竟什么才是真实的？那个多数人的世界，真的更好吗？

突然，我的眼前一片浑浊，随之而来的是越来越严重的头晕。我吓了一跳，赶忙闭上眼睛。我听得见自己的喃喃低语，安慰着自己这只是幻觉，再用僵直的指关节敲了敲自己的太阳穴，然后睁开眼睛期待光明——还是没用。

所有的颜色都消失了。黑暗包围了我。

难道就这么瞎了吗？

从未有过的恐惧中，我终于体会到了什么叫做度日如年——甚至度秒如年，我几乎已经看到了那个倒在地上后被人送去医院，躺在病床上虚弱无助的自己。滤镜，调整镜，色盲，视觉异常......纷乱的词语在我的脑中回旋飞舞，然而在真正的黑暗面前，什么都了无意义。

我怎么还未到生命的中途，

就已耗尽光明，走上这黑暗的，茫茫的世路。[15]

如今还会有盲诗人吗？在失去意识前，我莫名地想起荷马。

＊＊＊

"艾米......你听得到吗？艾米......"

黑暗中似乎有遥远的呼唤。一只冰凉的手轻轻放在我滚烫的前额上，又移开了。

我很久没有像现在那样渴望那个声音，那种触感。像是渴望黑暗中的一道光。

"妈妈......"

"别怕。"  她紧紧握住我的手，"没事的，你只是因为眼压不稳导致的短时失明。"

我战战兢兢地睁开眼睛。四周渐渐亮起来。

而我的视野因为泪水，再次模糊了。

"我不知道.......爸爸.......我......"  我泣不成声，"为什么......不告诉我？"

"你是多么害怕自己的特别啊。孩子。所有人都害怕。我也曾经害怕过。"  妈妈叹息道，"我只是想保护你，不过，我错了。"

我惊讶地抬起头，难道妈妈也......

镜框后，她疲惫的眼睛闪着光。

"我们每个人都很特别。但又没那么特别。"  妈妈将我的头发拢到耳后，"妈妈也花了很久，才明白了这一点。"

她为我戴上了一幅耳机。

"现在你的眼睛还需要休息。闭上眼睛吧，孩子。用耳朵去听。"

---

15《哀失明》，弥尔顿

333

　　我颤抖地重新躺下，耳机里传来妈妈的朗读声，就像很多年前，她在我床前朗读童话和传奇一样。　　不过，和过去的夜晚不同，这次的故事，让我的呼吸渐渐急促，内心翻江倒海，我时而忍俊不禁，时而泪水涟涟，像是荷马的第一批听众。

　　那是妈妈的日记。

＊＊＊

　　……2024年，1月25日。

　　今天我在滑雪场遇见了乔。我几乎是一下子就被他的眼睛吸引住了。浅淡的冰蓝色，里面还有那么多不同层次的绿色，丁香色，青金石色……怎么可能有这么漂亮的眼睛？我呆若木鸡的样子，在他眼里一定很可笑。

　　不过我很快发现，他可能是个色盲。他的滑雪服是我见过的最丑的绿色，像一个放了半年的牛油果，还掺杂有脏兮兮的土橘色，我在他面前忍不住咯咯笑个不停，搞得他莫名其妙。看来我以后必须帮他打理衣橱……　　不过，至少现在，我不用担心别的姑娘会在雪道上跟他搭讪了。


　　……2028年，5月30日。

　　谢天谢地，最后一批花总算在婚礼前送到了。白色的芍药，早上刚刚从费尔班克斯的农场里采摘下来。我的手捧花则是含苞待放的白色栀子花。白色的蜡烛，白色的蕾丝桌布，白色，白色，全是白色。

　　乔小心翼翼地问我，真的不用别的颜色吗？哎，我该怎么向他描述呢，他总是看不见，白色不是白色。就像我见到他的那天，雪地的颜色一样。我让他想象蛋白石的样子，在半透明的白色石头上有比红宝石更柔和的火彩，紫水晶的绚丽紫色，以及祖母绿的绿色之海，所有闪闪发亮的元素汇聚在一起，就像普林尼说的那样，像硫磺燃烧的火焰，可与画师最深广最丰富的色彩媲美。那就是我的白色。

　　他像往常一样，不知道我在讲什么，却还是频频点头。好像看见了，就像……他装作听懂的样子，一脸严肃地搜肠刮肚，想要找一个形容词，让我不得不去吻他的唇。

　　就像我爱你的样子。


　　……2030年，11月1日。

　　艾米来到了人间。第一眼看到裹在襁褓里的，小小的她，我竟然不相信那是我的女儿。

　　她不像我。我的皮肤是浅橄榄色的，可她却是那么苍白，

334

透出细小的血管，像奶油覆盖的蓝莓。她的颜色不对。我一遍遍对护士重复，她们费了好大力气才听懂我在说什么，又再三保证，让我平静下来。我知道这蠢透了，她并不一定要跟我的皮肤色调一致，但我还是忍不住这么想。

颜色对我来讲是如此特别。我早就知道，并不是所有人都能像我一样，看到这么多种颜色。从七岁起，我就是美术课上最特别的孩子。我画的其实并不好，但是所有人都说那些画一看就是我画的——别人画不出来那种颜色。而我只是将眼中所见的百分之一画出来了而已。

我希望艾米也能像我一样。如果她也是个"正常人"，她的世界将是多么平庸乏味啊。


…...2035年，7月6日。

乔真令我郁闷。他不小心将一块苹果掉在地板上，却无法分辨苹果块与木地板的边界。而对于我，那醒目得像块青柠色的火腿，难以置信他竟然看不见。

为了这个，我差点和他吵了起来，我不知道自己是怎么了…...听说有一种视网膜调整镜技术正在实验，也许至少可以让乔成为"正常人"？

我开始在画画时把艾米放在一边，让她学着看。尽管有点儿早，但是塞尚和莫奈的颜色是那么丰富而生动，我希望她能够早点发现颜色的魅力。

不过，目前看来一无所获。


…...2037年，9月2日。

我不知道该说什么。艾米抱怨，看不清楚老师在墨绿色黑板上用蓝色粉笔写下的数字。我忽然有种可怕的预感。

我让她识别印象派作品中的细微色差。她看不出来。

艾米无法完全分辨蓝色与绿色。与乔的红绿色盲相比，这并不算严重，但是，也远远算不上"正常"。更不要说，像我一样。

艾米。在她诞生的那一天，我就抱有的希望，如今变成了巨大的讽刺。

我和乔激烈地讨论，到底要不要给艾米植入调整镜。我简直无法想象女儿在一个色彩缺失的世界里生活，但是乔说，并没有那么可怕。他并不觉得自己比我少了哪些生活的乐趣。

那是你没体会过。我试图解释。想想看，看到一个完全不同的世界，更丰富，更清晰，更生动，充满了难以穷尽的可能性。一旦看到这样的场景，你将无法忍受之前的一切。

不，亲爱的。我也看到过你从未看到过的东西。他微笑着说。拉格朗日力学可以让你对整个世界的存在产生新的看法。一旦理解了那些公式和符号的语言，你会觉得这个宇宙和谐得可怕，也脆弱得可怕，人们的喜怒哀乐，生老病死都了无意义……但是这并不妨碍我听你讲述那些我永远看不见的美妙景象，去感受艾米躺在我臂弯里的温度。

语言也是一副眼镜。我记得他说，它可以让我们看到往常看不见的东西。但是何时戴上，何时摘下，需要我们自己的选择。

我们决定再过几年，把选择权交给艾米自己，她需要做出自己的选择。在此之前，尽量不让她感受到自己的异常。我的特殊或许能带来赞许，但是艾米的特殊不是。

我和艾米的老师通了电话。

……2043年，4月12日。

我的朋友并不多。在以前，和女伴们聚会时，我就常常因为被那些令人屏住呼吸的色泽吸引了目光，而显得格格不入。我记得，她们抱怨说，不得不重复喊我的名字，才能把我从无休无止的凝视中拉回来。

也许只有乔能忍受我。谢天谢地。

我曾经希望艾米在植入调整镜后，能看到和我一样的景象，体味到那些幽微的感触，但是我错了。我能感受到她在一点点离我远去。她不再阅读我钟爱的那些书籍。我听不懂她那些时髦的用词，就像她也听不懂我的话语一样。

乔不会要求我去学习拉格朗日力学。我又能要求艾米什么呢？

她宁愿凝视着虚无，也不愿意和我一起画画，看画了。我知道，在她的眼睛里，是一个我所无法达到的地方。

今天我去咨询了成人植入调整镜的手术。在初步检查后，医生对我特殊的颜色感知很感兴趣，表示需要等待进一步的实验报告。

……2043年，4月20日。

四色视觉。我第一次听到这个词。

极其罕见，医生说。人只有三种视锥细胞，负责加工红色、绿色和蓝色，而四色视觉者眼睛里的第四种视锥细胞还可以对其他颜色进行加工。这种状况通常是由X染色体变异导致，发生在男性身上可能引起色盲症，而女性则多是四色视觉者。

相似的变异，让我和乔走上了不同的方向。他能看到的颜色，比正常人能看到的一百万种要少得多，而我却可以看见将近一亿种颜色。而艾米继承了糟糕的那一种。

目前，四色视觉者无法接受调整镜的植入。我本身的视觉神经通路已经过于复杂，调整镜的算法无法整合。

我无法看见艾米的世界了。

也许是该放手了，她已经是个亭亭玉立的少女，粉红色的青春痘从她白皙的面颊上悄悄冒出来。有了调整镜的修饰，她并不太在意。不像我，曾经为脸上的青春痘痛苦不已，它们是那么的触目惊心，直到现在，我也必须化妆之后再出门，皮下血管的青绿色，深紫色，酒红色，在我的眼中过于清晰了。

也许，她能看到的，是一个比我眼中更好的世界。

……2047年，12月19日。

乔离开了我。

他躺在那里，紧闭着眼睛，脸色灰白。所有的颜色都消失了。红宝石，紫水晶，祖母绿。那是死亡的颜色。

甚至是黑色都太丰富了。我在黑色里能看见紫罗兰，深蓝，翡翠，那让我想起椋鸟的翎羽和太阳刚刚落下的大海。

而我的心是一把燃尽的灰。

……2050年，4月25日。

艾米马上要毕业了。她健康，聪明，自信，几乎完美。她也懂得照顾自己。有了调整镜，她的色觉感知"正常"了，我再也不用担心，她会像乔那样，在某个更新了调整镜交通信号的国家，看不清红绿路灯。

我已经老了。我们的时代已经过去，就像所有的世代一样。如今我只能从那些越来越陌生的词语里捕捉那些旧日的气息。它们像一个个沉睡在黑暗中的矿洞。

人也一样。近来我有个可怕的念头，为什么每个人喜欢的颜色都各不相同。

那一束束光线，在艾米和乔的眼中，是近似到乏味的色调，在我的眼中，则是令人屏息的异彩，在"正常"人的眼中，难道，就是一样的吗？

没有人知道。每个人也是个黑暗中的矿洞，每个人都是特别的。我们永远无法得知物质世界在不同的洞穴中映照出的影像。物理世界的真实，犹如一团无所定型的灰白色云雾，而使其凝结下来的，是每个人的心灵。人们的认知本身重塑了世界，也是某种意义上，我们所能认识到的，唯一的世界。

黑暗中的一个个洞穴冷漠而疏离，而将他们勉力联系在一起的，不是眼中所见，而是口中所言。人们无法定义个人心灵中的独特体验，但是可以为那些体验赋予统一的名字。我们就凭借着这些名字，在这个疯狂而混乱的世间相知相爱。多么神奇啊，即使荷马的暗酒色的时代早已逝去，即使乔的白色和我的白色完全不同，我们仍然可以分享一丝同样的感受。

艾米。我看着你飘得越来越远。我无能为力，也安然接受。我们都太注重看到的东西，忘记了倾听，也忘记了述说。爸爸懂得这一切，但是他已经离开了。

日记结束了。我紧闭的眼睛早已温热。

我明白了盲诗人的诗篇为何动人。

***

"现在，你看见弥漫的苍黄云层被闪电击穿，扰动了远方的天空。随着视角渐渐移动，从天上回到了人间，视线聚焦雷暴在云层下造成的破坏。你所驾驶的旋翼机就正处在雷鸣闪电间，机身因为强风上下摇摆……"

"什么是旋翼机？"　杰克问道。在这些无法植入调整镜的客人中，他的年纪最大，却对沉浸式游戏或者影视最感兴趣。

"呃……"　我一时语塞，不知道该如何解释这个常见词汇。"就是一种单人飞行器，造型精细，不过稳定性一般……"

"就像罗伯特·弗罗斯特写的，暴风雨中七歪八倒叶残瓣破的花儿？"　妈妈问道，她现在是我们这个小小的"心目"俱乐部的管理员，茶点供应人，也是第一位"观众"。每个周末，我们都会为他们举办一场特别的体验会。

"嗯……对。"　我努力回想起那些诗句，以及它们在我心中留下的痕迹。"这个场景的数据模型来源于国际空间站拍摄的地球大气变化，不过，的确，这个场景想要表达的，就是类似的感受。"

我不确定这样的讲述到底会产生怎样的效果。这当然与调整镜中的视觉体验有所不同，我们的"观众"也并不多，但是，我知道，有些人不惜乘车两三个小时，从郊区赶到这

338

里，也有些人，会在我的讲述中，攥紧手中的茶杯，像握住过山车的扶手。这对我也绝非易事，很多时候，我不得不关掉调整镜，甚至蒙上眼睛，去寻找合适的语言，向他们展示一个个从未体验过的世界。

他们说，我就是他们的眼睛。但是我知道，是他们，教会了我如何用自己的眼睛去观看。

"哎，其实就有点像那幅画。"　　　比尔扬扬下巴。场景中，他正处于跟随视角，不过，他似乎对这间我长大的老屋更感兴趣。

我回过头，倒吸了一口气，那是《暴风雪中的汽船》。那幅妈妈喜欢的画。翻卷的旋风把海浪高高卷起，空气中夹杂着雪花和海雾，天地一片混沌。所有事物的形状消失了，所有的颜色都混杂在一起，但画家也有意在它们之间保持了细微的差别。虽然我无法细细辨识，但我现在知道，在妈妈的眼中，那是一种极其丰富，极其鲜明的壮丽景象。而那种超越了人们日常经验的，大自然的壮阔和崇高之感，正是我在设计这个场景时，想要达到的效果。

"透纳为了作画，曾经把自己绑在桅杆上，驶入暴风雪中的大海。"　妈妈说，眼神飘得很远。

"就像奥德赛一样……"　　我和她异口同声，目光碰上，相视一笑。这一刻，我觉得，我们的世界有着相同的颜色。

Colour the World

by Congyun "Mu Ming" Gu

Translated by Sarah Huang

Mu Ming's works have been published in various Chinese science fiction and literature magazines and journals as well as various online literature platforms. Some of her works have been translated into English, Japanese, Italian and other languages. Her most representative works include "Color the World", "The Serpentine Band", "By Those Hands", etc., and she has published her personal collection "The Serpentine Band" and "Colora il mondo" (Future Fiction, 2021). Award: Best Short Story of the Galaxy Award 2020

> And now am I come to shore, as thou seest, with ship and crew, sailing over the wine-dark sea, unto men of strange speech, even to Temesa.

I was eleven when I first read The Odyssey. Athena brings to Telemachus the news that his father Odysseus has returned from Troy. Samuel Butcher's elegant translation was full of troublesome Greek names and foreign inflections, but one word jumped out at me.

"What is wine-dark?" I asked Mom.

She winked at me. "What do you think?"

"I think Homer was using it as a metaphor," rhetoric lessons at school came to mind, "the sea's blue, isn't it?"

"Homer was blind." Mom let out a sigh. "And the sea isn't always so blue. The word blue didn't exist in Ancient Greek. Remember the beach in Long Island? How did the ocean look at sunset?"

I tried to recall those summer days when I rode by the beach. The sky would be turquoise-green, like the water, but it turned violet and agate-coloured where it met the sea. On the horizon, milky white clouds shaped themselves into an Olympian palace while crimson-gold rays, like heavenly rivers, poured into a darkening sea.

I liked those summer vacations. During those months, I was surrounded by seagull cries and the sea breeze's murmurs instead of my classmates' knowing whispers.

To be honest, I didn't find ancient poetry and oil paints all that bad. When I was even younger, I used to sit in a stroller and watch as Mom painted—she would often lose track of time until I began to bawl, but by the age of eleven, I understood that life wasn't about verses and pigments.

I had learned this the hard way.

"I don't know what wine-dark is." I shrugged.

Mom was quiet for a while. "Homer used the same word, oinpos, to describe bulls. In the Iliad he talked about how 'two wine-dark oxen both strain their utmost at the plow, which they are drawing in a fallow field...'"

"It's okay, Mom," I cut her off. "You can just say that you don't know, either. For all I care, you can say that Homer got Retinal Adjustors. Who cares? Everybody has them—everybody except me."

Mom closed the book. "Amy, I hope you will at least wait until—"

"No, Mom! Why can't I get RAs like everyone else?"

"But you're still so young ..."

"Mom, you just don't get it!"

Mom knew five ancient languages and could recite page after page of epic poetry. She understood the minute differences between dead words from extinct tongues, but she didn't speak a language that could describe the world we lived in.

I didn't understand why she was so against Retinal Adjustors. She made me too self-conscious to invite my classmates over. I was already the weird kid with no RAs, and the bizarre grey painting hanging above the fireplace would confirm that the weird kid had a weird Mom.

Snow Storm: Steam-Boat off a Harbour's Mouth. As far as I was concerned, Turner must have painted it after going blind like Homer.

Much like my life back then, it was dominated by gloomy colours and crude strokes that obscured actual shapes.

"Hey there, dork!"

Someone slammed into my elbow and made me drop my pencil. By the time I picked it up, half of the writing on the whiteboard was already gone.

"Come on, don't—"

The boy who had slammed into me threw the eraser at me. I dodged and it struck the corner of my desk. "Having trouble seeing, huh?"

"There's nothing wrong with my eyes…"

"You can't even tell blue from green!" He looked down at me, quite smug.

"I just don't have RAs…" I tried to defend myself. "And I can tell them apart. I just need a bit of extra time …"

"Yeah whatever. Why don't you wear your Mom's ancient glasses? They'd suit you." The boy circled his eyes with his fingers, his beautiful green irises full of mockery. "You ugly frog."

"Shut up!" I couldn't take it anymore, so I grabbed the eraser and threw it back at him, but I wasn't nearly fast enough, and he ducked like it was nothing. Not a single speck of dust got on his clothes.

"Alright now, let's go." Angela stepped over the eraser with easy grace. The boy blew a raspberry and took her school bag.

I looked at Angela. Her blond hair glinted in the winter sunset, and her ears were so white they were nearly translucent. Even without Retinal Adjustors she looked stunning to me. It was no wonder they all adored her. She turned and gave me a sweet smile, and it was a sight straight out of an oil painting.

But I could read the exaggerated, deliberate movements of her lips.

She said, "Bye, Froggie."

Now alone in the classroom, I stared at the rhetoric class notes in my notebook. I always got good grades, even if I sometimes had trouble reading the text on the whiteboard and had to copy it down after class. But where did that get me? I was a straight A student as Mom expected, as all Asian American Moms expect, but at that time, in those kinds of situations, it was not helping me.

I never told Mom any of this for some reason, but at that moment, I realized it was time for a change.

I slowly tore the unfinished page out of my notebook. Then, bit by bit, I ripped it up.

When I was twelve, Mom finally agreed to let me get Retinal Adjustor implants. I woke up early on the day of the operation. Opening the closet without turning on the light, I dragged my fingertips across thin laces and silky ribbons, picturing all the blooming colours I'd be able to see. In the end, I chose an ivory-coloured knit slip dress; the RA's colour filter effects showed up best against a background of white.

"Don't be afraid, sweetheart. It's a small operation." Dad was holding my hand, and I could feel the sweat on his palm.

"It's okay, Dad. It's just going to make me normal," I said playfully, all the while pointedly ignoring Mom. She stood in a corner, wearing a familiar gray rabbit fur coat. Too much foundation on her face made her look like a mannequin. She always wrapped herself in gloomy colours; the whole of her person, like her books and paintings, was perennially covered by a layer of ancient fog.

"Here," the doctor pointed to a cross-section model of the human eyeball. The transparent vitreous, looking like a crystal ball constituted about four-fifths of the organ. The gold-coloured membrane right behind it was the retina.

"The science behind Retina Adjustors isn't all that difficult. We know that the retina is made up of rod cells that are sensitive to light and the three kinds of cone cells that are sensitive to colour. In the old days, when people walked in dark woods on a moonless night, the rod cells within their eyes would capture photons and enlarge them, all without interference from the other cells. When they visited the beach on a sunny day, the colour-sensitive cone cells enabled them to quickly adapt to the bright sunshine." The doctor seemed used to giving this explanation; she was looking at her monitor as she spoke. Every word she said sounded unquestionable.

"With our newest Retinal Adjustors, we implant these biological multielectrode array chips into your retina, right between the layer of rods and cones and the pigmented layer, so that your rod cells and cone cells can receive light better. The retina's coder and decoder then convert the neural signals into visual recognition. It's just like changing your digital camera's image sensor—you will still use your own lens."

"But they are so much better than my own lenses," I cut in, eager to show off all the tidbits I'd learned from my classmates. "They can capture so much more visual detail, and they automatically adjust for lighting and colour saturation. I'll never have trouble reading the whiteboard again."

"You might never be able to take them off, either." Mom shook her head. "Think about it, Amy. These aren't traditional glasses. They might be your new eyes ..."

"I don't want to get stuck being blind forever!" In my mind's eye, I kept seeing Angela mouthing that word at me. Froggie. Froggie.

"The RA technology is really quite safe. We've come a long way over the last thirty years, and visual system enhancement technology has matured considerably." The doctor's voice was even and measured, she was obviously on familiar territory. "In fact, most children receive RA implants at an even younger age. They're like the hottest mobile phone model, the hottest social network app, and the hottest fashion trends all rolled into one. There is no fighting it. Of course, it's not a purely business decision, but RA technology is the future."

"Everyone in my class already has it. The adjustors have this shared filter function, too, you just need to get in sync to use it." I withdrew my hand from my father's palm and stared at the inner side of my wrist. Once the implant was done, I knew a dot of light would appear there.

"That's right. The adjustors can, through programmable interfaces, program the electronic signals in real time." The doctor nodded. "In a way, you might say that they open up an infinite number of worlds for you—and you can share them with everyone else."

"Yeah, isn't it amazing?" I was loud and that was on purpose. Maybe Mom was content to hide from the real world in her dimly lit study, but I wasn't. She had no idea how cruel—and how wonderful—the world was for kids. Or maybe she just didn't care.

But the thing is, we are the future.

"May I have a word with you in private, Doctor Chau?" asked Mom.

I don't know what was said between them. Dad kept me company and neither of us spoke a word. Dad only left when the doctor came back into the room. The doctor began to input adjustment parameters into the operation system and the nurse injected me with anesthetic: an icy pinch under my eye, then total darkness. The operation was about to begin.

"I'm wondering, Doctor Chau ... is it possible for adults to receive RA implants?"

"It's possible, but adults often have a harder time post-op than children." The doctor's voice sounded a little far away. "Not to mention our current technology doesn't support certain cases. For example, those who have issues with transplant rejection, and..."

That's all I heard before sleep overtook me. Inside the dark dreamscape a thousand brilliant colours were beckoning me over.


"Hey, Angela." I mustered the courage to wave at the girl coming my way. Her pale pink skirt had mint-coloured ribbon bows on it. It looked like a blooming tulip. "I like your pink skirt."

"Oh yeah?" She arched her blond eyebrows. "So, you finally got it, huh?"

"Yeah." I straightened out my hemline all casual like. The dark blue fabric, with glittering star lights, matched my hair—no longer black like my Mom's but a light brunette. A faint green light flickered on the inner side of my wrist. I knew that I had become a wholly different person in her eyes, as my RAs have been synced automatically with hers.

"Not bad. You know, before this, we all thought that you had a bit of a problem with this..." She tilted her head and pointed to her eyes.

"No! I didn't! I just ... I just didn't get the RAs!" I said in a hurry. "But it's different now. It's all different now. I'm the same as you guys."

"Not quite. There is one thing left." She squinted at me, grinning.

"What?"

"We don't call this colour pink. It's Rose Ashes from the Thorn Birds Filter Collection. Rose Ashes, the perfect combination of tenderness and cruelty. Likewise, your skirt isn't blue. With the Filter Collection, it's called Royal Midnight, the colour of melancholy."

"Oh ..."

Suddenly I realized that the adjustors didn't only change the colours and degrees of lighting. They had changed the very language used to describe the world.

And language ...

Mom's bedtime stories came back to me in a haze. From fairy tale curses to Greek mythical prophecies, language always had the power to transform everything.

Those stories are for suckers, a voice whispered to me. I blinked and tried to drive away those random thoughts—unnecessarily, in fact, because my field of vision would always be 100 per cent clear now that I had the adjustors.

"Okay, Rose Ashes." I nodded. "Sure thing. Want to try my Royal Midnight? I think it will match your hair great."

I majored in Human-Machine Interaction in college. After graduation, I joined a startup that produced filter plugins for Retinal Adjustors. Human Biological Engineering is the hottest thing out there now. Individuals with RFID chip implants no longer have to worry about forgetting their keys or wallets, while

3D-printed hearts, lungs, and kidneys have dramatically short-ened the organ transplant waiting list. Young people are flocking to bio-hacking, but I remain most interested in RA-related tech-nologies. Visual connection is one of the most powerful channels of communication we can establish with the outside world. I will never forget how, before my operation, I was denied entrance to that world.

Nobody objects to upgrading their physical hardware any-more, Mom excepted.

She tried to convince me to go to graduate school for Art or Literature, but after Dad passed away in a car accident while on a business trip, I moved out and rented a small apartment of my own. After that, she could no longer make me do anything.

Actually, ever since middle school, I had begun talking to her less and less.

The adjustors were a part of the reason why. In the ten years since my operation, as RA technology reached increasing heights, its visual impact came to defy all previous human experience, and it could only be communicated through the filters' own language. I couldn't really explain to Mom what Super Atmosphere III—the colour that you might get from light rays rising through the atmo-sphere, shifting through light blue, dark blue, purple, dark purple before finally settling into a velvety black, laced with indescribable strands of light—was. It was my favorite sleep environment. Nor could I describe to her the boy who was my first crush—he had a tiny galaxy in his eyes, with stars falling down around the edge of his irises. Only the newest chips could achieve that kind of effect.

Electronic monitors, initially geared for traditional human vi-sual perception, also made the shift to RA technology. Instead of Pre-Information Age graphics with jagged pixel edges, we had hy-per-realistic images produced by RA algorithms. These were a bit like the old 3D images, but far more lifelike. In fact, if it weren't for the monitor frames, we'd have a hard time telling the world inside the monitor apart from the one outside it.

Mom wouldn't have anything to do with it. In a way, I think it was her altitude, rather than the adjustors themselves, that sealed the uncomfortable silence between us. She wouldn't even use electronic readers or non-invasive reality-enhancing glasses, choosing to bury herself in those ever-duller classic books and artworks instead. I know that she took up painting again after I left for school. I've seen her works—old-fashioned still life and landscape pieces, nothing to boast about. The adjustors' dynamic lights don't show up on congealed oil paint.

"Do you like them?" she looked at me expectantly, a little girl waiting for a pat on the head. "Umm ... they're pretty good," I tried to sound as sincere as possible, "but really, Mom, are you seriously not going to try—"

"Amy, I wish you would turn those things off and see the world with your own eyes, say it in your own language." She peered at me from the other side of her old tortoise shell glasses, her voice dull and dry. "Listen to your mother, you can learn from my experience. Remember, the colours you see ..."

"Black isn't always black, and white isn't always white. Okay, fine, but is that why you showed up for the funeral dressed in grey?" My voice rose as a long-dormant emotion began to break through. "Mom, I'm all grown now, but you just haven't changed at all. You have to realize that these days people value actual experiences, not the kind that supposedly comes with age."

"You mean those mass-produced artificial experiences?" Mom twisted her hands. "You were such a special child, Amy. Remember how—"

"No, I wasn't special. You just wanted me to be. I never liked those classic stories and oil paintings." I turned my back to her because I didn't want to meet her eyes, "I just want to be normal."

"Amy ..." She stopped. I could hear the unbearable surprise and disappointment in her voice.

"I'm not a kid anymore." I forced myself to get it all out, lest the guilt held me back. "I've seen more things than you have, and I understand more things than you do. By leaps and bounds. Don't fence yourself in with all those hogwash clichés—and don't try to keep me there with you. Get out there and take a look at the new world."

She finally went quiet for a moment, I thought I heard a stifled sob.

I turned my back and left that dim, old house. It was drizzling and I turned on Turrell No. 7 in panorama mode, a visual simulation of Venus' Girdle. The gloomy sky softened under the reflected Rayleigh scattering rays. I took a deep breath and felt my frantic heartbeats returning to normal. Sorry, Mom, but I'm all grown up now.

It was raining like this on the day of Dad's funeral too, icy raindrops dripping from black woollen coats. A pair of luminous cherubs, made by the priest, holding up an arch of light on top of the cross. Amidst the foggy rain, a heartbreakingly familiar projection floated in the middle of the bright halo. I told myself that Dad would always watch over me from inside that halo, just as he had held my hand in his back then, so long ago.

All of this was alien to Mom. Even as she stood right next to me, she had hidden herself under her thick foundation and antiquated sweater. She could neither hear nor understand the priest's speech about the Three Crowns in the Kingdom of God. She only looked up at the lonely, ashen-white sky, her glasses wet in the rain.

I could hear people's whispers between the priest's words. I was no stranger to the deliberately lowered tone of voice and the awkwardness in avoiding eye contact. The adults played by secretive rules, but I understood what was hidden behind those considerate smiles and turns of phrase. I knew that I shouldn't be thinking about such things during the funeral, but rationality is no match for emotions.

Nobody was going to shelter me from the rain anymore. Mom couldn't be counted on.

"Please accept my condolences." Marc shook my hand. His obsidian suit was crisply pressed, as impeccable as ever. We had just started online dating and I hadn't expected him to be there.

He took my hand and leaned in. "It must have been tough for you."

"Thanks, I'm holding up." The warmth from his hand made me feel just a bit better.

"I mean, I had no idea that ..." He paused, trying to find the right word. "Your Mom ... your family is very special."

My hand went numb.

"It's not like that. She's the only one ..."

I wanted to explain, to argue, but his strange look of sympathy made me realize that I was still mired in the swamp I had tried so hard to crawl out of.

"We're all special, my child." Mom turned to look at us, rain dripping from her glasses. Her voice was loud enough to make me ashamed. "Amy—you, me, everyone. We are all special. Don't put all your faith in your lens—"

"Mom, stop, please."

Marc shrugged and left, leaving me to put up a façade and deal with the rest of the guests. Mom sat on the sidelines, indifferent as ever. She never had many friends.

I didn't know if she really even cared about Dad's passing and I almost completely gave up on her after that. Inside our house the doors were often closed. Our mother-daughter chats stopped and communication gradually dwindled to a minimum. I moved out not long after.

No, Mom, I probably can't change how you think, but I don't want to turn into you either.


When technological advances alter the language we use to describe this world, it changes the way we perceive the world itself.

Language alone is powerful enough to mold the human mind—back in college, a linguistics professor told us about the Sapir-Whorf hypothesis, the basis for much science fiction about acquiring superpowers by studying extraterrestrial languages. I feel that in this age of relentless change, the hypothesis has far more real-world implications than people might imagine

"Yo, need to expand the vocab DB again for audio assistance." An IM from Tariq pops up on my monitor and drags me back to the present. "RA user data from last week popped. 70+ new high-frequency words."

I turn around and scan the cubicles for Tariq's silver-gray mop of hair. A senior engineer of the company, he is my current partner in pair programming.

I know that the colour of his hair is as real as it gets, no filter required. "Genetics," he had explained at our initial meeting.

"That's pretty cool." I didn't want to make a big deal out of it. "I know people who don't use adjustors either."

"I'm not that cool." He grinned as his wild hair strands morphed into tangled mini rainbows.

"Yeah so ... feels like we should take another look at the whole setup." I key in my response in a flurry. "New filters bring new words in, and old words faded / filters deleted. We've updated the DB 3x times already in the past quarter. The turnover rate is too fast."

"You might want to calculate the acceleration." He adds a string of numbers at the end of his sentence, the code for a grinning emoji. "Coffee?"

"Sometimes I get the feeling that things are gradually ... spinning out of control." I open a bag of Skittles and empty its contents onto a paper plate. "You've probably heard how our choice of language affects the way we think," I start poking at the candy, "and we are helping to accelerate this process—"

I try my best not to think about my mother's face. "Think about it. RA technology has become entrenched in every aspect of our lives. From cinema screens to mobile apps, from commercial slogans to internet media, everywhere people are bending themselves to match their language to what they see through the filters ... It won't be long before—actually it's already started. People can't communicate, can't think without RAs. But what about the people who don't have them?"

"Skimmed or whole milk?"

"Come on, Tariq. I'm being serious here."

"Skimmed it is, then." He shrugs. "It's not a big deal, Amy. We invent technology, and technology reinvents us. It's a tale as old as time."

"Still, this is going way too fast ..."

"Why the pessimism?" He shakes the foamy milk and draws something on it. "Weren't you the one who said, during your interview, that adjustors, like all advanced tech, bring people closer together? By sharing the beautiful world we see with one another—"

"Maybe I was totally wrong." Deflated, I can feel the Skittles melting on my fingertip, growing into a sticky mess, just like my thoughts.

Tariq hands me the latte. On its surface, he has drawn a face with two eyes but no mouth. Something hits me from the inside, and I almost can't bring myself to look at the thick milk bubbles floating on top of the brown liquid.

"I majored in Physics back in college," says Tariq slowly, "even now, I believe that rational reasoning is the way to understand the physical world, but I also believe that if we limit ourselves to Newton's colour theory and abstract algebra, we will never understand what the ancient Greeks saw when they looked out to the horizon on a wine-dark sea."

"So, what did they see?" A Skittle squeezes under the tip of my finger. I have forgotten our initial topic altogether—I just want to solve the long-forgotten riddle.

"Um, I was just trying on the new Eyes of Homer ..." He looks surprised. "It's the first thing that comes up when you open the app store."

The blind poet had brought colour to that long-gone age with his words, the same words that will now lead me to the truth. How can I describe what I have seen? The ancient Greeks had no trouble telling the myriad colours of this world apart, but they cared more about lighting than palettes. Wine-dark didn't just denote a colour between red and blue; it meant an ever-shifting combination of brightness and movement. An ocean shimmering under a setting sun, the oxen's sweat-glistening bodies ... what I see, what I feel, is the thick liquid inside the paper cup, sparkling and whirling.

"This is incredible. Reverse engineering through language. It's like ... seeing the world through the eyes of the ancient Greeks."

This algorithm, in a sense, reflects both the physical reality and what the people of old learned from it, and it's all rooted in language. The Sapir–Whorf hypothesis didn't tell us the whole story. The choice of language hasn't obscured our vision, nor has it deprived us of the ability to think. It's just a pair of glasses that we wear.

I turn off my adjustors. How long has it been since I last did that? I'm trying to summon those archaic adjectives to my mind—or rather, I'm trying to forget the new words that came with the adjustors. You need to take off your glasses before putting on another pair ... you need to forget your native tongue, however temporarily, so that you can better learn a new one—yes, Mom is giving me the look again, from the other side of those tortoise shell frames.

"Amy? Are you okay?" Tariq's voice floats in from somewhere, "So Peter Pan's Journey is your colour, too. I had no idea."

My heart skips a beat.

My wardrobe has long been dominated by swathes of Pele's eye, Yuki Onna, and Mermaid song, with or without adjustors on. I don't like any colour that has a hint of green. It reminds me of a certain slimy amphibious animal and a certain pair of unkind eyes.


"Mom, there's something that I want to ask you ..."

I hesitate as I stare at the voice message that I've just sent. Eventually, I opt for the "delete" button. Maybe Mom will hear an unfinished sentence, or maybe she will see the indicator of a recalled message. I'm not sure what she will make of this, but we both know I stopped going to her for help a long time ago.

But what should I do?

My apartment is beyond messy. The floor is littered with take-out boxes and balled-up dirty clothes. The curved desktop monitor has both the Munsell Colour Wheel and the visible light spectrum on display.


I have piles of print-outs, too: Democritus' theory about colour, Dalton's "Extraordinary Facts Relating to the Vision of Colours", and Mark Rothko's abstract paintings of solid colour blocks.

None of them can tell me if the colours I see are the same as everyone else's.

Could I really be ... colourblind?

As farfetched as it may sound, it's far from impossible. I have a hazy memory of Mom saying "blue" while pointing to a clear sky, of her telling me that the new leaves in the garden are green. I have learned to match each colour with a name, but what if my cone cells are in the wrong place? What if the wavelength for blue, when it reaches my eyes, is translated into what is commonly understood as green? Would I even realize the difference?

I would believe that the colour blue simply looks green. I've learned to associate certain perceptions with corresponding linguistic symbols, but it hasn't occurred to me to ask what these symbols really mean. Perhaps what they represent are not physical properties but mental perceptions. I will never know how the world appears in the eyes of others.

To use the computer as an analogy—my eyes would be like the input end, my brain the black box, and my mouth in charge of output. When other people receive the signal for green, they perceive green and utter the word green; the same signal reads blue to me, but then I say "green" all the same. My own peculiarity is thus buried, hidden. I'm different from them, not just because of my eyes but because of how I've internalized my response to outside stimuli. I'm different on the inside.

You can't even tell blue from green.

Froggie. Froggie.

I'm besieged by fragments of childhood memories. Unlike my peers, I was slow to pick up on the subtle differences in colours. I always thought it was because I didn't have the adjustors, but the truth could be far more terrible.

The adjustors have allowed me to see what the others see. I've embraced its vocabulary and thought myself a part of the "normal" world, but do I really belong there? Mom went on and on about how I was special. She must have known all along. But why didn't she ever tell me?

So, I'm not normal, after all?

I suddenly remembered a post on the company's Disqus. We had designed the in-game interface for an enhanced-vision game, and a player was complaining that it wasn't user-friendly: "I love this game, but I'm really having trouble seeing the targets' glowing outlines. Everything looks the same to me."

The post didn't gain much traction. One of the few replies it received was: "The new UI is sooo cool. Are you colourblind or something? If you don't have RAs, don't troll here just quit and find some s**t for yourself."

The OP didn't take kindly to that: "F**k RAs. First the traffic lights got 'upgraded' so I couldn't drive anymore, and now you have to ruin my favorite game, too? I didn't ask for any of this!"

At the time, I didn't spare a second thought for that post. I simply marked it as N/A, No Action. We receive hundreds of user requests every day, and we only respond to the most important issues—"most important" being defined as things that affect the largest number of people, or have the most impact on the company's earnings report. Special requests like colourblind accessibility are not a priority for us.

Now though, staring at the account's registered location, I feel like somebody has punched me in the heart. The dull pain makes me want to throw up.

The Disqus account originates from the country where my dad had the fatal car crash. Like Mom, Dad never got RA implants. He was always careful on the road, and I thought it was a cruel stroke of fate. It had never occurred to me that maybe he was like that video game player, maybe he was simply overlooked by someone like me, someone who marked his need down as No Action.

Maybe I could have seen the world as he saw it. At least, I could have got close to him. Every single cell in my body is still carrying his DNA, and my eyes are the same colour as his. What kind of world did my dad see? Had he ever talked to me about it?

I can still catch a glimpse of the distant past through the words of the ancient Greeks words, but I have ceased to hear the voices around me. I should have been one of them.

Maybe I could have stopped it from happening.

No ...

I disconnect the adjustors as guilt sweeps over me. Re-connect. Disconnect again. The world now looks different ... or maybe not. What is real in all this? The world that the others see ... is it really a better one?

My vision grows murky as dizziness descends. I shut my eyes in alarm. I can hear me whispering to myself, saying that it's all in my head. I tap my temple with stiff knuckles, then open my eyes again, fully expecting the light—but it's no use at all.

All the colours are gone. I am surrounded by darkness.

Did I just go blind?

I've never known such fear. Now I get what people mean when they say how minutes pass like hours—no, like days and months and years. In my mind's eye, I see somebody picking me up from the floor and getting me to the hospital, I see myself lying in the hospital bed, weak and helpless. Filters, adjustors, colourblindness, abnormal vision ... a bunch of definitions whirl in my mind, but the darkness is absolute and it defies all words.

When I consider how my light is spent

Ere half my days in this dark world and wide

Is it still possible to be a blind poet in this day and age? The name Homer springs to mind before everything turns dark.


"Amy. Can you hear me, Amy?"

Someone calls for me from afar, in the darkness. A cool, tender hand strokes my burning forehead before moving away.

For the first time in what seems like forever, I find myself yearning for that voice and that touch, a light in the darkness.

"Mom ..."

"Don't be scared." She holds tightly onto my hand. "It's going to be okay. You just had a temporary bout of blindness because of unstable eye pressure."

I open my eyes with trepidation. Then there is light.

And tears blur my vision once more.

"I didn't know ... I mean, about Dad ... I ..." I can't even get out a coherent sentence. "Why didn't ... why didn't you tell me?"

"You were so afraid of being different. Everyone was scared. I was, too," Mom sighed, "I just wanted to protect you, but I was wrong."

I raise my head in surprise. Mom?

Her eyes, tired as they are, are glinting behind the glasses.

"Every one of us is special, but at the same time quite ordinary." Mom brushes my hair behind my ears. "It took me a long time to understand."

She puts a headset on me.

"You still need to rest your eyes. Close your eyes, Amy, and listen."

I lie back down on the bed, still shivering. Mom's voice comes through the headset, just like how she read fairy tales and legends to me at bedtime, all those years ago, but this time she is telling me a different story, one that turns my world upside-down. My breath catches and, like Homer's first audience, I can hold back neither laughter nor tears.

It's Mom's diary.


January 25th, 2024

I met Joe at the ski resort today. And just like that, his eyes had me mesmerized. They are coloured a light icy blue laced by a thousand different shades of green, and lilac, and lazurite ... How is it even possible for someone to have eyes like that? He probably laughed at me though, because I looked so dumbstruck.

The thing is, I quickly realized he's probably colourblind. His ski suit is green, the ugliest green I've ever seen. It looked like an avocado six months past its "best before" date. And it's got these dirty-looking orange streaks. I was giggling in front of him the whole time—I couldn't help myself—and that confused him no end. I think I'll need to take charge of his closet. But the upside is that I don't need to worry about other girls hitting on him on the trails.

May 30th, 2028

Yes! The last batch of flowers got here in time for the wedding! White peonies picked fresh from the Fairbanks Farm this morning. Budding white gardenias for my bouquet. White candles, white lace tablecloth ... white, white, white for each and every thing. Joe was apprehensive and asked me if I was sure about my colour choice. How can I make him understand? He can't see that white is not white, like how the snow looked when we first met. I told him to picture the colour of opal—a colour that is, in Pliny's words, "a refulgent fire of the carbuncle, the glorious purple of amethyst, the sea green of emerald, and all those colours glittering together." It can hold its own against even the deepest, richest colours in a painter's arsenal. That's what white looks like to me.

And once again, all that went completely over his head. He kept nodding, though, as if he really did see it. I had to kiss him, then and there. White ... white is how he looks when he tries to pretend that he "gets it", when he earnestly searches for a word to describe what I see.

White is how my love looks.


November 1st, 2030

Amy has arrived in this world. When I first laid eyes on her, all wrapped up and tiny, I couldn't believe that she came from me.

She looks nothing like me. I'm olive-skinned, but she's very pale, her tiny blood vessels look like cream-covered blueberries. She's the wrong colour, I kept telling the nurses. It took them quite a while to understand what I was talking about, and even longer to calm me down with their reassurances. I know, it's absurd, she doesn't have to share my skin colour, but it just keeps bugging me and refuses to go away.

Colours are special to me. I've long understood that most people can't see as many colours as I do. By the age of seven, I was already the most singular student in my art class. I wasn't that good at drawing, but anyone who's ever seen my paintings said that they could instantly tell they were mine—nobody else could use those colours like I did. And I hadn't even managed to convey a hundredth of what I saw to the canvas.

I hope that Amy will take after me. If she turns out "normal", she will be confined to such a dull and boring world

July 6th, 2035

I've had it with Joe. He dropped a slice of apple on the floor, but he couldn't tell where apple ended and where the wood flooring began. To me the piece stood out like a chunk of lime-coloured salami, but he just couldn't see it. Unbelievable.

We almost had a fight over it. I don't know what's wrong with me ... I've heard that they're doing trials for some kind of retina adjustment technology. Maybe that will make Joe normal?

I've started putting Amy next to me as I paint, hoping that she can soak some of it in. She might be a little too young for this, but Cezanne and Monet have such vibrant colours, and I hope she will embrace their magic. So far, it hasn't worked.

September 2nd, 2037

I'm at a loss for words. Amy is complaining that she can't recognise which is her teacher's writing on the board—blue chalk looks the same as dark green. I am seized by a terrible sense of premonition.

I asked her to spot the subtle colour differences in the Impressionist paintings. She couldn't.

Amy can't tell the colour blue from green. It's not as bad as Joe's red-green colourblindness, but it falls far short of normal vision, let alone mine.

Amy. When she came into this world, I had such high hopes for her ... hopes that now sting with irony.

Should we let Amy get the adjustors? Joe and I had a heated discussion. I couldn't imagine my daughter living in a world with missing colours, but Joe said that it wasn't that big a deal. He didn't feel like he was missing out on life.

That's because you don't know what you're missing. I tried to tell him. Think about it, a completely different world, with more details, more clarity, more vividness, full of endless possibilities. Once you see it, how can you confine yourself to anything less?

"No, Mieko, sweetheart, I've also seen things that you've never seen." He was smiling as he said this. "Lagrangian mechanics can open up a whole new world for you. Once you understand the language of those equations and symbols, you'll understand how the universe exists in a state of terrible harmony and equal fragility. Human emotions—indeed, human lives—hold no meaning … but none of that can stop me from listening to you as you describe the wondrous sights of this world, Mieko, or feeling Amy's warmth as I cradle her in my arms."

Language is like a pair of glasses, he said. It lets us see things that otherwise escape us, but we need to decide when to put it on … and when to take it off.

We decided to wait and let Amy choose for herself in a few years. It needs to be her own decision. Before then, we'll do our best to keep her condition from her. My peculiarity might have won me praises, but Amy won't be so lucky.

I made a call to Amy's teacher.

April 12th, 2043

I don't have a lot of friends. Whenever I met up with those ladies, I was always distracted by the spectacular colours on their persons, so I really couldn't fit in at all. They complained about having to repeatedly call my name to bring me back to earth.

Maybe Joe is the only one who can put up with me. At least there is that.

I had hoped that Amy, after she received the implants, would be able to see the same things as me and appreciate all the subtle touches. But that hasn't come to pass. I can feel her drifting away from me. She no longer reads my favourite books, and I can't understand her trendy words, just like she can't understand the language I'm using.

Joe doesn't try to make me learn Lagrangian mechanics. What, then, can I ask of Amy?

Now she doesn't want to paint with me or even look at the paintings at all. She'd rather stare into nothingness. I know that she is now in a world that I can never reach.

I had my initial consultation for adult adjustor implant today. After the preliminary check-up, the doctor said she was very interested in my abnormal colour perception. She is now waiting for the complete test results to come back.

April 29th, 2043

Tetrachromacy. I've never heard of that word before.

An extraordinary condition, according to the doctor. Normal humans only have three kinds of cone cells, one each for processing the colours red, green, and blue. People born with tetrachromacy, however, have a fourth kind of cone cell that allows them to process other colours. This type of X chromosome mutation causes colour blindness in males and, usually in the case of females, tetrachromacy.

A similar chromosomal mutation has sent Joe and I in opposite directions. A normal person sees about a million colours, Joe far fewer than that, while I can distinguish nearly one hundred million colours. As for Amy, she got dealt the worst hand possible.

Current technology doesn't allow for people with tetrachromacy to receive implants. My visual nerve pathways are far too complicated for the adjustors' algorithm to meddle with.

I will never see Amy's world now.

Maybe it's time to let her go. She is growing up fast and blooming into a young lady. Pink acne has appeared on her fair face, but with the adjustors' filters, she doesn't mind it too much. My own acne caused me endless torment because it looked so grotesque to me. Even now I can't leave the house without putting on makeup. Without a thick foundation layer, my hypodermis blood vessels stand out far too much with their turquoise green, plum purple, and burgundy red.

Maybe the world she sees is one that's better than my own.

December 19th, 2047

Joe has left me.

He just lies there, his eyes tightly shut and his face a pallid white. All the colours are gone. Carbuncle, amethyst, and emerald. The colour of death.

Black is far too rich for death. In black I can see violet purple,

Prussian blue and jade green. It reminds me of starling feathers and the ocean just after sunset.

And my heart is nothing but a fistful of ashes.

April 25th, 2050

Amy will graduate soon. She's a healthy, intelligent, and confident young woman. Just about perfect in every way. She also knows how to take care of herself. With the retina adjustors in place, her colour perception has been normalized. I no longer worry about how she might end up like Joe, unable to tell the red light from green in a country with adjusted traffic lights.

I am old now. My time has passed, like it does for everyone. Now I can only try to recapture the bygone days with increasingly foreign words. They are like mine caves sleeping in the darkness.

It's the same with people. A terrible thought has been haunting me of late—why do people like different colours?

To Amy and Joe, the same lights translate into similar colours bordering on dull but, in my eyes, they are so stunning I can hardly breathe. Do people with normal vision really all see them in the exact same way?

Nobody really knows. Each of us is like an isolated mining cave in the dark, and we will never know how the physical world is reflected in the cave next to ours. The truth of the physical world is like a formless grey fog, and it's our individual minds that give it its actual shape. Our perception re-molds the world for us, even though it's the only world we can ever know.

What connects the cold, isolated caves isn't what we see but what we say to each other. We can't define our individual experiences, but we can give them a standard name. It's with the help of these names that we fall in love with each other in such a mad, chaotic world. What a miracle it is that, even though Homer's age of wine-dark has long passed, even though Joe's white is nothing like my own, we can still share a trace of common feeling.

You are drifting further and further away from me, Amy. There is nothing for me to do but to accept this and make my peace with it. All of us are too occupied with what we see, so much so that we forget how to listen, and how to speak. Your Dad understood all of this, but he is gone.

The diary ends here. And my eyes, though tightly shut, are brimming with tears.

I understand now. I understand why the blind poet's words can touch us so.

"Now you see lightning tearing through mustard-yellow clouds as the sky rumbles in the distance. The angle of view gradually shifts from the heavens down to Earth. You focus on the damage caused by the thunderstorm, right beneath the clouds. The gyrocopter that you're piloting is caught inside this web of thunder and lightning, and its fuselage bounces in the squall ..."

"What's a gyrocopter?" asks Jack. All our guests are people who can't, for whatever reason, receive RA implants. He is the oldest out of the bunch, but he's also the one most interested in immersive games and movies.

"Uh ..." I'm briefly stumped, unsure how to explain such a common term to him. "It's a single-person aircraft. Really nice build, but not great in terms of stability ..."

"And then, the rain and the wind—" Mom chimes in, "to quote Robert Frost, 'they so smote the garden bed, that the flowers actually knelt.' Right?"

Mom is the manager-cum-caterer of our little "Mind's Eye" club, not to mention its very first audience member. We organize a special "experience scenario" for the club every weekend.

"Umm ... that's right." I try my best to recall those verses and all the traces they left on me. "To create this scenario, I used the International Space Station's atmospheric record data. But yes, that's what I have tried to convey through this experience."

I'm not sure what I can actually achieve with my words. Listening to me is, of course, a far cry from seeing the actual sight with adjustors. Besides, it's not like we have a big audience, but I know that some of them make three-hour treks from the suburbs to come here, and some of them grip their tea cups so tightly when they listen, like they are riding a rollercoaster and hanging on for dear life. It's not an easy job for me. Often, I have to turn off the adjustors, or even use a blindfold, in order to find the right words and lead them into a world they've never known.

They say that I'm their eyes, but I know it's them who have taught me how to see for myself.

"Ah, so it's actually kinda like that painting, isn't it?" Tariq points with his chin. He's on auto-follow mode for this scenario but seems more interested in my childhood home.

I turn and suck in my breath. It's Snow Storm: Steam-Boat off a Harbour's Mouth, Mom's favorite painting. Whirlwind and gigantic waves, snowflakes and sea mist. The canvas filled with nothing but chaos. Every shape has been obscured, and every colour has been meshed together, but the artist still manages to preserve the most minute differences between them. Even though I can't really tell them apart, now I know that when my Mom looks at this, she sees a spectacle that's beyond our human reach. The nature's transcendental grandeur and majesty—that's what I wanted to convey when I designed this scenario.

"To paint this, Turner had the sailors tie him up to the mast as the boat sailed into the storm," says Mom with a faraway look on her face.

"Just like Odysseus," the two of us say in unison. Our eyes meet, and we smile at each other. In this Moment, our worlds contain the same colours.

# 目录



# TABLE OF CONTENTS

封面插画：刘军威
Cover art by Liu "Sharksden" Junwei

排版：Alda Teodorani
Typetting and design: Alda Teodorani

英文校对  Eileen Herbert-Goodall
English text proofread by Eileen Herbert-Goodall